David Gilbertson read English and Modern Languages at Cambridge University before beginning a career in journalism and business information publishing. He was editor of Lloyd's List and managing director of The Lancet and went on to head two of the UK's largest information groups Informa and Emap. He now advises media companies as a non-executive director. Born in Wallasey, he and his wife now divide their time between London and Provence.

For Donald and Jocelyn

David Gilbertson

A Fine Line

AUSTIN MACAULEY PUBLISHERS™

LONDON * CAMBRIDGE * NEW YORK * SHARJAH

A CIP catalogue record for this title is available from the British Library.

ISBN 9781528935265 (Paperback)
ISBN 9781528942072 (Hardback)
ISBN 9781528950077 (ePub e-book)
ISBN 9781528945486 (Audiobook)

www.austinmacauley.com

First Published 2023
Austin Macauley Publishers Ltd®
1 Canada Square
Canary Wharf
London
E14 5AA

With my huge gratitude for all of your reading, believing and guiding.

BB, BC, SC, CC-M, DD, SE, ADG, DG, PL, IM-M, DM, AN, SK, LV, RV-M.

Cover illustration by Bill Butcher
https://www.billbutcher.com

a fine line

- *the slender division between two states where one is worse than the other*
- *a notable succession of related people*

Foreword
Wallasey 1945

The wooden trestle tables that lined the full length of Limekiln Lane groaned with food. Meats, pies and cakes; pastries, biscuits and sweetmeats; and huge bowls of pink blancmange and red fruit jelly were laid out in abundance as far as the eye could see. Bathed in the early June sunshine, children were hanging up paper chains, draping them from drainpipes to pillars, and decorating lamp posts with interweaves of coloured paper streamers and balloons.

Women were putting out plates, napkins and cutlery, squeezing in as many places as they could to accommodate all the folk from the surrounding streets, who were already starting to emerge from their doors, eager for the four o'clock start of the celebrations.

Men were carting into place an assortment of seats, volunteered up by many of the neighbourhood houses and shops: benches, kitchen chairs, stools of every shape and size. It made for a motley collection, but all the seating they could muster between them would be needed for this party of all parties, the party that would finally end the war.

The master of ceremonies for the day was Joseph Steggle, the grocer. He of the matinee idol looks had been, for many years, the apple of the eye of many of the lady customers to his large shop, which stood as the centrepiece of the road above the docks on the River Mersey. Clean shaven, naturally tan of complexion and with a head of luxuriant once black hair now flecked through with steel grey and tamed into place with oil, he was more than 80 years old but still cut a handsome figure. Successful businessman, town councillor, member of the masonic lodge, Joseph was spry, courteous, always immaculately turned out and a proper gentleman: a pillar of the local community. He had never spoken much of his background, but the common word was that he had come from nothing, worked himself up. Such a slender narrative only added to the frisson around the man.

Joseph and his son-in-law David Simpson had laid on most of the food for the party. Joseph had helped David to get started as an independent baker and confectioner by loaning him the money to open his own shop a couple of doors down from the Steggle's grocery. David together with his wife Florence, Joseph's second-born daughter and assisted by their three children, Douglas, Dorothy and Josephine, had worked through the previous two days, making all the pies, cakes and biscuits that were now being laid out across the decorated tables.

David hailed originally from Scotland and had come to the area after the end of the First War to join his mother Elizabeth and his sister Janet, who had first led her family from Dundee to the banks of the Mersey when she had been taken away from her Scottish home by the offer of marriage from a Liverpool man named Archie Rogers.

Elizabeth's lifelong friend Jane Garston lived just a few streets away with her two children: Ethel, a talented musician and piano teacher, and Albert, the deputy manager of a Cooperative store in the town. Albert and his wife Lilian had one son, Stuart. He and David and Florence's youngest daughter, Josephine, both 16 years of age, were new young sweethearts. They had met several months earlier in an after-school dance class to which Josephine, already an accomplished dancer, had been dragged reluctantly by two girlfriends, eager for male company. Now Josephine and Stuart never missed a dance class together.

Josephine's brother, Douglas, pin sharp in his army officer's uniform, was crouched at the top of the road rigging up a gramophone to a loudspeaker he had borrowed from the church hall. He passed a long wire through the downstairs window of a neighbouring house ready for the afternoon's musical accompaniment. A little further down the road, Ethel could be seen seated at one of the two pianos that had been brought out into the street, arranging the sheet music on both, all ready and in good order for the organised singalongs to come.

These families had been lucky in the Second War. The Liverpool docks had been repeatedly strafed by the German Luftwaffe in the Blitz raids, and many children, including Josephine and her sister Dorothy, had been evacuated to the safety of the North Wales countryside to avoid what was, for a time, near-nightly bombardment. But despite these terrors, the casualties these few families had suffered in Wallasey had somehow been mercifully few. Of all of them, Albert

Garston had come closest to losing his life when a bomb dropped directly on the unoccupied next-door house as he was enjoying his regular evening meal of ham and egg salad. As his wife, Lilian, and their son, Stuart, emerged alarmed but unscathed from their sheltering place beneath the stairs, they found Albert stoically finishing off his meal, parting the dust on the kitchen table with his broad forearms, his appetite seemingly unimpaired by the shower of fallen plaster that covered him and most of the room.

The most grievous loss sustained by any of them had fallen upon Janet, whose son Harry had been killed in action when the naval ship on which he was purser was sunk by a German U-boat in the Irish Sea. That sole tragedy was a far cry from what the families who now inhabited these few roads had suffered during the earlier conflict. It was almost as if some divine hand was balancing out the final price they had to pay after the heavy toll the First War years had taken of them.

Elizabeth and Jane, 'the Scottish ladies', as they were known reverentially around these streets, were among the first to take a seat at the trestle tables, as the place layers and the decorators fussed around them. Douglas, seeing his grandmother and her greatest friend making their way to the middle of a table directly opposite the picture window of Steggle's Grocery, quickly made sure the two elderly women were poured a large glass of the party punch, which Elizabeth accepted for both of them by brushing her hand gently across her grandson's cheek.

Seeing them suitably seated, and with refreshment already laid on for them, Joseph Steggle moved over from the door of his shop and sat down opposite the two women. "How are my two favourite customers?" he opened as he joined them. "I hope we are getting ready for some song and dance?"

"I think our best dancing days are long behind us, Joe, but we're glad it's a sunny afternoon for the party," said Jane. "We've waited long enough for it."

"It's true," said Joseph. "And it feels like the three of us have travelled a long way to get here, doesn't it? We've come through a fair lot, haven't we? But somehow, this does feel like a new beginning to me. Let's pray it really is the end of war—but more than that. I mean new government, economy getting back on its feet, talk of a free health service, new world. We've all seen our fair share of hardship to get here," he said, nodding as Stuart and Josephine passed by their table, smiling shyly hand-in-hand. "But these young ones have finally got good reason to hope for something better now."

"You've always been very quiet on where you came from, and what you saw before you came here, Joseph," said Elizabeth. "I'm sure Jane and I would be intrigued to hear the real story. And maybe, then we'll tell you some more of ours, if you're lucky and we think you deserve it," she said with a mischievous wink in her friend's direction.

Joseph smiled back broadly at her and replied.

"That sounds like by far the best offer I have had for a long time, Elizabeth. I'll come and join you both in a few minutes. I'll see if I can get David to come and join us, too. Be sure to save us those couple of chairs."

As he stood up and stepped away towards his shop, Joseph turned back towards the two seated women.

"I'm looking forward to it, ladies. I hope you can both keep a secret, mind."

Book One
Joseph Liverpool 1845–1865

One

Ranelagh Hall, once proud, stood in the village of Everton in the midst of the rolling countryside one mile east of Liverpool.

The home of Hugo and Emily Ranelagh, the mansion house had been built in the classical style in the last year of the 18th century by the lion of the Ranelagh family, Hugo's grandfather Oswald. On the perimeter of its 50-acre estate, under the canopy of a hundred mature elms, stood 12 stone-built workers' cottages, erected to house the Hall's servants and their families.

Sir Oswald, who was knighted by King George III in the year 1776 for his services to the African trades, had selected this land on which to build his family seat because it was far enough removed to provide him with a rustic retreat from the hustle of the Liverpool port while still allowing him easy access to the town's commercial heart only a half hour's carriage ride away.

Now, 45 years on, with Liverpool's population fast expanding and mounting pressure on housing provision seeing new built dwellings creeping ever closer to the estate's outer reaches, Sir Oswald's descendants at Ranelagh Hall were no longer experiencing the splendid rural isolation he had originally acquired.

Nor was the new generation living in quite the same comfortably cushioned circumstances which Hugo's grandfather enjoyed. The family fortune, amassed by Sir Oswald over a 40-year merchanting career of spectacular success, was now two generations old and depleting. Hugo and Emily, mercifully, were still able to answer the frequent calls made upon them to support good causes and they still lived well compared to most. But life was no longer as it was in Sir Oswald's day. Now only ten of the servants' houses were occupied, and Hugo and Emily were running the estate with the support of only 24 helpers.

Oswald, the son of a Lancashire farmer, had been a self-made businessman. A keen and able student, he gained a place at Brasenose College at Oxford University where he studied Classics—'The Greats'—before returning to his home city with a thought-out plan to set himself up in business. A number of his

Oxford contemporaries had opted to pursue a career in the Law but Oswald was excited by the opportunities of commerce and in particular in the rising demand for two much-loved and addictive commodities: tobacco and sugar.

His first tentative trading forays into buying small amounts of both products did not prove very lucrative. But that early experience showed Oswald that buying and selling goods at a market price that everyone knew was going to be a thinly rewarding business. Trading could only be really profitable if he speculated heavily by buying large quantities at the right time and then managed to sell it all on successfully in small lots for more than he had paid. Such an approach, however, carried with it huge risk. If he got his timing wrong, and prices then fell for any reason while his warehouses were full, he could find himself having to sell at significant losses. If ever his luck was well and truly out, he could find himself bankrupted.

As he wrestled with this conundrum it became clear to Oswald that, in order to make worthwhile profit from trading, he would have to find a sustainable commercial advantage over the parties he would deal with. If putting large amounts of his own money at unknown risk was neither a viable nor a sensible option, he would need to be better informed than those with whom he would trade.

In order to be able to predict whether the market was moving towards shortage or surplus, and whether prices in the near future were therefore likely to rise or fall, he would have to be very well read and keep himself constantly in touch with the best intelligence available in the marketplace. He would have to build relationships with well-connected sources. Knowledge, he saw clearly, was the key to profit in the commodity trades.

The second vital ingredient of success he identified was trust. All the best knowledge in the world would not suffice if people did not honour the commitments they made to buy and sell at the prices he agreed with them. He consequently espoused two resonant Latin phrases he had acquired at Oxford: *fidentia* and *uberrimae fides*—trust and utmost good faith. He lost no opportunity to promote them by word and in writing. Those were the standards he would follow himself and to which he would hold those who would trade with him.

This led Oswald thirdly to placing an absolute faith in the rule of law. The law was there to protect honest citizens and to establish a framework of common rules for their interactions. If something was lawful therefore, that meant it was allowed and acceptable. If it was unlawful, then it was not. There could be no doubt at all about that. In the commercial world, as long as you operated within the law, then whatever gains you made were entirely legitimately to your account. To Oswald that was quite black and white.

These principles became forged into a trinity by which Oswald governed and guided all his business affairs from then on: superior knowledge, secured by commitment to honest dealing and protected by the rule of law itself.

On this triangle of certainty, Oswald Ranelagh built his trading fortune.

Two

"Excuse me, madam, but there is a Mrs Edith Butterworth who has called without invitation and she would like your permission to present herself to you with a view to a brief conversation. She says she is a representative of the Society for the Redemption of Fallen and Distressed Females."

The speaker was George Mannion, the Ranelagh family's butler now in his 62nd year, 25 of which he had spent on the estate. He had joined the household in Sir Oswald's time as a footman and had been raised to the senior house role ten years previously when the previous incumbent, whom George had respectfully addressed from his first day to his last as 'Mr Armitage', reached his appointed retirement age.

"Certainly, do show her in, Mannion," said Emily Ranelagh, the lady of the house.

"Yes, madam. Further though, if I may, also waiting in the hall is a Reverend Stanley Peacock, accompanied by a Mrs Matilda Barnaby, who I understand are from the Temperance Society. They have informed me that they will be only too pleased to wait if you might be willing to grant them a short audience in due course. And finally, madam, Murdoch from the stables wishes to know whether you or Mr Ranelagh will be requiring the carriage to be prepared this morning?"

"Mannion, so many pressing issues!" cried Emily. "Yes, please ask the Reverend and Mrs Barnaby to make themselves comfortable while I meet the first caller and do offer them tea while they wait. And yes, please also have Murdoch prepare the carriage for Mr Ranelagh and myself. We have a luncheon appointment in town and we will need to leave at noon."

Mannion closed the door gently as he retreated, before returning momentarily with Mrs Butterworth from the fallen women's group bustling in closely behind him. She was a plump lady of rosy complexion dressed from bonnet to toe in austere black.

"Thank you so kindly for seeing me, Mrs Ranelagh," she began breathlessly while barely though the door.

"I do know that your time will be most pressing but I am sure you know of the work of the Society for the Redemption of Fallen and Distressed Females. You are such a kind supporter of so many of our local charities, and our work to help women who have fallen upon the hardest of times and are living on the streets of our town is so pressing and deserving of your grace. While I hope that you will have had little occasion to see the unfortunate plight of these benighted women on whom shame has been brought and who, in turn, by their own most reprehensible behaviour, bring further disgrace upon our menfolk and on the good name of Liverpool itself…"

"Yes, Mrs Butterworth." Emily interrupted not only to break her guest's babbling flow but also to spare the poor woman the task of describing her good cause in any more gruesome detail. "May I say two pounds?"

Mrs Butterworth returned her an agonised look that suggested she was less than fully delighted with the sum offered. She returned to her theme with a slightly firmer tone.

"Well, that is most kind of you, Mrs Ranelagh, but ours really is a most deserving cause to help the most needy in our society. You and your husband, whose own good fortune, as I know you are the first to acknowledge, owes much to the past cruel exploitation of those who had no voice to protest against their hardship, I know you will want to do all you possibly can to help this different but very oppressed group today."

"Very well, Mrs Butterworth," replied Emily. "Of course I recognise the importance of your work. Shall we say five pounds?"

Again the aspiring beneficiary paused, still looking pained.

"Well to save me bothering you again, Mrs Ranelagh, and I am so grateful to you, could I perhaps beseech you to possibly make it ten?"

Emily looked at Mrs Butterworth, who had now finally fallen silent, to await her completion.

"Yes, very well," Emily Ranelagh replied, reaching for a cheque.

Three

After serving five years in a merchant office on the Liverpool dockside, learning the basics of the sugar and tobacco trades, Oswald Ranelagh was ready to take his decisive step and form his own company. He had accumulated savings from his salary and his share of successful trading outcomes over the five year period, and he had also forged a strong relationship with a local banker, one Ernest Pybus, who, impressed by Ranelagh's energy, ambition and evident intelligence, had agreed to extend him a limited line of credit to enable him to pursue mercantile transactions as a principal. With this financial backing, in September 1746, Ranelagh Trading opened its doors for the first time.

In all that he did, Ranelagh was guided by his three-point principles. He chose his trading partners with great care and dealt only with those he had proved he could trust. He never permitted anything that crossed the line of the law and, before entering into any transaction, he first tested rigorously the basis on which he was proceeding.

Above all, Ranelagh sought to eliminate the role of luck in what he did. For him, luck was an entirely different thing from fortune. Fortune was the success that arrived when a well-reasoned plan came to fruition. Luck was random chance. Fortune was earned, luck came along when it chose. The two were never to be confused. Over a lifetime, Oswald reasoned, good luck and bad luck would likely even out, like the surfacing of reds and blacks in the dealing of a pack of cards. You could never rely on which way it would fall next. Good fortune, on the other hand, was the product of rigour and the application of science. If these were executed with enough care, you could predict good fortune. Ranelagh intended to be a fortunate merchant, not a lucky one.

To ensure that his knowledge of the markets in which he worked was kept at its keenest, he built up strong relationships with a range of market participants with whom he would converse daily. He became highly skilled in using those informal conversations to form a clear picture of sugar and tobacco availability and demand, and how that was likely to change in the coming days or weeks. He would keenly discuss rumour and occasional selective facts with those who spoke with him, but he never shared his broader assessments with anyone. He was happy to share gossip and minor snippets of information. What he never shared was his informed thinking, his accumulating trading intelligence.

As he developed his involvements with other merchants, he would test them by trading with them regularly in small lots until he satisfied himself of the second of his triptych of requirements. Could he trust them to honour their word? To establish this, he allowed varying outcomes to arise from an initial series of small trades and observed closely how his new counterparties behaved when they came out on top, when they lost a little money and when they lost heavily. Only if their behaviour was constant through all three outcomes would they make it through his proving filter to become trading partners he would trust to deal with at scale in the future.

Finally, he confirmed his third test: was the trade lawful? In truth, this typically proved a far less challenging hurdle for Oswald to clear than the other two points of his trinity. Of course, he would not deal knowingly in stolen material or with criminal parties. He followed the law assiduously. That was clear. As long as it passed the legal test, he was comfortable that justified everything. Nothing to see there.

As time progressed, it became evident to Ranelagh that he needed to diversify his sources of supply. It was not enough to be buying and selling with traders like himself. He needed to establish his own direct relationships with growers of sugar and tobacco: people who were permanent sellers of the commodities they produced and from whom he could buy reliably when he chose, at prices he could agree simply with them. He began to travel regularly to the British colonies of Barbados and Jamaica, and to Virginia and Maryland to open up his supply lines for sugar, tobacco and now also cotton, too, in order to establish the personal connections on which he could count.

During those visits, Ranelagh witnessed at first-hand how the growers' plantations worked, their economies entirely dependent upon slave labour brought to the Americas from Africa by the London based Royal African Company, which had held a monopoly over such trading until 1698. In the 30 years since the ending of that monopoly, private enterprise in London and Bristol had established those two ports as Britain's major slave trading centres. For Oswald, Liverpool had been unforgivably slow to become involved. Of all the ships that set out from Britain to Africa to collect slaves for the America plantations before 1730, only one in 15 had come from his home port.

But that picture was now beginning to change rapidly as Liverpool merchants like Ranelagh woke up to the wealth creating opportunities of the emerging transatlantic trades. Approaching 200 ships for this trade had left Liverpool in the ten years to 1750, but that number then more than doubled in Ranelagh Trading's first full decade of operation, with ten ships a week leaving Liverpool's docks bound for African ports en route to the West Indies and America.

Ranelagh became an active participant in what came to be known as The Triangular Trades. He chartered and eventually owned ships that would leave Liverpool with cargoes of manufactured cotton and linen textiles, copper and pewter goods, glassworks and potteries and other British products bound for the African west coast. Once set out from Liverpool, his ships would call next at Douglas in the tax haven of the Isle of Man to pick up additional duty-free cargoes from the East Indies such as beads, cutlasses, pistols and gunpowder. Once they reached the African coast they would then exchange those goods for a human cargo of black slaves for the next leg of their journey across the Atlantic—the treacherous Middle Crossing—to the labour hungry plantations of the Caribbean islands and America.

As the decade progressed, Liverpool's stranglehold on these highly lucrative physical trades increased hugely, at the expense of Bristol and London. Liverpool suddenly seemed to have all the competitive advantages and it pressed them home ruthlessly.

Liverpool boasted a bristling port brimming with ship's captains and sailors already hardened to the challenging Atlantic crossing and hungry for work. It had dockyards housing a first-class shipbuilding industry capable of building the ocean going vessels equipped for all three legs of the triangular trade. It had deep draught dock facilities in the port capable of accommodating and handling the largest slaving vessels. Importantly, it also enjoyed a geographic location sufficiently far north to be beyond the reach of privateer and pirate ships from Europe that frequently harassed and attacked ships exiting from Britain's southern ports. This important geographical advantage was a crucial contribution in making Liverpool ships far cheaper to insure than rival vessels sailing from its competitor ports to its south. With lower costs of operation, they could afford to undercut their competition. To top it all, Liverpool's hinterland was now connected with a world-leading canal network to the industrial powerhouses of Manchester and Leeds, which meant the movement of goods in and out of the Liverpool port was both easy and fast.

Liverpool merchants' relationships with African entrepreneurs, tribal leaders and middlemen became unrivalled. Ranelagh and his contemporaries ambitiously developed new slave trading centres beyond the Bight of Biafra, Gold Coast and Angolan ports that had been opened up by previous generations of Bristol traders. They moved into Sierra Leone, Gabon and Cameroon and built communication lines and personal bonds that were far stronger than their rivals had ever managed. They also opened up new options to supply slaves to sugar growers in the Caribbean beyond the two established destinations of Jamaica and Barbados. Growers in islands such as St Lucia, Trinidad, Martinique and Guadeloupe, San Domingo, the Virgin Islands and Cuba all became clients of the relentless Ranelagh and his fellow new generation of Liverpool entrepreneurs.

Armed with all those advantages, Liverpool became the hugely dominant British force in the slave trades, leaving Bristol and London trailing in its wake. In the final ten years of the 18th century, the decade when Ranelagh Trading was at its peak and Oswald Ranelagh's fortune quadrupled, Liverpool vessels carried more than a quarter of a million slaves across the notorious central passage to the Americas, four times the combined number that disembarked from London and Bristol ships in the same period.

Peerless and pitiless, Liverpool had become the metropolis of slavery.

Four

As Sir Oswald Ranelagh's long life ebbed towards its final chapter, he was driven one warm day in May 1807 to a luncheon appointment at The Athenaeum, the library and gentlemen's club in Liverpool's Church Street that he had helped to found as a proprietor member ten years earlier.

The club had quickly become famous as the home of one of the most prestigious reading rooms in the country. Set up expansively to "procure a regular supply of newspapers, all the periodicals of value and all the pamphlets that have reference to subjects of local or general polity or commerce," the Athenaeum had become an important place for obtaining the superior knowledge that Ranelagh had identified as vital for trading success at the outset of his merchant career.

As their two-horse carriage pulled up outside the club's imposing oak doors, Sir Oswald's coachman Edwin Steggle expressed the hope that he would find his lunch enjoyable and his guest companiable.

"Thank you, Edwin," the old man replied. "I am sure I shall. I have known William Roscoe for more than three decades and, despite our many differences, I have always found him a stimulating and courteous companion. He is a man of little formal education but nonetheless one of the cleverest I have ever known. We share a love of the arts and the classics. Yet we have found ourselves in matters of politics in profound disagreement throughout all our lives. But despite that, we have never lost our respect for one another nor mislaid the ability to agree to disagree while always parting on cordial terms, ready to meet again."

Making his way on foot to the Athenaeum simultaneously, the politician William Roscoe was charged with adrenaline. He had recently resigned as Liverpool's Member of Parliament after serving just a few months in the position. But in that brief tenure of office he had played a pivotal role in delivering the most important parliamentary decision of the new century. He had voted alongside the reformer William Wilberforce to abolish the transatlantic slave trade on which so much of Liverpool's economic success of the previous hundred years had been built. The vote to end slave trading when it came had been overwhelming, passing by 283 votes to just 16.

Roscoe's well known lifelong opposition to the slave trade, and the role he had played in the final vote to end it, had deeply divided popular opinion in the town. Wilberforce himself had praised Roscoe's speech in which he condemned slavery as 'this inhuman traffic' and said his vote was 'worth twenty of anyone else' because he knew that, as a Liverpool representative, Roscoe would be bound to pay a heavy price for his controversial stance among his own constituents.

Over the entire slave-trading period, Liverpool interests had been responsible for sending almost one and a quarter million captured Africans into conditions of slavery on American and West Indian plantations. From the grand commercial and mercantile interests that conducted that business to the ordinary men serving on their ships or loading them with goods on its docks, the trade Roscoe had just helped to close down had created the new fortune of Liverpool.

By no means everyone saw him as a hero in consequence. For some, Roscoe was a traitor to the local cause. On his first return to the town after the abolition became law, just ten days before this appointed lunch date with Ranelagh, he had been set upon and beaten to the ground by a mob of sailors who had earned their living in the now banned trade. They had joined up in an unholy alliance with a group of religious zealots who disapproved of Roscoe for a different reason: his condemnation of government oppression of Irish Catholics. Bloodied but unbowed, the politician had come through an emotionally charged month.

Ranelagh and Roscoe met in the atrium of the Athenaeum and greeted each other amicably. Sir Oswald was the first to speak.

"I am not sure we shall have much to discuss today, William," he said. "We know the game is done and its course is run."

"Come now, Oswald," came the politician's reply. "I am sure we will find some good ground for discussion." "It has been a long time coming."

They made their way through to the oak panelled dining room and ordered a dozen oysters each to be followed by beefsteak washed down with jugs of the club's renowned Hock and Claret.

As the two men ate, Ranelagh, dabbing the corner of his mouth with his napkin, opened the conversation.

"I am not sure whether we will meet again William. Not because I bear you any animosity for what you have done to bring down the curtain on this long play. I have known your opinions about it very well for many years."

"No, the reason I am not sure we will meet again is because I feel my days are now drawing to an end and I don't know how many more such opportunities we will have to meet. I can tell you also that since I lost my son Peregrine, who you will recall lost his life bravely trying to preserve the lives of others on our ship that sank so tragically in the Middle Passage, I have lost my appetite for the business. I now just wish to bring it all to a close. No words can express what it means to lose a son in the prime of his youth at just 28 years, and he already the master of his own ocean going vessel after just four previous voyages to sea."

"My sole consolation, William," Ranelagh concluded, "and it is a scant one, is that Peregrine has left behind a young son, my grandson Hugo, who will take our family name forward after I am gone."

"You have my deep sympathy, Oswald," Roscoe replied, "but I must point out to you that you were not the only parent to be bereaved that day. Not only were Peregrine's crew all lost, but his precious human cargo perished there, too. Three hundred African mothers and fathers lost sons and daughters when the *Achilles* went down, and those Africans died a second time that day on Peregrine's ship. They had already been dead to their parents and their families when they were taken from their homes, however it was done and by whom, into that ghastly trade."

"I am sure you also heard the rumours, Oswald," Roscoe continued, "that Peregrine overloaded the ship in the Bight of Biafra with excess cargo on top of its already overflowing human complement, and it was the extra bulk that cost the ship its buoyancy when it ran into that mid ocean storm?"

Ranelagh snorted in response. "I heard those remarks, William, but they are lies put about by those that wish our family ill, and I shall not dignify such poisonous tittle tattle with comment."

"I should tell you, William," Ranelagh went on, "that when I look back upon my life and my career, I feel I have nothing to answer for to my Maker. I played by the rules that were set by others. I learned them carefully and I worked always within them. I did nothing illegal. I always abided by the law. I travelled in this country frequently to London to meet with the insurers and the financiers to whom I was close and I journeyed extensively in Africa, in America and the spice islands, building true personal relationships with the real people with whom I traded.

I am proud, for example, when I hear that Antera Duke, the chief of Efik Calabar in Biafra who brought me so many slaves, now calls me his friend. I am proud when Africans say they preferred to deal with Liverpool merchants rather than the 'small country vessels' that came to them from London and Bristol. I am proud of what we achieved and the British goods we took into Africa to Biafra and Sierra Leone and the commodities we brought back from the Americas, from Virginia, from Jamaica and the spice islands for British people to enjoy. I am proud of the Triangular Trade that has benefitted this town and this country so richly over the last century. I was honoured for it and I am honoured to have done it."

Roscoe looked across at his companion and replied.

"Let me say this to you, Oswald. I do know that you believe that and I know that you always looked to follow the letter of the law in what you did. But the law is capable of being an unreliable friend. You have always held the view that, because everything you did lay within the law, it meant that everything you did was justified. But sometimes in life, the fact that you *may* do something does not mean that you *should* do it. Sometimes, there is a higher calling to reckon with. Sometimes, the question we should be asking ourselves before going down a certain path is not just 'is this allowed?' but rather 'is this right?'."

As they summoned a decanter of port to bring their lunch to a well-lubricated close, Ranelagh returned to the subject one more time.

"Let me ask you one final question then, William," he said. "Why do you think it took so long to bring this trade to a halt? Have you ever stopped to think whether that was because it benefitted this country hugely and was never such a bad thing as you have always contended?"

Roscoe looked across at the deeply lined face of his white-haired companion and replied.

"The reason it took so long to end it, Oswald, is not at all because it was not such a bad thing. It was because we could not see it. The worst excesses of the Triangular Trades—the inhumanity, the degradation and its other evils—all took place outside these shores. The ordinary people of Liverpool, of Glasgow, of Bristol and London never saw men and women being led in chains into holds and laid flat packed tight. Nor were they ever obliged to accompany them in the holds on the Middle Passage. They never saw the working conditions in the sweltering heat of the plantations or the brutality of treatment to which those people were subjected. They were never forced to consider what it really means to be a slave in perpetuity, with no escape possible even in death because, even when you were called to meet your Saviour, your children and your children's children forever more would remain enslaved, the permanent chattel of other men."

"Instead, all people here ever witnessed of the Triangular Trades was the wonderful sight of their own textiles, their glass products and their brandy being loaded up onto ships to set off to be sold to unseen buyers in countries so far away that they would never visit or even be able to place upon a map. And then they could stand and cheer on the docksides as they saw sugar for their tea and tobacco for their pipes arriving on their return, bringing them delicious foreign tastes from faraway worlds."

"That is why this evil trade lasted so long, Oswald," Roscoe said. "It was because its shame and its cruelty took place out of our sight and out of our minds."

The two men at length parted, exchanging a warm embrace. "Take good care, Oswald, and farewell," said Roscoe. "You, too, William," the old man replied. "I thank you."

Edwin Steggle was waiting dutifully outside the club doors, his carriage door already opened, ready to help guide Sir Oswald Ranelagh up into his black leathered seat.

"A good lunch, sir?" Steggle enquired respectfully as he took up the reins. "Just move on, Edwin, just move on," came the old man's curt reply.

Later that week at Ranelagh Hall, Sir Oswald Ranelagh, veteran commodity and slave trader, passed away peacefully in his sleep.

Five

Murdoch took Edwin Steggle's job when the unfortunate cuts happened. He had joined the estate only two years earlier as a groom working for Edwin in the stables. Tall, swarthy, well-muscled and with a demeanour verging on swagger, he boasted a rich mane of blue-black thickly oiled hair.

He first came to the estate when he walked up to the door of Ranelagh Hall unannounced, knocked boldly on the brass lion's head, which in those days the housemaid Mary kept constantly gleaming, and asked to speak with Mr Hugo Ranelagh himself.

Hugo, whose established policy was to turn away no-one in need of help, had Mannion bring him in. The stranger sat down opposite him and came quickly to the point of his visit.

"Mr Ranelagh, sir, thank you for granting me audience. I come in search of employment. I am skilled in rearing and working with horses and I am here to seek a role as a groom in your stables. I have especially come to you because I am the son of an African slave who, while working on a plantation in the Americas, was found to be in a relationship with a white lady, my dear mother, whom he had got with child. Indeed, you see him here before you today, for that child is myself."

"Sadly, such an irregular union of the colours was not approved or permitted by the owners of the plantation and I regret to tell you that on hearing of it they despatched my dear father, God rest his soul, without delay or mercy. My mother then begged to be allowed to take her child, being my good unborn self, away from the plantation, and I am pleased to tell you that my mother succeeded, may the Almighty bless her, but only on the payment of a hefty sum to free me from my enslavement before my very birth."

"My dear mother is now greatly aged, sir, and I owe her not only my limitless gratitude but also to pay back those monies she was required to give up to secure my freedom. So I am here today in the hope of opportunity to show you my worth so I might earn enough to be able to send regular funds to help salve her in her final years. I have heard tell that you have a particular interest in paying off the debts of slavery, sir, and I very much hope that you can help me to settle mine."

Hugo, clearly moved, replied, "That is a dreadful tale and I am sure we can help you Mr…?"

"Please just call me Murdoch, sir. I am a modest man and I go by no other name."

Hugo rang his small brass table bell to summon Mannion, and asked him to bring Edwin Steggle to his room. While they waited for the coachman to arrive, Hugo remarked, "You have a fine countenance Murdoch but you seem different in aspect from the African figures depicted in my grandfather's paintings."

"I believe it's the mixed blood, sir," Murdoch replied. "I am blessed with my father's black hair, my colouring is a sweet mixture of my parents' white and black skins, but all my facial features I owe to my blessed mother's side, lovely woman that she was."

At this point, Steggle knocked and entered the room. "Good morning, Edwin," said Hugo. "We are hiring this man today. His name is Murdoch. He will work from now on as a groom with you and Edward in the stables. Please show him to the workplace and have Mary prepare a room for him in the vacant quarters."

Murdoch did not prove a popular addition to the servants' number. Work-shy, deceptive and given to drink, he was a poor fit with the time-served team who worked closely together to ensure the much loved Mr Hugo and Mrs Emily had all that they required and that the estate functioned properly.

Murdoch was loathed in particular by the butler, Mannion, who never uttered his name without adding the words 'of the stable'. The trusty Steggle found Murdoch such an unwilling collaborator, despite his obvious great facility with horses, that in time he disregarded him from tasks, preferring to entrust what needed to be done with the animals, the tack and the maintaining of the two estate carriages to his son, Edward. Edward had worked alongside his father from a young boy and was now at 21 years old newly married to Amy, one of the Ranelagh's chambermaids.

Edwin, long a widower, his wife Sarah having died of consumption a dozen years previously, shared his modest servant's house on the estate with Edward and his new bride, and with his daughter, Ann, Edward's sister three years his junior, who worked as an assistant in the Ranelagh Hall kitchens to Betsy Heathcote, the cook.

Six

At the age of 17, Ann Steggle was in the first flush of womanhood. Pale and fresh of complexion, she kept her beautiful long flaxen hair tied and knotted discreetly under her white kitchen cap whenever she was seen in public. Her most stunning feature though was not for such easy concealment—a radiant ivory white smile of such brightness it made all who saw it respond instantly to her warmth. Ann was her father Edwin's pride.

For all her striking looks, Ann was a quiet young woman, softly spoken, diligent and hardworking. Her role at Ranelagh Hall was to keep the kitchen pans and crockery spotless, to get the cutlery gleaming and to ensure that the kitchen itself was 'ready for a visit from royals'. This she did assiduously even though those ultimate possible visitors had never yet arrived to test her state of readiness.

In addition to her own tasks, Ann took every opportunity that time allowed to learn the art of cookery at Mrs Heathcote's side. The house cook, now 65 years of age, was gratified to have such an attentive student and happy to share with her some of the secrets of her craft, much of which she had learned from her own mother. She had told her young protégée on one occasion that, provided she continued to apply herself to her learning, then maybe when the current incumbent had gone to her long awaited retirement, Ann might step into her place and become the next cook at Ranelagh Hall. From that moment on, that prospect had become installed as Ann's life ambition.

Mrs Heathcote liked to keep her kitchen 'for those who work in it'. She, Ann and the young maid Charlotte Jones were kept busy all day long from their early morning rise for the preparation of breakfast, through the selection and cutting of the day's vegetables from the garden, to the delivery and the serving of the midday and evening meals for the staff and the Ranelaghs themselves, before the day's final job of restoring the kitchen to get it gleaming and ready for the resumption and repetition of the whole exercise the next day. It required focus and attention for the three of them to get done what was required. There was no room for distractions.

The rest of the staff knew very well that Mrs Heathcote's domain was not for entering without good cause. But the groom Murdoch, who seemed always to have time on his hands and possessed an appetite that never seemed satisfied, was a frequent intruder.

He would come in quietly unannounced and tip toe soundlessly over the flag stone floor to inquire whether he could see 'a slice of succulent pie' or there was a 'delicious sweetmeat' he could sample. He pronounced himself a man who loved the 'sweet taste of sugar'.

Betsy Heathcote herself, whenever she encountered the trespasser in her space, had little truck with him and sent him packing with a few choice stern words and occasionally the threat of a raised rolling pin. But the girls who worked with Betsy found ridding themselves of Murdoch's glowering presence altogether more difficult. No match for the redoubtable sexagenarian who had "seen his sort many times before," Murdoch increasingly began to time his kitchen visits to periods when he could be sure the cook would not be present, when she was upstairs discussing menus with Mrs Ranelagh or out selecting and picking the basket of vegetables and herbs for the day's meals.

When he could catch the two younger women together, Murdoch would take great pleasure in stealing up and standing up close up behind one of them, peering over their shoulders "so I can see just how you apply your special kitchen skills." In time, he seemed to tire of harassing young Charlotte and began to leave her alone. But to Ann he became a constant stalking presence. She made it as clear as she could that she didn't want him breathing over her or standing close behind her brushing into her skirts but her protestations fell on deaf ears. It was noticeable that it was only when Mrs Heathcote returned to the kitchen that Murdoch would beat his retreat with the words, "I must let you get on now, ladies. I know the excellent Mrs Heathcote does not permit interruptions."

"I hope that man is not bothering you, Ann?" Mrs Heathcote asked her quietly on one occasion. Ann, who wanted no trouble, replied simply, "No, I can manage, Mrs Heathcote."

Though his employment was supposed to be in the stables, Murdoch seemed to find much time and reason to be present in the house itself. He had quickly placed himself on intrusively familiar terms with Hugo and greeted him every day with the same expression of gratitude.

"Mr Ranelagh, I must again thank you for helping settle the debt." Murdoch never qualified his remark. It was never 'my debt' or 'my mother's debt', just 'the debt'. He might as well have said 'your debt'. But the truth was he didn't need to.

Hugo knew the former slave's debt was his. Murdoch's dues were just one tiny fragment of the overwhelming burden of Hugo's life, the reparation he believed he owed to all those who had suffered directly, or even indirectly, as a result of his grandfather's depredations. All the money that Sir Oswald and his late son, Hugo's father Peregrine, had made was, to Hugo at least, as stripes taken from the backs of those they had delivered so cruelly into perpetual servitude. Not only should that money never have been made in the first place, but it now fell to him, like a martyr tried by unending punishment, to decide how it should be returned correctively to those who rightfully deserved it. Hugo's greatest satisfaction was to give employment to those people who through several generations had served his family.

Hugo was also delighted that his wife Emily had found personal vocation through the work she did treating with all the good causes who called at their doors, each one always confident of leaving with handsome donation. Emily, though she had been born into the well-to-do Biddle family who had made their money in the Liverpool glass industry, and had no direct involvement in the now contemptible Africa trades, accepted her share of Hugo's ancestral burden as her own. As a couple, they bore their family responsibility heavily and equally. They attended the Unitarian Chapel in Mount Pleasant each Sunday to honour those who had suffered wrongly at the hands of others, to beg the Almighty that injustices be righted, to wish for special blessing to be granted to those less fortunate than themselves, and to ask, in pulsing silent prayer, for their own forgiveness.

In the midst of all this, the opportunity to settle Murdoch's freedom debts seemed especially fitting to Hugo. Murdoch was the progeny of a wronged and enslaved African who had been rescued from a life of enslavement that awaited him before he was even born. Hugo acknowledged that Murdoch was an uncomfortable individual to be around, but correcting the sins of his forefathers was never supposed to be easy. Any discomfort Hugo experienced from Murdoch's awkward presence in his household he treated as one of his daily due doses of divine penance and a recurring reminder of just how much more correction for the sins of the past he still needed to make.

At times, it seemed an overwhelming task to know how to manage it all. But, one thing seemed clear to Hugo stretched out on his rack of guilt: the people who certainly did not deserve to be fortunate were the Ranelagh family itself.

What fortune they had remaining was borrowed money, and it was living on borrowed time.

Seven

Arthur Meggs was brought up in a modest household. His father Cuthbert worked his whole career as a clerk in a shipping office in one of those unfortunate employments which are somehow deemed menial in importance and of low social standing, but which nonetheless require those performing them to fulfil their responsibilities to highly exacting standards.

A calligrapher of no little talent, Cuthbert was entrusted with the penning of all the firm's shipping contracts. To do this he had to capture their terms of agreement precisely and accurately, secure the necessary signatures of confirmation from each of the trading parties, wax and engross the finished documents with the firm's seal, and file them safely and carefully in the office cupboards so they could be instantly retrieved if ever need arose, through dispute or other reason, to refer to the commercial details they enshrined.

When it came to determining the wages for this role, Cuthbert's work was assessed by his employers as so humble that it might be done by anyone literate. It therefore merited minimum financial reward. When it came to tolerance for any error that Cuthbert might make in carrying out this work, however, they found they could actually afford no error at all. Any mistake that Cuthbert might make in the composition of his documents would immediately expose the fact that complete precision and accuracy on his part was actually of the greatest importance. Cuthbert's employers were therefore very fortunate that the standard he consistently achieved met their expectations and greatly surpassed their generosity.

When the time came for Arthur to start out in his working life, Cuthbert gave his son an important piece of advice. "Try to stand close to men who have money, Arthur. If at all possible, help them to look after it. If you serve them well in that capacity, then you should find you are well served in return."

Arthur, good with numbers and with his father's eye for detail, took that advice closely to heart. He trained to become a bookkeeper with a firm of

Liverpool lawyers who offered accounting services to merchants and shipping companies and their owners. Arthur progressed quickly in the legal practice and developed a reputation for speed and accuracy in his recording of incomes and expenditures, matched with a reliably trustworthy discretion in his dealings with their important clients. His name in time began to be mentioned favourably among the notable families and businesses of the town and his practice grew with his rising reputation.

Meggs had been the accounting financial adviser to the Ranelagh family for more than five years when he appeared at Ranelagh Hall one foggy morning in late September. He had wrapped up well against the unseasonal chill in the air. Stepping from his hackney carriage outside the house, he wore a plainly anxious expression. Met at the door by Mannion, he deposited his hat, overcoat, gloves and cane with the butler and was shown through to the drawing room where Hugo stood, expecting him.

"Good morning, Arthur, please do sit down," said Hugo.

"Most kind, Mr Ranelagh," replied the bookkeeper. "It is, as always, a great pleasure to see you, and I do hope you and Mrs Ranelagh are both in good health. I am afraid though, sir, I come with concerning news and this cannot be an easy conversation between us this morning."

"Having completed the 'thorough review' of your financial situation which you asked me to undertake, I have to tell you that it does not make for good reading," Meggs said. "Your levels of expenditure have risen sharply in recent years and are now cutting very heavily into the family capital which remains to you. These high outgoings fall into two categories: the costs associated with employing your full complement of staff at Ranelagh Hall and the steadily rising level of philanthropic donations which you and Mrs Ranelagh have been good hearted enough to authorise."

"How bad is it, Arthur?" asked Hugo, visibly paling. Meggs drew a breath before answering with gravity.

"In my considered opinion, sir, if you continue with the current rising level of outgoings and do not mitigate them very significantly without delay, then within two years your family fortune will be almost entirely depleted. If you are to avoid the unthinkable eventuality that you might be bankrupted, you would need to be ready to sell Ranelagh Hall within one year."

Hugo stood up and walked across the room to the fireplace, looking aghast.

"I am truly shocked, Arthur," he said. "I knew that we were taking on an increasing toll on our resources, and that it could not continue indefinitely, but I did not expect the position to be this severe." He paused for a moment in thought before turning to Meggs and asking, "So what is your advice?"

Meggs, a strained look still written large across his face, said, "My advice to you is as follows, sir. Two things need to happen and in short order. You must cut your staff outgoing at the very least by half, and you must halt immediately all but the smallest and most essential donations to good causes. Some of those you have already made I know carry future commitments so they may take a little time to unravel. This means on both counts that time is of the essence here."

"If you do this, it will restore your outgoings to a supportable level and you might reasonably then expect to be able to keep Ranelagh Hall and a comfortable standard of living for perhaps ten more years. At that point, you and Mrs Ranelagh, who hopefully in continuing good health would still look forward to at least another decade of happy life together, would have sufficient funds from the sale of the property to enjoy your final years in good circumstances, albeit in inevitably smaller and more modest accommodation."

"And is there any alternative to this plan?" asked Hugo.

"None that I can see, sir," replied Meggs. "I am afraid to say the alternative is to allow things to continue as they are today and if you were to be imprudent enough to do that I believe things will spiral out of your control within the next few months. That would be a ruinous course you would be set upon."

"Thank you, Arthur," said Hugo. "Your message is a harsh one but it is clear. There are some hard decisions which we will have to take and promptly. I will let you know what we have decided within two days for your confirmation that the changes we intend to make are adequate, first to allow us to keep Ranelagh Hall as our family home, and second to enable me to continue to provide my wife with a safe and certain future for the remainder of her days."

Meggs stood up and made his leave of Hugo. Gathering his belongings from Mannion in the hall, he walked out into the cold air towards the main estate gates and immediately lit up a small cigar from his pocket case. He had been dreading the conversation with Ranelagh for days and now it was done he felt sick to the pit of his stomach. He felt desperately sorry for his clients who were among the most good hearted of any he had dealings with. But he had done his painful job like a good physician. He had diagnosed the disease and he had prescribed the only treatment. It was the only way they could be saved from themselves.

Eight

Observing the bookkeeper as he walked from the house was Murdoch, the Ranelaghs' occasional groom.

Lurking outside the kitchen door earlier that morning, he had overheard Mannion referring to 'Mr Ranelagh's accountant' as he ran through the list of the day's expected visitors and appointments with Mrs Heathcote.

Now concealed among the hoar frost coated bushes that adjoined the estate driveway, Murdoch was interested to observe from close quarters as Meggs walked slowly away. He registered the unmistakably pensive and strained look on the departing visitor's face, and he did not fail to note the long deep breath Meggs had drawn before he stopped to light up his cigar.

Hugo meantime lost no time in heeding Meggs's dire warnings and acting on his advice. As Murdoch walked past the main entrance to the house as he stole back from his hiding place, he witnessed a flurry of activity inside. Hugo had already asked for all his records and papers to be brought upstairs to his study on the first floor where he planned to begin to address the pressing issue of expense reduction. Servants were scuttling here and there holding piles of papers and carrying them quickly up to Hugo's reading room.

Murdoch continued past the house over the frontage's closely mowed lawns and carried on down the long decline towards the stables. There he saw Edwin the coachman polishing and buffing the brass of the main carriage in the courtyard, and his son Edward brushing down one of the mares inside the number one stable. He slipped inside, picked up a brush and started to help Edward with the grooming.

"I've been meaning to ask you, just from interest, Edward, how long has your father worked on Ranelagh land?"

The young groom wasn't rightly sure but replied he thought it must be nearing 40 years. Murdoch whistled as if from respect for such a length of service.

"That's just about my whole age, Edward," Murdoch said, "and remind me how old are you now?"

Edward was little used to such affability from Murdoch who generally barely exchanged the time of day with him other than to point out some task that he should be sure to get to next. He was flattered to be asked. "I'm nearly 22, Murdoch, the exact same age as my Amy."

"How perfect is that!" said Murdoch. "I expect you'll be starting a family soon?"

"Well, yes, we're trying now," said Edward with a shy smile.

"I'm sure you'll not be long," replied Murdoch good-humouredly. "Now your father, I couldn't even guess how old he would be," he continued. "Would he be 70 years old by now?"

"No!" laughed Edward in reply. "And best you don't let him hear you say that, he's not 65 until his next birthday."

Hugo pored over the books for several hours. The donations were easier than the staff costs to adjust. He could console himself with the good causes that the family had given to generously over many years. It was in the nature of all donations that they could only be made if they were affordable and money was available to let them take place. It would be a sad task to tell these organisations their contributions would have to stop and he would look to spare Emily from any involvement in that unpleasantness. But it could be done, and it seemed to Hugo that the most awkward aspect of that would be to stop unhelpful rumours flying once these various charitable bodies, who probably all spoke to each other regularly, shared the news that Ranelagh donations were suddenly ending. But that could not be helped. Needs simply must, he concluded.

Far more taxing though was the issue of the house staff and finding savings of at least a half of all expenditure as Meggs had prescribed. Hugo, as he struggled with it, went first to the thought that he could let the junior and more recently recruited staff go and keep loyalty with as many of the long-serving seniors as he could. He permitted himself a momentary wry smile at the unworthy thought that such a plan would enable him to dispense with that man Murdoch who would really be no loss to anyone in the whole establishment.

But when he looked at the money paid to the junior staff and the newly arrived recruits, taking them out of the expenses sheet didn't make anything like the difference he needed. He recognised, cursing his own slowness, that if he took out only those staff who earned the least, he would need many more than half the total number of staff to leave to reduce the financial costs by half. Some of the higher paid people, the loyal stalwarts of Ranelagh Hall, would have to go to make the figures work. That was a truly dreadful prospect but it looked as though it was unavoidable. Hugo looked at his watch and saw it was time for him to get ready for dinner. He would have to return to this agony tomorrow.

There was a dinner party at the house that evening with Emily's parents Arnold and Charlotte Biddle and four other couples attending. It should be a merry occasion that Emily had been much looking forward to and which Hugo recognised he must not allow to spoil. His mood, though, was hardly convivial.

The dinner party in fact passed off quite well. Hugo did not for one moment forget the woes of the day, but he successfully pushed them to the background of his mind and managed to engage in small conversation and even join in some laughter as the evening went on. As his guests' carriages arrived at eleven o'clock, he was though very glad for Emily and he to retire to their bed. It had been the most harrowing day and tomorrow would be no easier.

Mrs Heathcote, Charlotte and Ann were left hard at work finishing off in the kitchen. Betsy Heathcote had been up since five that morning and was fit to drop, Charlotte had been run off her feet all day doing all the little things that her two seniors hadn't time to address, and she had done all the legwork to go with that, too. Her eyelids were sagging as the three women set about the washing up together.

"You two go to bed," said Ann, looking over at her two flagging workmates. "You have both been proper heroines today, and I can take care of this. Get off the pair of you."

Betsy and Charlotte were both so far on the point of exhaustion that their polite resistance to Ann's suggestion was only mild and short-lived. They accepted her offer eagerly and with gratitude.

"I'll owe you this one, Ann," said Charlotte as she and Mrs Heathcote trooped off to their beds and to the restoring embrace of sleep.

Ann was just putting the last of the dried glasses back onto the shelf when the back door to the kitchen eased open noiselessly and the figure of Murdoch appeared from the night shadows. Ann stepped back with a start and said, "Can I help you Murdoch? It's right on midnight, and I'm just about finished up here."

Murdoch, it seemed to her, had taken drink because his speech was slurred and she could see from his open mouth that his teeth were stained blood red as if he had drunk wine.

"I'm here for a taste of something sweet before bed, Ann," he said as he moved directly across the kitchen towards her.

Within a second, he was upon her. He gripped her hard by the throat with his powerful left hand and forced her to the floor. She went down under his weight and felt her breath draining immediately away under his fearsome grip of her windpipe. As he squeezed her neck seemingly ever tighter, she recognised that she was in the clasp of a man who knew how to kill, who had killed before. Ann was quite powerless to resist and was on the verge of losing consciousness under the fell clutch of his fingers.

When he had her flat on the ground, with his free hand he tore away at her lower clothing. Ann, her breath denied, felt only half present in the room and was longing for the mercy of the only escape she could foresee, into unconsciousness. Then, with expert timing, Murdoch released his hand from her throat and allowed her for a moment to gasp for air to fill her lungs. As she did, he moved his palm flat over her mouth to prevent her from crying out, but Ann could not have screamed if she had tried. She was frozen, paralysed, only half sentient and filled with such terror that the only thought now in her mind was the same four repeating words: let this be over.

As he lay on top of her on the kitchen stone, Ann now naked from the waist down, Murdoch unbuttoned himself as he pinned her to the floor with the weight of his thighs. Ann heard him whispering breathily into her ear.

"I'm just showing you the way, Ann. I know there will be many a man lying between your legs in the future, so I will be simply the first and all I'm doing is clearing the way for those that will follow."

He took his hands away from her face and set them either side of her head to support himself as he entered her. As he heaved and thrust and moaned, Ann lay unmoving, staring up at the beams in the kitchen ceiling above her where the six gleaming copper pots she was proud of hung down in a row over the cutting bench.

A few sweating moments later, gasping, Murdoch reached his end and slumped upon her, his hot wine-soaked breath covering her face. Ann lay, still motionless, gazing upward, daring to hope that it was done and that this man would now go without killing her. But she was, in her stupor, preparing for that possible worse moment of ending, too, and she had readied herself for it.

Murdoch, after what seemed to Ann an age, stood up and fastening himself above her, he spoke, still in hushed tones.

"Let's be clear, you don't breathe a word of this to anyone, Ann. You know I work closely with your father, and those horses we work with can be terrible frisky at times, and your father is not as young as he once was. It would be a dreadful pity if he were to meet with some unfortunate accident at work, especially at his elderly time of life."

"So you keep this to yourself, girl, unless of course you would like us to make a repeat occasion of it in which case I, together with some other gentlemen of my acquaintance, will be only too pleased to come and oblige you again and regularly."

With that, he departed through the back door and into the night leaving Ann, her heart hammering, her stomach wrenching, to drag herself up from the kitchen floor.

The next morning, Hugo woke early and returned to his study to continue his dreaded task of saving his family funds at the cost of other people's livelihoods. It was now clear to him that there was no way this could be achieved without devastation to many of the people of his household who had served his family so long and so well.

Dipping his quill pen into the inkwell on his desktop, he was about to begin the sickening act of drawing up the list of those who would have to leave his employ when there came a tentative knock at his door.

At his 'come in' call, Hugo was greatly surprised that his early morning visitor was the groom Murdoch who was looking conspicuously tidier than was his custom. His mane of black hair, which normally flowed unkempt on his shoulders, was hard brushed flat against the top of his head and pulled back tight behind his ears. It was tied behind to form a small pigtail, which sat at the nape of his neck, resting on the collar of a white shirt that looked like it had been freshly laundered. Hugo also saw that Murdoch's untidy grey black stubble, which normally smothered the whole of the bottom half of his face and throat, was this morning quite disappeared. He presented clean-shaven.

It was a transformation in appearance in his servant that Hugo could hardly let go unremarked, so he commented favourably, "You look well this morning, Murdoch. I am very busy today but how can I help you?"

Murdoch replied, "Sir, I wonder if I could beg a few moments of your time to seek your help and also, if I may, to put forward a proposition for your consideration?"

Hugo was pressed to return to his task in hand but so unpleasant was it that even this unwanted interruption was preferable to tackling it. He was grateful for the excuse to put it off at least for a short time. "Very well, Murdoch, let me hear you," he said, leaning back in his mahogany captain's chair.

Murdoch began obsequiously. "Forgive me, sir, if I have this wrong, but I have a sense that all is not as it should be with the fortunes of Ranelagh Hall. Would I be correct in surmising that the financial health of our enterprise is requiring of some urgent correction and improvement?"

Hugo was surprised to hear Murdoch so accurately describe his current plight but he was not about to deny it when very soon the whole household would have to know the truth. Murdoch's question at least gave him opportunity to try out the explanation he would soon have to give much more widely.

"Yes it is true, Murdoch," he said. "And I am afraid some very unpleasant and unfortunate consequences must follow from the very poor, even desperate, financial plight in which we find ourselves. It will mean expenses and other outgoings must be cut back severely, and that will mean that a number of individuals, including those most recently arrived, must leave our employ in the next few days."

Murdoch responded to this dramatic news with surprising calm. "I am very sorry but I am not surprised to hear that, sir," he said. "And it is with that prospect in view that I bring you a proposition. May I continue, sir?"

Hugo silently nodded his assent, and Murdoch went on.

"It seems to me to stand to reason, sir, that if a certain sum of money must be saved from the costs of all the staff of the house, that sum of reduction will be more readily achieved if those to leave are the more highly rewarded individuals. For it will surely take many more of the lesser paid to go in order to reach the looked for saving, and in consequence more of the household number will therefore have to depart. Further, since the more junior staff typically perform many of the most lowly but necessary chores of the household, it seems hard to imagine how a small number of the grander senior staff could possibly manage the running of the house without them."

"It seems to me also, sir," Murdoch continued, "that in terms of the debt that you are settling for the excesses of the past, in terms of what you owe and to whom, your family's long employment of many of the senior servants might be said to have paid off that debt quite fully with regards to each of them. Whereas others, who have spent rather less time in your employ, have received far less recompense. But of course I do understand there is still the terrible difficulty of your explaining that to the senior staff after all their loyalty."

At this point, Murdoch paused to allow Hugo, who was plainly listening carefully, to ask him the question he was now ready to answer. On cue, his employer fell into his hands.

"So what is this proposition you have, Murdoch?"

"My proposal, sir," said Murdoch, "is that you regretfully dismiss all the senior staff and their families, with perhaps a small number of exceptions, retaining as many as possible of the lower paid servants, and that you tell all those that remain that in return they must expect to do much more work than they have been."

"My suggestion would be that you should express this in terms of the continuing important debt to society that you and Mrs Ranelagh have dedicated your lives to repaying. You would do this by explaining that you remain committed to continuing to pay off that debt to the greatest of your ability even in the new, more trying circumstances."

Murdoch paused to allow his employer to absorb his words before continuing.

"It is there that I believe I am uniquely placed to help you, sir, because of my special indebted status. So it is my proposition that I put myself forward to you as the new Manager of the Ranelagh Estate."

"What stronger and better message could you possibly send that the Ranelagh family remains committed to righting the wrongs of the past than by appointing the freed son of a wrongly enslaved and cruelly dispatched African as the Steward of your estate?"

"In this role, sir, I will take on the responsibility of handling the departures of all those who must leave and selecting those to remain and informing them of what shall be expected of them in the future. I will take this unpleasant and unsavoury task out of your and Mrs Ranelagh's hands and, in so doing, I will spare you from the painful and iniquitous decisions of choosing among a close group of individuals who are in each and every case so meritorious and have served you with such fidelity for so long. How can you, who have been so close to them all, possibly be asked to perform such a thankless deed?"

"My proposition means your announcement then can be a mercifully short one. I recognise also that time is of the essence and that you are resolved to acting quickly. So I wanted you to know that I am ready and willing now to take up these responsibilities and to commit myself wholeheartedly to helping you and Mrs Ranelagh achieve the changes in expenditure and the running of the household that are required," Murdoch continued.

"I have taken the liberty of writing a short announcement to this effect, sir, in the hope that if this idea finds favour with you, that it will be of immediate assistance to you." Murdoch reached into his pocket where he retrieved a folded sheet of paper, which he handed to Hugo. Hugo read the brief paragraph.

"The Ranelagh family commitments remain undimmed but our financial position is such that there have to be economies made immediately and, to that end, the necessary changes will be overseen by the new Steward of the Ranelagh estate, who I am appointing today in the form of Mr Murdoch. He will be talking to each of you later. My wife and I would like to thank you all meanwhile for all your years of service to this family."

Hugo thanked the groom courteously for his proposal and told him that he would consider it along with all the various other options he was reviewing. At this, he had Murdoch withdraw.

In truth, as the day progressed into evening, Hugo was finding his other options not very various at all and very unclear. He finally lay in his bed that night unsleeping and still unresolved, his mind replaying repeatedly the enormous existential problem of the estate and his vicious dilemma.

He did not seem able to find any financial adjustment that met Meggs' recommendation of cost reduction which also produced any sort of palatable outcome for the estate and its loyal workers. Hugo considered asking for more advice of Meggs, but he reflected that his trusted accountant had done all that he reasonably could in spelling out very clearly what was needed. Meggs had rightly left the detail of the actual decisions to achieve it in the hands of his client. Hugo concluded that it would be an abdication of responsibility on his part if he asked Meggs to decide where the axe should fall. He was not even sure that Meggs would feel at all qualified to accept such a burden of decision.

Hugo also desperately wanted to ask Emily for her opinions. She was always a kind and sincere counsel, but again Hugo concluded that this decision was really his and his alone. It was his family estate and his forebears' money at stake. It would not be fair to ask Emily to be in any way accountable for such an horrendous course of action. He owed her protection from all of this as her husband. As head of the family and the heir to the Ranelagh fortune, Hugo had to deliver his own conclusions as to how things now had to be. He could not pass this poisoned chalice to anyone else.

Hugo did not much care for Murdoch, that was for sure. But he reminded himself, as he lay in the darkness of his bedchamber, that his life of atonement for the actions that his family had taken before he was old enough to understand them was not meant to be convenient or a matter for his personal preferences. His grandfather and his father had in their time exercised their personal preferences quite ruthlessly. It had fallen to Hugo now to try to make up for the untold harm they had caused. That was his calling, his duty.

Perhaps indeed, he began to ponder, it was God that had sent him Murdoch, a man whose cruel beginnings were so typical of the widespread sufferings among disadvantaged peoples that his family had been responsible for. Perhaps Murdoch had been sent to Ranelagh Hall, when he had appeared unannounced that day, for a higher reason. Perhaps through Murdoch, a near perfect emblem of all that was wrong that had gone on before, deliverance could at last be brought to the Ranelagh family. Perhaps he could become their salvation, finally lifting the yoke of responsibility for the untold sins of history from their aching shoulders.

It was notable after all, Hugo mused, that in this moment of acute crisis, it was Murdoch, and Murdoch alone, who had stepped forward to give him not only some support but a solution. None of the other members of the household was capable of understanding the implications of the situation, of advocating a way through it, or of playing any role in effecting the necessary changes. Murdoch had emerged as the only candidate. He had shown himself to be *primus inter pares*.

The more he considered it, the more Hugo began to believe that Murdoch and his proposition was a sign from above. He could think of no viable alternative to it, and it was also the only way he could see that would spare poor Emily and himself from the traumas of having to dispatch so many much beloved servants themselves. Hugo could not even picture how he would get through those horrific conversations.

Perhaps Murdoch had been sent to him precisely to be the agent of the change that was needed to allow the estate to survive, Hugo reflected. This might be an instance of divine intervention, he realised, his heart jolting at the thought. If this was indeed God's will, then for him wilfully to reject Murdoch's proposition without some clearly better alternative might be to court a catastrophe.

The case was becoming progressively more compelling in Hugo's mind. Murdoch did not have any friends among the staff, there was no emotional complication or any issues of favouritism for him to consider. Murdoch already stood apart from the rest of the household. Was it really such a big step to have him stand above them? The estate was now going to have be much more business-like, much more hard-nosed. It could no longer continue as a gentle charitable organisation for worthy causes externally and its own comfortable, deserving staff at home. Who better than a forceful outsider like Murdoch to change the nature of the household and bring about the new order that was required?

As the hands on the bedchamber clock edged up towards four in the morning, Hugo arrived at his decision. Exhausted and relieved by it, he fell quickly into a profound sleep.

The following day, as the house clocks finished striking midday, Hugo Ranelagh, with his wife Emily standing tearfully beside him, read out haltingly a short paragraph from a handwritten paper he held in his trembling left hand to a full gathering of the household staff in the otherwise silent atrium of Ranelagh Hall.

"Good afternoon to you all and thank you for attending. The Ranelagh family commitments remain undimmed…"

Nine

Murdoch, the newly appointed Steward of the Ranelagh Estate, lost no time in holding his promised conversations with all members of the household. He did not move swiftly to confirming his decisions as to whether individuals would go or be invited to stay. Instead, he seemed to rather enjoy prolonging the excruciation he was causing, inviting each individual to tell him how much they hoped to be kept on and how much more they would be prepared to do and what reduction in wage they would be prepared to accept should they be allowed to remain.

He explored with both men and women whether they could think of anything special they could offer him personally to encourage him to give them preferment. For those who stood in his way, or with whom he had clashed, he was, however, particularly vindictive. He saved his most cruel and unyielding treatment for the coachman Edwin Steggle and his family, his two children: his son Edward and his daughter Ann.

"The whole family will have to leave," he told Edwin bluntly in their first meeting. "Not just you but your son and his wife and your daughter, too. She will not be long finding gainful employment I am sure," he said with a leer.

The effect of this warning was to send Edwin into a paroxysm of fear. Bad enough that he would be cast onto the streets himself at almost 65 years of age, but the prospect of his whole family facing ruin simultaneously was too much for the old man to bear. He dropped to his knees to beg Murdoch to spare his children and allow them to remain in the Ranelagh employ though he himself would accept his fate and depart.

"I am not a cruel man, Edwin," Murdoch said after several further days had lapsed.

"I have listened carefully to your heartfelt words about your younger family members. I cannot of course keep them both, but in Christian kindness I will allow Edward to remain in sole charge of the stables on half his previous pay and

51

his wife Amy may remain as a chambermaid but on five shillings less a week." You and your daughter Ann will depart by the end of this week, and I shall come to check that you are gone. That is the decision. "I wish you well in the future."

Edwin, despite his pain, was grateful at least for the reprieve of his son and his young wife, though Murdoch's motivation for retaining Edward's service was hardly philanthropic. The new Steward of the estate had quickly reckoned that if he moved both Edwin and Edward out at the same time, it would have left Murdoch himself as the only man with any real experience of horses on the estate. That would have required him to perform work that he had hitherto shown no willingness to fulfil, even when he was being paid to do it.

If that self-interest informed his decision to retain Edward, Murdoch's lack of clemency towards Ann was altogether differently motivated. Neither Edwin nor any other member of the household was aware of what had taken place between Murdoch and Ann in his midnight assault upon her, so no-one had any inkling as to why Murdoch was now especially keen to be rid of her. Having taken his pleasure of her, Murdoch wanted her out of the way to remove any threat of Ann exerting some hold over him. Murdoch now answered only to Ranelagh, and that was the way he wanted it. Everyone else lived or died at his say-so.

Ann, with some history with him from before his appointment, had become a distinct inconvenience, a potential threat, best quickly dispensed with.

Ann's ghostly pallor about the house in the weeks since the night of Murdoch's attack would in normal circumstances have attracted much attention and concern. But coinciding with the shock that had descended over the whole of Ranelagh Hall since Hugo Ranelagh had made his announcement, Ann's deathly look was one shared by almost everyone. No-one expressed any concern or surprise at her particular demeanour or appearance. They were either too obsessed with their own cares to notice or believed they recognised in Ann's distant stare just the same acute distress they were feeling themselves.

As the time for the departures approached, the Steggle family met in the family cottage in the estate grounds for a tearful farewell meal. Edwin put a brave face on his own prospects and said he was sure the stables of another Liverpool estate would surely need a man of his great experience with equines. His children were really not to worry about him. He also pronounced himself sure that Ann, a young, fit, intelligent, hard working girl would soon find work and lodgings elsewhere.

Ann had no experience whatever of life and work outside the cloistered world of Ranelagh Hall and she smiled weakly at her father's encouraging words. Edward and Amy meanwhile, the lucky family members who would be allowed to continue to earn a living, albeit a reduced one, and keep a roof over their heads, could offer little more than a few warm but ultimately empty words of comfort to Edwin and Ann. With expressions suggesting they feared otherwise they said they were sure that all would turn out well for both of them in the end.

After a time, and with awkward silences beginning to descend over their discourse, Edwin and Amy retired to their beds leaving the siblings Edward and Ann to finish off together in the small sitting room of their servants' cottage.

"I hope you will quickly find a new position, Ann," said Edward.

"I am sure I shall," replied Ann, who was sure of no such thing. "But I have something further to share with you in strict secrecy before I leave."

"What?"

"I am not certain as yet but I have reason to believe I may be with child."

Edward was dumbstruck. He looked at his imminently to be displaced sister whose troubled new circumstances had now just taken a sickening turn for the worse. An unmarried mother with a child would not only have so much more practical difficulty in working and earning while trying to care for her offspring, she would also carry with her the stain of her child's illegitimate birth.

She would be treated by society as a low pauper of loose morals, a shameful individual who had brought disgrace onto herself and her family. She would be shunned by all polite people. This was not a time when women finding themselves in such predicament were embraced sympathetically and cared for. On the contrary, they were held to be fully responsible for their own depraved actions and worthy of nothing but scorn. There was no suggestion that anyone, least of all the father of her child, owed such a woman any financial or other support. She really ought to have known better.

Moreover, this was not just a matter of private opinion or squeamish public prejudice. It was now written into the law of the land that, where providing succour to illegitimate children of the poor had once been the province of the Parish, it was now to be left entirely to the mother of the child to take full financial responsibility for the raising of her unlawful progeny.

What better and more effective way to discourage degenerate and irresponsible behaviour? Let immoral women pay for their sins. How would they and others learn the true responsible path otherwise? Ann had not yet seen it at first hand, but as a consequence of the new Poor Law, which had passed into force in 1834, the low streets of Liverpool were now swamped with such abandoned souls and their children.

Edward, his throat dried, took a draught of water from the jug on the table and composed himself.

"Can I ask who the father is and…"

"No you cannot," Ann said before he had finished his sentence. "You can just know that he is nothing to me and that he will have no part in this child's upbringing."

"Well, we should have something to say about that…" Edward began earnestly. "We do not, we must not and we will not," his sister replied.

Edward saw the uncompromising look of steel in his sister's eye and he saw that was an avenue down which for some reason he could travel no further.

"Will you keep the baby?" he asked.

"That is my intention, yes," Ann replied. "But all this means I shall have to move quickly to find work and lodgings so my child can be brought up healthy and in safety."

Edward looked over earnestly at his sister and said, "Listen Ann, if Amy and I can ever help you, then you know where we are. We have been trying to start a family for more than a year now without success. If for any reason you ever change your mind about keeping the baby, we could give it a loving home here and we would raise your child as if it were our own."

"Thank you, Edward," Ann replied. "That is a kind offer, and it is a comfort for me to know, but I want to be able to raise my child myself."

"One more thing," she added. "Do not tell Father. There is really no point in worrying him at this anxious time. He has more than enough on his plate thinking about his own future. I shall be fine."

Ten

Beyond the varnished gates of Ranelagh Hall, lay the streets of Liverpool, a town of violent contrasts. Vast mercantile riches shared its pavements with abject penury. It was as if the port stood on the confluence of two mighty rivers rather than just one. It was a place where a great stream of unadulterated wealth met a matching torrent of poverty, disease and degradation, and the two flowed powerfully into each other, co-mingling constantly, in a whirlpool.

When the pregnant Ann Steggle, her worldly belongings gathered together in one modest bag, walked out through the gates of Ranelagh Hall, she was crossing a line, exchanging her sheltered upbringing behind those tall black iron estate gates for the real world outside, a world without filters. Her tearful father had pressed five pounds into her hand to tide her through her first months as she crossed the threshold of the estate. That gift, together with a few shilling coins she had managed to save from her wages, was the only wherewithal, beyond her own wits, that she had to take with her.

Nothing that she had experienced working for the Ranelagh family could give Ann any preparation for life on her own. She was, though, not fearful. As she headed out towards the town on foot, she bolstered herself with questions she could answer with confidence. How hard could it be to find work in such a busy place? She was young and resourceful and not yet at the stage where the baby forming inside her would hinder what she could do. She was willing to try new things, to embrace new adventures. This was a moment to make a new life for herself. She would not have chosen this path, but perhaps it was a good thing, forcing her to seek out new opportunity, to embrace new experience.

It began to rain, and Ann pulled her bonnet down over her ears and drew her shawl more tightly round her shoulders. As she made her way down the road, she was passed regularly by carriages pulled by trotting horses carrying men wearing top hats, and ladies in their finery sheltering under covers. The wheels of the carriages, and the horses' hooves as they caught the gathering puddles between the cobbles of the roadway, threw up great splashes of water as they made their speedy and purposeful way into town.

By the time Ann reached the outer reaches of the port area, the rain was falling heavily and, if she was to avoid a complete soaking, she had little choice but to take refuge in a doorway, resting her bag on the ground beside her. A few minutes later, a hunched man, his collar raised against the rain, passed her and, turning as he saw her, asked, "Have you got somewhere we could go?" Ann, unsure of the question, replied that she did not and in fact was looking for somewhere herself. The man looked at her piteously and hurrying on in the rain called back "You'd best try out Lime Street, there's rooms there for a girl by herself like you."

"I need work though, too!" Ann cried out after him as he headed on.

The man called back to her laughing but without turning around, "You'll find plenty up there!"

Lacking any better or other guidance for either employment or accommodation, Ann resolved to seek out Lime Street. It was at least a place to start. The afternoon half-light was turning to October's early evening darkness. The steel grey reflections of the clouded sky and the shades of the turbulent river to her left were being gradually overshadowed by the brown hues of the streets and the dark stone of the forbidding buildings of the port road. Ann made her way onward into what was plainly now the outskirts of the centre of Liverpool.

As she turned up the hill, leaving the hubbub of the dockside behind her, Ann was startled to see the sheer numbers of people that confronted her. At first, she feared there must be a commotion afoot: some incident, which had brought together such a throng. There was perhaps an accident ahead of her or was it, she wondered, something else fearful: an arrest, a robbery, some violent protest or even a riot?

She cowered in a doorway afraid to go further and watched for a few moments what was by some distance the largest number of people she had ever seen. But as her eyes became accustomed to it, she saw it was not a single group or gathering at all, it was simply the vast comings and goings of the town. Groups of sailors heading into the centre from their ships in search of the taverns; street vendors selling fruit and small bunches of flowers; business men heading for home at the end of their workday; police constables pushing their way through loiterers and passers-by; and many, many people who looked desperately poor. Dirty, under-fed, ragged children and young women, presumably their mothers, trying to keep hold of them as they ran between the legs of the adults on the move. Some standing, some scurrying amid the crowds, begging, pulling at coats, and some, Ann noticed, just sitting in the wet, their backs leant up against walls, watching the world go by and letting the rain fall upon them.

Ann was daunted by the prospect of pushing herself into this swirling sea of humanity, but she recognised that her doorway offered nothing more than brief and inadequate shelter, and her purpose today had to be to find work and lodgings. She saw a middle-aged woman with a basket over her arm, standing holding out small posies of flowers for sale to the passing crowds, none of whom seemed to have the slightest interest in buying from her. Ann approached the woman timidly.

"Excuse me, Ma'am. I have just arrived here and I am looking for work. Do you happen to know anyone who is looking for help?"

The woman looked at her and replied, "My God, girl, don't you know there's little or no honest work for womenfolk here? This is Liverpool. All the work for ordinary people here is in the docks and that is only for the men. There's no factories here with jobs for women. There is nothing. In Liverpool, if you've got no man to keep you, then you live on your wits and you make whatever money you can to keep yourself alive, anyway you can. You have got to be ready for that, girl. That is the truth of it."

"Have you got an address you're heading for?" the woman asked seeing Ann's forlorn expression.

Ann, suddenly feeling very alone, her sense of adventure fast giving way to a grave sense of foreboding, realised the only street name in Liverpool she knew was the one mentioned to her by the passing man she had spoken to an hour before.

Not wanting to sound more innocent and vulnerable than she already had, Ann made her destination sound firmer than it was. "I've been told to go to Lime Street," she said.

The woman snorted in apparent astonishment and replied. "The best thing a girl like you could do in Lime Street is go in the railway station, buy yourself a ticket and get on a train out of here. But if you do want to stay in Liverpool, then Lime Street on a Saturday night is just about the best place for a newcomer to get to know what this town is really about."

"Thank you," said Ann. "Will I be able to find affordable lodgings there for the night, would you expect?"

"Listen girl," the woman replied, "taking one look at you, I'd say that would be the surest thing in the world."

Lime Street took its name from its origins as the site in the late 18th century of a row of lime kilns owned by the local builder, bricklayer and brewer William Harvey. Harvey's kilns were now long gone, taken down after the local hospital complained about the unsupportable stench they gave off, but the name had outlasted the stink. The street was the now famous site of the new railway station which opened in 1836, a proud symbol of Liverpool's status as a world port of great importance, a railway destination.

If the modern railway station had made Lime Street familiar to those previously unfamiliar with Liverpool, it had added little to the area's long-standing notoriety for something entirely different. As a thriving seaport, Liverpool had always overflowed with sailors newly put to shore, their pockets stuffed with months' worth of wages at their voyages' end, looking for drink, food, merriment, and company. Women flocked to the port in their thousands to help relieve this never-ending tide of briefly enriched mariners of their new found wealth.

In the year after the new railway station opened, the Head Constable of Liverpool had estimated there were 400 brothels in the city, each housing on average five women. In addition, 2,000 other prostitutes lived in lodging houses, he believed. The police, trying to assess the scale of this huge private enterprise, set it consequently at 4,000 women in total. Those rather closer to the reality than the force that had been newly charged with trying to police it, thought the actual number two to three times that figure.

The entire waterfront area, from Lancelot's Hey to Parliament Street, was inhabited by prostitutes. Some thought the Sailors' Quarter alone was home to around 3,000.

Williamson Square, littered with gambling dens and taverns, was a centre of licentious entertainment and behaviour, with 100 brothels in its immediate neighbourhood. One street alone boasted 22.

But Lime Street itself was the beating heart of this trade, its narrow streets and dark alleyways playing host to hundreds of 'night rooms' where assignations procured in the immediate area's many pubs, bars and taverns could be consummated.

It was to this section of the city that Ann Steggle now ascended in search of shelter, warmth and gainful employment.

Eleven

Ann had never imagined such a place. Lime Street was as if a hundred travelling circuses had arrived simultaneously and started performing all at once. The din was unbearable, music rang out from the taverns, there was carousing, singing of obscene songs, shouting, screeching, laughter, crying. Drink was flowing everywhere, women were darting in and out of bars offering company to any man who would take it, drunk men staggered from drinking den to tavern with painted women draped on their arms.

Ann eventually made out a coffee shop that was only half full. She went tentatively inside and asked for the owner. "That's me and who wants to know?" said the sour faced matron behind the counter.

"I'm looking for work," said Ann. "Are you in need of any help?"

"Listen to her!" roared the woman in reply. "She's looking for work! It's not hard to find work here, girl, but there's none serving coffee if that's what you're asking. But a good looking girl like you won't be long without custom in Lime Street, I'll wager."

Her request denied, Ann stepped out the shop and was immediately caught up in a group of four men, whose day of heavy drinking had clearly begun several hours earlier. Before she knew it, she was seized round the waist by one of the men who, plunging his unshaven face into hers, made to plant a kiss on her mouth. Ann shrieked and hit out at him, half pushing, half striking herself away. The man doubled up as if poleaxed, and as Ann froze, momentarily wondering whether she had done him some harm, he rose up and hit her forcefully across her face with the back of his hand, sending her flying backward into the wall.

"Not good enough for the likes of you, am I?" bellowed the man. "Well don't come to Lime Street showing off your wares if you're not ready to sell." Two of his three companions took him by the arms and carted him off, one saying, "Leave her Jack, there's plenty more where she came from."

Ann, her head still spinning, and tears sliding down her face with the pain from the blow and the confirmed new misery of her circumstance, suddenly realised she had let go of her bag as she fell. She peered through the legs of the multitude pushing and shoving through the crowded street. She could not see it. It can barely have spent two minutes on the ground. It had been long enough. The bag, with all her few worldly possessions in it, including five pounds that her father had given her as she left Ranelagh Hall, had just vanished into the night.

Ann drew her legs under herself to avoid being stepped upon and rested her back against the wall which she looked up and saw was the outside of a tavern called The Traveller. She buried her face into her hands and, lost in despair, she sobbed.

The cacophony of the narrow alleyway filled her head. She was aware only of noise. Not definable words, nor speech nor strains of music, not celebration nor argument. Just an hysterical drowning racket from which she could decipher nothing distinctly but the sound of her own heaving grief.

Suddenly, she was aware of two women crouching either side of her. "Now, now," said one, a young redheaded woman of alabaster white complexion not two years older than Ann. "Cheer up, love, it's Saturday night and the evening is only just starting."

"Yes, come on, girl," said the other, a striking high cheek-boned ebony-skinned woman perhaps a couple of years older again. "What's happened? We've not seen you round here before, have we?"

"No," said Ann, trying to compose herself to respond to the first kind words that had been offered her all day.

"My name's Ann Steggle. It's my first day here. I am looking for work and lodgings, but I have just lost my bag with everything I have and also what money I had. I really don't know what to do next and what will become of me now."

As the younger girl put her arm around Ann's hunched shoulders, Ann noticed both women were, by comparison to those around, quite well dressed. The black girl in a bright blue cotton dress, and the pale red haired girl in vermilion.

The younger girl spoke.

"Well, maybe you've had a stroke of luck bumping into Bonny and me like this. My name's Molly by the way. Nice to meet you. We live round here just a couple of roads back in Hotham Street. We're dress lodgers at Mrs Midgeley's, or Aunt Joanna as she likes us all to call her. She's a kind soul who likes to look after young girls. She's bound to take a shine to you looking like you do."

"I know, I'm sorry. I must look terrible," said Ann, trying to wipe the residue of her fallen tears from her face.

"Not a bit of it. You look just perfect, so don't you worry about that," said Bonny.

"Why don't we take you to meet Aunt Joanna now and see if she can sort you out somewhere to stay?"

Twelve

Aunt Joanna was the embodiment of charm itself to Ann from the first moment she saw her that first evening when Molly and Bonny brought her to her house. She could see instantly she was a beauty, even if her looks were not flattered by the wretched expression she wore as she stepped across the doorwell. She was also soaked from the rain and splattered with mud from head to toe by her bruising encounter and fall outside The Traveller Inn.

"Let me run you a nice hot bath straight away," said Aunt Joanna, a handsome, full bosomed, woman around 45 years old wearing an extravagant wig of thick dark brown curls that dropped onto her shoulders. "We'll soon set you right."

Aunt Joanna stayed with Ann solicitously as she undressed and stepped into the tub. The lady of the house poured hot water over Ann's back from a large copper jug. When she was done, and as Ann stood up, fully washed and restored and ready to step out of the bath, Aunt Joanna paused momentarily before meeting her with the towel she held outstretched in front of her. "Oh yes, my girl, you do make a pretty picture," she said.

Aunt Joanna offered Ann a room for that first night as her guest. As Ann slipped gratefully between the welcoming sheets, drawing her knees tightly into her chest, she fell quickly into deep sleep. She was only passingly aware of the constant comings and goings on the staircase and noises from the neighbouring rooms, which punctuated the rest of the evening and continued into the early hours of the morning.

The next day, when Ann awoke and put on her clothes, still damp from the night before, she went downstairs cautiously to the kitchen and found Aunt Joanna, Molly and Bonny sitting around the table drinking tea. Aunt Joanna welcomed her with enthusiasm and immediately seeing her in her dirty and bedraggled garb, said, "Come and sit down, drink some tea, and Molly will get you something more cheerful to wear to get the day off to a good start."

"Won't you, Molly??" she said, darting a look across the table at the young redhead who had not registered the implied instruction.

Molly jumped up, left the room and returned five minutes later with a yellow cotton dress, low at the front with short quarter sleeves. Ann had never worn anything like it, but it was clean, bright and cheering, and certainly a huge improvement on the damp and torn service dress she was wearing. She accepted it with grace.

"So the girls tell me you are need of both lodging and employment, Ann," said Aunt Joanna.

When Ann confirmed that both pressing needs were true, Aunt Joanna replied.

"We would be delighted to have you come and stay here with us and, in time, you could perhaps learn the role of dress lodger from Molly and Bonny. They earn their keep here by sewing and embroidery as well as by entertaining my house guests. And in return, they have room and food, the finest dresses a woman could hope for, which they help me to keep in the very best condition. And on top of all that, they earn some pocket money for those little extras that we all enjoy in life."

"But I'm not sure you've yet got much experience of entertaining gentlemen guests, and I think it would be a short while before you'd be ready for that."

Anxious that this adverse assessment might see her ejected from the house, Ann was about to protest that she would be more than keen to learn the entertaining work quickly when Aunt Joanna continued.

"I do though have some contacts in the town who I know are looking for young ladies like yourself, without much experience, to appear on stage. I don't know if you have ever done any public performing or acting?"

Ann said she had not but, desperate not to displease her benefactor, confirmed she would be willing to try. Ann then decided this was the opportune moment to share the other aspect of her current predicament.

"I should tell you, Aunt Joanna, I am with child and in the next months I fear I will become less able to work as well as I can now. Can you help me to get through until I can bring my child into the world?"

Joanna stroked her chin and looked across at her closely. Her answer delighted Ann.

"I was wondering if that might be the case, my girl. Yes, I think we might be able to come to an arrangement that could work for us both. I can introduce you to people who I can share your circumstances with and who may well be able to employ you through your pregnancy. Their theatre is called The Parthenon in Great Charlotte Street. My friend Mrs Ruby Dean is the mistress there. I am sure she would be interested to offer you work.

While you work for her, you can stay here."

Ann had never heard the French entertainment terms *poses plastiques* or *tableaux vivants*, and since she had never learned a word of French, even had she heard them she would have been none the wiser. But in Ruby Dean's employment at The Parthenon she agreed to appear naked on stage as part of a series of elaborately staged nightly theatrical scenes. Some were recreations of famous paintings, some depicted scenes of history, while others were seemingly new creations composed just for that evening.

Ann proved a popular artiste with the packed audiences from the very start. The shy coyness she showed in her first few tentative appearances seemed only to win her increasing encouraging approval. As she slowly progressed from participating at first only in the unmoving *tableaux vivants* portrayals to stretching out naked in various flexible positions in the *poses plastiques* scenes, her enthusiastic following rose steadily and her applause grew deafening.

As the months progressed, Ann's popularity did not decline at all as she entered the middle and latter stages of her pregnancy. Indeed, her first lightly rounded and then fully pregnant naked form made her the most successful and sought after of all the artistes to appear at The Parthenon. Ruby Dean could not have been more highly satisfied with the success of her new protégée.

Ann was escorted to The Parthenon and back each night to Hotham Street by a man Aunt Joanna referred to as 'my bully', an Irish strongman with the physique of a bullock who went under the name of Red Pat and who took care of all matters of security for the Hotham Street household. He brought Ann back each night with her handbag bulging with the tips given to her by the many men who thronged into the girls' dressing room each evening after the performances. They paid for that privileged access through the purchase of an over-priced bottle of the Parthenon's famously indifferent wine.

After going through Ann's bag thoroughly, Aunt Joanna left in it only a small amount at the end of each evening. She explained to her lodger that the money she took was needed to contribute to the costs of Ann's clothes, her food and her lodging.

For Ann, while this was not work she would ever have dreamed of, it did at least enable her to keep body and soul together as she went through her pregnancy. She was not proud of what she was doing but once her initial embarrassment had been overcome, it was hardly difficult work, and she was at least proving successful at it. Her audiences seemed to love her and her tips showed it. She had managed to find a way to get money and food and to keep a roof over her head. She could be thankful of that at least.

It was, however, becoming very clear to Ann that this was not a circumstance in which she could bring up a baby, still less a young child. And if she gave up her work to care for the infant, she knew she would find herself cast back immediately into the unforgiving world she had faced when she first came into the town. She would only keep a lodging at Aunt Joanna's if she could pay her way. The moment she could not, she would be thrown back on the streets—and with a baby this time. Aunt Joanna was running no charity. Ann also knew that if she could not support herself on the streets of Liverpool, then it would not be long before she would be carted off to the workhouse and incarcerated. She may have her child taken away from her. For Ann, that was unthinkable.

So when it reached the seventh month of her pregnancy, and with Aunt Joanna holding the pen and writing for her, Ann composed a letter to her brother Edward, referring back to their conversation about her unborn child when she was still at Ranelagh Hall. She told him simply that she had changed her mind. She gave her brother no details of her new situation, but she let him know that she had concluded she did not have the means to bring up a child safely. If his offer still stood, therefore, she would be greatly in his debt if he would agree to adopt her baby.

Two months later, in a back room of Aunt Joanna's house of delights in Hotham Street, Liverpool, Ann gave birth to a daughter weighing six pounds and two ounces whom she named for her mother, her father Edwin's deceased wife, Sarah.

Four weeks to the day later, Ann's brother Edward and his wife Amy Steggle arrived at the Hotham Street address in a hansom cab, as had been agreed, to take the baby Sarah back to Ranelagh Hall where they would raise her as their own child.

Thirteen

Seventeen years had passed since Edward and Amy collected Ann's child Sarah and first brought her to Ranelagh Hall. By announcing to the whole household noisily that Amy was pregnant as soon as they heard of Ann's agreement to give up her unborn child to them, Edward and Amy had managed to present the new-born baby as their own. When they brought Sarah back from Hotham Street, they smuggled her across the lilac blanket of heather at the bottom of the Ranelagh Hall estate. They darted through the woods behind the stables and made it back into their cottage without being seen. The following morning, Edward told the Ranelaghs, the servants, and Murdoch, who was by then well into his first year as Steward of the Hall, that his wife had given birth overnight to a beautiful baby daughter and that both were well. Their subterfuge went wholly undetected.

Now a young woman, Sarah was working as a housemaid in Ranelagh Hall. Edward was in sole charge of the stables and the carriages. Hugo and Emily Ranelagh were still owners of the house and the estate though their lifestyle was no longer what it had been. The house itself had had to be partly closed to save expenses, and that portion which remained open was no longer being kept in its previous pristine state of repair. But at least they had managed to keep a hold of the property, and there were still sufficient funds in the family account for the Ranelaghs to see a future into their old age.

Murdoch was now a well-to-do man. He had seen his own wage increase by two and a half times when Hugo had agreed to make his lowly slave-descended groom the master of his estate, and he had continued to enjoy annual increments to his remuneration ever since.

From the first day of his appointment, Murdoch had ensured he would be in sole charge of distributing the weekly wages to all the staff. After he had overseen the dismissal of all the senior servants—including Mannion, Mrs Heathcote and Edwin Steggle, along with the Head Gardener, the Cattleman, the Shepherd and three other long-standing members of the household—he presented Hugo with a list of all the remaining 15 staff and their wages. This showed that the total costs of employing the remaining complement of servants was reduced by half from what the total staff cost had been, even after allowing for Murdoch's own substantially increased pay.

Hugo showed this to his accountant Arthur Meggs, who confirmed all the figures and assured Hugo that this saving, along with a reining back of the donations to good causes, would be enough to shore up the Ranelaghs' sinking ship. Meggs also congratulated Hugo on his decisiveness and confirmed that it would be fully in order for Hugo to hand the new total weekly wages over to Murdoch in cash for him to distribute to each individual member of the staff as set out.

Murdoch had long since rid himself of any concern that Hugo or Meggs or anyone else would threaten his lucrative tenure. He had successfully farmed out all the work on the estate to the remaining workers, and all he was required to do to ensure matters continued in their highly satisfactory manner was to keep three secrets.

First, he needed to maintain his control over the wages. Second, he needed to ensure the staff were all so frightened of losing their jobs that they would never dare consider going behind his back to the Ranelaghs to complain at their treatment or their lot. The third item that Murdoch needed to keep concealed, and the most critical, was the truth of his own identity. As long as he kept those three things under wraps, he was home and dry. Living high on the hog's back, not at cloud on his horizon.

Murdoch meanwhile was keeping a watching and increasingly admiring eye on Edward Steggle's young daughter Sarah. She had a vivacious demeanour, bright eyes and a glorious smile, and there was something about the unusual mix of her pale complexion and dark luxuriant hair that drew Murdoch's lustful gaze. As he was the Steward of the estate, Sarah, like all the servants, worked for him. And what Murdoch wanted, Murdoch got.

Over the 17 years since his attack on Edward's sister Ann, when he was still the lowly groom, Murdoch had availed himself of many other young women on the estate. The others since Ann he had compelled to comply with his desires, not through physical force nor menace, but simply by making it clear that submission to him as the Steward was the price all young girls in the employ of the Hall needed to pay if they wished to remain. His threat to them was even greater than physical violence; it was the prospect of ruin.

It was a source of shivering delight to Murdoch that he could now achieve what he wanted with the co-operation and freewill of the women he targeted. He found it deliciously gratifying that he no longer had to overpower them to have them comply with his lusts. He simply needed to compose a few well-chosen sentences, and they would step out of their clothes and obey him obligingly. These, he noted with the sickly satisfaction of the self-entitled, were the trappings of the authority he had worked so hard to earn. He savoured these fruits of his power with even greater relish than when he had taken his pleasure by force.

Murdoch summoned Sarah to his rooms one afternoon in March and, locking the door behind her, gave her what was now his well-practised speech.

"Sarah, I have noticed that now you are 17 years old, you are now becoming a woman. It is part of my role as the Steward of Ranelagh Hall to bring all young women of your age into womanhood through performing the act of sexual congress. Compliance with my right to this is a condition of all young women such as yourself remaining employed on the estate. This legal right is referred to formally by an official French term: *droit de seigneur*. Today is the day when I wish to exercise that right here in the adjacent room." He pointed to his bedchamber, which adjoined his study.

Sarah, horrified, buried her face in her hands and dissolved into tears of fright and disgust.

"No, no, no," she said. "I do not want that to happen and you cannot compel me against my will."

"Of course not, Sarah," Murdoch replied with a deceitful grin.

"First, let us be clear that this conversation must always remain a secret between us or there will be the direst consequences for you and your family. But let me explain to you that you have three options here. You undress now and comply, and my right will be exercised. Or you refuse and leave this room, in which case my right is automatically increased tenfold and there will be ten such occasions to be satisfied in the future before your obligation is met. The third option is for you to refuse, which will immediately end your employment here today, along with that of your mother and your father. All three of you will then leave Ranelagh Hall tomorrow morning forever if you would seek to deny me my entitlement as the Steward of this estate."

"But whatever would we do if we had to leave?" Sarah cried in horror.

"I have no idea," Murdoch replied, "but I am aware that outside the protection of the Ranelagh estate many people have found it harsh in the extreme and have fallen quickly into degradation and destitution on the streets. I cannot believe that is a fate you would wish upon your loving parents who have brought you up so selflessly, even if you could contemplate bringing it upon yourself."

With that, Sarah fell quiet, a dread realisation of the desperate nature of her position descending upon her.

"Which choice will you make, Sarah?" asked Murdoch lasciviously, finally breaking the crushing silence between them.

"Your so called options give me no choice at all, Murdoch, and you know it," she said. "I will do it now."

Fourteen

After she gave up the baby Sarah to Edward and Amy, Ann had returned a few weeks later to her appearances at The Parthenon where she remained a popular performer even if not quite reaching the heights of fevered attention she had enjoyed in her late pregnancy.

After a few months, Aunt Joanna suggested to Ann that she was now 'ready to move up in the world' and escorted her one morning to Abercromby Square, then the most desirable address in Liverpool. Among the longstanding residents of the grand town houses on the quadrant were powerful Liverpool dynasties such as the Gladstones, the Littledales and the Earles. In recent years, some of the town's moneymen, among them the Langtons and Mozleys, and shipping magnates such as the Ripleys, the Doerings and the McIvers, had all come to live in the square.

Standing discreetly among those grand homes was a house run by a refined, always expensively perfumed, lady known as Madam Jessica who kept an establishment there preserved for the special entertainment of Liverpool's wealthy and most powerful. Because she served the local upmarket clientele, Madam Jessica received no troublesome attention from local busybodies or from the police. Indeed, the local constabulary, whose senior members included several regular clients of the house, helped to ensure that decorum and high standards were preserved by quickly moving on any undesirables who threatened to disturb the tranquil elegance of the square or soil the privileged pathway to Madam Jessica's door.

Over tea in her drawing room, Madam Jessica assessed Ann as a potential 'silken' hostess, fit to entertain her demanding and wealthy clients. She approved of her fresh complexion and her strawberry flecked hair. And dressed as she was in Aunt Joanna's best violet velvet dress, Ann successfully passed muster and was accepted into the embrace of the Abercromby Square establishment. Madam Jessica discussed the terms of Ann's employment with Aunt Joanna. Seventy per cent of Ann's earnings would be retained by Madam Jessica, 20 per cent would be remitted to Joanna, and Ann herself would be permitted to keep the remainder. Madam Jessica advised that if she worked hard, Ann's own earnings would likely exceed five pounds a week, or three times what she was earning as an artiste at the Parthenon.

So it was in the grandest style available in Liverpool that Ann was introduced formally to a life of prostitution. Her clients were all moneyed and mostly considerate in their conduct. Madam Jessica's establishment did not permit the entry of the inebriated, so Ann did not have to cope with drunkards. The best were very appreciative of her and treated her well. Many became frequently returning clients, her 'regulars'. A few, whose tastes and proclivities were more demanding, Ann would tolerate for a while for higher fees if pressed strongly to do so by Madam Jessica on account of the importance to the establishment of certain individuals. But after a while, Ann's standing and the demand for her company rose to a level where she was able to decide for herself which clients she was comfortable to see, and from then on she saw only those.

In all, Ann spent 12 years in Abercromby Square before Madam Jessica decided she had outlived her best years and should be replaced by a younger girl. She was little more than 30 years of age.

Ann then returned to Hotham Street and became one of Aunt Joanna's dress lodgers where she worked alongside Molly and Bonny. It was altogether a coarser and more demanding life than she had enjoyed in Abercromby Square. The clients were sailors and other working men, often looking for easy comfort after a night out drinking heavily in the taverns of the town. The manners and behaviour and standards of hygiene of many of them left much to be desired. Ann had to toughen up quickly and learn to hold her own. While Red Pat was never too far away on the Hotham Street premises, ready to intervene to turf out unruly or violent customers, Ann still had to be ready to defend herself with her fists when it was called for.

Ann found her new lowered circumstances, a far cry from her life as a courtesan in Abercromby Square, almost intolerable. To get through the days, nights and weeks, she began to drink. She started with beer and wine and then moved to spirits: gin, rum and whisky, until she was not too particular what she took. She would now welcome anything to deaden the experience of her life as a Hotham Street whore. With the increasingly heavy drinking went her complexion and her looks. She lost a front tooth after a blow in the face from one drunken and dissatisfied client, and she began to be passed over for other girls when clients came to the Hotham Street door and asked to choose a companion.

After a time, with Ann's income falling, Aunt Joanna threw her out, saying she was no longer bringing in enough to pay her way. Joanna told her she bore her no ill will and Ann could pay for a room by the hour if she brought back clients. This she did for a while, before the rate Joanna wanted to charge for the room was exceeding what she could earn by taking it. Ann then rented two modest rooms in nearby Gascoyne Street, where she received her few regular clients and supplemented that meagre income by soliciting casual trade in the inns and taverns of the town.

Fifteen

Sarah mentioned her degrading encounter with Murdoch to no-one. But when two subsequent months had passed by without a bleed, it became clear to her that she had fallen pregnant. Though the circumstances of the conception were dire, her maternal instinct and her sense of responsibility for her unborn child were immediate and strong. She wanted the baby and to raise it with love. But if she had hope of a supportive response from her parents to this ambition, she was to be disappointed.

When she broke the news to Edward and Amy, it was as if an explosion had hit their cottage. Amy let out a high-pitched scream and fell into hysteria. "Oh no, Sarah! What have you done? This is dreadful and terrifying, too. The shame of it! The disgrace you have brought on us and our family! What are we to do?"

Edward was stony faced as he sought to comfort his sobbing wife. His reaction was cold and instant. "I cannot believe you have brought this shame on us, Sarah. We really do not deserve it. Unless you agree to have the baby disposed of, you will have to leave our house. Even if we were to think otherwise for a moment, with an illegitimate child in our midst, Mr and Mrs Ranelagh would have to send us all away from their estate, and they would be quite right to do so. We could have no complaint at being cast out of their employ."

As Sarah sat listening, a stream of tears rolled down her cheeks. "I hoped that my parents would have been kinder. But I shall have the baby that God has willed to be mine."

"You are no child of ours, Sarah, not in the eyes of God nor the law," said Edward grim-faced.

Nonplussed, Sarah asked her father what was the meaning of his remark. Edward, standing with his hands on the shoulders of his wife, who was still weeping and seemingly inconsolable, replied, "You are not our daughter Sarah, and you never have been."

Sarah, unable to speak, waited for the elucidation.

"You are the daughter of my sister Ann, who had to leave this estate nearly 18 years ago, pregnant with you after also choosing to lie with a man outside wedlock. She, too, brought shame upon herself and this family, and Amy and I did what we could, what we thought was right, to give you, her illegitimate child, a decent home and upbringing."

"This now is how you have repaid us, with the same disgrace that your mother brought upon herself. All we have tried to do for you from a baby now counts for nothing. It's like mother, like daughter, it seems."

"What ever became of my mother?" asked Sarah, her mind coursing ahead. "Is she alive?" "Where is she now?"

Ann was sitting alone in her Gascoyne Street rooms, nursing a half bottle of rum, when there was an urgent knocking at her door. She recognised instantly that it was not the sound of another visiting client. The knock was neither the discreet tapping of a sober man nor the uncontrolled hammering of a drunk.

When she answered the door, it was Bonny from Hotham Street.

"Hello Ann, you're to come with me to see Aunt Joanna now. There's been a letter for you, and she says it's very important."

"It must be I have come into a large amount of money!" said Ann throwing her head back in exaggerated laughter.

The two women made their way together dodging through the close alleyways that led between Gascoyne Street and Hotham Street, and arrived at Aunt Joanna's to find her sitting at her kitchen table.

"Come in, Ann, and sit down. A letter has arrived for you, and it says I am to read it out to you. It is an important matter."

She unfolded the handwritten letter and began to read.

To whom this shall concern.

Please read this out aloud to Ann Steggle whom I last knew of at this address.
Dear Ann

This is your brother Edward writing to you. It is now nearly 18 years since we last saw each other and I hope you remain in good health.

I write with terrible news of your daughter Sarah who you passed into the care of myself and my wife Amy.

At this, Ann let out a cry of shock and fear, but Joanna held up her hand to her and said, "Wait Ann, it is alright. Sarah is alive and well. Let me continue." She read on.

Though she is but 17 years of age and has no husband, nor it seems any hope of one, Sarah has broken the news to us in recent days that she is with child.

She says she will not dispose of the baby and is determined to give birth and to raise it. In so saying, she has shown us that she is determined to bring her disgrace upon us and cause us in certainty to lose our livelihood and our home.

I cannot allow this to happen so I am writing to tell you that I intend to bring your daughter to the Hotham Street address from which we first collected her as a new-born and to leave her there at three o'clock this Tuesday afternoon.

I do not know if you will wish to see her but if you do then she will be there at that appointed time. We have explained to her that we are not her parents and that you, Ann, are her true mother. If anyone can help her in her shame, it is perhaps you.

Your brother Edward

Ann was dumbstruck for a moment. Her heart was still pounding from the momentary shock of fearing she was about to be told her only child was dead. The rest of the message required a deal of absorbing.

"What do you want to do, Ann?" said Aunt Joanna after a while. "The appointed day he mentions is tomorrow. Will you see her or do you want nothing to do with her? If you want us just to send her on her way, we can easily tell her we haven't heard of you for years and we know nothing of your whereabouts."

Ann looked up at Joanna and replied "Absolutely not, Joanna, thank you! She is my daughter and I will take her in and make sure she is looked after. She and I can decide together then what is best for her."

Sixteen

The hansom cab drew up on Lime Street outside the railway station, and from it descended a dark-haired girl in a bonnet, with a thin shawl wrapped tightly across her shoulders, followed by a tall man of around 45 years of age who took the girl by the arm. He wheeled her though the side streets and alleys, past The Traveller Inn, into Hotham Street and towards Aunt Joanna's house.

Ann was already waiting at the doorway and saw her brother and his ward approach. She noticed straight away that, since she'd last seen him, he had lost much of his hair and what he had left was greying heavily at the sides. Her eyes then went quickly to Sarah who looked pale and anxious, but that took little away from her beauty. Ann melted at the sight of her.

"Sarah?" she said, as they met, and the two women fell instantly, emotionally, into each other's arms. They held each other tightly and tearfully for several moments before Ann, still gripping her close, looked over her daughter's shoulder and dismissed her brother who was standing uneasily by, plainly desperate to be gone.

"Thank you, Edward. You may go now."

The man, muttering something inaudible, turned on his heel and scuttled away back down the alley in the direction from which he came as quickly as he decently could.

Ann took Sarah back to Gascoyne Street, where she made them both tea and they began talking. It was at once as if they were two old friends who had known each other all their lives, though before this meeting, they had only been in each other's presence for the first few weeks of Sarah's life. There was so much to find out and learn about who each was, and Ann was full of questions about Sarah's childhood and upbringing, keen to learn what she loved to do, and to hear her hopes and dreams.

There was no mention of the baby at first. Ann wanted her daughter to know that she of all people would pass no judgement on her. Eventually, it was Sarah who opened the way for that conversation with a question about her own parentage.

"What happened to my father, Mother, did he die?"

Ann looked at her daughter and replied after a moment's pause. She had long ago decided the story she would tell her daughter about her father if she were ever somehow to meet her.

"Your father was the kindest man in all the world who would have loved you with all his heart. He was a handsome sailor who went on many exciting voyages to wondrous places from Liverpool. He would bring back exotic fruits and sweetmeats and other rare things from abroad. But, tragically, he died at sea in a terrible storm when you were still unborn inside me. Without him, I did not have the means to bring you up alone, so my brother and his wife seemed the best and only way of giving you a good life. I pray now that you can forgive me."

Sarah replied, "Mother, I wish I had been with you and with my father, but I can understand why you made the decision that you did. You can know that I was loved and well cared for by Edward and Amy. Now I have found you, though, at last we can be together, can't we? I hope you will be happy to have a grandchild?" she asked, anxiously.

Ann reassured her daughter that nothing would make her happier, before asking her to explain how her own circumstance had arisen. "Please tell me, Sarah, what of the child's father?" she asked. "Did he abandon you?"

Sarah drew a long breath and replied to her mother. "I am sorry that mine is not such a happy story as yours, Mother. I can hardly bear to tell you, but I will never tell you a lie. There was a man at the estate, a despicable, revolting man, who obliged me to lay with him or he said there would be dire consequences for me and my paren—for Edward and Amy, too. He said we would all be cast out of the estate if I did not give myself to him. So I foolishly agreed. It was awful and I am ashamed that I allowed it, but I felt I really had no choice. I felt as though he was holding a gun to my head—and to Edward and Amy's, too. But kind fate has intervened, and the result perhaps now can be a happy one, because I have a child to come into my life now, and because this child is coming, I have also found my true mother today."

The blood had drained from Ann's face as her daughter spoke. She reached across the table and filling her empty glass with rum, took a heavy draught of it.

"What was the name of this man?" Ann asked.

Sarah responded, "He swore me to total secrecy, Mother, and warned me there would be a terrible price to pay if I told a soul, so I have told no-one. But I already feel that we have known each other forever, and I will have no secrets from you. So may I tell you? His name is Murdoch."

Ann choked on the sound of her assailant's name, who was now revealed as the despoiler of her daughter, too. She drained her glass, immediately pouring another.

"Are you alright, Mother?" said Sarah, concerned.

"Yes, of course, Sarah," Ann replied, composing herself and trying to recover her voice. "It is just that it is a shocking story to hear. But then as you say it has allowed us to find one another and we shall have a baby to look forward to. Good sometimes can come from evil."

The two women embraced, and Sarah unpacked her bag, with Ann making room for her things alongside her own.

Over the next months, they lived happily together side by side. It was soon clear to Sarah how her mother was making her living, but Ann reduced the number and frequency of her assignations, and Sarah took to leaving their rooms discreetly from early afternoon until the middle of the evening to 'go shopping' and thereby allowed her mother to continue to meet with her regulars.

Three months after her arrival, Ann decided it was time for Sarah to meet her long-time associates Molly and Bonny. They agreed to gather in The Traveller where they exchanged pleasantries in which Sarah told Molly that her baby was due in 'a few more months'. Molly explained she hailed from an Irish family who had come to Liverpool from Donegal 20 years prior. And Bonny told Sarah that her unusual name came not because she was born either beautiful or bountiful, but because that was the name of the African port her mother came from.

"My mother lived in Port Bonny in Biafra, and my story is that, one fine day, she made the mistake of catching the eye of a sea captain who was due to set sail bound for Liverpool that evening. He paid a trader a few pounds for her and took her back with him on his ship. When he got to Liverpool, he abandoned her in the port, with not a word of English or anything more than the clothes she stood in. He did leave her with one kind gift though; she was pregnant with me. So that's why she named me Bonny, after the home she never saw again. She died when I was eight years old."

At this point, a man came up to their table and stood over them. Short, hunched and unshaven, he cut an unsettling figure, so Sarah was greatly relieved when he addressed them with a friendly greeting.

"Good evening to you Ann, Bonny and Molly. It's my lucky day indeed to find three such jewels in the one setting. And who is this vision of loveliness?" he asked, his hand outstretched towards Sarah.

"That's my daughter Sarah, Uriah, she's just come to live with me. Would you like to join us and buy us all some drinks?" said Ann.

"I most certainly would, my dear," the man replied settling between them as the women shuffled around the table to create a space for him to sit.

"Allow me to introduce myself, Sarah," he said. "My name is Rathbone, Uriah Rathbone. I am a friend of your mother and these lovely ladies. Your mother in particular has been a great friend to me."

At this point, Ann, without the slightest change of expression or evidence of any movement in her upper body, delivered a sharp kick under the table to her daughter's lower leg. Sarah, startled and on the verge of crying out, recognised her cue just in time. She succeeded in turning what was starting out as an exclamation of pain into a clearing of her throat.

"Agh, it is a great pleasure to make your acquaintance, Mr Rathbone," she stuttered leaning forward. "I am so pleased to be meeting some of my mother's closest friends now for the first time. It's my honour to know you, Molly and Bonny, as well, of course." The two women, unused to such courtesies, gave Sarah smiling nods while raising their glasses of stout to their lacquered lips to take a swig.

"May I inquire, Mr Rathbone," said Sarah, growing a little more confident, "what is your occupation?"

If truth be told, Sarah's question was less a genuinely interested inquiry than the only thing that came into her head to say. But before Rathbone could respond the conversation was halted by Bonny spluttering ale copiously down her front. She then hurriedly attempted to mop herself up with her unoccupied hand before, head down, waving at her companions with the choking words, "Sorry, that went down a bit too quick."

There was then a silence around the table while Bonny dried herself before Rathbone leaned forward, playing his dark bristled chin in the fingers of his right hand.

"It is very kind of you to inquire my dear," he said. "I do appreciate your interest. I'd answer you in this way. I consider myself to be a private person. So I am pleased to say that my line of work is such that I have to answer to no man. I am what some would describe as a free*lance*," he said, placing emphasis on the last syllable.

"I can say, I believe, without risk of bragging, that I am exceptionally skilled in what I do. I like to think of myself as a technician of my craft. My work requires sharpness of eye, deftness of hand and quickness of foot. I'd liken it to the high standards of precision required of a well-qualified medical surgeon."

Sarah noticed Ann and her two companions were now staring resolutely into their own laps as Rathbone continued his discourse.

"I find my work very rewarding, and I am sure you will be impressed to learn that, working as my own master, I am able to obtain payment each and every day I put myself to work, unlike those poor souls toiling in the docks or on the ships who have to wait for a week or even months before they see a penny of their pay. It all means I am able to acquire some things of beauty," he said, opening his jacket briefly to reveal three hanging watches, two silver and one gleaming gold.

Reaching into his pocket, he then brought out something that he held tightly in his hand. "And this is an important trinket which never leaves my side which you might be interested to see, Sarah," he said, opening his hand to reveal a dark and shining wood carving with a club end big enough to fill a man's fist sitting over a thick stem maybe four inches long and two inches in circumference. Sarah saw the carving was of a magnificent African head.

"It's African ebony and it's a thing of great beauty and magical power. I bought it from a sailor on the dockside here when he'd just landed from Guinea. It has never left my side ever since," he said. "Most invaluable it is."

As the barman laid fresh drinks in front of them, Rathbone continued, "Anyway, I am fortunate enough in life to be able to treat my closest friends," he said waving at the three women, "to the occasional evenings of nourishment and entertainment."

At this, Molly and Bonny broke into guffaws, and Molly retorted, "which we do certainly most appreciate and look forward to, Mr Rathbone, we really do."

Ignoring her, Rathbone picked up again. "But as I mentioned, there is one friend to whom I owe a particular debt of gratitude, Sarah, and that is to your mother," he said looking over at Ann. "She has rendered me kind service on many occasions…" Molly at this again erupted into laughter before being instantly silenced by Rathbone bringing down his hand hard on the table and sending the women's ale glasses rattling.

Rathbone returned to his theme. "She has rendered me frequent service to ward off the unwanted attentions and inquiries of those who are jealous of my successes. Those who would wish to detain me elsewhere so as to extinguish the opportunities that my trade present and which my particular skills equip me to deliver. By confirming to such people that I have been in her company, while I may in fact have been elsewhere practising my private trade, she has ensured that those who would threaten my livelihood have been unable to do so. And for that I shall be eternally grateful to her. So, to Ann, your mother," he said raising his glass charmingly, "the very finest of ladies."

At the invited toast, Sarah echoed the single word 'Mother' while Bonny and Molly, grinning, chimed together "The very finest of ladies." Ann responded simply, "Thank you Uriah, you are very kind."

As the toasting glasses were placed back down, Rathbone, his eyes glinting, leaned across the table to Sarah and said, "So, my dear, I very much hope that you and I shall become the closest of friends, just as your mother and I are. Like mother, like daughter, I can so clearly see now. I would very much look forward to entertaining you privately at your earliest pleasure."

"Entering more like," Molly muttered unheard under her breath.

"That's enough, Uriah," said Ann firmly, raising herself up. "Sarah is altogether a different person. She has come from a privileged place with an education, and I can assure you she is destined to pursue a much grander walk of life than me."

Before Rathbone could speak, Ann continued.

"You will please remember that, Uriah, just as I have been pleased to recall, and have been able to recount when I have been interrogated by those who required to know, the many unforgettable occasions we have spent in each other's company at my home. So here's to both of us continuing to enjoy good memories."

With that, Ann stood and said, "Come Sarah, it's been a pleasant evening and it's time for us to go. Thank you for your kind hospitality, Uriah. Bonny, Molly, until the next time.

Goodnight all."

Seventeen

It was by now quite evident to Sarah how her mother was managing to put food on her table.

It was a way of life that did not sit at all well with Sarah, and finally she drew up the courage to challenge her mother on the choices she was making. Was there not another way she could make a living? Did she not feel abused by her profession and by the men who used her?

Ann drew a deep breath and replied to her daughter.

"When I was still a young girl a man took me against my will, Sarah. He told me I was nothing and he treated me that way. He invaded me. He stole my privacy."

"I shall never forget how I felt at that moment, and the shock of it afterward crippled me for a long while. But in time, I decided I would not allow it, I would not allow him, to define me. I would not permit his unspeakable intrusion to weaken me but instead I would use it to make me stronger. I resolved that I shall have my retribution. So I take it now, every day, from each and every man who crosses my path and who I make hunger for my company."

"When I first walked naked onto the stage at the Parthenon, I was so frightened and shy. But even that first night, I realised that the power in that room was all mine. Even the noisiest, the bawdiest, the most carousing of men in that raucous audience I could silence with just one look into their eyes. While they might pretend otherwise, they had all come there to see me, to feast their eyes on the contours of my body, to dream of me, to yield themselves to their basest desires. One knowing look to show I knew why they were there, who they really were and what they desired above all else in the world in that moment, placed each one of them into the palm of my hand."

"I was no longer the Nothing which That Man had told me that I was. Instead, I was the Everything to every man in that Parthenon room. And that is true of all of us, Sarah. Any woman can have just about any man she wants to if she chooses to put her mind to it. We are the very opposite of powerless, we are the source of all power, strong enough to bring any man to heel."

"So, now when I entertain these men, I assert my control over them. I make them wait on my whims until their desires are almost uncontainable. When I finally take pity on them and grant them what they crave, I watch them as their knees buckle and their faces contort and I can tell you, Sarah, I relish the power that I hold over them."

"When, at the end, I make them hand over their money, and I send them shambling out of my door, and by then they usually can't wait to escape, I put into my purse the latest instalment of my retribution. Another pound, another guinea of my restitution."

"In due course, one day, Sarah, I shall extract my ultimate apology from That Man who wronged me himself, in person. I know that I shall. But I am a patient woman, and meanwhile I content myself with taking a little from Mankind each day as I await that moment of final reckoning, whether that comes in this world or the next."

Sarah listened intently, only partly comprehending her mother's explanation but hearing her passion clearly enough. She did though venture a second challenge. "But wouldn't you be happier doing something more respectable, Mother?" she asked.

"Respectable?" Ann retorted instantly, her eyes flashing. "I don't even know what that word means. Respectable in whose opinion? Whose respect do I need and should I seek? If I had it by the barrel-load, would it give me shelter for the night or put a loaf on my table?"

"Tell me, Sarah," she said, "do I need the respect of the snuff-taking toffs riding in the horse-drawn carriages who have more money than they can ever spend? Do I need the respect of the fine ladies who want the likes of me swept from the streets because they don't like the look of me and they worry I might lead their husbands astray?"

"Or from the puffed up politicians who made the law that says a woman like you with a child but no husband should be given no support? Or the clever civic brains here who have created a town where the only work for ordinary people is for men and even they have to stand in line on the docks and beg for it every day?"

"Or from the policemen who if they find you out alone on the streets with no home to go to would rather lock you up to rot in the workhouse on Brownlow Hill than find you outside again the following night?"

"If I had the respect of all these people, and I could fit all of it into one of their top hats, I would rather have the respect of one single person than of all of them put together."

Sarah interjected, "Who is that single person, then, Mother?"

"That person is myself, Sarah," said Ann.

"Self-respect. That is what a woman needs and that is sometimes maybe all she can hope for. Doing what I do may not be 'respectable' to the grand folk and all the preachers, but at least it makes me the mistress of my own fortune. I may have no education in reading or writing, but I have something that men desire and for which they will pay me my price. I can live an independent life as my own person in consequence, not beholden to any man, not answerable to any person, not begging for the charity of others in order to survive. I make an honest living this way, Sarah, and believe me I see no other way."

"The truth is, Sarah," Ann added, "all those people whose respect you'd like to earn don't give a tinker's cuss whether you live or you die. So make sure you don't die trying to win it. They've a hundred grand opinions about how you and our sort should live our lives, but don't you dare hope for a shilling or a helping hand from any of them along the way. The only person you can rely on to look after you, my girl, is yourself."

Sarah could hear her mother's vehemence but she tried one final time. "But what about me, Mother, I am good with a needle. I was thinking after the baby is born of looking for work seamstressing?"

Ann smiled at her daughter. "Bless you, Sarah. If you think you can support yourself and your new baby on five shillings a week, then that is the course you should take. A young girl like you with your great beauty and in the right establishment can earn 20 times that in the same time. You would end up trying to supplement the pennies you'd earn as a seamstress out on the streets as a hawker, trying to sell picked flowers that no-one wants to buy, but without a home or any protection."

"Consider this alternative well, Sarah," Ann said. "You and I can become two of a trade, and because I know this world of old, I can ensure that the clients you see are only the best ones that can pay the highest prices. Between the two of us we can look after your child and bring in the money to ensure the three of us can live a life worth living, where we answer to no man. That is what I would call a 'respectable' life."

For Sarah, Ann's 'two of a trade' proposal was deeply unpalatable. But she had heard enough in her mother's words to be in no doubt of her determination to proceed in that way. She was also more than aware of her own lack of any viable alternative.

Expelled from Ranelagh Hall so unceremoniously by the couple she thought were her natural parents, only to find she had been living a lie, and with a baby of her own on the way, the sudden fortuitous appearance into her life of her real mother had been a godsend for Sarah. She recognised that if she were to reject Ann's proposal of how they should make a living together, it would probably mean taking her new-born child with her and casting both of them onto the mercy of the world. She knew she could not bring herself to do that. Not the least reason for that was it would mean losing her newly found mother in the process, the woman who had taken her in and embraced her so warmly, so openly, the only family she had. She could not walk out nor turn her back on her.

At least not for now anyway, Sarah reflected. She was not yet 20 years old and had her whole life in front of her. She still had her looks, her gumption and her ambition. Perhaps the lifestyle her mother was advocating could be a short episode in her life, a means to a better end. Perhaps, Sarah romanced wistfully, among the gentleman clients she might meet, there could emerge one who would love her and offer to take her and her child, and perhaps her mother, too, out of their sordid world and lift them into far better circumstances. She might one day marry a man like that and even become a lady.

Sarah consoled herself with that dream as she braced herself to embark on the new chapter in her life.

As the expected day of the birth of Sarah's child approached, Ann paid a visit to Aunt Joanna.

"I'm here to talk about the future," she said. "My daughter will give birth any day now and we will soon be in need of more money than I can possibly bring in to support three mouths in the family. I was thinking of asking you to introduce Sarah to Madam Jessica for me."

Joanna replied, "There is no doubt in my mind that Jessica would be very pleased to take Sarah. She is a rare beauty and would for sure be a high attraction at Abercromby Square. But I have been considering this for a little while myself, Ann, and I do have an alternative proposal for you."

"What is it?" Ann asked.

"If you bring Sarah to me here, I will take you back and give the two of you the two rooms on the top floor to live in permanently. I will also make you a business proposition that you can keep one third of what she and you will earn, and you pay me the remainder. That's much better terms than Sarah would ever get from Jessica."

Ann recognised that, even to contemplate making such a proposal, Aunt Joanna must believe that Sarah as a Hotham Street dress lodger would be capable of earning a great deal of money. Pounds turned to guineas turned to gold.

Ann responded, "two thirds to us, and one third to you." Joanna, her prize then in sight, responded instantly "down the middle, half, half."

"Done," said Ann. "And you pay for a replacement tooth for me so my sparkling smile is restored, too. I can't be entertaining the great and the good again looking a fright like this," she said, cracking her broken grin.

Their pact sealed, the two women shook hands on the bargain.

Ann and Sarah moved into the top floor rooms at Hotham Street that evening. The following week, Ann became one of the first patients of Liverpool's new Dispensary for Diseases of the Teeth, which had opened earlier that year. She emerged with the line of her top row of teeth handsomely restored, with an artificial tooth of ivory filling the unsightly gap left by the damaging blow to the face she had taken.

Two weeks later, on May the 17th, 1860, Sarah Steggle gave birth to a seven-pound son. She named him Joseph. He was a good-looking boy with bright blue eyes and a mop of dark wavy hair.

The period that followed was the happiest of Ann's life. She, with Sarah and the baby, lived comfortably on the top floor of Hotham Street. Sarah became one of the most sought-after prostitutes in all of Liverpool and she charged accordingly. She entertained fewer clients but they paid considerably more. Ann acted both as her Madam and as an alternative attraction for those for whom Sarah's high prices were beyond their means or else had a fondness for the more mature lady. Between the two of them, they shared the job of bringing up Joseph. When one worked, the other cared for the child.

The financial arrangement worked very successfully. Joanna's half share in their earnings doubled what she had previously made from working girls using those rooms by the hour. Ann and Sarah were able to afford good clothes and good food, and they lived well in their own private accommodation, which allowed them to give young Joseph a secure start to life. Their celebrity increased, and they were referred to in the local newspaper on several occasions as well-known local courtesans. Sarah and Ann were described together in one article as 'two popular prostitutes'.

That was an understatement. The two had become very popular indeed.

Eighteen

But it was not to last. Among Sarah's most devoted early clients was a young painter called Leonard Cartwright. He visited her frequently, paying her full price for each of his visits, and the two soon became close. Sarah began to look forward to his appointed days. She ceased to see him only as a client, and he, too, longed to be with her, wishing the time away between his visitations.

The relationship was no longer one of simple gratification and financial transaction. This had been going on for more than six months when Cartwright asked Sarah to come and live with him in his house in Rodney Street. He was so keen to secure her that he said she could bring with her not only her son but also her mother.

For Sarah, who loved him, this was the chance to escape from a life she found distasteful, though the trappings of her high popularity were considerable. Cartwright was a talented artist who lived comfortably from selling his highly regarded works, even though he was not yet 30 years of age. He could support the three of them with ease in a house that was among the finest in the town.

Sarah felt like her dream of escape from her lowly circumstances was coming true. But any hopes she had that her mother would welcome this new prospect were soon to be dashed. "Don't you see, Mother?" Sarah pleaded. "It is so perfect! We can go together. Leonard has told me you are welcome to come, too, and we will have a house of our own, a real family home. We can be well-to-do people and live like a proper family!"

Ann, though, was quite horrified that, no sooner had they managed through their own endeavours to make their lives comfortable and entirely self-supporting, than Sarah wanted to end it all and move them all into a kept house where they would become an instant, convenient, surrogate family for the painter.

She was deeply suspicious that Cartwright had not asked her daughter to marry him, but just to move in with her son and mother in tow.

"What does that say to you, Sarah?" she asked. "Why, if he loves you so much, and must have you with him, does he not ask you to be his bride? He has enjoyed your company so many times as a paying client, and now he wants to have that pleasure all the time but with no payment required? What sort of arrangement for you is that?"

Sarah did not see it at all in the same way. Cartwright told her he loved her and had promised her that they would see how things worked out. This arrangement would give them all the opportunity to see how they lived together and allow their relationship to flower, away from the unsavoury rooms of Hotham Street. It would enable Cartwright to develop his relationship with young Joseph and show himself to be a man worthy of being his father. At the same time, Cartwright confirmed he would happily afford her mother indefinitely a safe and clean home, removing the need for her to do degrading work while, most important of all, saving Sarah herself from a life that was so unworthy of her.

To Sarah, who was not yet 20 years old, this sounded like a type of heaven. Ann, defeated and under duress, gave notice to Aunt Joanna of their intention to leave, and they departed Hotham Street for what was to be the last time. Sarah, Joseph and Ann moved that day into Cartwright's home. The 1861 census filing made by Cartwright for the house described himself as a painter, Sarah as his housekeeper, Ann as a lodger and the infant Joseph as his nephew.

Sarah was delighted with the new arrangement, living in splendid surroundings in a beautiful home with no unwanted requirements upon her. Ann, on the other hand, was deeply unhappy, feeling she had been cheated. Cartwright had come along out of the blue, fallen for her beautiful daughter, and plucked her away from a world where, for the first time, she had opportunity to make herself a self-sufficient woman, to earn all the money she needed to build a good independent life and bring up her young son. She could have borne it better if Cartwright had done the honourable thing and married her. How could she not have? But this was intolerable. It all looked so ideal from the outside but underneath she felt it was abuse.

Ann was also very under-occupied. For the first time in her life, she did not have to work hard or struggle for her living. She had food laid on, she had clean sheets to sleep in but she had nothing to do. It did not take long for her to return to the drinking which had been held in abeyance while she and Sarah occupied the Hotham Street top floor rooms.

She began to drink solidly through the day and, her tongue loosened by drunkenness, there were frequent unpleasant arguments between her and Cartwright and between her and Sarah, who saw her mother's behaviour threatening to destroy the new idyll she had managed to create for them.

"She is all I have, and you have taken her away from me!" Ann told Cartwright during one heated altercation.

One morning, Ann came downstairs still drunk from the night before and, seeing Cartwright and Sarah with Joseph seated at the breakfast table, hurled a flowerpot at Cartwright, who had to restrain her physically. Ann complained to the police that Cartwright had attacked her, and the case went before the police court. Humiliatingly, Sarah gave evidence against her mother that she was in fact the assailant, not the victim, and Ann's case against Cartwright was dismissed with an order for her to pay the defendant's costs.

After that incident, Ann returned increasingly to the streets and plied her trade once again among the inns and taverns of Lime Street and the surrounding alleys, renting out rooms in the night houses around the station and frequenting the notorious sailors' quarter on the dock road. She remained as a lodger in the Rodney Street house, but now went back there to sleep only when she had no other room nor occupation for the night.

Nineteen

"Immorality assumes many forms but two are unusually prominent. They are 'intemperance' and what is called 'the social evil'. The former is often the parent of the latter and they increase and diminish together… We are entitled to expect as much order and decorum as one finds in the streets of Paris or London, yet it is perfectly well known we do not possess it."

Reverend Abraham Hume, vicar of Liverpool Vauxhall parish in his report on the Condition of Liverpool, Religious and Social, 1858.

It is a question that has perplexed mankind for centuries: which came first, the chicken or the egg? A variant of that age-old conundrum, when applied to the world's oldest profession has similarly defied an answer. Does the supply create the demand, or does the demand create the supply?

Liverpool in 1860 was awash with prostitutes and street-walkers numbering into their several thousands. But more than matching them were the sailors, with as many as 30,000 or even 40,000 in the town at any one time. While the women toured the streets and the taverns looking for custom, the sailors went looking for drink and comfort in the same places. Many seafarers would routinely spend three parts of their pay on alcohol and prostitutes. It all made for a ready exchange of desire and fulfilment.

The town's thriving twilight business needed no further encouragement from outside, but it received some from a most unlikely source: the Law. When, one night, a ship caught fire while berthed in the Liverpool dock, the civic rule-makers rushed to pass a new Dock Act forbidding fires and lights on any vessel berthed in Liverpool after dark, to ensure there should be no repeat.

Retiring to their dinners that evening, the worthy burghers who passed that new regulation will have been cheered by the thought they had improved the safety of the town. What they did not foresee was that no lights on docked ships meant sailors' berths were plunged into total darkness by nightfall. No fires on a berthed ship meant no food could be cooked on board. A more effective way to drive hordes of hungry and thirsty sailors into a town in search of sustenance and other comforts would, therefore, have been difficult for even the cleverest of lawmakers to devise.

One of the taverns on the Dock Road that Ann had taken to frequenting on the lookout for seafarer clients with money to spend, and appetites to satisfy, was named The Bunch of Grapes. One cold mid-evening in November, Ann, seeking trade, threw open the door of the noisy inn and saw every table occupied with drinkers. Some already had working girls pressing their charms upon them, but two tables, she saw, were still without female company. Around the first table sat four serious looking men engrossed in a game of cards, who did not look open either to interruption or diversion. At the second table were three men huddled together in conversation. With half a bottle of whisky inside her already, Ann made her way decisively across the room towards them.

Murdoch, or to give that man now his proper name, Pyramus Hearne, was drinking in The Bunch of Grapes that evening with two fellow members of the Romani traveller families from which he came. Their names were Neptune Rivera and Wisdom Garseer. Hearne, Rivera and Garseer had been close associates until that day two decades earlier in Birkenhead when Hearne had overheard a bar room conversation about a wealthy family in the village of Everton called the Ranelaghs, who were big charitable donors wracked with guilt about their history in the slave business and determined to pay off their dues.

On hearing that story, Hearne had immediately sensed an opportunity.

Blessed from his youth with an easy facility for spinning a tale, Hearne had wagered his two friends that night a guinea each that he could get himself a job with the Ranelagh family within 48 hours. When he did not return to his wagon in their caravan camp for two nights, Rivera and Garseer concluded Hearne had either gone before his time to meet his maker or, far more likely knowing him, he had won the bet.

Were one to cut Pyramus Hearne, a physician would find evidence of many different bloods inside him. He came from a rich blend of generations of Romani families, some Irish, some Spanish, some Turkish, some Italian, some north Indian. Mixed blood from all those heritages coursed through his body.

But blood that not even the most assiduous phlebotomist would ever find a single drop of in his veins was African. The heart-rending tale he had presented to Hugo Ranelagh when he first persuaded him to give him employment at

Ranelagh Hall was a fabrication, a fiction, a lie. The basis on which he had subsequently secured his position as Steward of the estate was pure invention. He had no enslaved father and no white mother who bought him his freedom. He had no honourable debt to pay off. The only debts Pyramus Hearne owed were those he had racked up himself gambling and walking out on unpaid bills.

Pyramus was regaling Neptune and Wisdom with the old hilarious stories of his grand deception of the Ranelaghs that night at The Bunch of Grapes, and the three men were engulfed in guffaws of laughter at his retelling of the old familiar tales. Accepting their hearty applause, Hearne told his companions conspiratorially, "But you should know that my time there is now nearly done. I have achieved all that I wanted and I shall soon be striking out to pastures new and acquiring a suitable property of my own." It was at this moment that Ann strode up brassily to their table.

"Good evening, you three fine looking gentlemen," she said, leaning over them, her breasts spilling out over the front of her dress. "Might any of you be looking for a little company tonight?" Hearne's two companions remained silent, ignoring the question and waiting for her to move on. But Pyramus lashed out at her.

"Get away from us, you harlot! Can't you see we're engaged in men's conversation?"

Ann looked at him full on and instantly recognised her old foe. Seeing him for the first time since she had left the Ranelagh Hall kitchen all those years ago, not long after he had violated her, her blood ran ice cold. But while she knew him well enough, it seemed that Hearne did not recognise her.

"Who are you calling a harlot, you filthy rat?" she shrieked falling onto him, scratching at his face and beating him with her flailing fists.

"You flea bitten whore, get out of here before I kill you," roared Hearne standing up as he threw her off him onto to floor.

As Ann was quickly hustled to the door by the bar keeper, who was well used to such exchanges and thought little exceptional of this one, decades of boiling hatred flooded through her head. This was the man who had raped her at 17, the man who had cost Ann her family and her honest living, her home. This was the man who had brought her to what she was now. More, and worse, this was the man who had forced himself on her daughter, his own daughter, too, if he only knew it, and ruined her also. This was that man who had brought misery and shame on her and her family through two generations. This man was the devil.

Having been pushed out of the inn, Ann hurried purposefully through the streets and within five minutes found herself outside a small house dimly illuminated by a single lighted candle lantern above the door. She knocked urgently and the door was opened narrowly to reveal the face of Uriah Rathbone.

"Ann, what an unexpected pleasure," Rathbone said with a broad grin, opening the door wide to let her enter.

"It's not about pleasure tonight, Uriah," said Ann. "Tonight is the night I will ask you to do something for me to repay those occasions when I have kept you out of jail and maybe more with all the alibis I have given you. I have something that should have been done years ago, which should be done now."

A few minutes later, Rathbone led Ann through the dark alleyways back towards The Bunch of Grapes, and once they'd arrived, the two crept to the grimy side window and, peering through it, Ann saw Hearne and his two confederates with fresh flagons of ale in front of them, again emitting their peals of laughter at the stories of artfulness and deceived innocence they were sharing.

"That's him, Uriah, the one on the left with the long dark hair."

"I have him, Ann," said Rathbone, handing her his latch key. "It looks to me like they have about another hour of drinking left in them. Go back to my house now and wait there for about 30 minutes, and then make your way back to me here. I will then have a small job for you to do."

With that, Rathbone drew his dark cap lower over his eyes and pulled the collar of his coat high up to his ears while he receded into the darkness to wait.

One hour later, their night's drinking done, the three Romani men found themselves standing unsteadily outside the door of The Bunch of Grapes. After bidding raucous farewells to one another, they separated. Two of them turned south down the road towards the river. The third man turned north and, 30 yards on, as he staggered waywardly over the cobbles up the hill, he was met by Ann who stepped out of the shadows and stood in front of him.

"How about a little entertainment for the end of the evening now that your friends have gone home, sir? I've been waiting especially for you," Ann said winsomely, her head tilted to one side, the inviting low cut front of her dress revealing her ample bosom to eye-catching effect. She saw Hearne's gaze fall upon her and she watched his resolve melting before her eyes as his ardour rose.

Ann took hold of one side of her skirt and raised it to show him a shapely calf clad in a white stocking. She now had his complete attention. She raised her skirt further to reveal a purple garter holding the top of her stocking in place and above it, a few inches higher, the naked white flesh of her thigh.

"Is there a room we can go to?" Hearne asked, watching her in the half light now captivated, his speech slurred by the drink.

"Of course, and it is very close by," said Ann. "Just follow me. It's only a minute away through this alley."

She beckoned him on with a flicker of her fingers as she looked back at him over one shoulder. He stumbled forward a few steps behind her before he realised she was gone, disappeared somewhere, lost somehow in the night.

His next sensation was the impact of a heavy dull blow to his temple, delivered by a short club held firmly in Rathbone's muscled hand. The next was to feel the slip of a garrotte around his throat, instantly clutched taut and then as Rathbone dexterously inserted the leg of his African carving inside the cord, with the carved head standing proud against the skin of his victim's neck, Hearne felt its tightening redouble.

Rathbone set his right thumb below the stem of the carving as he gripped the head tightly among his four fingers. Then like a clock winder at his task, he raised his thumb slowly and progressively to open out his hand, moving his thumb from the left through 90 degrees to the right, taking the hand from palm down, finally to palm up, all the time gripping the bull head of the carving, unrelentingly, in his fist. As he completed the twisting turn, the garrotte locked into total constriction on Hearne's neck and rendered him unconscious.

Rathbone, stooped calm and still, keeping his slumped victim upright by the tightened cord around his neck alone. He held the tie unyieldingly in place for two more minutes before he allowed the lifeless body of the being they had called Murdoch to fall away beneath him. As he did so, Rathbone slipped his hand deftly inside the dead man's jacket and drew out his bulging purse and watch, placing them noiselessly in one movement into the deep outer pocket of his overcoat.

With that he moved away, leaving his victim behind him lain out on the cold stones of the alleyway. Uriah Rathbone had relieved the world of a stain that none would ever lament.

Twenty

Hugo Ranelagh reported his Steward of the estate missing to the police after two days had elapsed without word nor sign of him. Events then moved quickly as the police were able to match the missing man's identity with that of their unidentified cadaver, just the latest victim of another highway robbery in Liverpool. The officers greatly sympathised with Mr Ranelagh at the loss of his trusted employee, but could only confess with regret that the chances of their ever catching the perpetrators were vanishingly small in this ever shifting transient town. The killer or killers would in all likelihood have slipped away on one of the next ships out of the port.

Ranelagh broke the news of Murdoch's death to his servants who greeted it without visible emotion. While the passing of any man in such gruesome fashion was to be treated with suitable respect, no-one in truth mourned his passing for a moment. For the men in the complement, they were finally rid of an overseer they saw as a ruthless slave driver and exploiter, while the women were glad to be freed of his constant menacing presence and frequently lecherous behaviour towards them.

Hugo Ranelagh unlocked the door to enter Murdoch's quarters to begin the process of removing the deceased's belongings. He noticed straight away a number of iron boxes arranged on shelves behind the door of the room and, opening one with its key, he was surprised to find it packed with folded banknotes. Closing the lid, he moved to the next and found similar contents. A third and a fourth with again the same fat and tightly packed bundles of notes inside confirmed that Murdoch had been hoarding a great deal of money.

Ranelagh moved across to the bookcases that lined the walls of the room with more than 60 volumes tidily arranged in rows. He took down one tome that caught his eye, a broad beamed medical textbook entitled *The Annals of Surgery*. As he opened it, he was startled to see the central portion of all the pages had been cut away with a knife, leaving only the outer inch of every page intact. The carved-out centre of the book created a concealment cavity into which more banknotes, once again wedged in firmly, had been carefully pressed. The next volume proved to have been similarly doctored and filled with banknotes. As did the next.

Ranelagh, aghast, had seen enough. He left the room and wrote a short message, and summoned Thomas, his young footman, to run it into town without delay for the urgent attention of Mr Arthur Meggs, accountant.

"Rathbone has delivered for you, Ann," said the highwayman as he slipped back through the door on his return to his lodging after the killing to find Ann waiting anxiously. "My gratitude to you is repaid. Neither you nor your daughter nor her young son have anything more to fear from that man. He has been dispatched to answer to his Maker."

"Thank you, Uriah. Knowing that he is gone from this earth and that justice has finally been served I will sleep now as I have not done for more than 20 years since I left Ranelagh Hall."

"I shall be moving on now for a few months to allow things to quieten down," said Rathbone. "The beauty of my trade is that I am not bound to any single place, but I can find opportunity to practise elsewhere at the drop of a hat. I think I shall head to Manchester for a little while to seek good fortune and will be sure to come to visit you when I return."

"I shall be waiting for you with the warmest of welcomes Uriah," Ann answered.

Arthur Meggs arrived in Hugo Ranelagh's living room within the hour of receiving his message and, locking the door behind him, installed himself in Murdoch's quarters to begin the substantial task of counting the money Murdoch had secreted away. After two hours, he went back downstairs to Hugo to suggest that he should send up a trusted man to take up the floorboards in the two rooms to search for more hoarded cash. It proved to be a prescient request because the lifting of the boards revealed another two dozen large rectangular wooden boxes all packed to the brim with still more carefully folded notes of currency.

Meggs worked behind the bolted door for most of the following day, collecting and meticulously counting the enormous hoard. Finally, he was ready to report his tally. He met with Hugo in the Hall's main drawing room.

"Mr Ranelagh, I am astonished to report to you that the total sum secreted in those rooms, barring any further discovery we have not yet made, amounts to more than £16,000. Or, to be precise, £16,337 in all."

Hugo was startled to hear the scale of the trove. "But where can such a sum have come from, Arthur? Murdoch was the son of a slave, he was not a wealthy man. That was the very reason he was here."

Meggs answered that he could have no clue as to the source of this money, but suggested that, if Mr Ranelagh would permit him to hold a series of private meetings with each of the members of the household staff, it was possible that some information or some clue may emerge as to how Murdoch might have obtained such a fortune.

Ranelagh readily agreed, confident of Meggs's total discretion in the matter. And over the next day, the accountant spoke at length with each member of the household staff to try to solve the mystery.

At the end of the afternoon, he was ready to meet his client with his findings, and the two men sat down together again in Ranelagh's drawing room.

"I wonder if I could be impertinent enough both to ask for a glass of whisky for myself and also to recommend that you might pour one for yourself before we start, Mr Ranelagh." Meggs began.

Never before in their relationship had the very proper Arthur Meggs made such a request, and Hugo duly poured two glasses from the ship's decanter on the sideboard and sat down opposite him to hear his report.

"It is plain," the accountant said, "that none of the staff has any knowledge of Murdoch's private life whatever, nor any clue about his financial circumstances. None of them has a good word to say about him, and it is also clear that they found him a heartless and most unpleasant man to work for. But none of them was able to help at all with the source of the money, sir."

Ranelagh, visibly disappointed that the inquiries had produced no result, was about to ask what then was to be done next when Meggs resumed.

"However, sir, while no-one could suggest how Murdoch might have acquired such a prodigious sum outside of Ranelagh Hall, I believe I may have solved the mystery of how this money arose rather closer to home."

"I asked each member of staff, by way of introduction before I spoke with them, to confirm to me their name, the nature of their employment, the number of years they had been in service with you and their weekly wage. As each answered, I ticked each reply off against the master records of all your employees that I hold for you."

"Every element in each and every case was precisely correct and in order, except for one which was wrong for every single employee. In each case, the weekly wage the staff reported receiving from you via Murdoch was between one half and two thirds of the sum which you withdrew from the bank on their behalf every week and entrusted Murdoch to pass on to them in full. So while you handed over to Murdoch a total cash sum of £48 a week, to be distributed at the various levels of wage among the 15 staff, in fact he passed on only £30 of that cash and kept the remainder of the money for himself."

"At that rate, in one year, he misappropriated some £936 and this it seems he has been doing ever since you first made him master of the estate 20 years ago. Taking that across the full term of his employment that would amount to the fraudulent retention of some £18,720. Judging by the amount we have recovered, it would seem that around £2,400 of these ill-gotten funds has been lost, presumably spent along the way by its procurer, but we have managed to recover almost 90 per cent by the very fortunate timing of his death. I suspect with this amount of money in his possession it would not have been long before Mr Murdoch would have been taking his sudden leave of you anyway."

The affair was of such significance that it was reported as a scandal in the local newspapers. Police took sworn statements from all the Ranelagh household. These, when put together with the formal reckoning and analysis of Mr Arthur Meggs, one of Liverpool's most respected accountants, and the high standing of Hugo Ranelagh and the family in the town, made the decision of the court on the matter when it came before them very straightforward.

The *Liverpool Gazette* reported the judge's ruling verbatim stating:

"It is clear from the evidence gathered by the police and presented in this case and confirmed by the statements of the accountant Mr Arthur Meggs that the sums recovered from Ranelagh Hall held to be in the possession of the estate Steward, Murdoch, prior to his untimely death earlier this year, were obtained by means of fraud.

The estate of the said deceased Murdoch is therefore deemed to be nil and all the recovered funds of £16,337 are to be returned to Mr Hugo Ranelagh from whom it has been proven they were stolen."

The newspaper added the following statement:

Mr Hugo Ranelagh, owner of Ranelagh Hall, Everton and the grandson of the late Sir Oswald Ranelagh, leading merchant of this town, thanked the judge for his decision. He stated, "This money was stolen not from me but from my employees and to them it shall now be returned."

Hugo Ranelagh took the recovered money, and from his own funds added £2,400 more to replace the amount plundered by Murdoch and repaid it all in full to his 15 employees in shares proportionate to the salary of each.

The *Liverpool Gazette* in a subsequent report referred to this resolution as:

"The action of a true gentleman, selflessly correcting the misdeeds of others."

Twenty-One

As the young Joseph Steggle approached his fourth birthday, he and his mother continued to live a largely happy life in Leonard Cartwright's Rodney Street home. To the outside inquirer, Sarah was the painter's housekeeper, residing at his house with her infant son and her mother. To all intents and purposes, she and Cartwright were living together as man and wife.

Ann, though, continued to be a troubling occasional presence in the household, drinking heavily and taking insufficient care of herself. Her increasingly reckless and licentious lifestyle was taking its visible toll upon her. She looked ten years older than her 41 years, sallow of skin and pockmarked, often unkempt and unwashed. She resisted all her daughter's attempts to keep her in the house and to bathe her.

For Ann, the case against Cartwright was now fully proven. He had still not offered to marry her daughter and, what is more, showed no sign of doing so. To her, his self-serving intent was now entirely clear. He had imported his preferred source of carnal pleasure into his home and would keep it there as long as it suited him.

This caused Ann huge distress and regret for the loss of what might have been. Reunited finally with her daughter and her young son, they had managed to achieve an independence as two adult women that gave them the chance of moving on from the streets into something far better. A few more years of the Hotham Street money would have set the three of them up as a family with a proper future.

Cartwright had denied them that opportunity in a cynical way, returning the two women to subservient dependency. They were now birds in a gilded cage, no longer in control of their own lives or their own fortunes, there at a man's convenience. While she was infuriated by what this had cost her personally, at the very moment she could at last see a pathway to true happiness, Ann was also deeply concerned for her daughter's future.

"I shall be long gone by then, I am sure, Sarah," she said, "but consider your own position in this arrangement. When your looks fade, or when your painter tires of bringing up your son, or he meets a woman of his own class who he sees not as a convenient housekeeper offering comfort, but as a proper wife, what will become of you and Joseph then?

We know what a fine line it is between Rodney Street and Queer Street, how quickly a woman by herself can go from riches to rags. We know what few chances a woman alone has in this town. Wake up and think about it!"

To Sarah, watching Cartwright teaching Joseph how to draw and to read, enjoying the well-appointed rooms of the house, adorned by Cartwright's exquisite landscapes and portraits on the walls, looking out of the tall windows onto one of the best appointed streets in Liverpool, sitting in its delightful garden on a sunlit afternoon, she was in Arcadia. Yes, she would prefer to be man and wife with Leonard, but that would surely come with time. She just needed to be patient. In the meantime, the last thing she wanted to do was to put all this at risk.

The only shadow that hung over her was her mother. She was increasingly erratic, always drunk or on the way there, quarrelling constantly both inside the house and outside, and a growing health risk both to herself and others. Sarah knew it would not be long before Ann's presence could threaten her continuing lodging in Cartwright's home. He had already tried to raise the subject with her on several occasions, but Sarah had successfully and firmly closed down the conversation before it could begin. Ann was her mother and she would remain loyal to her to the last.

Later that year, Ann fell unwell. She stopped staying away from the Rodney Street house and instead stayed locked in her room for more than a week, eating and drinking little and refusing company or help. Her symptoms, which started with aches and pains, backache, pain in her joints, headaches and dry coughing, turned worse with nausea, vomiting and diarrhoea, and finally, with a soaring temperature, she broke out in a dark rash which covered her whole body save her face, her palms and the soles of her feet.

Sarah, shut outside the room with her mother refusing to admit her or showing any willingness to talk, finally decided that she must take matters in her own hands. She had Cartwright break down the bedroom door and the sight that met their eyes was truly horrifying. Ann was in raging fever, covered in red spots with all the signs of her other distressing symptoms evident across the bed and the room.

Cartwright ran out of the house to summon his physician Dr Isaac Abrahams who kept a surgery just ten houses away. Abrahams came running back with his friend and neighbour and, having examined the febrile patient, stepped out of the room with Cartwright and Sarah and delivered his assessment.

"I am truly sorry, but there is nothing that we can do for Mrs Steggle. She is in the last stages of typhus, and I regret to have to tell you that I do not expect her to see out the day."

Sarah, breaking into tears, asked the doctor how her mother might have contracted such a terrible disease.

"Typhus is a severe illness caused by lice and ticks, which bite the sufferer infested by them. And their scratching of the affected areas causes pernicious bacteria to enter the bloodstream and infect the whole body. That is what has blighted your mother. Once this happens, it invariably leads to death, I regret to say," he replied.

"Despite its morbidity, it is not though a disease which can transfer from human to human, so you need not fear that it can be passed from her to you. You can safely give your mother what care and balm you can over her remaining hours to try to lower her temperature and to give her best comfort in her passing."

Sarah stayed with her mother, mopping her down with a water-soaked cloth, telling her that she loved her and was how happy she was to have found her and to have known her, and how especially important it was that Joseph had been able to know his grandmother.

Ann, so weak she could hardly speak, managed only a few intelligible words of response. "I love you, too, Sarah, with all my heart. Take care of yourself and of Joseph. He will make a fine man."

Shortly afterward, as the physician had foretold, Ann Steggle died in her Rodney Street bed.

Twenty-Two

Ann's epitaph came to be written in what remained of Sarah's life. Her mother's unwelcome warnings as to what Sarah should expect from Leonard Cartwright went unheeded by her daughter during Ann's lifetime. After her death, Ann's predictions proved sadly prescient.

For a time, Sarah remained, with young Joseph, in Cartwright's house living as man and wife in all but name. Cartwright continued to expect conjugal relations with her, but Sarah felt as time progressed that what he had prized so highly while he had to pay for the pleasure became progressively less valued by him once it was offered freely. Still there was no suggestion of marriage, and the prospect of it seemed to Sarah to be fading with time rather than becoming more certain as she had hoped.

One fateful morning, Sarah answered a knock at the door and saw a tall, well dressed woman in a wide brimmed hat standing on the step accompanied by two children and a small dog.

"Good morning," said the visitor. "My name is Daphne Venables and I have come to pay a visit to Mr Leonard Cartwright, who invited me to call at any time when I happened to be passing to view some of his paintings. Am I standing outside the correct address?"

Sarah confirmed that she was and went to fetch Leonard, who was in his artist's studio at work. He greeted the woman cordially and invited them in. The elder of the two children was a lugubrious boy of around ten years of age, the younger a highly energetic girl some two years his junior. The dog, an animal of some maturity, was a small over-fed creature whose short legs held its rotund stomach above the ground by only a few inches. Its face was of the flat variety, with features seemingly squashed into its head by some unseen opposing force.

"May I introduce my son Vincent and my daughter Vanessa and, of course, my darling pug Algy?" the woman said. She then issued some instructions. "Vincent, please find a chair to sit on while I am looking at Mr Cartwright's work. And, Vanessa, please keep a close eye on the dog. You don't mind if I unleash Algy do you, Mr Cartwright, he cannot escape from anywhere here, can he?"

Leonard assured the woman her animal would be quite safe as he showed her through to his studio. The boy took a seat as instructed in the drawing room and sat motionless and silently in it until the visit was over. His sister, by contrast, who appeared to have inherited all the energy of both children, gaily ran between rooms, climbed the stairs to the next floors, opened doors, cupboards and drawers and made herself greatly and instantly at home.

Sarah listened from the parlour as Leonard showed the woman a selection of his work. He asked whether she had any particular style in mind, was it a painting of her own preference she was seeking or was she perhaps looking for a gift for her husband?

"My husband has passed, Mr Cartwright," she heard the woman reply. "It was very sad but only to be expected. We did not meet until he was almost 65 years of age, more than 30 years my senior, and we were afforded only a few short years of happy life together. But my dear husband did leave me my two children, and because of his successes in business as the owner of a sizeable cotton mill in Manchester, he has left me comfortably off as a lady of some means."

"Oh now, this one I absolutely do like very much!" said Mrs Venables, suddenly alighting on a portrait of an artist at his easel. The subject was shown from behind and was wearing tight breeches and no shirt, as he stood brush in hand in front of a large casement window that overlooked a garden scene.

"Is this a self-portrait, Mr Cartwright? It's a most taking one if so, I must say, positively moving," she said.

"It is," Leonard replied "but it's not really intended for sale, Mrs Venables. It was a practice piece to try to convey movement in the human back and forearms."

"Nonsense!" said the woman. "It is an exciting piece of art and thing of great beauty that I should love to have on my walls. How much do you want for it?"

Leonard tentatively suggested that, if she insisted, he could possibly ask her for five guineas, but the woman held up her cream gloved hand and rejected the suggestion outright. "I will not pay a penny less than ten guineas for such a piece but that is on condition that you bring it to my house yourself and show me where best to place it. Are you willing to do that, Mr Cartwright?"

Leonard was about to confirm his acceptance when their discussion was interrupted by the young girl Vanessa bursting into the room.

"Oh Mummy, naughty Algy has made his frightful mess on the floor in the drawing room!"

Mrs Venables looked mortified at this news and, turning to Cartwright, said, "I am so sorry, Mr Cartwright, Algy does tend to want to make his special mark whenever he visits somewhere new. Could you possibly ask your girl, is she your housekeeper, to clean it up? It's not usually too awful."

"And while we settle matters between us over the painting, could I trouble you to ask the girl to bring me a cup of tea with milk and sugar and, if possible, two lemonades and perhaps a sweet biscuit for the children? They do get a little peckish at this time of morning, and it is still an hour from their lunchtime. Oh, and would you have her also fetch a small bowl of water for dear Algy?"

Sarah, hearing the whole conversation unfold from her seat in the parlour heard Cartwright reply. "Yes, of course, Mrs Venables, I will have Sarah attend to it all straight away."

In the coming months, Daphne Venables became a regular visitor to the Cartwright household. The children never again appeared on any occasion, but Algy the pug was an unfailing attendee. On each occasion, Mrs Venables would ask Sarah to take the dog for an hour-long walk, to give him his daily exercise. At first, Sarah was asked if she would mind, would she be so kind, could she be prevailed upon once again, but in time, with the familiarity born of repeated visits, it came to be the standing expectation that Sarah would fulfil this task unasked. Until eventually, as Sarah opened the door to admit her, Daphne Venables would simply hand her the animal's leash and offer only the barest of acknowledgements of her expected regular service as she moved past her into the house.

Sarah noticed on the occasion of her first return from stretching the dog's short legs that Mrs Venables' light brown hair, which had been tightly pinned under her bonnet when she had arrived, was now hanging loose upon her shoulders, and her previously pale cheeks looked a little flushed as Sarah found her sitting closely together with Cartwright in his studio.

After this, Cartwright started to leave the house most days for several hours without explanation and his demeanour towards Sarah became progressively colder. She felt herself becoming the housekeeper that she had never felt she was. Cartwright no longer came to her bed nor invited her to his. With overwhelming sadness, Sarah recognised the truth that she was now a lodger in his house, an unpaid servant. She began to realise that neither she nor Joseph meant anything to the man she had thought loved her. She had been, just as her mother had warned her, a convenience to him. Now she felt herself and her presence becoming daily a little less convenient.

Sarah, proud and heartbroken, desperately wanted to pack her bags and leave, but where would she go? Back to her old life in Hotham Street? She recoiled at that prospect and could not contemplate taking young Joseph into that seedy world once again now he was of an age to understand and to question it. But what other option did she have? Her mother had warned her against becoming dependent on this man. She had rejected that suggestion outright. She knew now that she had been wrong to do so. Her mistake was now clear. She was no longer the mistress of her own destiny. She now had little or no money of her own nor any means to earn. Dizzy with love and eager to escape a lifestyle she found repugnant, she had totally misread the signs. She had plunged in a few short months from complete happiness amid great comfort in Rodney Street to depression, alarm and anxiety within the now hostile confines of the same four walls.

Cartwright did not tell her to leave, but as time progressed his relationship with Daphne Venables completely supplanted Sarah. He no longer felt obliged to explain his whereabouts or his plans or to discuss anything with her and certainly not his future, in which she increasingly plainly would have no place. Sarah, unloved and disregarded in a home she thought was hers, began to look paler and frailer. She stopped eating properly once she and Cartwright no longer took their meals together. Depression and despair drained her of her strength. She lost weight and developed a recurring cough. Her clothes hung off her.

One night a few months later, Sarah awoke in a terrible sweat, one minute hot with fever and the next shivering with cold. She lay there until the morning light came when she called out weakly to Cartwright to ask him to come to her room and to bring a doctor to her. Cartwright walked down Rodney Street to his friend Isaac Abrahams, the physician who had attended to Ann on her last typhus-stricken day. Abrahams came to the house and identified immediately that Sarah had contracted the wasting disease tuberculosis, the scourge of their age.

Her end was not long in coming thereafter. After a short period of illness, Sarah passed away, barely three years after her mother. Her cause of death was recorded formally on her death certificate as Phthisis and was registered with the authorities by Dr Abrahams who certified that he had been with Sarah at her moment of death at an address in Rodney Street, Liverpool. In the box set aside on the certificate for the *Occupation of the Deceased* was written only the words 'Daughter of Ann Steggle'.

Later in that same week of Sarah's passing, Leonard Cartwright, a painter residing in Rodney Street, took Joseph Steggle, eight years old, an orphan, for admission to the Ragged School in Soho Street, Liverpool. This charitable organisation was founded to provide free education for destitute children. Cartwright informed the school as he handed over the boy that he was the son of his late housekeeper, Sarah Steggle, who had died four days previously, aged 26. The boy was in good health and he was literate.

The woman admitting the young Joseph Steggle remarked upon his fine head of dark wavy hair. Cartwright confirmed that he had no knowledge of the identity of the boy's father.

One month later it was reported in the local newspaper that Leonard Cartwright and his fiancée, a widow named Mrs Daphne Venables, had married.

Book Two
Elizabeth Dundee 1875–1912

One

Elizabeth Bentley and Jane Gemmill were firm friends. They grew up together in the Cambuslang district in the southeast of Glasgow and played together as children in the streets outside their family houses, which stood just four apart on Bushyhill Street. When they came of age to attend, they were admitted into the local Kirk school where they were two of just four girls in a class of 30 boys.

Their parents were also close. Elizabeth's father Malcolm was a chemist who ran the local pharmacy, three streets from their home, where he was assisted by his wife Rebecca.

Jane's father Thomas, known by all as Tommy, was originally a blacksmith by trade, but he had developed his anvil craft to become a specialist engine smith, making parts for engines and fitting and repairing them. His wife Mary devoted herself to bringing up their four children. Jane, their eldest, had been followed by three brothers, Andrew, George and Richard.

Both families were religiously observant though neither was especially pious. They adhered to the Protestant faith and attended the local church every Sunday, where they sat together in their regular pew. The Bentleys' attitude to religion was relaxed and largely unquestioning. Malcolm and Rebecca felt very much part of their neighbourhood community and saw their attendance in the church as a way of expressing that. They went to church primarily for social reasons. There they met friends, relations, neighbours and the customers of their medicine shop on a weekly basis.

Tommy Gemmill had an altogether more intense relationship with the church. For him, Presbyterianism was an integral part of how he defined himself and his tribe. The Kirk gave him a powerful sense of belonging. He was a staunch propounder of the Protestant faith, he was a member of the Church of Scotland, he was a proud Scot and he was British. He was also a committed Unionist and a Loyalist. For Tommy, his membership of all those clans was all important. He believed in hard work, in diligence and in the responsibility of all people to make the best of themselves. Brought up in a family of impoverished farm workers, he had determined as a young boy that he would build a better life for himself than the one in which he grew up.

He placed huge importance upon education, having had very little himself. Through learning, people could improve themselves and find pathways for betterment. That message he had passed on loudly and clearly to Jane. Tommy was adamant that his daughter's education would not be confined to home crafts. He wanted her schooled in the subjects that the boys learned as well as the handicraft skills that teachers thought most fitting for girls. He was determined his daughter should be advantaged, where he had not been.

Jane learned to read from the age of four. Her father encouraged her to develop her handwriting and from her sixth birthday onward he insisted she regularly write short letters to relatives and friends who lived further afield. He also schooled her in basic number. By the time Jane first went to the Kirk School, she was far ahead of the rest of her class and already instilled with a passion and a hunger to learn. Jane had also inherited her father's competitive gene. She wanted to be the best.

To the young Elizabeth, who sat next to Jane in elementary class, her friend was both an inspiration and a teacher. If Jane saw Elizabeth struggling with a word in a reading passage, or a sum she could not fathom, she would quietly lean across from her desk and guide her friend towards the answer. Jane quickly became Elizabeth's reference point. She did not aspire to surpass her, but she did try to follow her. She couldn't bear to look foolish or idle in Jane's eyes, and that drove Elizabeth on as they progressed through their school years to become the best reader and arithmetician that she could.

Elizabeth was very adept at needlework, which she learned at home with her mother Rebecca, who made and embroidered all her daughter's dresses and knitted her guernseys and socks. In that domestic discipline in school, Elizabeth excelled and she frequently had to return the favours Jane was extending to her in their academic subjects by patiently unpicking Jane's clumsy sewing or showing her how to save a dropped stitch mid row.

The two girls stood head and shoulders in all subjects above almost all the others in the class. This of course meant they drew regular sneering abuse from some of their boy classmates, through the truth was most were rather in awe of them.

When they left school at 14, Elizabeth obtained a position as an apprentice seamstress working for the talented local dressmaker and milliner Agnes Whyte. Jane, much to her father's satisfaction, found a position as an assistant in the public library. Both girls were therefore working within a few hundred yards of each other on Cambuslang's Main Street. When the weather was clement, they gathered to sit and eat their lunchtime sandwich together in their half-hour break.

Shortly after they had each completed two years of work, they met at their customary bench for their usual lunchtime rendezvous. Jane on this occasion had news to share.

"Elizabeth, I have something to tell. It's exciting and sad at the same time," she said. "What is it?" said Elizabeth anxiously.

"We are moving away. We are leaving Glasgow."

Elizabeth's face fell. It had never occurred to her that something like this could happen and so suddenly. Jane was her one true friend. This was where they lived, where they had both always lived.

"Pa has got a new employment," Jane continued. "It pays more money and has better prospects and he is very thrilled. It is with a shipbuilding company. They want his engine knowledge and his skills with molten metal. It's a company called Cammell Laird."

"But where is it?" asked Elizabeth, quite forgetting to congratulate her friend on her father's good fortune.

"It is in a town called Birkenhead across the River Mersey from Liverpool," she answered. "We are leaving on the train next week. I know I am really going to miss you."

At that, the two girls hugged as tears welled in Elizabeth's eyes.

Two

Separated by more than 200 miles, Elizabeth and Jane corresponded regularly over the next two years. "Let us write to each other little and often!" Jane had exhorted. "No essays!"

Elizabeth found maintaining their written exchanges much the harder of the two. Not only did she lack Jane's practiced letter-writing fluency, she also struggled to think of things she could tell her now distant friend. Life at home with her parents was grindingly uneventful and there was little beyond small talk from the chemist's shop or polite conversation at the church that she thought even barely worth sharing.

Her career with Mrs Whyte was progressing well enough and she was certainly meeting her employer's approval, but there was not so much she could write about every day dressmaking that was likely to excite or entertain Jane. Though Elizabeth was delighted to share with her friend the day Mrs Whyte sold the first dress Elizabeth had made singlehandedly and without the slightest assistance or correction. The two happy occasions Mrs Whyte had increased her wages also made it onto the page in her correspondence.

Jane, on the other hand, always seemed to have lots of adventures to report from somewhere new, which sounded so much more colourful and vibrant than the drab streets of Cambuslang. She reported their moving into a new house in Birkenhead and gave regular progress on their family life and on Tommy's progress at the shipyard.

Pa is so happy with his new job he comes home every day with a big smile on his face.

Pa has learned some incredible stories about important ships they've built at Cammell Laird. David Livingstone's ship for the expedition up the Zambezi River! The first steamer ever to cross the Atlantic! Ships that fought in the American Civil War!

Pa feels like he really belongs in the yard. Everyone there is a Protestant. They don't allow any Catholic workers there you see. Pa says it's because they don't have the skills.

Then, a few months later, she shared stories of local visits she'd enjoyed.

We walked in Birkenhead Park on Saturday afternoon. It is so grand and beautiful. They have big arches at the entrance and many pretty buildings in the grounds, including a beautiful covered wooden bridge. Bands play there, too. Pa says when it opened 30 years ago it was the first public park anywhere in the world.

We went to the seaside on Easter Monday. New Brighton is only a few miles from us and it has all sorts of attractions. There is a big pier out over the river. You can watch the ships go by from very close. You can swim and paddle, there is music and all sorts of entertainments. We ate ham and eggs in one of the tea rooms. Such a crowd though! There must have been thousands of people there.

Several months later again, Jane wrote to Elizabeth.

There are so many people in Liverpool! Pa says it is because there are too many Irish. Like the Irish in Glasgow they all came over to escape the famine in Ireland. But there are so many more of them here! Pa says there are more than 300,000 of them in the town now. He says most of them live in bad conditions and don't wash properly and that's why they have so many diseases.

Pa says he is very glad he is working in the shipbuilding yard in Birkenhead instead of in the docks in Liverpool. Because all the Irish are really poor and need work, there are far too many people trying for the jobs they have on the docks each day so the wages are very low. Pa says proper Liverpool people find it hard to get work and he blames the Irish.

He says the Irish people don't want to be British. They don't want Ireland to be part of our country. I really don't understand why there are so many of them here if they feel that way.

Then six months later, Jane had more news.

Such excitement this week! Pa has joined something called an Orange Lodge. It is named after King William of Orange who won the Battle of the Boyne, which maintained Protestant rule in the country. He says the Lodge have marching parades here and they organise socials and dances too. He says the next time there is a dance, he and Ma will take me! Everyone in the Lodge has to be a Protestant. He is very honoured to be a member.

Another six months on and Jane had a family success to report.

Ma and I are so proud! Pa has been elected to be the Secretary of the Orange Lodge. He has been a member for still less than a year but he is already one of the most important people in the whole club. He gets to sit at the big table now. So does Ma when she goes with him. He is really getting on in the world!

Three

Elizabeth was finding life in Cambuslang very humdrum. Jane's letters, so full of news and enthusiasm, only served to remind her of the monotony of her existence. Unlike her friend, she had gone nowhere and she was going nowhere.

She was now 18 years old and still living at home with her parents. Her routine never changed. Up at six to help Mother set the fire and prepare the breakfast. Breakfast with Mother and Father at seven. Clear away and wash the dishes at half past seven. Leave the house at a quarter to eight and be in her seat at Mrs Whyte's shop by eight o'clock sharp. She took her half-hour break for lunch at one, and since Jane had moved away she spent it alone watching the world go by as she ate her sandwich. If it rained, she took it in the back of the shop. Home after the shop closed at six. Tea at seven. The evening spent reading. Sometimes, Father would play the piano, and she and her parents would sing together before bed at nine. Elizabeth loved her parents but she desperately wanted more than this.

One wind-swept afternoon in late autumn, Elizabeth was working alone in the shop. Mrs Whyte had gone into the centre of Glasgow to carry out a dress fitting for one of her regular and better-off clients. Elizabeth was working on a gown that she and Mrs Whyte were making together, with Elizabeth given the main stitching work to do and her patron adding the more intricate decorative elements on the bodice, collar and sleeves.

The door opened, ringing the small brass bell above it to announce an arriving customer. It was a young man who was probably, Elizabeth guessed, in his late twenties. He was dark haired, moustached and of medium height and athletic build. He came in hurriedly, eager to get out the wind, and shut the door firmly behind him. When he'd composed himself, he greeted her with a wide smile.

"Good afternoon, Missy," he said. "I don't know if the lady of the shop is here or, if not, if you could maybe help me?"

Elizabeth stood and explained that Mrs Whyte was away performing a client fitting and would not be back until the following day. "I would be pleased to try to help, though," she said. "Are you looking for something in particular?"

The young man replied that he was looking to buy something he could give his mother for her birthday. "She is 50 years old next week, and I want to give her something special if I can. I wondered about a dress?"

Elizabeth could not help but warm to this young fellow who had turned up wanting to buy his mother something special to wear but clearly had very little idea of what it should be or how to go about it.

"Have you brought with you, or do you by any chance know, your mother's measurements?" she asked.

The young man looked abashed. "No, I'm afraid not, though I'd guess she is a wee bit bigger than you are."

Elizabeth smiled and said, "May I offer you some advice? I'd suggest we could try something less ambitious. You would not want to buy something that would not fit her well. Unless you could perhaps bring her here into the shop?"

"No, I cannot do that, I'm afraid," he replied. "We don't live here you see. I am a Dundonian, just staying in Glasgow with a friend for a few days, and she is away at home in Dundee with my father. Do you have anything which doesn't need measurements?"

Elizabeth went to the drawer of the glass demonstration cabinet she sat behind all day and took out a pair of fingerless gloves knitted in light grey wool and decorated with small purple embroidered flowers.

"I made these," she said, "and I think they should fit. I think they are quite pretty and I hope she would be pleased with them? They are two shillings."

The young man's face lit up. "They are really canny. Would you mind trying them on for me so I can see?"

Elizabeth obligingly put both gloves on and held out her hands in front of her so he could inspect the gloves. He took hold of her right hand and raised it as if to look at the embroidery more closely, but as he did, his gaze moved up to meet hers.

"I'll take them. But on one condition. That if I invite you to come with me to the dance at the Kirk Hall tomorrow evening, you'll say yes. Unless you're already going with someone else, that is."

Elizabeth blushed and found herself replying shyly, "No. I mean, no, I'm not going with anyone else."

"Very good! So is that a date then?" he asked. "I shall come to meet you outside your shop door at seven o'clock tomorrow evening, and we can walk down there together."

Elizabeth wrapped the gloves, and he handed over the two shillings. "I hope she likes them," she said.

"I'm sure she shall," the young man replied as he made for the door before turning to add, "Oh my name is James, by the way. James Simpson."

"I'm Elizabeth. Elizabeth Bentley."

"I'll see you tomorrow then, beautiful Miss Elizabeth," he said. "Outside the door here at seven. I am looking forward to it. Until then, I'll bid ye a fond good evening."

With that, he left the shop, smiling towards her as he set himself against the gusts of wind that continued to blow outside. Once he had disappeared from view, Elizabeth sat back down on her chair, her heart pumping, to recover her breath.

Four

Over the next months, their relationship grew steadily stronger. James was 28 years old and a cabinet maker, born and raised in Dundee. He was making a reasonable living working for various local builder contractors whose practice was to hire in carpenters by the day. He did what he could to supplement that irregular income by making furniture pieces for private commission and by producing some items in wood for general sale. He explained to Elizabeth that it was up and down money. For periods his pockets were full, while at other times he had to tighten his belt a notch or two.

He came to visit her almost every weekend over the next months, staying with his friend Hamish Grey in his rooms behind Sauchiehall Street. He spent each Saturday evening and Sunday afternoon with Elizabeth. His custom was to return her home each Saturday by ten o'clock and then collect her again after church the next day's lunchtime.

Malcolm and Rebecca found him a polite and respectful caller and were delighted to see the change he had brought about in their daughter. Her manner had been transformed from listless and melancholic to joyfully energetic in the space of just a few weeks.

Elizabeth looked forward all week to James's visits. She found him a funny and charming companion, and endearing in the way he appeared one moment very confident and self possessed while the next he was seemed awkward and shy. He gave her a reason to look forward. Suddenly, she had a shape to her life, a purpose.

After six months of polite courtship, James proposed to her.

"Will you marry me, Elizabeth, and come and be my wife in Dundee?" he asked. "It is a joy to come to visit you here each week, but I long for us to be together. And if we are man and wife, we can maybe look to get a home of our own and think about starting a family together?"

Elizabeth, her heart overflowing, answered yes the instant James finished speaking, but she reminded him that he would need to seek her father's permission first. That proved to be a mere formality. Malcolm, who had seen nothing but good in his daughter's young suitor, and the effect he had had on her happiness since they had met, was only too pleased to give his consent for their marriage to proceed. Both he and Rebecca thought Elizabeth should have a husband who was older than her, but also one who was still young enough to enjoy the pleasures of young adulthood. James, at 28, ten years older than their daughter, seemed to fit that bill perfectly.

They married in the Cambuslang Kirk four weeks later. Elizabeth wore a pretty white dress with head-dress and veil, made for her by her employer, Agnes Whyte, and wedding gifted to her as a thank you for her years of service as her apprentice and assistant. Mrs Whyte had now to find a replacement for her. "It will be no easy task to find someone of your diligence and talent, Elizabeth," she said.

Jane travelled up on the steam train from Liverpool for the occasion. It was the first time she had been back to Cambuslang since her family had moved south. Jane was Elizabeth's maid of honour. Also dressed in white, with a short veil, she was escorted by Hamish, the groom's best man, on the wedding procession to the church as Elizabeth walked on the arm of her father Malcolm. Seeing her friend's evident joy, Jane congratulated her on her choice of groom and sincerely wished them both every happiness in their new life together.

Malcolm was a charming host to James's mother Ellen, who wore the grey gloves her son had bought from Elizabeth on their first encounter. James' father Duncan accompanied Elizabeth's mother Rebecca and showed himself to be a graceful dancer in the celebrations that followed.

Duncan confided in Rebecca as they danced that when his own late father, James, for whom he had named his eldest son, had married his mother Margaret in Perthshire in 1823, they had neglected to arrange for the banns to be read out in church in advance. They declared themselves man and wife straight away, but were then rebuked by the Kirk session, which only formally blessed their marriage six weeks later after they had expressed contrition for their oversight and paid up the necessary fees.

"I am glad my son has exhibited more God-fearing respect for the ordinances of the Kirk than his grandfather managed," Duncan quipped.

John McCarthy, the local butcher whose shop neighboured Malcolm's pharmacy, provided a whole mutton for the wedding breakfast as his gift to the couple. He was also given the honour of filling the ceremonial loving cup, the Quaich, with whisky and handing it ceremonially to the groom. James unconventionally took that as an invitation to drain it completely, and without a moment's pause, before handing it back to be refilled. Only then was it explained that he and Elizabeth were meant each to take a sip from the cup to toast their marriage. James, laughing, said he was happy to try again. Hamish later gave a witty address referring to the traditional role of the best man as the friend who was there to help the groom capture his bride and run off with her. James had needed no assistance in captivating Elizabeth, he said to peals of approving laughter. It was a happy start to Elizabeth and James's marriage.

That night, they stayed as man and wife at Elizabeth's parents' home and were taken by Malcolm and Rebecca for a farewell lunch the following day at the Grand Central Hotel in the centre of the city. The following morning, Elizabeth's parents waved the young bride and her groom off from Glasgow station as they began their 80-mile train journey to Dundee, passing through the towns of Sterling and Perth. They were to stay for the immediate time being with James's father and mother Duncan and Ellen at their house in Princes Street. They had returned the previous day to prepare to welcome the newly-weds to their home.

It was not a journey Elizabeth had ever made before, and the Dundee that greeted her when she arrived at the Dundee West railway station that afternoon was not a town she could ever have imagined. It was July the eighth, 1882.

Five

As she peered through the carriage window as the train pulled in, Elizabeth saw what looked to her like a vast forest of tall chimneys, each belching out smoke that, coalescing, hung like a great pall over the town. As far as her eye could see were dark, forbidding factories, pressed close together and seemingly combining into one heaving, straining hive of industry.

"Welcome to Juteopolis," said James cheerfully. "A hundred and twenty five textile mills and factories all squeezed into this little town hidden away on Scotland's east coast.

Have you ever seen such a concentration of industry? Spinning and weaving jute into products ready to send right across the world."

Elizabeth looked on dismayed as her eyes adjusted and she began to make out the form of figures moving through the murky town, the factory fog thick all around them. "What is jute?" Elizabeth asked. "Is that the material they make sacks and bags from?"

"It is," James replied. "The world's goods nowadays are pretty well all carried in it. When you see cotton or coffee, or grain or flour or sugar or sand being loaded on and off the ships, those bags are all made from jute. Sailcloth is jute, wagon covers are jute, tarpaulins, anything hardy and tough that has to stand harsh conditions that you can think of can be made from jute, and Dundee is the world's capital of it."

"It is big business here. There are more than 30,000 people working in these factories, it's more than half of all the jobs in the town. But do you know what is extraordinary?" James continued. "Three quarters of the jute jobs here are for women. The men really struggle to find employment in Dundee. It's the women who have plenty of work if they're prepared to do it. Single and married both, the women all work. There's no marriage bar here. And 60 hours a week guaranteed. That's why they call this place 'She-town'. It's the men folk who stay at home here. It's the boys who are the kettle boilers in Dundee."

At the time Elizabeth arrived there, Dundee's Juteopolis was enjoying a boom time with demand for its products soaring all over the world. The wisdom the Dundee industrial families had shown in converting their factories—which had previously been dedicated to producing coarse linen—to the manufacture of jute products was regularly trumpeted in the local newspapers as one of the greatest industrial success stories of the age.

Hand spinning and weaving had been replaced by steam-driven spinning frames and power looms, and the appetite of these new monsters of automated manufacture had seen production increase sevenfold from its first beginnings. Dundee now imported 200,000 tons of raw jute from India each year and exported jute products all over the world, to the grain farmers of America and Canada, to the meat packers of Argentina, and to the wool producers of Australia and New Zealand.

Workers from far and wide had flocked to Dundee as its jute production expanded rapidly, including many from the famine-hit population of Ireland. The mass influx of the last 30 years had seen the population of the town almost double in consequence to 140,000.

It was now overflowing.

Six

Elizabeth and James moved into Duncan and Ellen's Princes Street home for a few weeks. James had promised his new bride that this would be just while they 'sorted themselves out'. Several months later, there was no particular sign of things sorting themselves out. Elizabeth, who had imagined a new beginning in their marital home on Scotland's east coast, found herself instead having to accommodate to life in her husband's parents' house.

James had mentioned to her earlier in their relationship that his income as a carpenter relied on his being hired to work on projects by the day and that meant his wages were 'up and down'. Since they had married, Elizabeth now observed, they had been more down than up. James was rarely called away from the house and, available work seemed very scarce. He didn't seem to have earned more than ten shillings in any given week and over several weeks he brought in nothing at all.

"Surely, with all these people in the town, all these thousands flocking here to find jobs in the mills and the factories, there must be carpentry work to do building homes for them to live in?" Elizabeth asked.

"They're all squeezing into the places that are already there," her husband replied. "There's little or no new building going on. The new jute workers go into buildings that are already crowded and they just share rooms. Some of them live eight to a room and sleep four in a bed. That doesn't make for lots of call for new joinery," he said.

Mercifully, living together with Duncan and Ellen, their living costs were low. They shared their in-laws' food, and Elizabeth made sure she paid for her continuing welcome by keeping the whole house spotlessly clean. But she saw no money from James and, lacking any income of her own, she had only her own modest savings to draw on if she wanted to buy any item for herself. Recognising that her husband's income was unpredictable in the extreme, she was loath to spend a penny of what she had put away. Her father had advised her from the day she started work with Mrs Whyte to ensure that she kept money by for a rainy day. She had in truth encountered very few of those in her life so far, but she could see them coming thick and fast now.

She asked Ellen if there were seamstresses or dressmakers locally who might need assistants, and her mother-in-law gave her the names of two women who she knew ran their own shops in the town. Elizabeth went with samples of her sewing to visit both. The first, a Mrs Ida Montgomery, admired her work and told Elizabeth that, while she could see she had a talent, she sadly hadn't enough work of her own to be able to afford an assistant's wage.

The second shop, run by a woman named Jean McCourt, stood on the crescent at the foot of Dundee Law, the hill that was the high point in the centre of the town. It seemed to Elizabeth a slightly bigger enterprise than Ida Montgomery's, and Mrs McCourt, too, was impressed by the quality of her work.

"I can see you're a talented seamstress, Mrs Simpson, and I would be very happy to have you work for me. But this is a poor town and there just isn't the money among the working people to spend on fancy clothes. Those that don't work have little or nothing, and those that do don't have that much more."

Elizabeth was about to turn away in disappointment when the proprietress continued. "But wait, I have work making aprons for one of the factories at present, and I could do with a helping hand with that if you would be interested? It is not the most satisfying work for a seamstress of your skills, and the prices I can charge for it are very low, so the wages I can pay might not be enough for you."

"How much could you offer, Mrs McCourt?" Elizabeth asked.

"It would be only seven shillings and six a week for an eight-hour day with a half day on Saturday," she replied.

It was poverty money, but Elizabeth needed to get out of the Simpsons' house during the day. She was desperate for something to occupy herself with, and she simply had to bring in some money so she and James could at least start to pay their way.

"I'll take it, Mrs McCourt, thank you," she said. The women shook hands and it was agreed that she would start the following morning.

Despite the great scarcity of paid work that he faced, James always seemed able to find a little money in his pocket. He would disappear from the house for long periods and frequently come back smelling strongly of whisky. Elizabeth put this down to his drowning his sorrows. It must be hard for a proud man who was able and ready to work, but who was not able to ply his trade through no fault of his own, was her sympathetic assessment. She was glad she could now contribute at least something to the slender marital wallet.

A few months later, Elizabeth was overjoyed to discover she had fallen pregnant. Duncan and Ellen were delighted at the prospect of a first grandchild, and James seemed proud of his achievement of impending fatherhood. "I hope it is a boy!" were his first words to Elizabeth on hearing the glad news.

During the months of her pregnancy, Elizabeth continued to work in Mrs McCourt's shop, and James's work fortunes seemed to take a turn for the better. He was given employment constructing wooden buildings, structures and benches in Baxter Park, the town's new public recreation facility that was being paid for by Sir David Baxter, the owner of one of the prominent jute factories. James was earning eighteen shillings a week. Suddenly, the new family had money coming in. Steady work for a year was promised.

James got his wish. Elizabeth's first born was a boy whom they named Robert. Elizabeth was enraptured but she had relatively little time to adjust to new motherhood. Three months later, she found she was pregnant again.

Seven

Jane's letters had become less frequent now. Elizabeth was not sure why, but she accepted the reality that they were living very different lives. It was almost inevitable they would pull apart over time. Jane was still unmarried and would naturally want to keep her private life to herself. She was probably enjoying herself to the full and had neither the time nor the interest to share that with an old married friend now so remote. It was not easy to be on intimate terms so far apart when the only communication means was the occasional letter.

Elizabeth also did not feel totally at ease sharing her innermost thoughts about her marriage and her relationship with James now she was a mother and soon to be of a second child. Relationships move on, she thought, while reflecting that Jane and she would always have their treasured years of youthful friendship. That at least could never be taken away from them.

After six months of good money from his work in the park, James's job there came to an abrupt halt. He was reluctant to discuss why the promised year of work had ended prematurely, but it had. He would just have to look for something else, he said matter-of-factly. Elizabeth, now heavily pregnant with her second child, continued her daily and increasingly laborious climb to the foot of the Law Hill to her sewing job with Mrs McCourt. James, now again unoccupied, resumed his uneasy friendship with the whisky bottle.

Their second child was born in October, a dark-haired, dark-eyed girl they called Ada. Her arrival meant they were now a perfect complete family but they were still living with their children's grandparents and existing on a single paltry income that could not support them independently.

Duncan and Ellen had been tolerant hosts to them now for almost four years and had never really questioned the couple on what their plans for the future were, still less put them under pressure to find a place of their own. But Duncan was becoming increasingly concerned at his son's lack of work and troubled by his consuming fondness for escape through liquor. Duncan was too proud a man to cause friction in front of womenfolk, but matters came to a head one evening when Ada was some six months old. James, having disappeared for the day, stumbled into the house late in the evening, clearly drunk.

"This can't go on, James," his father said as they met in the hallway as James fumbled with his latchkey. "You have a wife and two children and you are almost 33 years of age. You should be prospering with your young family, but you are living on your mother's and my charity and you appear to have no prospect of improving your lot."

"I'm doing everything I can to find work," blustered James. "As soon as I find regular income, we will move out into a place of our own."

"But when will that be, James?" said Duncan. "What is ever going to change while you have the comfort of living here in Princes Street? Think on it. Your life is slipping away as quickly as the whisky is slipping down your throat."

At this slur, James staggered across the hall menacingly towards his father. The older man stepped forward towards him, gripped his son's two arms and held them tightly to his sides.

"Go to bed, James, before something regrettable occurs," he said.

The uneasy co-existence in the Princes Street household continued for another six months with no sustained improvement in James's wayward behaviour. After the incident with his father, he seemed for a brief period to be more purposeful in seeking work and he successfully obtained three short-term assignments. But again none of them developed into longer-term employment. His determined focus soon gave way again to easy resignation.

Elizabeth could feel the rising tension between the two men making life increasingly uncomfortable in the house. She wanted instinctively to side with her husband and not with his father, but she knew deep down that Duncan and Ellen owed them nothing.

Elizabeth's relationship with Ellen had always been cordial but never especially close, so the topic was not an easy one for the two women to discuss. The fact they both knew very well they were living in an atmosphere of growing bitterness made it less easy for them to communicate with one another, not easier. They both elected stoically not to mention the new awkwardness. So their conversation became more sterile, and their eye contact less frequent.

Elizabeth's patience with James was also wearing thin. The dutiful tolerance and supportiveness that she had seen as her wifely calling was clearly not helping either her husband or her family. She decided that her brushing their issues under the carpet was now serving no-one.

When James again returned to the house after another workless day, his breath overpowering with its familiar reek of alcohol, Elizabeth steeled herself to challenge him.

"James, what has happened to you and what is to become of us?" she cried. "You have no work and no money. The work you do manage to get is short lived and even when you are promised continued employment, it gets brought to an end before its due time. You drink heavily each day, and with that goes your chances of being able to find work the next day."

"Shut up! Shut your nagging mouth, you harridan!" James bawled at her.

"I won't be quiet, James, no. I have been quiet long enough," said Elizabeth. "You are failing yourself, you are failing me and you are failing your children!"

That was the first time he hit her. He took three strides across the room and with the back of his right hand dealt her a heavy blow across the left side of her face sending her sprawling backward into the fireplace. She cried out involuntarily in pain and the sound of her cry and the general commotion sent both Duncan and Ellen running up the stairs to their room. As they opened the door, they witnessed their son standing astride his wife, shouting down at her as she lay prostrate across the hearth.

"Don't you ever speak to me like that again, you little hussy," they heard James snarling. "I am the master here."

"I am afraid you are not, James," said his father, standing in the doorway. "You will get out of this house straight away!"

Eight

Cedric Blumenthaler was a correspondent with America's leading newspaper, *The New York Times*. Chicago-born, he was an Ivy League literature graduate of Columbia University who was now in the tenth year of his career in journalism. He had managed to persuade his editor to allow him to visit Britain, partly, it must be said, at his own expense, to produce a series of colourful feature articles that would appeal to the newspaper's readers by offering insight into life at the centre of the British Empire.

His brief was to seek to shine a light in particular on areas that an American audience would be able to relate easily to their own everyday experiences. America was the largest market for the jute manufactures produced in Dundee, and Blumenthaler had decided that an article from Juteopolis, profiling the extraordinary industry on Scotland's east coast through the eyes of some of the people who owned it and worked in it would be a worthy inclusion in his 'From the Heart of Empire' series.

He was staying in London at The Travellers Club where he had so far produced three well-written but rather worthy articles on British Royal Palaces, the working of The Stock Exchange and Prime Minister William Gladstone's Speeches in Parliament. They had been received with subdued enthusiasm by the *Times'* features desk, whose views on his output to date were made painfully clear when his Editor telegrammed him at the Club with his customary terseness.

Anything happening outside London? STOP.

Cedric's Dundee idea was potentially a good one, but he knew no-one in the town. He was starting to come under pressure from New York. The article he hoped to write needed to work out and it had to be successful. He was beginning to fear if he did not produce something soon that lived up to the billing of a true colour article about modern Britain and its Empire, he would be recalled to his desk in Manhattan and put on six months' court reporting duty as a penance. He decided to follow the well-trodden recourse of all newspapermen when they are in serious doubt of anything: ask another newspaperman.

In the Travellers' library, he found to his great encouragement that the editor of the local newspaper, the *Dundee Advertiser*, one John Leng, was clearly a pioneer of newspapers in the town. He was also very promisingly a prominent Liberal party member and speechmaker. Blumenthaler took out a sheet of Travellers' letterhead notepaper from the library desk and penned a letter to him.

For the urgent personal attention of: John Leng Esquire
The Editor
Dundee Advertiser
Dundee, Angus
Scotland
March 15, 1885

Dear Mr Leng

We do not know one another, but my name is Cedric Blumenthaler and I am a correspondent with The New York Times. I am here in Britain for a short period producing a series of articles under the heading 'From the Heart of Empire' for our American readership. I am planning to visit Dundee next week for the purposes of researching an article about the remarkable Scottish jute industry. I wonder if you would be willing to help me? I would very much like to meet you and wondered if in addition you could introduce me both to one of the leading representative industrialists of jute in your town and perhaps also someone who can tell me what it is like to work in one of the factories that are now so important for the traffic of the world's trade?

I very much hope you will be able to facilitate these introductions for me and I shall of course be delighted to do anything I can to reciprocate your favour by helping the Dundee Advertiser in any way that I can.

I await your reply with impatient excitement and hope I can look forward to making your acquaintance personally next week.
Cordially yours

Cedric Blumenthaler III
The New York Times
c/o The Travellers Club, 106 Pall Mall, London.

Blumenthaler signed it with a flourish of ink, blotted and then folded the page before inserting it into one of the club's crested envelopes. He walked over to the front desk to commit his missive to the liveried doorman for postage.

His father's command for him to leave the premises straight away seemed to pierce the alcoholic fug inside James Simpson's head as he loomed over his stricken wife. He turned and blundered past his parents in the doorway, and to the sound of his two children crying in alarm in the next bedroom, stumbled down the stairs. Pausing only to gather his coat and cap, he lunged out of the front door and into the street.

Ellen hurried over to tend to Elizabeth, who by now was sitting up and clutching the side of her face where a great red weal was already surfacing on her left cheekbone. She was dazed but at least she was conscious.

"Fetch her some water, Duncan," Ellen told her husband. "I need to go and attend to those children." Duncan returned momentarily with a glass of water, releasing his wife to go to comfort the wailing infant and baby in the next room. He helped raise Elizabeth to her feet and over to the bed where he laid her down, propped up with two pillows.

"I am so sorry, Elizabeth," said Duncan. "He will not bother you again tonight. Ellen will bring you a poultice for your face, and you should then try to sleep. Ellen will make sure Robert and Ada are settled." Elizabeth, still in shock, mumbled a few words but she nodded in compliance and whispered a quiet "Thank you" to her concerned father-in-law as he made his way from the room.

Duncan went downstairs to the kitchen where he sat deep in thought for almost 20 minutes before he was joined by his wife. "The children are calmed, Elizabeth has a dressing on her face, and I have put her properly to bed," Ellen said.

Her husband, who was 71, looked drawn and aged as she sat down opposite him. "What is to be done do you think?" she asked.

Duncan drew breath and said, "An already bad situation has just become considerably worse. James has committed an offence under the law—a common assault, battery of his wife—under our roof. We cannot ignore that because we have a duty to protect her, the mother of our grandchildren, while she is in our household. God forbid that such a thing were ever to happen again with more serious consequences, and it were to emerge that we had failed to report an earlier incident. We, too, would be guilty then in the eyes of the law. I believe we have no choice but to report this matter to the police."

Ellen gasped and said, "We must report our own son to the police? Is there no other course?"

Duncan replied, "I think not, unless you believe for some reason that Elizabeth is safe in his company and that such violence will never recur. We have failed to change James's behaviour these last years. We have failed to get him to see what is becoming of his life. We have failed to keep him away from the demon drink that is killing him. So I hardly see that we can have any reasonable confidence that this incident will somehow mark the beginning of a change for the better, and that his wife and children are not at risk of further violence. It is for greater authority than we as his parents to make that decision anyway. Perhaps that is what is needed to bring him to his senses. I am at a loss, to be honest, to think what else will."

"So what will you do?" Ellen asked.

"I will bolt the door of the house against him tonight. He can sleep elsewhere. I don't greatly care where. Tomorrow, when he returns, I will summon the constabulary to the house to report the incident and have Elizabeth give her full account of what happened."

The following day, James reappeared mid-morning at Princes Street dishevelled and contrite. He was full of apology, both to his mother and father and to Elizabeth.

"I don't know what came over me," he said, his head bowed. "It was a momentary madness. I have come to my senses now. It won't happen ever again, I swear it."

He went to embrace Elizabeth whose swollen face bore angry blue testimony to the severity of the blow she had sustained the night before. She uncomfortably accepted his approach, and Ellen across the kitchen table breathed a shallow sigh of relief at the sign of tentative reconciliation between the two.

Duncan sat still grim-faced and paused before he spoke. "That is a good thing, James. I am pleased that you have apologised to your wife and your mother. I welcome the assurances of the future that you have made. But this is an incident in my house, which I am duty bound to report. There are also children here to whom I owe a duty of care as the head of this household. You and Elizabeth must both give an account of yesterday's events to the police, and we must abide by their decision on any action that needs to be taken."

James was taken aback and pleaded soulfully with his father to forget the matter and accept his promises as to his future behaviour. He begged Elizabeth to say she forgave the unfortunate occurrence.

Elizabeth had many things spinning through her mind. She had not previously been frightened of James, but the previous day's experience now made her so. She was alarmed not only for herself but also for her two small children. If her husband was capable of such violence in anger towards her, what might he do in a moment of frustration at the little ones?

Part of her absolutely wanted to forgive and forget. The last thing she wanted was the indignity of an interrogation by the police. But she also looked across at the concerned face of her mother-in-law, and the stressed but dignified resolution of Duncan, and recognised that this for her was a moment of truth. If she were to side with James in the face of his father's stated intention of how this should be handled, she could see matters quickly running out of control. What would Duncan then do if she refused to cooperate with his proposed plan of action? He could easily decide to have them all leave his house immediately. She, the children and James could find themselves out on the street. Such a thought filled her with horror. They had virtually no money, James was out of work and, at times, seemingly out of his mind. While she had work, her earnings were meagre and certainly nowhere near enough to pay for food and rent for her and the children, let alone her volatile and thirsty husband. She had looming and desperate visions of the doors of the workhouse in a town where she knew almost no-one. It decided her.

"I will accept your apology James," she said. "But I also accept your father's reasoning that we should report this incident to the police. It is right and in the best interest of all the people living in this house that we do." James's head dropped into his chest as he saw the chances of his behaviour escaping unchecked disappearing, and he prepared to face the consequence.

"Very well. You are all decided against me then. Do your worst. Call the bloody police."

Nine

Cedric Blumenthaler was enjoying a breakfast of two Scottish kippers with a squeeze of lemon and two pieces of brown bread and butter at The Travellers Club three days later when the doorman brought him a letter marked as Urgent for his attention.

He opened it in a mix of excitement and trepidation. He had received a further telegram from his editor this previous night saying only *News? STOP.* He feared the next message he would receive from Manhattan, if he couldn't report positive developments in the next 24 hours, would be *Come back NOW. STOP.* He slit open the letter on the platter before him with the club crested ivory handled paperknife that had been presented alongside it and he read.

March 17, 1885

Dear Mr Blumenthaler

It is an honour to receive a communication from a correspondent of the august New York Times and I would be pleased to meet with you and to assist you in your inquiries. I am pleased that you will be bringing the Dundee story to your readers and I am sure they will find it an impressive and most interesting one.

I should be delighted to invite you to lunch and to introduce you to Mr Edward Cox who is the head of Cox Brothers the local family firm which owns the Camperdown Works, the largest jute factory in Dundee. More than 5,000 people work there. I will also invite Mr Robert Ritchie to join us. Mr Ritchie is the president of the Dundee Trades Council, the body which represents the interests of workers of the town. Between the three of us we should be able to give you a good picture of Juteopolis and the proud position in world trade that it enjoys.

If it is convenient to you to come to my offices at the Advertiser next Wednesday at twelve noon, we can meet for a brief discussion before walking over to meet our lunch guests at the Royal Exchange.

I trust this is satisfactory to you and I look forward to welcoming you to Dundee.
Cordially yours

John Leng, Editor
The Dundee Advertiser

Blumenthaler wiped his mouth with his napkin and broke out into a broad smile. *Mr Editor, sir, please prepare yourself!* he thought. A real story is on its way, he whispered to himself with a blend of self-congratulatory satisfaction and relief.

The police sergeant and constable called at the Simpson's Princes Street address after a Mr Duncan Simpson, the head of the household, visited the constabulary to report a domestic incident. The policeman separately interviewed both the victim and her alleged assailant, her husband, and the two other adults present in the house at the time.

Their notes showed the following. There appeared to be no contradiction among the four accounts. The two older witnesses, the alleged assailant's parents, confirmed they had not seen the incident itself but had heard a commotion and, on rushing to the scene, saw their son standing over his wife who was lying on the ground with signs of a facial injury. The victim said there had been an argument between her and her husband. She declared she had not been violent, but her husband had hit her. This was borne out by the alleged assailant who confirmed that he 'lost his temper' and struck his wife in the face, knocking her down. He confirmed that he had taken drink that day and he admitted that his judgement was 'impaired by alcohol'. He stated he regretted the matter and that no such incident had occurred before. The wife corroborated this statement.

After no more than 20 minutes in the house, the two officers of the law thanked the inhabitants for their co-operation and told them they would be hearing from them shortly. Showing them to the door, Duncan asked what the next steps were likely to be and what they should expect.

The Sergeant replied, "This will be referred to the Police court, Mr Simpson. It will likely go before the magistrate, and I expect your son will be fined. It is possible but unlikely that he could face a few days of imprisonment as an alternative, but as a first offender it is more likely that he will be given the opportunity to pay a penalty and be cautioned as to his future conduct. It is clear that you are a good family with no history of misconduct and this will count in his favour, as will the fact that you reported the incident voluntarily and that nobody in the household is disputing the facts of the case."

Duncan thanked the officers and professed himself relieved at that outlook. "It is unfortunately a common occurrence in this town, Mr Simpson," the sergeant replied. "There is a lot of frustration here on account of the lack of work for men. It has reversed the natural order of things in my book how we've gone here with this so called 'She-town'. The men sit at home all day or loaf around the Greenmarket with nothing to do but drink or cause mischief. The wives come back tired from a hard day's work, and there is often trouble in the evenings. The magistrates are run off their feet with domestic assault cases. We are hard pressed to keep up with all the arrests. I don't know who's to blame for it really. Keeps us busy in our work though, I suppose. Good day, sir."

Duncan went back inside where James, Elizabeth and Ellen were waiting for news of his conversation. "The police think you will be called before a magistrate in the police court, but the fact that you have no previous record and the fact you come from a good family should mean you will only be fined, though they did warn there could be a short sentence of confinement. But they said if there were ever to be a repeat, it could be very different."

"But we need a separate conversation also James," his elderly father continued. "I have concluded that it is not good for you, or any of us, for you to continue to live here with your mother and me. You are not supporting your family financially, and the comfort we grant you in this house gives you no incentive to find the work you need to put your family on an independent footing. Your self-indulgent drinking is weakening your resolve to work and making it less likely employers will engage you or keep you on if they do give you a chance. So I am giving you notice that you must be ready to leave this house with Elizabeth and the children not later than six months from today. That is plenty due time for you to find work, find rooms to rent and prepare yourselves for independent living. The days of easy hospitality for you here are over, James."

Elizabeth, looking across at her husband, was surprised to see him looking chastened but also somehow emboldened by his father's ruling.

"Thank you, Father," he said. "We will get ourselves ready by that time."

That night, James stayed in the house. When the children were soundly asleep, James, seemingly invigorated by his prospective escape with only light punishment, and cheered by his father's invitation to stay on for a further six months, pressed enthusiastic amorous attentions upon Elizabeth. When she discovered six weeks later that she was pregnant once more, she worked out that was the night that she had conceived again.

The police court magistrate found James guilty of assault and fined him seven shillings and sixpence or four days in gaol. In passing sentence, he advised James Simpson to be careful of excessive drinking in the future.

Elizabeth gave him the money to pay his fine so he could avoid prison. That was one week's worth of her wages.

Ten

Cedric Blumenthaler arrived promptly at noon at the offices of the *Dundee Advertiser* for his appointment with John Leng. The two newspapermen greeted each other warmly, confident immediately in their shared trade though they could hardly have differed more starkly in appearance. Blumenthaler, in his early thirties, was tall, angular featured, and immaculate in his starched collar and patterned bow tie and razor sharp pleated trousers. He wore his straight blond hair slicked right back. Leng was a short stocky man with a thick unruly beard some 25 years his senior. Shod in a pair of stout brown shoes, he was dressed all in tweed, his paunch straining at the buttons of the waistcoat he wore beneath his jacket.

Blumenthaler was still in the early phase of his journalistic career. Leng, the longstanding editor turned proprietor of the now daily *Dundee Advertiser,* had a glittering record of publishing success. As well as transforming the fortunes of the newspaper he had also founded a successful news weekly—the *People's Journal*—and a popular literary weekly, the *People's Friend.* He had become the most prominent force in journalism in Dundee, a town renowned for publishing prowess. With all this achievement already on his record, many felt Leng would soon now leave the newspaper—which he liked to refer to fondly as his 'inky mistress'—and enter the world of politics full time. By contrast, Blumenthaler's journalistic pinnacles still lay ahead of him.

Leng suggested the two should walk and talk to be sure of not keeping their guests waiting. He gave Blumenthaler a brief pen portrait of their lunching partners as they left the building.

"Edward Cox has not long succeeded his late father James as head of the Cox Brothers firm. His father was at one time the Provost of Dundee. You could not have a better representative of the Dundee jute industry than him to talk to. He runs the largest factory at the Camperdown Works. They call the industry 'King Jute' here, and they call the bigwigs who run the firms the 'Jute Barons'. He is one of the biggest Barons of the lot. Academic, loves fine art, much involved in philanthropic and religious work. He's a Unionist and an ardent free trader."

"Thank you so kindly for arranging this meeting, Mr Leng," said Blumenthaler. "He sounds the perfect lunch companion. And Mr Ritchie?"

"Robert Ritchie is the president of the Dundee Trade Council and he is just about the nearest thing you will find to a representative of the jute workers in the town. But between you and me, he is not that close to the mill and factory workers."

"Not that close?" spluttered Blumenthaler. "He's the head of the Trades Council and he isn't familiar with the biggest trade? How can that be?"

"It's not so much that he isn't familiar with it," said Leng, "but he finds it by far the hardest industry to deal with here. He is much more at home with Dundee's other trades such as the shipbuilders, the engineers, the railway workers or the town's famous marmalade makers. Why? Because the jute workers are different. For a start, they are almost all women, they aren't formally organised, there are no trade unions, they don't have formal agreements and their motivations are not the same as the male workers in the town."

"I suspect Ritchie and his few Council officials really dread having to address jute workers' meetings," Leng continued. "The job for two or three men standing up trying to address a jeering, sneering, wolf whistling crowd of 200 or more hardy jute girls is not one for the faint hearted."

"What did you mean by their motivations are different, Mr Leng? Surely in the end women workers want similar things from work and their employers as the men do?" Blumenthaler pressed.

"Before you leave the town, you might want to see if you can talk to some of the women as they are waiting to go into work or as they leave," said Leng. "You will find them a feisty bunch. They don't take orders easily and, don't get me wrong, they will fight hard for their rights. But the things they value are just different. For a start, many of them are single girls. So they can accept far lower wages than men who have to bring up a family on their pay. They see their money as just for their food and lodgings, drink and entertainment. They are mostly happy with what they can earn and with the financial independence from men that it gives them. The married women, on the other hand, are often bringing a second wage into their houses. As long their husband earns reasonably elsewhere, they can live comfortably on their pay packets from jute. What none of them wants is to rock the boat. The last thing they want is to put their jobs at risk. Jute gives them what they need, and they are suspicious and resentful of any interference in it from outside. They want to protect what they have. They don't want jeopardy."

"I suppose what you are saying in a roundabout way is men just wouldn't accept those terms and wages?" said Blumenthaler pointedly.

"Men lost that battle long ago when they resisted the introduction of steam power into the spinning and weaving trades. Now they are not at all in competition with women for the jobs in the industry. The women have wiped them out of it completely. Barring very few overseer and maintenance jobs, which are still reserved for men, the mills and factory workers are all women. Women and children, that is. There are a couple of thousand young lads and lassies working half time as shifters in the mills, alongside the women, taking the full bobbins off the spinning frames and replacing them with empty ones."

"Ah, we're here," said Leng, as they walked up to the doorway of the Exchange Coffee House. "Let me take you in and introduce you to Edward and Robert. I hope I've given you some sense of who they are."

Edward Cox and Robert Ritchie, both white-bearded men, were sitting already at the table awaiting their arrival. The two men stood as Blumenthaler and Leng were shown to the table. "Good afternoon, Mr Blumenthaler and welcome to Dundee," said Cox. "Won't you please be seated? We thought we should toast your arrival with a little Scottish wine, of the grain variety of course, before we perhaps proceed to the grape with our meal?" The waiter appeared with four large crystal tumblers of whisky and placed them on the table before each man.

The three Scots raised their glasses in toast to Blumenthaler, who responded simultaneously. "Your very good health."

Leng made the courteous introductions and, noting that both Mr Cox and Mr Ritchie were busy men and pressed for time, said he was sure that Mr Blumenthaler had a number of questions he would wish to put to them. "We have taken the liberty of ordering the food already and I hope it pleases your palate. So there no need for us to worry about a menu," he said. "We have kept to a Scottish theme so we will begin with a plate of the finest local smoked salmon and then proceed to a haggis and neeps. Good for you to sample proper Scottish fare while you are here, Mr Blumenthaler," Leng said with a broad grin.

Blumenthaler, not sure whether he was being played for a fool or not, smiled and said, "I am ready for just about anything." This appeared, judging by the Scots' responses, to be entirely the correct reply.

"So first," said Blumenthaler, "may I thank you both for the great kindness of your time. I am honoured to meet you all. I thought I might open by asking you for context where the jute industry of Dundee came from. I presume it was not an overnight sensation?"

It was Cox who replied. "Far from it. The history of the town in textiles started with wool but really began in earnest with coarse linen about 100 years ago. We were early to embrace steam-driven mills and power looms. In the first 50 years of the century, the town became established as the country's leading linen producer and the biggest importer of flax, which is linen's raw material. We were huge importers from Russia and the Baltic lands of Latvia and Estonia."

"I understand from Mr Leng," Cox continued, "that your series of articles is to be headlined 'From the Heart of Empire'. That is a propitious heading indeed for an article about this town, for Dundee is very much an Empire town. I would go further. While Mr Dickens' notable novel of Paris and London was entitled *A Tale of Two Cities,* the story of Dundee, I would suggest to you, is *A Tale of Two Empires*. In the first half of this century, we were a crucial outpost of the Russian Empire. We are now a manufacturing pillar of the British Empire, importing raw jute from the Empire territory of Bengal in northern India, which is the only place in the world where it grows. We process and manufacture it here, and we send British Empire finished jute products all over the world."

As the side of smoked salmon arrived to be carved at their table, Blumenthaler, scribbling furiously in his notebook, asked what it was that had driven the local industry to switch from linen to jute?

Cox again responded. "Multiple factors in truth. The middle years of the century, as you know, saw several wars—notably the Crimean and the American Civil War—as well as the Australian gold rush. Those events all drove up the demand for sacking, tarpaulins and canvas tenting materials, for all of which jute is ideally suited. At the same time, we had growing concerns here about our dependency on Russia for nearly all our raw material for linen. Relations between Britain and Russia were not good or stable, and we felt vulnerable to a single source of supply which we did not control and which might quite easily be turned off completely in the event of a conflict."

"So, the attraction of a much cheaper raw material—a ton of raw jute is usually about half the price as the same amount of flax—which we could obtain from a connected source located within the British Empire, was unassailable. When it was discovered that this very coarse, hardy raw material could be softened by saturating it in whale oil for a few days, so it could then be spun in our steam-driven mills, the case for jute was made. We already had an existing whaling fleet based here so their regular catches provided easy access to that crucial softening oil for us. Almost all our linen production capacity was then switched to jute. Though one of the biggest firms in the town, our colleagues Baxter Brothers' Dens Works, is still devoted to linen. As it turned out, despite the periods of great political tension, flax supplies from Russia have never been turned off as we feared. But we are now no longer exposed to that risk. We have become the British Empire powerhouse at the centre of the world jute trade."

"Do you have virtually all the world market to yourselves then?" Blumenthaler asked, as he noted down the jute baron's words. Cox was about to reply again when Leng interceded and said, "Let me allow Edward to enjoy some of this delicious salmon while I shall try to answer the question for you."

"There is competition in Europe, the Germans have a domestic jute industry which they seek to protect with tariff barriers, for their product is far inferior on many grounds to what we have here in Dundee. But the real competition that we face is from within the Empire itself. In Bengal, on the Hooghly River, close to where all the jute crops are grown, a number of mills and factories have sprung up and are highly productive. Indeed, several of them are based on investment from Scotland. They use machinery built here and managers trained here. Of course, India also benefits from very low costs of local labour, so they can produce jute products very cheaply to compete with us. Not on quality we would say still, but certainly on price. It means the industry here has to be very careful to keep a tight control of its costs of production, or cheaper prices offered by Calcutta jute producers could make us uneconomic and drive the works here completely out of business."

"So Scottish men trained in Dundee are using expertise they gained here to compete against Dundee in India?" asked Blumenthaler.

"They are," said Cox, returning to the conversation. "But we have to recognise it is a free market, Mr Blumenthaler. It is up to us to ensure that we remain competitive."

"That sounds like a good opportunity to ask you then, Mr Ritchie," said Blumenthaler turning to his left, "what do the jute workers here feel about the wages they earn and the conditions that they work in here?"

"May I pour everyone some white wine?" Leng interjected at this point, drawing attention away from the question and thereby giving Ritchie a moment or two to consider his answer. The Trades Council president responded once their four glasses were filled.

"There will always be an aspiration for higher wages," he said, "but in my opinion the jute workers here consider they receive a fair wage for a fair day's work. On conditions, I am sure Mr Cox will tell you that conditions in the mill are not the easiest, not with the noise and all the dust fabric clogging the air, but you don't see jute workers giving up their jobs easily or putting them lightly at risk."

Edward Cox, now addressing his haggis with gusto, again rejoined the fray.

"I would say we have successfully educated the workforce here to understand that we are an international business though we stand on Scottish soil, on the banks of Scottish water. The jobs here are not really local jobs at all, they are totally related to the fluctuations of the world market. We buy our raw material from India 9,000 miles away by sea. There, it is subject to regular fluctuations in price. Sometimes, that's because demand is rising or falling, at other times it is to do with to crops being plentiful or scarce due to the weather conditions in Calcutta."

"We also now have to compete, as Mr Leng has explained, with Empire workers in India who are content with local wages far below the expectations here. And we have to supply customers across the world, who are keen to buy their jute bags and other products at the lowest possible prices. So you will see it is a complicated affair with many factors that are outside our control. In order that we can continue do all that profitably, we sometimes have to reduce the workers' wages here when times are hard and raise them again when we are doing better."

"Is that a frequent thing?" asked Blumenthaler. "How often have wages had to be adjusted up or down in the last years?"

"In my recall," said Cox, "maybe twenty times. Eleven or twelve times down and may be eight or nine times up."

"That can't be too popular," said Blumenthaler.

"It is very popular when they rise," said Cox with a wry smile, "less so when they drop. But we are not about being popular, Mr Blumenthaler, we are about being successful and surviving to see another day. If we fail in that, there will be no jobs in jute here at all."

"I can see you're enjoying your haggis and neeps, Mr Blumenthaler," said Ritchie. Blumenthaler hadn't the slightest idea what he was eating and he didn't care to ask for details for fear of a troubling answer. "My first time and I must say it is delicious," he said dutifully.

The conversation continued with a discussion of the differences between the Dundee industry and its newly established competition in Calcutta. Blumenthaler learned that, until half way through the century, there hadn't been a single jute mill in India though all the raw jute in the world was grown there. He discovered that the Indian factories today needed many more workers than the Scottish works, but Indian workers earned barely a quarter of the wages expected in Dundee. Blumenthaler was also interested to inquire whether Dundee jute owners were investing their money into India and fuelling their own increasing competition. Cox and Leng both maintained that this was not the case.

Dundee jute families were already fully invested in jute in the town and did not need to redouble their existing capital in the industry. Many were certainly putting money they made in Dundee into America, they explained, but into other industries, such as the fast-growing railroad companies.

The four men then discussed the philanthropic contributions of some of the leading Dundee owners in endowing local parks and hospitals, before matters turned to more general discussions. Blumenthaler politely reciprocated by sharing with his hosts some of his perceptions of modern New York. At the stroke of two o'clock, Leng brought the agreeable luncheon to a close.

"May I thank you all, gentlemen, for attending today. I am sure Mr Blumenthaler has found the conversation very informative and, sir, I remain at your disposal if further questions arise in the coming days. Mr Ritchie and Mr Cox, thank you both very much for your time. I wish you both a good afternoon." The two men rose, thanked their host graciously and bade Blumenthaler a safe journey home.

Leng and Blumenthaler took a cup of coffee together after the American had politely declined his host's suggestion of one more whisky to close.

"I'd suggest you'd find it worthwhile to go talk to some of the jute women," Leng said. "The best time is probably first thing. They gather in front of all the workplace gates from around five thirty each morning. The shift starts prompt at six, so you'll catch them standing around waiting to be let in at that time. When the bell goes for the end of the shift in the evening, you'll find it a lot harder to hold them in conversation. They're away like a shot then. Good luck anyway and don't hesitate to get in touch if I can help you further."

"Thank you, Mr Leng. You have been most kind. I cannot thank you enough for what you have done," said Blumenthaler as the two men parted ways at the doors of the coffee house.

Eleven

The next morning, Cedric Blumenthaler rose at five, washed and shaved and, with notebook and pencil in hand, set out in the direction of the jute works. It was not a challenging navigation. The heavily clustered forest of chimneys, some of which, even at this early hour, were already beginning to belch out smoke into the air above, was plainly visible from miles around.

He walked up from the docks onto the Lochee Road, and as he got closer to the smoking stacks, the streets around him became progressively busier. Hundreds, maybe thousands, of women were pouring out of doors onto the roads, all then hurrying purposefully in the same direction through the dark and dirty roads and alleys. The buildings from which they emerged, mostly tenement dwellings, were all heavily blackened by the soot, the smoke and the filth that billowed out all day from the factories and darkened the entire area.

Hardly a man was to be seen. Instead, a ceaseless sea of drably dressed women, some with shawls pulled tight around them over their dark dresses, some wrapped up in heavy coats against the falling morning drizzle, surged like a tidal wave through the town. Above them towered the tall mill chimneys, dwarfing the thousands of tiny creatures that scurried beneath them, thrusting skyward, each seemingly vying to outdo the next in scale and daunting presence.

Now as he got up closer, Blumenthaler noticed that many of these stacks were not as he had imagined them to be: brutal, bald brick structures. On closer inspection, he saw many were richly decorated and seemed to have taken inspiration from the beauty and traditions of Italianate architecture. He passed the Lawside works, which boasted a large cupola. The Gilroys' Tay Works, which stretched along Marketgait, was highlighted with magnificent obelisks and pediments. Outside the Bowbridge Works of the Grimond family, he admired an exotic camel and a rider, seemingly a tribute to Lawrence of Arabia, on the top of the factory gates.

Proudest of all, standing as a great landmark above the town in the distance, was the chimney of the giant Camperdown Works, owned by Edward Cox and his family. It was a magnificent Renaissance campanile in its decoration, an industrial megalith in its purpose. Standing 288 feet high, and reportedly made of one million and one bricks, it loomed large as a towering masculine symbol over a town whose wealth was being made by women's hands. As Blumenthaler gazed at it, taking in its majesty, he narrowed his eyes and fancied he saw the giant stack as a tall man in a top hat, his tailcoat adorned with polished buttons right down the front. It reminded him somehow of Robert Howlett's iconic photograph of Isambard Kingdom Brunel standing before the launching chains of the *SS Great Eastern*, which had appeared in so many newspapers all over the world, including his own. Cox's Stack was brute industry made almost human.

On Hawkhill, close to the Blackness Road, Blumenthaler paused outside the Ashton jute works, owned by the Caird family, where a huge crowd of women were gathered outside the still closed high iron gates, waiting to be allowed into work. He decided this was as good a place as any to meet his first jute workers. He was in two minds at first whether to head for the clutches of women who were already engaged in animated conversation in groups, in the hope he might break in and get several impressions of life in the jute at once; or aim instead for the solitary figures, the quiet ones keeping themselves to themselves, who were waiting silently for the great doors to open and who might be glad of the attention and prepared to share some secrets in relative privacy.

He decided he could not know which was the better course until he engaged, so he headed straight for a group of ten or twelve women standing up close to one another, huddled against the cold and chatting among themselves animatedly.

"Pardon me, ladies, may I beg a few moments of your time?" he opened.

The women all turned as one, surprised by his accent, his tone and an unexpected male presence.

"Well, hello handsome," said one. "Glory be, it's a Yankee Doodle Dandy!" said another, "Oh yes, pardon me, sir, do tell me what I can do for you!" said a third as the others around them dissolved into giggles of ribald laughter.

Blumenthaler had decided on his way to the works that he would not introduce himself as a newspaperman, for fear of his audience clamming up when confronted by a journalist who, for all they knew, might write something damaging to them. So he took an alternative tack, one that was the truth, if not quite the whole truth.

"I'm a writer researching the jute business in Dundee, and I wondered if I could ask you a few questions to help me understand what it's like to work in these mills and factories, and how you feel about working in this industry?" he asked.

A tall sassy woman with a cigarette hanging between her lips answered him "Sure. Fire away, lover boy, what do you want to know?"

"Is it easy work or hard, do you enjoy it, what are the conditions you work in like, and what do you think of the wages? Those are my main questions," he said.

"No-one would ever say work here is easy Mr… er?" said one. "My name is Blumenthaler, and I'm from New York," Cedric answered.

To mocking wolf whistles from two of the women, a second girl spoke. "It's a full 12-hour shift here, and you're working all the time, there's no time for breaks or slacking or sleeping on the job, you have to have your wits about you the whole time."

A third chimed in. "If you haven't, there's two mortal dangers you face. One, you'll get a finger or your hand taken off by a machine because those belts stop for nothing that gets in their way. The other is if the foreman sees you leaving your workplace, or you're not totally on your job, he'll haul you off the shift and you won't know when you'll see work again."

"Is there not even time for you to relax and enjoy a little conversation among your workmates?" Blumenthaler asked. The women roared as one in laughter. "Conversation?" said one. "You've never been in a jute mill, have you, Mr Bloomingtiler?"

"It's Blumenthaler, ma'am, and, no, I have not," the American admitted.

"That's clear as day because, if you had ever been over the door of one, you wouldn't have asked that question," she continued. "The din in there is fearsome. I suspect someone with your educated way with words might call it 'deafening'. For some women, that is what it truly is. Some have gone stone deaf because of the terrible racket of the machines all day long. What we say is, at least it lets them work in peace now. Most of us get used to the noise in the end. It gets to the point where eventually you don't even notice it. So no, there is no social chit-chat going on, but we do have a sign language we've worked out between ourselves which lets us communicate a bit by hand. But it's never by voice. No-one would hear a word that was said anyway even if you were to shout your blooming head off."

Blumenthaler, writing down their words as fast as he could, then asked the women how they would describe the atmosphere in which they worked. They described it as hot, greasy, heavy with sick-making oil fumes. The air all day was thick with jute dust—'the stour'—they said, explaining that was the word they gave to the small floating specks of jute that broke away during the spinning process and floated through the air, invading their eyes, mouths and nostrils. "A lot of us bring in snuff to take," said a round ruddy-faced woman in her fifties. "It's just about the only thing that will clear it."

Blumenthaler was trying his hardest not to comment on their replies or to betray his views on their lot, not least because he was trying his best not to interrupt their flow with any comment that might slow or alarm them—or worse, make them shun him. Instead, he tried to keep the pace of his questions up with their appetite to answer them.

"Do people sometimes get sick because of that?" he asked.

A short woman at the front of the group, who hadn't so far spoken, said, "Yes mill fever affects a lot of people, especially the ones who haven't worked here so long. Seems like you get hardened to it over time, but it makes a lot of people too ill to work and then they don't earn, so they try to get back as soon as they possibly can, sooner than they should more often than not."

"Thank you so much, ladies, you have been so kind, but just one more question if I may," said Blumenthaler, as he saw the works clock edging to five minutes to six, the moment when the bell would sound and the great gates would be swung open. "How about the wages, do you think they're fair?"

The tall woman who had spoken in answer to his first question took his last. "If you want to hear all the views on that, then you'll need all day and we don't have that to give you," she said. "We're all women, and the men wouldn't work for what we get paid. We know that, and it's part of the reason why the jobs here are all reserved for females and the kids. We're mostly smaller than the men, and the bosses can fit more of us into the spaces and they don't have to pay us the rates a man and his union would demand, the money the head of a family needs to bring home. But for a young girl, ten or eleven shillings a week is enough to give her independence, enough to put food on her table, a shared room to sleep in, and leave her with a bit of money for enjoyment. Where would she be without it? For the married girls, it works for them as long as their man is making decent money somewhere else. Then her wage can make all the difference that lets a family live with some dignity rather than in hunger and need. But if a mill girl's got a family with bairns of her own, and her man is idle, those are the ones that really struggle on the skinny wages here. You can't live on them. So it all depends on your circumstance."

At this, the Ashton works bell rang loud and repeatedly, the gates swung open and the mass of woman started moving as one, their halting progress dictated by the shuffling advance of the crowd.

"Good luck, Yankee Doodle!" said the tall women as she turned to bid Blumenthaler farewell. "Be kind to us in what you write. We're not bad girls, you know."

Cedric Blumenthaler remained in Dundee for three more days continuing his researches and speaking to other factory owners and workers before he returned to London to compose his article. When he telegraphed the finished piece across to New York, it was received with great delight by his newsroom and by his editor, who described it as 'a beacon of all that our journalism should be'.

When the article was eventually published in *The New York Times*, it was spread over two full broadsheet pages side-by-side, including photographs Blumenthaler had taken of some of the mills and crowds of their workers.

It was set under the banner headline:

Heroines of Jute: A Tale of Two Empires
The Story of the Women of Dundee who Make the Carriers of World Trade

The article was envied by the *Times'* competitors, applauded by writers and commentators alike, and it produced a huge number of readers' letters. For two days, the newsroom editors selected from among them those most suitable to print.

The letters were all considered and read carefully, each one picked reverentially from a large sand-coloured burlap sack placed in the middle of the newsroom floor.

The article and its reader response did more than justify Blumenthaler's ambitiously self advocated trip to Britain, it made his name on the newspaper. He returned to his Manhattan desk to spontaneous applause from around the floor.

His reputation made, he went on to serve as a distinguished reporter for *The New York Times* over the next three decades, first at home, and then on foreign soil.

Twelve

Elizabeth and James were now five months into the six-month extension of their permitted stay in Duncan and Ellen's house. Elizabeth's work was continuing well in the shop at the foot of Law Hill. Mrs McCourt continued to get regular orders from a number of the jute works, who were pleased with the quality and reasonableness of price of the aprons she produced. To cope with the workload, she hired two more girls and put Elizabeth in charge of them. She raised her weekly wage to eight shillings to reflect her new responsibility.

"I'm sorry, it can't be more, Elizabeth," she said. "I know you're worth more, but there just isn't the profit in this work for me to be able to pay you more." Elizabeth, now entering the last stage of her pregnancy with her third child, was glad of the security of the work and pleased with the recognition of the small raise. With her husband's money still unpredictable, it was a certainty she valued hugely.

For her part, Jean McCourt trusted her implicitly. She had Elizabeth opening the shop in the morning for her, and closing it in the evening, and she prized her work as a seamstress highly. It was the shop owner rather than Elizabeth who raised the issue of the approaching birth.

"When the baby comes, I can understand you may not be able to come into the shop for a while. What I can do, Elizabeth, is give you piece work. Then at least for a time, if you would like to continue to work for me, you can do it from your home. You can come in to collect the linen at the start of the week and deliver me the finished aprons at the end. I think I could manage sixpence for each dozen you complete," she said. That took a huge weight from Elizabeth's mind as her father-in-law's deadline approached.

James's demeanour and work performance had improved somewhat in the months since the assault and his brush with the police and the court. He seemed more resolved to go out and find work than he had previously, and he had proved more successful in the last five months than he had in the previous twelve. In all, he had worked for ten weeks in the period and earned on average around 18 shillings a week. Had that sum arrived for each week of the five months, Elizabeth and he would have had a reasonable living. But since he had only found work for half the time, it rounded out as little more than nine shillings a week when taken across the whole period. That, together with Elizabeth's eight shillings, was still poverty money. It would be a challenge, even impossible, to find lodgings for a family of four on that level of income, and Elizabeth knew it.

With just a fortnight left of their allotted time remaining, Duncan asked James and Elizabeth to come for a discussion about the future around their kitchen table. The two children, Robert and Ada, were sleeping soundly in their beds upstairs. Elizabeth had been dreading this moment for some time, almost since the deadline ultimatum had been given. And she couldn't fail to notice the pallor in her husband's complexion as he sat down opposite his parents. Both Duncan and Ellen looked sternly across the table. This was not to be a light-hearted conversation, Elizabeth could instantly see.

"It is time now for us to talk about the future and the next stage of your lives," Duncan began. "I made it clear to you almost six months ago that your time in this household must come to an end and that you must, as healthy and fit young people, find a way of living independently from your mother and me. I am no longer working and we cannot continue to support you here as we have done since your marriage."

James sat in silence as his father continued. "I had hoped that in these six months since I made that deadline clear that you, James, would have secured a regular income which would enable you to support your family, your wife, your two young children and the third one who is shortly to arrive," he said with a nod in Elizabeth's direction, her pregnant swelling clear for all to see.

"We are pleased to see that you have applied yourself to this search for work in a more diligent way than you evidenced before, but it is also clear to your mother and me that this has produced at best only half-time work. You have not yet obtained a consistent wage, which would allow you to support your family, especially as your pregnant wife may soon, at least for a time, be unable to work."

"Father, would it then…" began James, seemingly clinging to a forlorn hope that his father was about to relent on their notice to leave.

"If you are about to ask if you can be permitted to stay longer, let me stop you and state clearly to you that, no, you cannot," said Duncan with finality. "I have explained to you very plainly why I think it is essential that you both leave our house. It is not only because we cannot afford to support you, but because you need the driving responsibility of creating a home of your own. You must leave in two weeks' time, as was agreed."

The shock at this, which registered on James's face, was evidence that he had not believed that his father would hold to his resolution. Duncan was made of sterner stuff than his son, however, and, once decided on a path, he was not a man to be shaken from it. For Elizabeth, while she might have hoped for a different outcome, this was neither a shock nor a surprise. It was merely confirmation. She knew Duncan rather better than did James.

What came next, however, Elizabeth certainly had not anticipated.

"Your mother and I have discussed the situation at some length," said Duncan. "We are not cruel people but nor can we continue as now. We are deeply concerned, however, that if we send the four of you, soon to be five, from this house, that you will fall into ruin, that you will not be able to feed the children properly or support yourselves. If that occurs, there can be only one outcome for both of you and that would be the workhouse. You would then stand to lose the children to the care of an institution that would take over responsibility for them."

"Your mother and I could not bear to see that, so we wish to make you a proposal. It is for you to accept or reject as you see fit. You should, though, think very carefully about it for, once made, there is no going back upon it."

Elizabeth and James looked in consternation at Duncan's resolute features, still not knowing what was to come.

"Our proposal is that you two leave this house and find somewhere where you can live with your new baby and give your new child a proper healthy upbringing, living within whatever means you can obtain. Your mother and I would continue to provide a place here to bring up Robert and Ada to ensure they are fed and schooled and brought up to be healthy young people in a loving family home."

Elizabeth and James sat both dumbstruck by the suggestion, Elizabeth's mind racing in one direction and James' in another. For Elizabeth, the prospect of surrendering her two children seemed unthinkable, a dreadful outcome, almost the worse possible. James immediately saw merit in it. They needed to be reasonable, and his father's idea would ensure their two eldest children would have their childhood assured. If he and Elizabeth insisted on taking Robert and

Ada with them into an uncertain new place, adding their two mouths to feed—and sets of clothes to provide—it might be too much for them to support.

"Please give us your decision tomorrow because we all need to decide what are to be the next steps," Duncan continued.

"I wish to make one further thing clear though," he added. "Your mother and I will not do this on a temporary or an unclear basis. It will serve none of us, most importantly not Robert and Ada, for them to think their parents have gone to live elsewhere but will come to see them sometimes, only then to disappear out of their lives again. Uncertainty and instability of that sort would be very damaging to such young children."

"From the point of view of the two of you, also we believe that if you are looking at one moment to your own livelihoods, and then looking over here at the other half of your family, that divided attention will prevent you concentrating on building a new future with your new child that you can make healthy and lasting."

"So our proposal is we will become the formal guardians of Robert and Ada and take your place as their parents. We will not deny to them that you are their natural parents, but we will explain that you have had to go away, and that we are their family now, that we will look after them and that they are staying here in their own home, just as safe and secure with us as they were before."

"It is now for you to decide. Should you decline this offer, which we hope very much that you will treat seriously, then you will all leave this house in two weeks, and I am afraid we will not entertain requests for financial or other help which might follow upon your decision. You would have then chosen a course for which you must accept the full consequences as grown people and parents. My strong advice to you is to accept our suggestion, the decision though is entirely yours."

Elizabeth was silent. There was so much information to work through and consider. She knew she should certainly not rush into a heated or relationship-ending reaction to her parents-in-law's proposition. This needed calm reflection and discussion with her husband, the children's father. She did not know how he would see the suggestion and she needed to hear him speak.

James stood up from the table and said, "Thank you, Father, that is clear. And a generous offer for you and Mother to make. Elizabeth and I will indeed consider it carefully. We will give you our decision when we have done so and, in any case, by this time tomorrow."

With that, James held out his hand to Elizabeth to lead her from the table. She stood up and took it, silently, the handkerchief in her other hand pressed hard to her face as they made their way from the room.

Thirteen

For James, there was nothing to discuss. He had not anticipated his parents' proposal but, now it was put before him, he seized upon it as his solution.

As the day of their departure had approached, he had been turning back increasingly to the solace of the whisky bottle to calm his rising panic about how he could possibly get by with a wife and three children to feed, given his uncertain prospects of work. Now his parents, in offering to take on the two eldest children, were handing a lifeline to him and Elizabeth and their soon-to-be new-born. He could begin to picture their having a place of their own that they could afford. He could see them starting out afresh. Robert and Ada, meanwhile, would continue in the only home they had ever known, with their grandparents who would ensure they wanted for nothing. To James, there was nothing there to question. It was the alternative that was unthinkable.

Elizabeth, by contrast, was torn apart by the prospect of losing her two children. It was an emotional rupture she felt so hard she did not know if she would be able to survive it. It plunged her into an agony of misery and loss. But, at the same time, she also recognised, amid her anguish, that the prospects for Robert and Ada in staying with their grandparents were undoubtedly better than if she insisted on their coming with James and herself. The evidence before her, despite all her hopes to the contrary, was that James was an unreliable breadwinner. For her part, while she at least had regular employment, she was not bringing in anywhere near enough to sustain what was soon to be a family of five. She thought of writing to her father Malcolm to ask him for some financial help but she could not bear the humiliation of begging her parents for charity.

That would be something she would only consider as an absolute last resort. Had she truly fallen so low?

So while James saw the picture very clearly, his wife was flayed by the conflict between her intense motherly instincts and the harsh reality of their circumstances. It took her all her powers of self-control not to allow her throat to well up with a bile of resentment, frustration and anger towards her husband. He had not provided for her and for their family, and now, directly as result, she was being faced with this heart-searing dilemma.

She could see by the look in his eye that James had found great relief in Duncan and Ellen's solution. His mind was already made up. He would not truly regret their family being split into two. So, Elizabeth reasoned, the only interests left for her to consider were her own and those of Robert and Ada. In a slow and excruciating process of logical thought, she came to the conclusion that the infants' interests were better served by staying with their grandparents than by coming with James and her. Her personal needs and interests were the exact opposite. But she could not put her selfish concerns before her children—and she would not. She had, in truth, nothing to offer them but her love and a life of likely poverty, perhaps not even with her, confined in some awful institution.

As Duncan had pointed out horrifyingly, she could quickly lose control of the whole situation if she insisted they all stayed together, if they then were to become destitute. Her children would be taken from them and sent away to the Ragged School. Robert and Ada could then lose both their grandparents and their parents in a matter of months. Could she guarantee that would not happen? No. Could she say it was unlikely to happen? Again she thought, in all honesty, no.

The more she considered it, the more the right course seemed obvious and set. She had to stand aside in the best interests of her children and consent to her husband's request that they agree to the grandparents' pact. As that finality dawned, Elizabeth dissolved into an engulfing flow of grief. Staggering, her stomach heaving, to the bathroom basin, she was violently sick.

At noon the next day, James and Elizabeth, composing herself as best she could, made their way to the kitchen where Donald and Ellen awaited them around the table. She noted her father-in-law had a pile of neatly handwritten papers to his right hand.

"Sit down, please," Duncan said to his son and his wife. "Have you reached your decision?"

James looked across earnestly at his parents and replied.

"We have, Father, yes. And though it is with heavy heart, Elizabeth and I both agree that it is in the best interests of Robert and Ada that we accept your and mother's kind proposal and that we convey them to your loving care. We can know that they will be well looked after by you in good circumstances. At the same time, it gives Elizabeth and myself a chance to start out anew, God willing, with a new baby arriving in a couple of months. You have given us the opportunity to make a success of living independently together as man and wife."

Ellen reached across and squeezed Elizabeth's hand in a gesture of sympathy and comfort. Neither woman could find words fit for the moment of this decision. Lips tight, they made a fleeting misty-eyed connection. It was Ellen's gaze that fell away first.

"Very well," said Duncan. "I am sure that will not have been an easy decision for you to make, but I do believe you have made the right one and taken the sensible course. You can rest assured that we will take good care of Robert and Ada and that is the greatest gift that your mother and I can make you in helping you to make a success of your marriage together."

James and Elizabeth both whispered the words "thank you."

Duncan turned to the papers on the table and said, "I did not know what your decision would be today, but in case you decided to accept our proposal, I had lawyers compose an agreement between us along the lines we discussed. If you would both then read this page, and if you are satisfied with it, sign it at the bottom. Your mother and I will then sign to confirm the agreement."

James took the letter from his father and, reading through it for two minutes, took up the pen and inked his signature in the space provided for it before passing the page to Elizabeth. She read the letter slowly, her eyes blurring as she made her way slowly through the sentences. She realised on several occasions, having reached the end of a paragraph, that she had retained none of its meaning. She had registered the words but none of the sense. Again and again, she revisited the words on the page. Until finally, after what seemed an age to all four around the table, she picked up the pen and, with trembling hand, signed her name.

"Thank you, Elizabeth," said Duncan, handing the letter to Ellen who confirmed her assent to the agreement with the single mark of a cross where she was guided to place it by her husband. Duncan then signed his own name and, blotting the inked paper, folded it and placed it into an envelope. "It is done," he said.

Ellen stood up and asked, "Would anyone like some tea?" James replied instantly that he would, but Elizabeth declined saying, "Thank you, Ellen, but if you don't mind I would like to take a little fresh sea air. I think I will take a walk down to the port."

"Of course, dear," said Ellen, adding "James, will you go with her?" Before her husband could reply, Elizabeth interjected.

"No, stay and take your tea, James. I am sure there's lots for you to discuss with your mother and father. I'd like to take some private time."

With that, she stood and was making her way to the door when Ellen cried out, "Oh, I am so sorry, Elizabeth, it completely slipped my mind with all this to go through today. A letter arrived for you this morning. Let me fetch it for you."

She stepped out into the hallway and returned with Elizabeth's letter. She had expected it might be from Jane. She had not heard from her for several months and she was her only regular correspondent. As she took it from Ellen, Elizabeth saw instantly that it was not Jane's well-formed hand on the envelope. The writing was recognisably her mother's. She had not written a letter to her before but the feathery script was unmistakably hers.

"Thank you, Ellen," said Elizabeth, slipping the letter into her pocket. Wrapping her shawl around her shoulders, she stepped out into the cold Sunday afternoon.

Elizabeth went out onto Princes Street feeling like she had been struck with a heavy blow to the back of the head. She was dizzy and weeping uncontrollably. She had to pause to steady herself with a hand on a wall as she reached the junction with Marketgait that would take her down to the dock road. She breathed as deeply as she dared to draw in the sea air as the great Tay Bridge hoved into view. One of Dundee's proudest landmarks, it had been the scene of great tragedy ten years earlier when it collapsed in high winds, killing all 70 passengers on a train that was crossing it. The new bridge that replaced it now stood across the Firth as a symbol of hope for the industrial future but also as a shrine of sadness.

Elizabeth walked on the waterfront towards the railway station. This was where she had arrived two days after her marriage to James, when she saw Dundee for the first time. She recalled how optimistic and excited she had been that day to be starting her new life with James. What had happened since to tarnish so many of those dreams? Feeling her baby kicking inside her she remembered that there was still hope for the future. There was, amid all the pain, the chance of a new beginning.

She found a seat looking out of the water. Seagulls screeched overhead, and the hive of activity in the busy docks was plainly visible all around her. She remembered her mother's letter, took it out from the pocket and slipped her finger in to open it. She unfolded the single page and read.

My darling girl Elizabeth

I am sorry to be the bearer of some terrible news. Your father has passed. He was struck down with consumption only three weeks ago but the dreadful disease hit him very hard and all hopes of a recovery for him faded in these last days. He had good physicians attending him but sadly they found they could not save him. They believe he probably caught the affliction from one of the customers to the shop who came in for medicines. There was one man I remember a week or so before your father fell ill who had a pallor and was coughing and wheezing as though he was near his last. Your father of course attended to him solicitously and gave him what medication he could to help. We can never know but I wonder if he contracted the consumption from him.

I am sorry not to have written to you sooner but I have had many things to do since your father passed away. Because I am not certificated as a chemist, we had to close the shop straight away. I am happy to say that your father's society of pharmacy have found a new chemist and his wife to take over the lease so I have, thank God, been relieved from paying the rent for the shop. Your father has left me some money, not a great deal for sure, but I hope I shall have enough not to need to seek charity in what years remain to me. I shall for sure though need to move to a more modest dwelling now there is no income any more.

Please forgive me for these sad tidings Elizabeth. I am grief-stricken at the loss of my Malcolm, your father, and I am sure you will be terribly sad to read this letter, too. I hope though that all is well with James and with Robert and Ada and that you are in good spirits awaiting the new baby.

What a sadness that your father will not know your new born. Yet this shows us that with God's blessing life goes on. I am comforted in my loss to know that you have the blessing of your young family growing up around you.

With kindest wishes
Your sorrowing mother

Elizabeth stood up and felt the buffeting wind blowing in towards her from the sea, which rocked her back on her heels. Was there any further torture to be inflicted upon her? For all mankind, the death of a parent serves as a *memento mori*, a reminder of the inevitability of death and of now being next in line. Elizabeth felt that cold realisation chilling through her as she contemplated never seeing her loving father again.

But she also felt a second sensation, one of a trap door closing over her head. She had resolved not to ask her father for money to help her in her plight. She was too proud to do that after all he had done for her and all the encouragement he had already offered her.

But it is one thing to choose not to ask for help, it is quite another to realise that all possibility of help is gone. Even in extremis now, her mother was not in a position to help her. She was really on her own. She had to make her marriage work to provide a home for the young life stirring inside her, readying itself to be born.

There was no alternative.

Fourteen

Some ten days later, as their final day in Princes Street approached, Duncan informed James and Elizabeth that an old work acquaintance of his, a man named Robert McLennan, had let it be known he had two modest basement rooms to let in his house and he was looking for a rent of six shillings a week. The house was in Crichton Street, just up from the docks. Duncan suggested James and Elizabeth might care to go to take a look.

When Elizabeth saw the rooms, her heart sank. They were dark, dingy and dirty. The word 'modest' was a flattery they did not deserve. McLennan, a short balding man of around 60, seeing the expression on her face, and anticipating her objection, said, "You'd want to clean them, and perhaps a lick of paint would not go amiss around the place to brighten it up but, if you do that, you'd have a bargain at six shillings a week in this town."

"We'll take it for four shillings," said James, suddenly, and with equal speed, McLennan responded, holding out his hand. "At five shillings, you have a deal, Mr Simpson." Without the briefest glance towards Elizabeth, James took the man's hand and shook it.

"Five shillings a week is agreed then," McLennan said. "Rent is payable one week in advance, so I shall need the first five shillings from you at your earliest convenience and the place is yours from that day."

James agreed they would return the following day with their belongings and the money. "All it needs is some elbow grease," said James to Elizabeth as they left McLennan's house and walked out into the street. You can clean it up and I'll take care of the painting. "At last, we will have a place of our own."

Elizabeth's thoughts had moved on from the grime and the dirt in the ill-lit rooms to the five shillings a week it would cost them to live in them and how they would afford it. It would leave them only three shillings for food from her weekly wage from Mrs McCourt, and that would be barely enough to exist on. If they weren't to starve, James would have to be bringing regular money into the house. Even that fragile position meant that, after the baby was born, she would have to be sure to sew enough aprons on a piecework basis to match the wages she had earned regularly by going into the Law Hill shop every day. Her head was awash with these whirling concerns until she calmed herself with the thought that this was what living independently required. This was what independent living was going to mean.

The next day, her last in Duncan and Ellen's Princes Street home, Elizabeth gave Robert and Ada their midday feed and carried them upstairs where she laid them down for their afternoon rest. She sat on the side of the bed, with the two of them lying side by side, stroking their hair, caressing them off to sleep. As first Robert's, and then Ada's eyes closed, she kissed both her children gently but lingeringly on the side of their heads. She then stood and, with tears running uncontrollably down her cheeks, made her way softly across the room before closing the door of the bedroom noiselessly behind her.

As she made her way downstairs, she gripped the banister tightly in her right hand for fear of toppling, her eyes clouded with her tears. She held her left hand folded beneath her heavily swollen pregnant stomach. At the foot of the stairs stood James, with three bags at his feet, and Duncan and Ellen standing with him in attendance. Both his parents wore solemn expressions, aware of the gravity of the moment for the young mother of the two children now asleep upstairs.

"Do you have everything? Mind that you do," said Duncan, managing to convey both concern and closure in those few words. "We will take good care of them, Elizabeth," said Ellen simply. Elizabeth nodded silently in response and picked up the smallest of the three bags.

"Farewell, both of you," said Duncan. "We wish you every success and happiness in your new lives." James embraced his parents briefly, and with that the two of them stepped out of their house for what was to be Elizabeth's final time.

When they arrived in Crichton Street, Elizabeth handed over to McLennan five of the six shillings she had in her purse, and he gave them in exchange two keys, one to the front door on the street, which would give them access to the inside of the house, and one to the outer door of their below-ground rooms. They descended to their basement abode and recognised at once that, even though it was still daytime, the rooms needed artificial illumination to aid the limited light that entered from the window which faced onto a grimy outside wall barely four feet away.

Elizabeth lit up a lamp and, as its light filled the room, the scale of the cleaning task that awaited her became clear. The place hadn't seen soap or water for a long time.

Every surface felt greasy to the touch, and the floors, sticky with grime, were outright filthy in the corners. There was an acrid stench of airlessness and rotting dirt filling the room. Elizabeth, taking off her shawl, had James fetch her a pail of water straight away and, dropping to her knees, she began the long job of making their first marital home habitable.

Two weeks later, in their spotlessly cleaned, but still unpainted, Crichton Street home, Elizabeth gave birth to her third child, a bright-eyed girl whom she named Janet. She and James were parents once again. Beside Elizabeth's bed, as she lay nursing her new baby, was the pile of linen she had taken from the Law Hill shop two days prior. This was so she could be ready to start sewing completed aprons at her agreed piece rate of sixpence a dozen, as soon as she felt ready to resume her work.

Fifteen

Elizabeth took up her needle and thread again two days after Janet was born, and set about producing aprons at a number that would at least match the eight shillings she earned before. That meant she had to produce almost 200 aprons a week, or almost 30 a day if she worked every day. She resolved instead to try to produce three dozen a day on Monday to Saturday and take a rest from the work on Sundays. The ill-lit room, which was starved of natural light, meant she had to perform all her work by lamplight while attending to the feeding and other needs of her baby daughter at the same time. Her eyes would surely need a Sunday rest.

James over the next weeks earned very little. There were a few days where he returned home and emptied his pockets to show only a couple of shillings. One memorable day, he came back with four shillings but it was the exception. While he went out every day, there were many days where he returned home with nothing at all to show for his absence.

Elizabeth managed the household budget like a hawk. She kept two small pots side by side on the mantlepiece to hold what money they had clearly in view, so she could be sure they would not run out. In one pot, she put five shillings, set aside to cover the next week's rent to McLennan, and in the second, she put whatever remained on top. If she worked flat out on Mrs McCourt's aprons all week, that would give them four or even five shillings more on which to manage food and clothing for the baby and feed the two of them. What money James brought home went into the second pot. Elizabeth accounted for both pots carefully. She needed to for, if a mistake was made and an over-expense was incurred, it could mean they had nothing for food at the end of the week. They were living on the edge of hunger.

Elizabeth was increasingly suspicious of James's failure to bring home more than a shilling or two for his labour. What work could he be doing that paid so little? Was he only working for a few hours? Or was he losing the work he was given to do and being sent away with less than a full day's wages? She was reluctant to put further pressure on him for fear that would put paid to even the meagre sums he was bringing back. But they were a long way from being able to live comfortably, and what they had was almost solely down to the money she earned from her piecework. One evening, she decided once again to force a conversation with her husband.

"Is there really no more work out there that you can find, James? We are living so poorly on what I can earn while I am raising Janet, and your few shillings are barely enough for us to put anything other than bread on our table. It is two weeks since we had a piece of meat, and it would be good to see a change from porridge and the odd piece of fish we can buy cheaply at the end of the day from the fishermen's catch."

"Do you think I do not want to earn more money, woman?" James snarled back. "Do you think I enjoy having so little? Until I go out to look for employment each day I cannot know what the day will hold and what rate I can earn. It is not helped by your complaining. I am not going to find it easier to get work with a witch on my back." With that, he stood up, walked out of the room, and she heard the heavy tread of his boots on the stairs outside and the sound of the front door of the house slamming behind him.

One week later, with no improvement in their circumstances, Elizabeth was sitting sewing her aprons with the baby Janet lying contentedly in her crib on the floor, when there came a knock on the door. Elizabeth rose to answer and saw her landlord Robert McLennan on the threshold.

"Good afternoon, Mrs Simpson," he said. "I am here to collect this week's rent. Your husband did not pay me yesterday as he is bound to do, so I am calling to collect the monies due from you."

Elizabeth was mortified. The payment of the rent was a task that James had fulfilled since they first moved in, using the money that she carefully set aside and placed in the rent pot on the mantlepiece every week before it was due.

"Pardon us, truly, Mr McLennan!" she said. "I will attend to it directly. Won't you please come in?" McLennan entered the room, and Elizabeth turned and went straight over to the rent pot and, removing its lid, emptied its contents into her hand, fully expecting the five shilling coins she had put there to drop into her palm. She looked down and, to her dismay, saw only three shillings in her hand.

McLennan saw the look of startled consternation on her face. "Is there some problem, Mrs Simpson?" he asked.

"No, no, Mr McLennan," she blustered. "I have other money here." She reached across to the second pot in which she kept the rest of what funds they had. By her last accounting, she expected there to be three shillings and sixpence in there. She found to her great alarm that it was a shilling and sixpence short. The pot contained only one shilling coin, together with one sixpence and six pennies. She put all the money together into her two cupped hands and gave it to McLennan.

"Three shillings, four, four and six and the pennies make five. Thank you, Mrs Simpson." said the landlord, relieving her of every last coin they had. "I'll bid you good day and may I please ask you to remind your husband that your rent is due promptly every Monday morning. I would ask that it be paid to me on time. I do not wish to have to come to collect it from you. It is an unsavoury thing for me to be required to do."

"I shall of course, Mr McLennan. Please will you accept my apologies? We shall not allow such an oversight to happen again," said Elizabeth. McLennan bade her goodbye and Elizabeth, pale from the experience and perplexed and frightened by the unexplained shortfall, fell back into her chair.

How could it possibly have happened? Had they been burgled? There was no sign of any break in, and surely, if someone had come to steal from them, they would have taken all the money and probably other things, too. Perhaps James had hidden the money somewhere else for safekeeping for some reason? He would surely be able to explain where it was when he returned, she decided.

That evening, James did not come back at his usual time. There was little food in the house and the most Elizabeth was able to bring together for a meal was a hunk of bread, some cheese and a small apple. She divided the humble fare into two portions and placed it on two plates, with a jug of water and two glasses to wash it down. Feeling her own hunger rising, and with still no sign of her husband returning, Elizabeth began slowly to eat. She was just finishing the last morsels on her plate when the door swung violently open and James staggered in, uneasy on his feet and smelling strongly of alcohol.

"What is this? Have you eaten without me?" he bellowed at her.

"I was hungry and I did not know when you would be coming back," replied Elizabeth.

"And what do you call this?" said James, seeing the scant food laid out in his place at the table. "Do you call this a meal, woman?" He swept his arm across the table, sending the plates crashing onto the hard floor. Elizabeth gathered up the baby Janet, who had begun bawling at the noise, and stooped to pick up the pieces of scattered food and broken crockery.

"It is all we have, James and, what is more, we now seem to have no money at all unless you can explain why the rent pot had only three shillings in it and the other pot had just two shillings more. Mr McLennan came to collect the rent from me today, saying we were already one day late in paying. I had to give him every last penny that we had to settle our dues. Unless you have brought money home today or you can tell me where the missing money is to be found?"

"You gave him it all?" screamed James. "Are you a mad woman? What are we going to live off for the remainder of this week, do you imagine, you idiot?"

"Are you drunk, James? You stink of whisky," said Elizabeth, looking James straight in the eye.

"Of course I am not. I have no money for drink," retorted James boorishly.

Elizabeth set Janet down again in her basket on the floor and walked across to James and stood in front of him and spoke calmly to the raging man.

"James. You have stolen our money haven't you? You have taken our rent and food money and you have spent it on whisky to put down your throat. You have robbed our daughter, you have robbed me, and you have robbed our family. You have done a terrible thing, James. You should be very ashamed."

That was the moment when James Simpson hit Elizabeth for the second time. Clenching his left fist, he drew back his arm and struck her viciously across the cheekbone and high on her face, knocking her off her feet and backwards. She dropped heavily onto her back, banging the back of her head heavily on the floor as she landed. Mercifully, where she fell was some two feet to the right of the crib where the baby Janet lay, now screaming with alarm.

James stumbled through into the bedroom and fell senseless onto the bed. Elizabeth, her head throbbing and her heart pounding, curled up next to her baby daughter on the floor and, drawing her knees close into her, wept until she fell deeply asleep.

Sixteen

The next morning, Elizabeth awoke early and felt her face, which was swollen and painful to the touch. Her head was still aching blindingly from the impact it had taken in her fall. She took out from the pocket of her dress the small oval hand mirror that her mother had given her for her 18th birthday and held it up to her face. Her right eye was closed, and the skin all around her eye socket up to her forehead and down half her cheek was a mass of red, black, blue and sickly yellow flesh. Looking down at Janet, still asleep in her basket, Elizabeth found herself saying:

"I have been lucky. I might easily have fallen on my baby girl and killed her. If his blow had been a few inches the other way, he could have killed me. I am lucky."

But at that point, she stopped. How lucky had she really been? Was her swollen and battered face good luck? The thought made her consider her whole life with James. Had she been lucky that day she met him? Had it been a kindly wind that had blown him into her shop that day? She had seen some happy times with him, for sure, but was that really good luck? He had given her two children but she had now lost them because he could not support their family. They were penniless, hungry and struggling to survive. He was a serial drunk and a deceiver. At times, he had shown he could be a brutally violent man. Was she safe with him and was her baby daughter?

She considered whether she actually deserved good luck and found it a hard question to answer. If she had any right to expect good luck, then it was hard to see that her life with James was bringing her much or any. If, on the other hand, she deserved bad luck, then that was seemingly coming aplenty. Should she then stay in such a cursed place? If she was neither deserving nor undeserving of luck, then would this poisonous cocktail of poverty, misery, loss and mortal danger which she was having to drink again and again be likely to change for any reason? Did she really believe something would happen by magic to change her fortunes and realign the stars?

Again, Elizabeth looked down at her new-born child. What if something terrible were to happen to Janet because her mother ignored all the evidence of her own eyes and took no steps to get her to safety? She had already lost Robert and Ada. She could not bear the thought that one day she might lose Janet, too.

She picked up the now stirring baby, cleaned and fed her, and, wrapping her up in her own shawl against the morning cold, she slipped out of the room, closing the door quietly behind her, leaving James, still out to the world, sleeping off the skinful of whisky he had taken the day before. She hurried through the morning streets, already crowded with women jute workers heading out to the factories, and made her way to the police station.

The constabulary arrested James Simpson two hours later after recording Elizabeth's complaint against him for assault. The sergeant in charge recorded her statement that this was the second time that her husband, when beside himself with drink, had attacked her with brutal intent, causing her serious injury. When James was taken into custody, Elizabeth went home and wrote him a short letter.

Dear James

For all the reasons that were true last time, I felt it necessary to report your attack upon me to the police. I am frightened not only for myself but for our daughter and for you.

I cannot continue with you. It is too dangerous for us all and I could never forgive myself if I allowed something dreadful to happen to Janet because I did not act on the clearest of signs. I am resolved that we must separate. You are not able or fit to look after our daughter and our two older children are being cared for by your parents already. I will take care of Janet now and bring her up safely alone.

One of us must leave Crichton Street. I believe it is easier if you are the one to leave. As a single man you will find it easier to find lodgings in this town than I as a young mother on my own with a new-born. I would prefer not to have to answer the questions that would surely be put to me about my circumstances. But if you will not leave, then I shall have no choice but to take Janet and leave today.

Please reply to tell me your decision. Whichever it is, I am decided. You must know this. I cannot go on with you and I will not.

Elizabeth

As she signed her name at the foot of the letter, she felt some strength and spirit returning to her body. The decision was the right one for all concerned. Writing it down gave it form and reality. It offered her and Janet a future that could be based on her own resourcefulness. They would be dependent on no-one else and on nothing else. Amid so much instability and uncertainty around her, she was confident in herself and what she could achieve. She felt strengthened that she would be in charge of her own destiny finally. With her baby bound in a sling in front of her, she carried the letter round to the constabulary to be delivered to their detained suspect. One hour later, there was a knock on the door and a police constable handed Elizabeth an envelope with a single page inside containing James's written reply. It was brief.

Elizabeth I will go.

Please put my things into a bag and hand them to the constable to bring to me. I am sorry.

Your loving James

With an engulfing sensation of relief, Elizabeth gathered James' few belongings together and placed them into a hessian bag, which she handed to the waiting policeman.

Two months later, the newly independent Elizabeth Simpson and her daughter vacated the Crichton Street property and moved into a room in the neighbouring suburb of Broughty Ferry, four miles east of the centre of Dundee on the north bank of the Firth of Tay.

Standing on a beautiful stretch of sandy beach, Broughty Ferry was a well-to-do area where many of the wealthy jute dynasties, including the Gilroys and the Grimonds, were building palatial mansions away from the grime of the city. For a time this earned the area a reputation as the richest square mile in all of Europe. Yet its distance from town made it not a convenient place for most ordinary folk, who needed to live close to the workplaces in the mills and the factories. So the cost of renting lodgings in the more modest properties of the area was sometimes less than in the densely packed and overcrowded tenements of the centre of town.

Elizabeth had been directed there by her employer Jean McCourt, whose long-time friend, Mary McKinnon, was looking for a reliable and trustworthy lodger to take a room in her house. Mrs McCourt, apprised of Elizabeth's new circumstances, had no hesitation in recommending her. Mary was the Shifting Mistress at the Grimond family's Bowbridge jute works in Hilltown. As Shifting Mistress, she was in charge of the child workers in the mill. She was pleased to offer her friend's trusted employee and her new baby her lodging.

With Janet still needing her near constant supervision, Elizabeth continued to work for Mrs McCourt on a piece work basis from her new abode. For Elizabeth, the flexible work was critical, her essential lifeline. Were she to lose it, then it was not clear how she could survive. With it, especially now newly installed in an upper floor room with natural light, she could be more productive than she had been working in the Crichton Street gloom.

Over the next months, Elizabeth's sense of well-being improved immeasurably. Aided by her new place and surroundings in the tranquil seaside beauty of Broughty Ferry, away from the hurly-burly of the smoke-filled town, she felt her spirits lifting daily. She was still living on a small budget but, freed from the costs and the stresses of life with James, she actually took pride in managing on a few shillings a week, and joy in seeing Janet growing bonnier each day.

When she finally again felt calm and safe, and no longer constantly feared the prospect of James re-emerging at her door unannounced, she began to think about a new beginning. As she did so, her thoughts turned to her oldest friend, Jane. They had lost touch altogether in the last year, and Elizabeth recognised that, now she was in a new address, if she did not write soon to tell her the news of her changed circumstances, she would likely never hear from her again.

She had for so long been too humiliated and anxiety-ridden to write to Jane. She could not think of an honest sentence she could bring herself to set on a page, so she had remained silent. Now, however, it felt different. She had acted to make a change and, while she could not know how Jane would react to the events that had befallen her and the decisions she had taken, she could at least for the first time now write with her own hope of better prospects. She took up her pen and wrote.

127 Long Lane Broughty Ferry

My dear Jane

Forgive your old friend for such a long time of silence! I have been in a dark place and I am only now emerged from it with a hope of a brighter future.

I have much to tell but will try to put it into few sentences. No essays, we always agreed! James and I have separated. We tried hard to make our marriage work but it proved too much. He was given to drink, he earned little money and he can also be a violent man, I am sorry to say. I could not go on with him.

I have just had a baby, our third, a lovely girl who we have called Janet and she is with me. James' parents adopted Robert and Ada to give James and me a chance of making a new life. It broke my heart to agree to that but with James earning so little we could not hope to keep a family of five together. I feared we would end up in the workhouse and the children would be taken away if we did not find a new arrangement. As it proved, another bad incident with James a few months ago showed me we were not able to manage things even as three. Now it is just Janet and me, I feel happy and safe for the first time for a long time. She is a lovely baby and I long to introduce her to you!

I am continuing to work at the same shop as before as a seamstress but I am now sewing the aprons from home so I can look after Janet. My work there is good and stable though I would like to earn a little more if I could. I am wondering whether I can persuade my employer to give me some material to make a proper dress so I can show her what I am capable of. The work she gives me is really very simple. My new plan is to save enough money to buy some material of my own so I can show her a finished dress in the hope she will trust me to do a little more!

Anyway I hope that you are well and have happiness and that your Ma and Pa are doing well. I am sorry to say finally that my father passed away recently. He was taken by consumption, so that was a further great sadness for me. It makes me feel more blessed than ever to have Janet.

My own troubles I hope are now behind me and I would love to hear your latest adventures if you can understand why it has been hard for me to write to you for so long.

I am lodging at the above address with a very caring woman who has an important position in one of the factories in town.

With my kindest thoughts
Elizabeth

Elizabeth did not have to wait long for her reply. Jane's letter arrived three days later. She opened it hurriedly, anxious to know her friend's thoughts.

My dear Elizabeth

What news! I am so glad to hear after all that has befallen you that you are now settled and happy after what must have been such a very difficult time. I am very sorry to hear that your father has passed but so pleased to hear of your blessing with your new baby Janet. I am sure James' parents will take good care of Robert and Ada and I understand what a hard decision that must have been for you to make. You have acted in their best interests though to leave them in what you know for sure are safe and good circumstances.

I am very sad to hear about what has become of James. At the wedding, I noticed that he had a fondness for the drink but I hoped that could be put down to the celebrations of the day. It is a shame that the relationship has been so challenging but your safety and your baby girl's must be the most important thing. Maybe James will come to his senses over time.

Families are so difficult! I have my own troubles here but I do not yet know how they will resolve. I have met a man I love very much. He is tall and handsome but it is complicated on the family side. Indeed, it is complicated on both family sides to be honest so I do not know what will become of us. It is certainly not easy. I will write to you when matters are clearer to tell you how it unfolds.

In the meantime, how good that you continue to work with Mrs McCourt and what a good idea to show her your real dressmaking talent! You are a very talented seamstress Elizabeth and I am certain that you deserve more reward for all your hard work. I have included something in this envelope, which I hope will help to shorten the time you have to save to buy the material you need. It comes from my savings. When you have earned enough to return it to me, I shall be pleased to see it again. But not before!

Good luck and my best wishes
Your always friend

Jane

Elizabeth went back to the envelope that was lying where she had left it on her kitchen table as she read. She picked it up and held it open. A crisp, newly-minted ten shilling note lay inside.

Seventeen

For the next five years, Elizabeth and Janet lived at Mary McKinnon's house in Broughty Ferry. They lived a simple life but they had a loving home. Elizabeth's work with Jean McCourt had expanded and she now produced dresses for occasional sale in her shop in addition to her regular apron work.

That new arrangement began when Mrs McCourt had agreed to obtain four yards of black velvet for Elizabeth for ten shillings. The dress that Elizabeth produced from it, a simple high-necked full-length gown with leg of mutton sleeves, had been on display in the window of the Law Hill shop for less than one day. Four women visited the shop during the morning to try it on, the last of whom it fitted perfectly. She was happy to pay the one pound and 16 shillings price that Mrs McCourt thought the dress merited. She subtracted a commission of eight shillings for selling the piece and returned to Elizabeth the princely sum of one pound and eight shillings for her creation and her skilled labour.

It meant Elizabeth was immediately able to return the money she had been sent by Jane, which she increased to 12 shillings to thank her for her kindness, so her friend could share in her success. That left with her 16 shillings. Ten shillings was set aside to buy more material and the six shillings she then had left went into the second pot on her mantlepiece. It was the first time in her life that Elizabeth had earned any money that had not come from wages. She was delighted to have found a way she could supplement her modest income and afford Janet and herself a slightly less frugal life. Regularly from then on, in addition to her weekly wage, she put what she always called 'Jane's ten shillings' to work again with a purchase of new material and put a dress up for sale in Mrs McCourt's window. Her work brought more customers to the shop and allowed Elizabeth to start to save a little money each week, instead of living entirely hand to mouth as she had previously.

Elizabeth had not once seen James during these five years, though she had heard reports from mutual acquaintances that he had found regular work as a seafarer on merchant vessels. He was employed as a ship's carpenter on long haul voyages. These apparently took him away from Dundee for many months at a time.

Then on the 24th of May in the year 1891, Janet's fifth birthday, James suddenly reappeared in Elizabeth's life.

He arrived unannounced at her house with flowers and a gift in his hand and asked Mrs McKinnon politely if he could be admitted to see Elizabeth and his daughter. The child was delighted to receive a visitor who made such a fuss of her on her special day, and especially a kind man who gave her a rag doll. Elizabeth, too, was pleased to see him.

She had not been alone in male company for a long time, and all her happy memories of him flooded into her head as he sat drinking her tea.

"It has been a long time, Elizabeth," he said. "I am ashamed of what I did, and I thought it best to leave you in peace for you to bring up Janet in your own good time. I went to see McLennan in Crichton Street, and he gave me this address which thankfully is still your home so I was able to find you."

"I am changed man now, Elizabeth. I have found regular work on the ships and I have voyaged far afield, to America and to Australia. I have had plenty of time to consider the error of my ways, the mistakes I made, and I have come to ask if you will take me back. If you will give me another chance. We are still man and wife after all. Will you forgive me?"

It was all too sudden and too much for Elizabeth to take in after so long apart. But she did feel torn. She had wanted to be a married woman with a family, not a woman living alone with an infant. She still wore her wedding ring and she had never had thoughts of another man. In his long absence, James had always remained her husband.

"I wondered," said James, "if I were to take lodgings near here in Broughty Ferry, could I come to visit you and Janet when I am ashore? What do you say?"

Elizabeth could find no good reason to refuse his request. She was flattered by his attention and the thought of Janet being able to know her father was a heart-warming one to her. He would be away much of the time, he seemingly now had a good income from his work, and perhaps things could be different between them, she thought.

"I am sure if you wish to do that, then it would be a nice thing," she found herself saying. James duly found a room nearby and came to visit them every day for the next week.

Each day he brought Elizabeth flowers, and sweets and trinkets for Janet. Elizabeth felt like she was being courted all over again. James was charming and humorous. He had lost none of his good looks, and his old attractive blend of modest confidence had returned. The sullen, crestfallen and abrasive man she had known while they were living at Princes Street appeared to have gone.

On the seventh evening, James told Elizabeth that he would be sailing the next morning. He was bound for New York on this occasion and would be gone for three months. "I shall miss you, Elizabeth," he said looking into her eyes. James had not yet touched his wife in the week of their reacquaintance, but he took her hand and kissed it now. "I shall miss you too," said Elizabeth as she gave herself to him in an embrace.

James stayed with her that night, and they made love together, reawakening their dormant marriage. He awoke early the next morning, before six o'clock, to head to the docks ready for his nine o'clock sailing, leaving Elizabeth with a fond kiss of farewell and a promise to see her again in three months' time. He left the house noiselessly so as not to wake their sleeping child.

Elizabeth was enthralled. She had not understood how much she had missed him nor realised how she warmed to the loving attention of a man. Her heart lifted at the thought that their marriage might be restored. When Janet awoke, she was delighted to find her mother in such joyous mood as they played together with the new rag doll that the kind man had given her.

Before James Simpson again set foot in Dundee on his return three months later from New York, his marriage had taken a further important step towards reconciliation. Elizabeth had discovered she was once again with child.

Her new pregnancy advanced what had been set in motion before James departed. The case for their getting back together, which had been only touched upon in principle, now seemed to have been made in practice. Time that might have been set aside to prove their re-acquaintance with one another seemed to have been overtaken by events. As well as a young child, they would soon have a baby.

James, on hearing the news, suggested he move back in with Elizabeth immediately, but something made her push back on that instant restoration of the marital home, at least for the time being. She made him continue to keep his own lodgings nearby but allowed him to be a daily, and sometimes nightly, visitor to their house. James was not best pleased by their continuing separation but he accepted his gradual process of redemption. Two weeks later, he departed on another voyage, again to America but this time to Virginia. On this longer trip, he would be away for nearly four months. Their relationship was being steadily advanced by short bursts of time together followed by longer periods spent apart. Recurring absence was making their hearts grow fonder.

Shortly before her period of confinement was to reach its natural term, Elizabeth finally relented and allowed James to move back in with her. Her landlady had no objection to a husband and wife being brought back together under her roof. Indeed, the kindly Mrs McKinnon, who had proved medically unable to have children of her own, was pleased at the prospect of a young family enlivening her house. Both Elizabeth and James were delighted when she gave birth to a baby boy whom they named Donald. Having had to give up their two eldest children in such sad circumstances, they had now produced a second perfect family; a father, a mother, a daughter, a son.

After the birth, James told Elizabeth he did not plan to take the next two voyages he was due to embark upon, but instead would stay with her in Broughty Ferry to help her take care of both children for the next few months. Not until things were settled, and she was able to work again, would he sign up for his next voyage.

His attentiveness to domestic matters was however short-lived. It lasted for only around one week before he started to leave the house for long periods during the day. At first, Elizabeth thought little of it. Donald was a docile and contented baby, fond of feeding and sleeping and scarcely a concern to her. Janet was now attending the local elementary school in the daytime, so Elizabeth really did not need James's assistance and, for a time, she was pleased that he had the resourcefulness to entertain himself outside the home.

He told her that he was away keeping in contact with some of the ship's masters with whom he regularly sailed while they were ashore. He did not want them to forget him when they were next hiring their crew. He explained this involved him drinking with them in the wharfside inns 'to keep his face familiar', so Elizabeth should not be concerned if she sometimes smelled a little whisky on his breath. It was all in the interest of ensuring his reliable future employment.

He started to return home frequently in the early evening, or sometimes later, the worse for drink. At first, Elizabeth accepted his explanations and did not protest or express any concern. One night, however, two months after Donald's birth, there was serious escalation as James returned, wild-eyed with drink, and forced himself on Elizabeth. He took his pleasure of her in a brutal and vengeful way. Deaf to her cries of protest, he overpowered her struggles without the least sign of care. As he rolled off her afterwards, and instantly fell into a drunken stupor, Elizabeth lay shocked alongside him, trembling at the experience, and now deeply apprehensive.

James did not refer the next morning or again to that drunken coupling. But it was to prove an incident of profound moment in their lives. Little more than four months after giving birth to Donald, Elizabeth now found herself pregnant yet again. What should have been a matter of joy, however, now filled her only with trepidation. Her second brief honeymoon with James had ended that night he had forced himself upon her. She now felt no pleasure, and indeed only apprehension, at the prospect of breaking the news to him that she was once again with child.

Elizabeth kept the news back from James for several weeks, putting it off as long as she could until the last night before his next sailing arrived. Even then she toyed with allowing him to go on his voyage without telling him. But this voyage was a longer one to Perth in western Australia, and that meant it would be five months or more before he would learn the truth if she did not break the news that evening. She decided eventually that not to tell him would be both cowardly and wrong.

"James, I have something to tell you," she said, as they sat around the kitchen table eating their final meal before his departure. "I am having another baby."

James's expression darkened and his face filled with thunder. "What! Who's is it, you slut?" he roared as he stood up, his chair tumbling backward behind him.

"What do you mean, who's is it, James? It is yours, of course," she answered, standing up and backing away from the table.

"You bare-faced liar," shouted James. "It is just another one of your filthy traps. You are trying to snare me, to keep me here against my will, bringing more and more mouths for me to feed until we are once again plunging into poverty. It is not my child. It cannot be, and I will have no part of it!"

With that, he caught hold of Elizabeth's head with both his hands and struck it forcibly three times against the wall. At the violence and the upheaval, both Janet and the baby broke out into desperate crying, and the pandemonium brought Mary McKinnon scurrying upstairs calling out, "Elizabeth, is everything alright?" Elizabeth, dazed by the blows she had received, was barely able to respond, but the arrival of the landlady at the door shook James out of his violent delirium. He grabbed hold of his knapsack, which was already packed for his departure the following day. Putting his flat cap hastily onto his head, he brushed past the anxious Mrs McKinnon on the stair, flattening her against the wall, as he passed her and made his way out into the night.

Elizabeth never saw James Simpson again. He died 12 years later, washed overboard from a British-built steel barque off the port of Fremantle in western Australia. The captain's log of the date reported that the ship's carpenter had been lost at sea, while believed to be under the influence of an excess of alcohol.

James Simpson's last known address was in Reid Street, Govan, in Glasgow. He died intestate, leaving probate valued at £51. That money was collected from the presiding Glasgow court by his daughter, Ada Simpson of Causewayend, Coupar Angus, near Dundee. She presented herself as her father's next of kin and declared that, since nothing had been heard of her mother for more than 17 years, she was presumed to be dead.

That £51 was the equivalent of approximately two years' worth of a woman's wage in a Dundee jute mill.

Eighteen

Elizabeth's fortunes meanwhile had come full circle. Prior to James's return she had managed to establish a way of life that kept her and Janet in reasonable circumstances. She had then had their son Donald and, for a brief moment, she had glimpsed the prospect of a family home with two incomes with two children to raise. Then James had disappeared from her life and she had given birth to another boy, whom she had christened David, in the November of 1893, the year of her husband's disappearance.

She was once again on her own, but now she had three children to support: one infant and two babies.

She remained in Mrs McKinnon's Broughty Ferry house and continued to sew for Mrs McCourt. She also carried on producing dresses, which gave her added income, but she was dependent on selling each one she produced so she could release 'Jane's money' to buy new material for the next one. If a dress failed to sell quickly, she had little choice but to wait until it did. Sometimes, if a piece did not attract a purchaser, she would have to reduce the price until it did. That ate deeply into the profit she made over and above the cost of the material. It made the dressmaking a welcome but unpredictable source of additional money. As time went on she began to wonder whether, with four mouths to feed and clothes to provide, she would need to find more lucrative work. Her new family was a happy one with young Janet a boon to her mother in helping with the feeding, cleaning and entertaining of her two younger brothers. But they had little or no money beyond meeting their most basic needs. Elizabeth realised also that, as the children grew, their demands would only increase and the cost of meeting them could only rise.

After two years of struggling on, Elizabeth resolved to make a change. Janet was now nearly eight, Donald was three years old and David just two. She had few people to whom she could turn for advice. Jean McCourt was a good friend to Elizabeth but she was also her employer. She had already allowed Elizabeth to sell her own dresses in her shop. She had provided regular work and reliable pay for several years. She had given her the flexibility to work at home rather that come into her shop while she had small children to raise. Elizabeth could hardly ask her for any more. She decided instead to speak to Mary McKinnon.

"Mary, you know I am hard pressed to make ends meet on the wages that Mrs McCourt can pay, even with the little extra that comes in from time to time on the dresses I make. The children's needs are growing as they get older, and I am wondering if I need to consider other work. Do you think I could find employment in the jute mills and would you advise me to try?"

Mary McKinnon replied, "I am sure if you want it, you would be an attractive employee for the jute, Elizabeth. You are a skilled and experienced seamstress, you understand all types of materials. You are a mother needing regular employment. I think you could find a job in one of the better factories as a weaver. That money is better there than on the spindles in the mills, the area I work. You'd be looking after four power looms. But it is not easy work, Elizabeth, know that. It is not for everyone. I wouldn't say it is a pleasant place to toil, and it is 60 hours a week, but the wages are more than you are making now. You'd be making 13 shillings and seven pence a week. Do you want me to put in a good word for you at Bowbridge?"

That was more than half as much again as Elizabeth now earned. She ran through the implications of taking such a job. She could perhaps continue to make occasional dresses as now for Jean McCourt. Janet was almost of an age where she could leave her in charge of the little ones. She was a sensible girl and Elizabeth already called her a little mother. They would have to move closer into town though. She couldn't possibly leave the children in Broughty Ferry and work nearly four miles away, where she would be unable to get to them in under an hour and a half's walk. As she put answers to those difficult questions, in her mind the big difference the extra money would make to their lives loomed large.

"Thank you so much for the offer, Mary," she said. "I would be grateful if you would ask if they need someone."

As the most senior female worker in the Bowbridge works, the Shifting Mistress Mary McKinnon was totally trusted by the company's owners and their managers alike. After 20 years of overseeing the production of the jute yarn, which then made its way out of the mill into the factory shed and onto the huge power looms for weaving, she was regarded as a most highly reliable employee. Her advice was respected on all matters relating to the workers and production.

When she recommended a potential new employee for hire, her word counted. Elizabeth was recruited after a short interview of confirmation with the manager of the weaving shed, a man by the name of Angus Chalmers.

Elizabeth moved with her three children from Boughty Ferry into two rooms in Milne's East Wynd, a small side street between Lochee Road and Blackness Road right in the centre of the industrial town. The lodgings were surrounded by jute works, with all the dirt and overshadow that brought with it, but somehow Elizabeth no longer found the press of humanity in the area so overpowering or intimidating. She now felt part of the hustle and bustle of industrial activity and felt strangely comforted to be back in the centre of things.

The location of their humble lodgings meant Elizabeth could be at the factory gates within five minutes of leaving home and, more importantly, she was back at home only moments after the whistle blew for the end of the day's work. Several families lived in the building, and Elizabeth struck up a good relationship with her closest co-habitants, the Deans, who lived on the floor above them. Margaret Dean worked in the Camperdown mill, and her husband George was a maintenance engineer at the Verdant works. Margaret's mother Dorothy lived with them and she stayed in the property each day while they were at work. Dorothy was happy to keep an eye on young Janet and the children, and would not accept a penny for her trouble. She was pleased just to help.

"We all look after each other here, Elizabeth," she said.

For the next six years, this was how they lived. Elizabeth was now earning a reasonable wage, though, as the sole breadwinner of the household, she was still far from wealthy. Her children were all now of school age. All three were enrolled in the Balfour Street school, just half a mile away from their lodgings. Janet, at 13, was entering her last year of education and preparing for a life of work. Donald and David were in the same group at school. The elder boy was proving a slow learner, while the younger one was a sharp student with proficiency beyond his age in both reading and arithmetic.

Donald and David were good boys but they were very different in almost every way from each other. Donald was a gentle and well-meaning boy. Good with his hands, he was a keen carver and worker with wood, having inherited his father's talent for carpentry and practical things. David was a keen reader of whatever he could lay his hands upon. He was hungry to learn and quick of wit. Donald, altogether slower and a kindly soul, found himself easy prey for some of the bullies at school. On several occasions, it took his younger brother who, though he was much smaller than his elder sibling, was nimbler and readier to use his fists, to rescue Donald from uncomfortable scrapes.

Donald found the schoolwork taxing and dispiriting and he had made few friends in the class. It made him a reluctant scholar.

Nineteen

On November 27 in the year 1901, four men hitherto unknown to Elizabeth and her family made an abrupt entrance into their lives. Their names were Septimus Quine, Fraser Douglas, John Campbell Smith and W.W. Dickson. These four individuals were only loosely connected with one another, but for Elizabeth they combined on this day to devastating effect.

Septimus Quine was a reformed criminal regularly to be seen in the backstreets and alleyways of Dundee. He was a man of saturnine appearance, his hair long, unwashed and bedraggled. His murine-featured face was unshaven, and his naturally crooked smile was further disfigured by the absence of several teeth. His most notably troubling feature, though, was to be found at the end of his right arm. He had lost his hand in a vicious knife fight before he gave up his criminal ways, and had chosen to replace his severed extremity with an iron hook. Screwed into a cup-like vessel, this fearsome appendage fitted snugly over the stump of his right arm and was held firmly into place by a leather strap attached to either side of the metal cup that he pulled tight over his shoulder and fixed around his neck. Quine had learned to deploy his hook highly effectively for catching hold of things and tearing them apart.

Sergeant Fraser Douglas of the Dundee constabulary was a career policeman who had had regular dealings with Quine when he was a young constable, having had cause to arrest him on several occasions. Now Quine was set upon an honest path in life, it was Sergeant Douglas of the hard-pressed Dundee police force who had retained his services as an informant. Douglas paid Quine to keep his ear to the ground to help reduce the levels of crime and misdemeanour on the town's streets. Douglas rewarded Quine each time he helped police to identify and apprehend a wrong doer of any sort and bring them before justice.

Substitute Sheriff John Campbell Smith was a grandee of Dundee society who meted out justice from his lofty post. A self-made man born into poverty, he had become an apprentice mason at 12 years of age and saved enough money from that employment to put himself through St Andrews University. From there, he went into the Law, first as a criminal barrister and now, at the end of his career, he was revered as one of the most important magistrates in the town. He administered the law with the vigour and certainty of someone who considered himself a shining exemplar to the poor. His own life provided proof positive that good attitude and a commitment to education were all any man, woman or child needed to get on in the world and contribute properly to society. His stated aim when culprits were brought before him was to seek 'reform rather than revenge'. Now 73 years old, with a most impressive pair of bushy white side whiskers, Sub Sheriff Campbell Smith was a prominent and respected Dundee figure.

The fourth man of the quartet, Director W.W. Dickson, was the head of an important educational establishment in the town.

It was Janet's job each morning to get herself and her two brothers up, washed and dressed in good time for school. This allowed Elizabeth to prepare a breakfast of bread, cheese and a glass of milk for the three of them before she set out herself for her morning shift at the Bowbridge works. On this morning, the children were a little late.

Elizabeth called to them to be sure to hurry on as she left the house to set off for her work. Janet and David had eaten their breakfast and were now ready to depart, but Donald was dawdling. This was often the case these days, as his sister had already had cause to note.

"Donald, David and I are leaving now," she called through to him impatiently. "Hurry up and be sure to pull the door shut when you leave." With that, David and his little mother set out for school.

Donald had decided he was not going to go to school that day. Instead, he would have a day of adventure exploring in the town. Two boys in his class had threatened to rough him up after an argument over a ball game the previous day, and his teacher had scolded him yesterday afternoon for poor work in his arithmetic. This would be a good day for him to be elsewhere, he had decided.

Donald left the house at ten minutes after six, already too late to make the school bell, and walked out through the busy Dundee streets. He didn't have a plan for the day, he thought he would just take a walk and see what he found. For three hours, he walked up and down streets watching the world go by and daydreaming as first the early morning shift workers headed out for work around him, to be replaced as the hour got later by those who had no work to go to or otherwise had cause to be moving on foot around the town.

At just after ten o'clock, Donald turned into a square next to the Dudhope Castle called Scrimgeour Place. To his great misfortune, leaning against a wall in that square with his arms pressed behind his back was Septimus Quine. As Donald sauntered past him, barely registering the man, Quine flashed out his arm and expertly hooked Donald's shirt collar from behind. As he drew him back, he reeled in Donald like a small fish caught on a line.

"Now, where might you be going at this time of day young, sir?" Quine asked the boy. Donald stammered in reply "I… I… I'm on my way to school, sir."

"Well, we'll see about that, because you've well missed your time today," his captor replied. "I think a visit to the police station is where you will be going instead."

Quine hauled the struggling Donald, whose scanty weight was no match for a powerfully built adult, into the police station and placed him down in front of Sergeant Fraser Douglas.

"Found wandering in Scrimgeour at five minutes after ten o'clock," he said briskly, as he handed the boy over to the custody of the officer. "Thank you Quine. I will be in touch later with your fee," said the Sergeant as he took possession of the hapless child.

After an hour detained in a cell, Donald was frogmarched into an oak panelled room in a grand building located several roads away. He was told to stand looking up at a whitehaired old man, with what seemed to him enormous furred whiskers, who was seated behind a highly polished dark wood table. The man, who was wearing a tightly sewn periwig on his head, fired a series of short questions that Donald strove to reply to as helpfully as he could so that he might be soon on his way.

He told Sub Sheriff Campbell Smith that he was nine years old, that he attended Balfour Street School, that he was born in Broughty Ferry, that he had lived in Dundee all his life, that he had never been apprehended before or convicted of anything and that he could read and write. He correctly gave the magistrate his exact address and his birthday. He told him, again correctly, that he was of Protestant religion. He gave him his mother's full name and said he knew she worked in a jute mill though he wasn't sure which one it was. He had one sister and one brother.

The magistrate looked down at the other details of the boy written on the police paper in front of him. He had been 'found wandering' when he was apprehended that morning. He was four feet tall and weighed four stones and eight pounds. He had grey eyes, fresh complexion, brown hair, and a short nose. He had no marks on his body, and his health was assessed as 'fair'.

"Where is your father, boy?" Campbell Smith then asked.

"He went away when I was just a baby," Donald replied, again truthfully. "Did he die boy?" the magistrate then asked him. Fatefully, Donald answered him that, no, his father did not die, he just went away. At this answer, Campbell Smith took up his gold-nibbed fountain pen and wrote in large script across the page: 'Father deserted the family eight years ago'. It was enough to decide him and to confirm Donald's fate.

Some appraisers of the facts of Donald Simpson's apprehending might have found causes for leniency in them. A young first offender who answered truthfully and politely, who had a fixed address and went to a local school, who could read and write, had a parent in regular work, and who had been caught playing truant from school one day, might have seemed to them a candidate for a telling off and a warning not to repeat their misdemeanour.

But Sub Sheriff John Campbell Smith took a different view. What he saw before him that day was a still innocent young child whose father was plainly a feckless individual who had abandoned his family. This child may not yet technically have committed any offence, but the child's instance of vagrancy on that day indicated of itself that he now very likely soon would. The Law had a responsibility to reform the children of the culpable poor before they followed the path of their forebears and drifted into delinquency and criminality; before they became a permanent burden upon society. For with such unreliable and untrustworthy parentage, this was the course they would inevitably take without public correction.

The next Donald knew, he was taken from the magistrate's office in a police carriage up through the town to the recently constructed Baldovan Industrial School in the Strathmartine Road three miles north where he was met by its director Mr W.W. Dickson, an immaculately dressed and stern looking man who admitted him.

"You'll be staying with us now, boy," he told the shaking Donald, as he took him over the threshold. "I am going to give you a number which is yours and you must remember at all times from now on. You are now number 172. What number are you?"

Dickson closed the door of the school behind them. Donald was not to know it, but the hirsute magistrate, acting, as was his societal calling, in the best interests of the impoverished innocent child and the wider community on whom he would likely soon prey, had committed him to be incarcerated there for seven years.

There were four legal criteria under which Mr Campbell Smith was able to consign a child to the Industrial School. Those were: if the child was found begging below the age of 14; if the child had committed an imprisonable offence below 12; if the child's parents had declared him or her beyond their control; or, simply as in this case, if they were 'found wandering'.

Convicted on the last count, and condemned in the eyes of the magistrate by his father's desertion of his family as a most likely future criminal, Donald was a clear-cut case for reformative training.

The training, which began that day, would over time equip Donald with such skills as tailoring, horse-hair teasing to produce stuffing for upholstery, firewood splitting, paper bag making for retailers and sack sewing. No idleness was permitted at Baldovan School, as the children needed to be taught to be industrious. Each working day was strictly regulated, from six in the morning until nine o'clock at night, when the inmates were put to their beds.

The gates of the Baldovan institution, which closed on Donald Simpson that day, were not to open for him again for seven years until he reached 16 years of age.

Twenty

When Elizabeth returned from her day's work, she was surprised to find only two of her children were there waiting for her.

"Where is Donald? Was he kept back at school?" she asked. It was Janet who replied with the anxious words, "We don't know where he is, Mother." David then interjected, "I didn't see him at school today, Mother. I thought maybe he felt sick and he stayed at home. I expected him to be here when we got back."

Elizabeth was both confused and perturbed by their replies and, turning to Janet, she inquired, "You did all go to school together this morning?" Janet looked down and confessed to her mother that today she hadn't done her job. She had called Donald to hurry him up, but she and David were worried about being late for school and they had set out without him. She thought he would be following them close behind. She admitted, with tears of shame rising in her eyes, that she did not know whether Donald had actually gone to school or not.

Elizabeth's thoughts were now racing and she felt a drying of her throat. Could he have had an accident trying to rush his way to school? Was he lying in the hospital injured or worse? Or could he have been snatched from the streets by someone of ill intent? She quickly decided to go the constabulary to report Donald missing and see whether they had news of him. He might even be sitting in a police cell in trouble for some minor misdemeanour, she thought hopefully.

Elizabeth ran the half mile to the station and was met on her arrival by a duty Sergeant sitting at the desk. "I am here to report my son missing, and to ask if you might have information about him," she said. The Sergeant asked her how old her son was and how long he had been missing. "Children often go astray and they usually turn up," he imparted. Elizabeth for her part explained that this had never happened before and expressed her acute concern. The Sergeant took down Donald's name and address and, on hearing it, he reached across to the day's ledger of incidents on the desk beside him.

Moving up the page with his finger slowly he reached the earlier entry and matched the name.

"We did have him here earlier, madam. He was brought in having been found wandering."

"Oh thank God!" exclaimed Elizabeth. "Where is he now?"

The Sergeant consulted the book and advised her that her son had been taken before the Sheriff who had been hearing cases that day. Consulting the ledger, he confirmed that the Sheriff had ordered that Donald be admitted to the Baldovan Industrial School.

Elizabeth had no knowledge of these procedures or of the Baldovan institution. "Can I go and collect him from there now then?" she asked.

The officer peered down at her and said, "I am afraid not, madam. The magistrate has ordered that your son be kept in the Industrial School for the foreseeable future. There he will be educated and trained in industrial skills at society's expense. He should consider himself very lucky to have been given such opportunity, and so might I say should you."

Elizabeth was simply dismayed by what she was hearing. "How long is the foreseeable future?" she asked.

"The judge's order is that it shall be seven years, madam. He ruled that it was in the child's best interest that he be kept in there until his 16th birthday."

Elizabeth felt physically sick. "No! That's just not possible!" she cried. "Can I do something to change any of this?"

"Not once an order of court is made, madam," the officer answered. "The law has already decided his case. If you hadn't wanted this to happen, you should have looked after him better. The law assumes there is no guilt in innocent children, but it will apportion blame to culpable parents who allow their children to run wild on the streets, causing trouble and problems in the town. Do you have any other children?"

Noting Elizabeth's silent nod of confirmation, the policeman continued. "You should take heed of this then and make sure to take better care of those you still have with you or you'll find yourself back here having the same conversation about them, too, I warn you. Now, if there's nothing else, I do have other work to attend to."

Elizabeth walked out of the station barely able to put one foot in front of the other. Agonised and humiliated, she walked home in a daze, her temples pumping and her chest heaving. She had to stop frequently to gather her breath.

She collapsed instantly onto the bed when she got in. She was able to say only one sentence to Janet and David, who were waiting anxiously for news.

"He's been sent to the Industrial School for the foreseeable future, and they say there's nothing we can do about it."

All four members of the Simpson family cried themselves to sleep that night. Mother and two children sobbed at their loss in their rooms in Milne's East Wynd. At the same time, Donald was also weeping, trembling in his iron bed as the nine o'clock lights were put out in his dormitory, plunging the whole room into complete darkness.

Elizabeth wrote Donald a tear-stained letter of love, comfort and reassurance the next morning and posted it to him. She received no reply to it so she wrote him another one week later. In the Baldovan School office, her letters were opened and read, and then carefully put back in their envelopes and placed in a cabinet into a file marked 172.

It was the policy of the school that no inmate was either to receive a letter or send one. Correspondence to and from the outside world was deemed only to distract, to weaken the spirit, to undermine focus and to slacken discipline.

The word 'family' was never used in the Baldovan School. It was simply excised from the language. The school dutifully retained any letters that it received for its inmates from outside and it kept them in files, to be handed to their addressees when they eventually left the school. Most children received very few letters. Some had no family left to write to them. Many had family who were not literate. A few had family who sent a few letters but then gradually stopped over time when they received no responses.

But the mother of inmate 172 never stopped. She sent Donald a loving letter of encouragement—with titbits of news of his siblings, often illustrated down the sides of the page by little drawings of people, animals, flowers and trees— every week during the entire time he was confined in the Baldovan School.

When they finally let him out, Donald Simpson was handed a large parcel neatly tied up with string to take with him. It contained more than 350 letters from his mother. Each one had been carefully slit open and read by the administrators in the office.

Not one had ever been delivered to the child.

Twenty-One

Elizabeth counted down every slow day of the next seven years, as she waited for Donald to be released. She tried to suppress the thought that, as each day went by, she was losing another unseen moment of his childhood until it was all gone. But for all her efforts to banish it, that haunting realisation chilled her repeatedly.

When she reached 14, Janet started work in the jute spinning mill at Bowbridge. She was positioned a long way from her mother in the weaving shed, but she had the familiar friendly face of Mary McKinnon to help her get used to her new surroundings. When David came of the age, he told his mother he wanted to work there, too. He moved to one of the town's Half and Half schools, which allowed pupils to work in the town's factories for half the day and then receive their education in school during the other half.

David began work as a shifter in Mary's crew and worked from six until one. He then spent the afternoon of his extended day doing his school work. He was a diligent and keen learner. He was determined to pack as much into half a day as others would manage in a whole day. He committed himself to extra learning in the evenings to make sure he could keep up. Most proudly, though, he earned three shillings and sixpence a week from the mill. He put half a crown each week into his mother's pot on the mantelpiece, and she allowed him to keep a shilling for himself.

It never once occurred to David to complain about the heavy demands that his new life placed upon him: working from early each morning in the mill, having to make his way quickly to school ready to pursue his lessons through every long afternoon, before retiring home to eat, study, sleep and start again. It did not occur to him to complain because he felt as if the whole of his young life had been preparing him for this moment.

He had never known his father, who had abandoned the family before he was born. All he had ever known was his mother as the only breadwinner in the household, straining to put food on their table and keep clothes on their backs. He had seen his elder brother locked away for reasons he still did not understand. Every time he thought about Donald's absence, he felt a shudder of guilt at what he might have done to prevent it. He had seen his sister join his mother at the jute works, and he could not wait to go with them there and take his part in earning the family living. That he got to keep a shilling of his pay for himself, he found exhilarating.

With that fortune, he could buy a couple of small bags of sweets each week, even some chocolate. Most of all, though, he could save, to add to his treasured collection of marbles. He aspired one day to own the rarest and most prized of those small glass balls: the alley, a white marble made from alabaster and flecked through with a gorgeous whirl of red or blue. He had only ever seen two. If, one day, he could own one of those, he would be the envy of all the children with whom he played regular street games of skill and speed, each pitting their own precious glass spheres against those of their rivals.

So, no, David did not complain. He did not protest at the jute mill's deafening noise or its constant sickening stench of oil in the air. He did not flinch at the stour, the fabric dust that hung in the atmosphere and wormed its way into his eyes, his nose and his mouth every hour he was in there. He never needed telling twice when he was told to crawl under the spinning machines to clear out all the dust beneath them. Nor did he baulk at having to step into the machines to lift off the full spindles, so laden he could barely carry them, and replace them with empty ones so the machine's relentless pounding never had to pause.

Not even when he was ribbed mercilessly by the sharp tongued, hard-bitten mill girls, when they discovered his mother was a weaver, did David raise objection. They called him *Little Lord Fauntleroy* after Frances Hodgson Burnett's entitled young aristocrat because weavers, of course, were the nobility of the jute works, paid so much more and esteemed far higher than the ordinary girls in the spinning mill. Weavers and spinners walked to and from their work on different sides of the street. The weavers, you could distinguish at a glance, always well wrapped up against the elements. Some of the spinners went without shoes. Haves did not mingle with Have Nots.

Some of the girls therefore lost no opportunity to take out their resentment on a weaver's son. They put on la-di-dah voices and told him how honoured they were that someone so hoity-toity would deign to come work with them. They would pinch him and twist his hair when there was no supervisor looking and they saw their chance to do it without reprimand. David took all their teasing without demur, responding only with a quiet smile as if he was sharing in their jokes. In time, the girls recognised the young boy's spirit and they desisted from their torment of him.

David did not complain about any of this because he accepted all these things as features of the adult world he was impatient to join. Working and earning had elevated him in his own eyes and given him the longed-for self-respect of adulthood. David felt he was now a man. At this moment of graduation, he was a little over ten years old. Now the whole family—Elizabeth, Janet and David, everyone save, of course, the still locked away Donald—was making their living from Dundee jute.

One year before Donald was due to come home, Janet fell head over heels in love. The man's name was Archie Rogers and he was ten years older than Janet. He lived and worked in Liverpool where he was a process engraver, a skilled tradesman in the photographic printing trade. He had worked first as an apprentice in the industry and was now a talented and well-paid young professional. He owned his own house in the Toxteth district of the city.

Janet and Archie met at a dance in Lochee while he was working at John Leng's *Dundee Advertiser* on an assignment for one month, helping them to establish new photographic reproduction facilities for the newspaper. Archie was entranced both by Janet's beauty and by her strength and independence of spirit. He proposed to her two days before he was due to return to Liverpool and they married a month later. Janet, who had known nothing but the boundless struggle of Dundee and her mother's fight for survival in the town, could not wait to leave and experience a new place, find a different life.

Elizabeth was delighted for her daughter. She found Archie a lovely man, kind, attentive, polite, witty and always well turned out. He was a professional tradesman with a good and reliable income and valuable skills, and he owned his own property. How could she possibly begrudge her daughter something she had always dreamed of for herself? It was also not lost on Elizabeth either that here was Janet leaving Scotland for Liverpool and the banks of the River Mersey at 18 years of age, just as her great friend Jane had done all those years ago. She was following in exactly her footsteps.

So as Janet headed south to begin her life as a newly married young woman in Liverpool, Elizabeth found herself with her youngest child David now coming up to 15, on the brink of setting out on his own adult life. David was deeply envious of his sister beginning a whole new life in an exciting new place. He, too, longed to escape from Dundee and to see the world. From a young boy, he had always been fascinated by the glamour and bravery of soldiers. He always watched enraptured when a military parade took place in the town. He told his mother that, as soon as he was of age, he planned to enlist into the army and to travel abroad, perhaps to India.

Elizabeth recognised that the footprint of her family in her adopted town of Dundee was shrinking rapidly. Her daughter had departed, her youngest son was readying himself to leave at his first opportunity, and her elder son was only still there because he was serving out the final months of his prolonged forced detention. It seemed to Elizabeth that the time was coming for her, too, to start thinking about leaving a town which had brought her so many tribulations. Perhaps it was coming time for her too to try something new.

Elizabeth stood outside the gates of the Baldovan Industrial School at six o'clock on the morning on the 13th of April 1908, Donald's 16th birthday. She waited for three hours until a young man carrying a parcel hove into view, as the great heavy door of the building opened and closed again almost instantly behind him, leaving him standing alone and motionless on its threshold. After a moment or two of hesitation, he began to walk slowly towards the outer gates of the school and out into the road. Elizabeth could barely recognise him. There was little or nothing of the four stone eight pounds child who had been hooked off the streets seven years before. He was a young man now. She hardly knew him and she knew nothing of what he had become.

Elizabeth ran across the road and flung her arms around him, showering him with kisses and hugging him tightly. Donald stood there holding onto his parcel, unmoving and unsure of what to do. He did not recognise her with complete certainty, but he accepted that this woman who seemed to have come to meet him must be his mother, and her embrace awakened some of the half-held memories he still had of her. Her scent now, as she held him, he thought faintly reminiscent. He seemed to have breathed it before. But it was a long time ago, almost half his young life. He had not been hugged or kissed by anyone in his time at Baldovan, and no-one had told him what the right thing to do was when you were embraced. He stood embarrassedly rigid until she had finished and composed herself. The two of them then set off walking slowly, side by side, down the hill to the town.

Elizabeth had put aside money especially for this occasion so they could have a breakfast together. They sat down in a cafe, which Donald looked around at in wonderment, taking in all he could of this totally unfamiliar setting. They ordered tea and hot buttered toast, and a pastry with jam. As he tentatively picked at the freshly made food, Donald made it clear to Elizabeth he did not want to talk about his time in the school.

"I am glad it is over, Mother, and I don't want to think of it any more. I have been looking forward to this day for a very long time, and now I can do what I want to do for the first time in my life. I am no longer an inmate. I am my own man. I am no longer '172', I am Donald again at last. I decided long ago what I am going to do now. I have had plenty time to think about it."

"How wonderful and quite right, too, Donald my love," said Elizabeth. "What is it that you would like to do?"

"I am going to enlist in the Army, Mother," said Donald. "I am going to join The Black Watch."

Book Three
Jane Liverpool 1885–1913

One

On the Scotland Road, which leads out of the centre of the Liverpool city towards Everton and the routes to the north, stood an unremarkable public house called The Dublin Castle. A single room establishment, it drew its customers from among the predominantly Irish residents of the area. It could not offer an extensive drinking area, but the room boasted a large and handsome plate glass mirror some six feet square, which was set upon the wall behind the bar. Its reflective effect made the Dublin Castle appear twice its actual size.

Since the huge influx of the famine refugees from across the Irish Sea almost 40 years earlier, most of the Irish incomers who had remained in Liverpool had gathered in the Scotland Road area. They packed into whatever accommodation they could find, in far greater numbers than the properties that housed them were ever intended to hold. In their many thousands, they squeezed into run down and often condemned buildings that had previously been earmarked for demolition. Overcrowding reached such a level that it was not uncommon for 50 or 60 people to be found in one house of three or four rooms, or for as many as 40 souls to be living cramped into a single cellar. They clustered, for want of anywhere better, into housing stock where the sanitation was inadequate or non-existent, reviving buildings that had been declared unfit for human habitation. Their teeming quarters in consequence became breeding grounds for disease and infection.

So concentrated did this huddling together of the Irish immigrants become in the area, that the scale of their presence began to serve as a powerful magnet for all new arrivals from Ireland who were looking for somewhere to settle in the city. Homeless, penniless, first footers could at least always count on finding a welcome from their own people somewhere on the Scotland Road. So most were drawn there as their first recourse. In time, this gave rise to a second effect, which was to make the former residents of the area who had no Irish affiliations feel it was no longer their home. In their hundreds, they began to move out of the road that the locals called 'Scottie'. Many relocated as whole families, together with their friends and neighbours, to the Netherfield Road district a couple of miles away.

So Scotland Road came to be seen as the place where the Irish were. Because the Irish immigrants were virtually all paupers fleeing from starvation at home, they brought their deprivation and destitution with them. They had nothing else to bring. Scotland Road became the part of Liverpool, as a result, which was the most poverty stricken and the most disease ridden. It was the place where Irish lived. Because almost all the Irish immigrants were Catholic by faith, Scotland Road then came to be seen as the place where Catholics lived.

This is the way a city first begins to divide and, in time, falls in upon itself.

The landlord of The Dublin Castle was a Catholic Irishman named Michael Murphy. Born in county Clare, he had been brought over to Liverpool by his parents when he was just two years old. He had no memory at all of his birthplace but, raised by an extended Irish family in Scotland Road, he had been regaled all his life with so many stories of the old country that he considered himself a fully paid up Irishman. He also spoke with the lilting accent of his forbears rather than the unmistakable and peculiar twang of the 'Scouse', spoken by native Liverpudlians, from the locally-born Prime Minister William Gladstone down.

Michael, who was a tenant landlord, ran The Dublin Castle with his wife Alice, who had borne him six children—three boys and three girls—in their less than ten years of marriage. They lived, more comfortably than most, in three rooms above the bar.

Alice came from a large English Catholic family in Crosby, a coastal town beyond Bootle, seven miles to the north of Liverpool. The Garstons had lived always within a mile or so of each other in that part of south Lancashire across many generations dating back hundreds of years. Alice's father Peter Garston had established a family building contracting firm, which had proved very successful. Peter had helped Michael to enter the licensed victualler trade by putting a little money behind him and Alice when they started out. Michael had become a popular barkeeper among the locals. He, too, was now doing well.

It was a quiet Tuesday night in the middle of March in the bar. There were only half a dozen drinkers in that evening. All of them were men. They were sitting at three separate pairs at tables spread around the room. The takings tonight would be low but Michael was not unduly troubled. He was looking forward to a bumper weekend ahead. This year, St Patrick's Day, March the 17th, would fall on a Monday, so he knew that he could expect his bar to be very busy from Friday afternoon onward right throughout the weekend and on into the Irish patron saint's day itself. There would be processions and celebrations all weekend, and this should ensure The Dublin Castle's biggest money-spinning week of the year. Michael could hardly be surprised, then, nor too disappointed, that his turnout tonight was so low. His customers would be saving up their money to blow it all at the end of the week.

Walking up Scotland Road that evening, with no such thoughts of goodwill, were four men. The leader of the group was Tommy Gemmill. Glasgow-born Scot, shipbuilding worker at Cammell Lairds, five years' resident of Merseyside, full-time Protestant, full-time Orange Lodge official, part-time trouble-maker, no-time friend of Irish. With him was his co-worker at the Lairds' yard, another Scot named Jocky Johnstone. A fellow member of the Birkenhead Orange Lodge, Jocky was Tommy's regular drinking partner. With them in tow were two Liverpool ne'er-do-wells named Billy Shaw and Jack Green with whom they drank occasionally. These were two fellows with too much time on their hands, given to petty crime, most regularly street robbery with menaces, who looked for any excuse to show how tough they were and take the opportunity to wield their fists. Billy and Jack liked going out with Tommy and Jocky because the two abrasive Scots could usually be relied upon to pick some mad argument that would result in trouble which the Liverpool boys could get involved in and earn from. This night, the four of them had set out purposefully to find an Irish bar or two in the Scotland Road. They were out to do a little celebrating of their own before the uppity Irish started their annual St Patrick's Day antics this weekend.

They had walked quite a way up Scotland Road without finding quite the opportunity they sought when the Dublin Castle hove into view. The provocative name itself made up their minds to enter. The four walked straight up to where Michael stood waiting to serve. Alice sat a little way from him on a low stool polishing up small glasses, the top of her head barely visible to the customers above the line of the bar. The reflection of the four men in their flat caps, lined up and now leaning on the bar as they waited to be served, drew the immediate attention of the other drinkers. Tommy watched in the large mirror as two of them hurriedly drained their glasses. "Sorry if we've disturbed you!" he called sneeringly after them as their heels disappeared out of the door.

Tommy turned his attention to the barman. "Right get us a drink, Paddy. If you've anything worth drinking in this shithole, that is," he said.

"My name is Michael, Michael Murphy," said the landlord, "and I choose who I serve here. This is an Irish pub you've come into, as you will know, and I sense you gentlemen are no great friends of Irish people. If I'm right, I'd take it kindly if you'd leave my bar and go find a place more to your liking. We don't want any trouble in here."

"Paddy, Mick, Paddywhack, whatever your fecking name is," Tommy rejoined. Reaching over towards Michael as if to whisper something privately to him, he said "a word in your ear." Michael leaned in towards him a little. It was enough. Gemmill caught Michael's open shirt at the collar in his clenched fist and, in a single downward violent movement, brought the landlord's head down with force, hammering his chin onto the zinc of his bar.

"Michael!" cried Alice, leaping up from her stool at the sight of her husband's plight and evident pain. Gemmill ignored her and, shifting his hand round to the back of Michael's neck to keep him pinned face down on the bar, he said, "Listen to me, you Fenian bastard. This city has shown you and your filthy likes unlimited hospitality over decades. Far too much hospitality, as far as my friends and I are concerned. So when decent people come in here and ask you to show them some respectful courtesy in return, then that is exactly what we expect you to do. Do I make myself clear?"

Michael mumbled in the affirmative, and Gemmill allowed him up. "Right. Then now we start again."

At this, the other four drinkers in the bar fled the premises, judging it as perhaps their last opportunity. "Goodnight ladies!" Jocky shouted in his broad Glaswegian rasp as the four men scuttled out through the door.

"Now, we will take a bottle of Scotch whisky and four glasses. None of your Irish shite, mind you well," said Gemmill to Michael. Freed from the Scotsman's clutches, Michael moved to retrieve an unopened bottle of Johnnie Walker's Old Highland Whisky. Gemmill then turned to Alice and said:

"Now you, Mousey, you get a bucket of soap and hot water and go and scrub down that table and those four chairs in the corner. I want you down on your hands and knees, cleaning underneath it all as well as on top so we four gentlemen can sit down without fear of catching whatever disease has been left by the lowlife you've last had sitting there."

"And you, Paddy Mick, you close the curtains and lock the door, and put up the Closed sign in the window. We don't want any more of your Irish tat coming in here polluting the place while we take a quiet drink in private."

Alice and Michael complied with Gemmill's instructions, Alice giving the corner table and chairs a thorough, if unneeded, scrubbing, and then crawling underneath to clean the floor and lower reaches of the chairs and the table. "Doesn't that look a pretty picture now," said Jocky, with a leering grin as the four men watched her from behind. Michael closed the curtains and locked up the door as he had been instructed.

When Alice's work was judged complete, Gemmill and his three companions allowed her up and went over and sat down at the corner table. Michael placed the whisky bottle and the four glasses along with a full jug of water in front of them. Then he retreated and joined Alice behind the bar. Once there, and despite their racing pulses, they busied themselves as best they could, quietly cleaning and putting glasses and bottles back into their correct places.

It took the four men a long hour to finish the bottle between them. Having finally drained it, and seemingly satisfied with the impact they had made on the establishment, they readied themselves to leave.

"Come over here, Mick," said Gemmill, calling the landlord over. Michael came out from behind his bar and stood in front of their table.

"So there you are, you see," said Gemmill, his face barely two inches from Michael's, his hot whisky breath flooding over him. "It doesn't hurt you to provide a little human kindness and hospitality to honest decent folk, does it? Let that be a lesson for you. Now we have liked this cleaned up table, very much, my friends and I. So much so in fact we'd like you to reserve it permanently for us from now on. Put my name on it. Write Mr Gemmill. Specially Reserved. You know how to write, don't you? And you leave that notice on the table there until we come back. We wouldn't want to come in next time and find some Irish filth sitting at our table after your little woman has been down on her knees fumigating it especially for us, would we? So you be sure and do all that for us, will you, Paddy. Yes?"

The four men stood and put on their hats and coats as Michael retreated once again to his post behind the bar. Alice stood behind him to watch the men leave her premises. Gemmill's three companions went over to the door together, and Jocky turned the key to the right in the lock as they prepared to let themselves out. Michael and Alice watched as Gemmill, lingering at the table, then slowly gathered up his coat and hat and prepared to follow them.

"Oh, just one more thing," he said to the Murphys. "Get some proper Scotch malt whisky in next time, not this cheap blended shite," he said picking up the empty and unpaid-for bottle of Johnnie Walker.

He weighed the empty bottle in his open hand, looked down at it for a second, and then, in one movement, his fingers closed over its neck and he hurled it head-height at the bar. The bottle spun in the air, missing Michael's head by barely a foot, and then, with a thundering crash, it struck the huge bar mirror near its midpoint, shattering it into thousands of flying smithereens and many dropping dagger-like shards of glass that showered the entire bar. Miraculously, and solely because neither Michael nor Alice had time to turn to face it, the explosion of glass behind them avoided seriously injuring either of them.

"You won't forget that now will you, Mick, you Catholic bastard? Proper Scotch malt next time."

With that, Tommy Gemmill and his three friends departed The Dublin Castle, leaving Michael and Alice to pick up the pieces from their visit.

Two

The next day, Michael and Alice, still shaken by the previous night's trauma, took a train to Crosby and went to visit Alice's father Peter in his contractor's yard. Peter was in his 51st year and a successful man. He had started his working life as a labourer but, smart and ambitious, he was drawn to the opportunities opening up from the newly patented material called asphalt, whose hardiness was making it potentially the roadbuilding surface of the future. He trained and qualified in the very first wave of the new trade as a master asphalter and had built up a thriving business in this age of necessary road improvement. The country's roads had seen many years of neglect, as almost all the country's transport investment had been poured into the railways. The rutted cobbled surfaces, which hobbled pedestrians and rattled wheeled traffic, could now at last be smoothed over.

Peter Garston Asphalt Company gave employment to Peter's three eldest sons, Alice's brothers, Edward, William and Jack. Peter hoped the firm, if it continued to thrive in the future, might also be able to support his two younger boys, both still scholars, John and Peter Junior.

Peter was also starting to have eyes on his own succession. He would not be able to carry on forever; he was not as fit as he once was. His wife Eleanor was already encouraging him to pass on more responsibility to the boys, so the two of them could enjoy more time together and spend some of the money his years of hard work had amassed.

Peter was not yet ready to hand over the keys to the family firm, however. He still had to decide finally which of his children was best placed to take it on. By rights it should be his eldest son, Edward. But Edward, it was very clear, was a physical force, not an intellectual one. A first class worker and as strong as an ox, he was the man you wanted there every time when a job needed hard graft to see it done. But Edward had no head for numbers and no idea about managing money. He entrusted everything he earned to his wife Catherine to look after. He was never going to be a businessman who could run the family firm.

Next in line was William, Peter's second son, the polar opposite of his elder brother, bright as a button and even now more than able enough to take over the company reins from his father. But did he have the drive for it? Would he live and breathe the asphalt as Peter had done and carry on in the way the founder thought was necessary to lead the business? Peter had his doubts. William had a tendency to take the line of easy resistance. Somehow, things didn't seem to matter to him enough.

If neither boy was suitable to succeed him, the next in line was Jack who was something in between his two elder brothers. A diligent worker but without Edward's prodigious strength and capacity for labour; no fool but a long way from possessing William's intelligence and quick wittedness. Was Jack potentially a better choice on balance than either of his siblings or was he actually less well suited than either of them? Again, Peter was not sure. It was a big choice for him because family was all-important to Peter Garston. He was determined to leave a strong legacy from what he had built up in the hands of one of his children who would ensure the firm would continue to provide prosperity for the Garston family in future generations. There was still plenty of time to consider all of this, though. For now, and for all these reasons, Peter remained firmly at the helm.

This morning there was a less important but rather more urgent family matter for him to attend to. Alice and Michael appeared in the office from which Peter could observe all the activity of his workers outside in the yards. Peter embraced them both and had them sit down in the two chairs that stood at either point of his oak desk in front of him.

"Now, this is a nice surprise!" he said to his second daughter and her husband. "To what do I owe this pleasure?" The office keeper, Peter's eldest daughter Martha, brought in a large china teapot and matching cups and laid it on the table in front of them. As she deposited the refreshments at the table, she let her hands gently caress the shoulders of her sister and brother-in-law and withdrew.

"We've come to ask you for some advice, Father," said Alice. "Michael will tell you the tale."

Peter sat silently as his son-in-law related the detail of the events of the previous evening. Peter stroked his chin from time to time as Michael spoke, plainly deep in thought. When he had finished, Peter asked whether they had heard any names being used by the four men.

"Well, there's the thing," said Alice. "He asked us to keep a table for him to come back to, and he gave his name as Gemmill. I don't think we heard a first name. He was the leader of them, for sure, and he was the one who smashed our mirror just as we were looking forward to preparing for St Patrick's, too."

"Gemmill?" said Peter. "Was he a short, stocky man, about my age, ginger red curly hair and with a strong Glaswegian accent?" he asked. "He was, Father!" said Alice.

"It sounds like Tommy Gemmill and his boys to me, Michael," Peter replied. "He is an Orange Lodge thug. He is secretary of the Lodge in Birkenhead. Dangerous and filled with hatred. He works in the shipbuilding yards in an all-Protestant workplace, and the distance that has given him has allowed his aversion to anything Irish and, from that, anything Catholic, to fester into total poison. He has caused repeated problems for Irish people in Liverpool and in Birkenhead ever since he first came down from Glasgow five or six years ago."

"I don't understand," said Alice. "How can you know so much about him, Father?"

"Alice," said Peter, "you know very well that our family has lived here in Crosby as Godfearing English Catholics for hundreds of years now. During that time we have known and survived many threats to our way of life and to our religion. Our ancestors were told at the stroke of the King's pen that their religion no longer existed, that their right to worship and to marry and be buried in their own sanctified places had been taken away. They were told overnight they were now part of another Church than the one they and all their predecessors had been brought up in. If they failed to comply fully, they faced potential death. Our family lived under that constraint and menace for hundreds of years. It's only in these last few decades that our rights to follow our religion here free of hindrance have finally been restored."

"That is who we Garstons are, and that is where we have come from. One thing all that hard experience over many generations teaches you is that, in order to survive, you must know your enemies: who they are, what they are thinking and what they are doing. You have to keep them close. Knowing who are the most dangerous among them at all times is an essential part of that."

"That's how I know about Tommy Gemmill. I have several friends high up in the Orange Lodge who keep me privately informed of such people as they arise within their organisation, so their threat can be contained, if not removed altogether. It is a favour that I return to them from our side, too, when I can."

Michael looked perplexed and put a question to his father-in-law. "I'm not sure I understand now, Peter. What interest would people high up in the Orange Lodge possibly have in helping Catholics identify threatening people in their ranks. Don't they wish all Irish, all Catholics, to Hell?"

"No, they do not, Michael," said Peter. "There are men of goodwill in all communities just as there will be a few rotten men in every community, too. The best in the Orange Lodge want to celebrate and proclaim their own religion, but not at the expense of another. They don't see that espousing one religion fervently has to imply intolerance of others. That has always been our family's view, too. As Catholics, we have been persecuted for centuries, but now our rights to worship in our own churches and follow our own doctrines have been finally reinstated, there is no reason we cannot live separately but peacefully with others whose Godly beliefs are different from ours."

At this, Peter paused and changed tack.

"But that is all the big picture," he said. "Down at the particular level here and now, we have to be prepared to act to ensure the likes of Tommy Gemmill and his crew are not allowed to terrorise you or your customers. I will arrange for you to have a few additional drinkers in your bar next week. I don't believe you will see Mr Gemmill again until after St Patrick's is over. Like all bullies, he is a coward at heart and he will not venture onto Scotland Road over this weekend when the Irish parades are in full throw and the police are everywhere. He will not come back sooner either because he will expect you to have mustered some reaction. Also, if I know his type, he will want to give you time to replace your handsome mirror so he can break it for you a second time!"

"So we won't expect him too soon but nor will we disappoint him when he does return," said Peter. "We should ensure that he and his comrades receive a traditional family welcome when he comes back, which he will, just so he is not then tempted to make it a recurring event."

"Now tell me," added the master builder, "how big was that plate glass mirror of yours? I'm thinking six foot by six foot? We'll need to get a new one to you and up and hung tomorrow in good time for the weekend."

When, one week later, just as Peter Garston had predicted, Tommy Gemmill and his companions returned to The Dublin Castle, they found the bar fully occupied. A new large mirror hung on the bar wall, just as before.

Their especially reserved table showing a paper with the words 'Awaiting Tommy Gemmill' written prominently on it was now pushed back right into the corner of the room and hemmed in by four smaller tables. Around each of those small tables sat two men quietly drinking. When Tommy called out for the malt whisky he'd ordered, Michael brought him a jug of water and four glasses.

"What the hell is this?" Gemmill roared at him in disgust.

"We don't offer credit here, Mr Gemmill," Michael calmly replied. "This is the hospitality of the high road, a glass of water for passing travellers before they go on their way. Unless, that is, you have come to settle your bill from your last visit?"

"And what bill is that exactly, Paddy?" Gemmill snarled.

"You owe three sovereigns here," replied the landlord. "Four shillings for the whisky you drank and did not pay for, and the remainder for the replacing and the hanging of the mirror you destroyed."

Gemmill stood up ready to confront Michael but, as he did, a large man more than six feet tall, who was seated at the adjacent table, rose up, stepped in between them and towering over Gemmill said, "You've heard Mr Murphy haven't you? Pay your dues like everyone else or be on your way."

Gemmill looked up at the huge looming presence of Edward Garston, and at the same moment he noted that every other eye in the house was now fixed upon him. He saw for the first time that the whole bar was lying in wait for him.

"What is this business to you? You're not even Irish," he blustered.

"No, I'm not Irish," said Edward. "I am one hundred per cent English, but Mr Murphy is very much part of my large family, as is everyone else you see in here this evening, Mr Gemmill. So, unless you would like an argument with all of us here and now, I would strongly advise you to take your leave peaceably and never return to this bar. Do I make myself clear enough to you?"

At this, an older man seated at one of the tables behind Edward stood up and came to stand alongside him. It was his father.

"We know who you are, Tommy Gemmill," said Peter Garston, looking directly at the Scot with cold-eyed intent.

"We know the people who matter in the yard where you work. We know where to come to find you, on any night, on any day. My son has given you some good advice. Now you drink up your glass of water, put on your cap like a good little boy and leave. Heed his message well. Consider as you walk down the road that there is always someone bigger, stronger, faster and better than you. You just have to hope that you never meet them. But unfortunately for you, Tommy Gemmill, you just have. Have a pleasant journey back to Birkenhead. I do hope you won't find the river crossing too rough and upsetting for your delicate stomach."

Gemmill darted a stare at his three companions, tilted his head towards the door and the four men hastily gathered up their coats, edged past the imposing figure of Alice's brother Edward and stumbled out of The Dublin Castle and into the night.

Three

It was now more than five years since Jane Gemmill had come to Birkenhead with her family: her father Tommy, mother Mary and her three brothers. She was into her twenties and living the same life that her friend Elizabeth had lived before she met her husband James. She was still in her parents' house and had a daily routine that never changed. She rose at six, helped her mother make breakfast for her father and brothers, and then set out to the Woodside ferry terminal to take the boat across the Mersey to Liverpool for her work. After work, she made the return journey and helped her mother prepare the evening meal and clear up afterward. She was usually in bed by nine, ready to start the round again the following day.

Her work was her salvation and she was fortunate to have secured a job that she loved. Her first working experience in Glasgow, in the library at Cambuslang, had enabled her to secure an enviable position as a junior librarian in the Liverpool Central Library on William Brown Street. First opened in the year 1860 as a library and museum, the Central Library had been funded by the local merchant whose name was now commemorated on the street on which it stood. Its benefactor had died four years after its opening, but his name now lived on permanently in the address of this magnificent classical building in the centre of the city.

The stunning building was, however, built upon ambivalence. William Brown had been the largest importer of slave-produced cotton into Britain in the first half of the century and he and his family had owned many slaves on their plantations in the southern states of America. At one time, it was said the Brown family had been responsible for one sixth of the trade between Britain and America. By the time the Liverpool Library was erected, however, Brown had judiciously sold off the family plantations and moved all his family money into banking.

The Library had been extended a decade ago with the addition of the Picton Reading Room, a glorious semi-circular space adorned with Corinthian columns. It was lit by modern electric lighting, the first to be installed in any library in the country. It was in the Picton Reading Room that Jane Gemmill worked.

She loved books with a real passion. She loved the feel of them, the texture, the scent of the pages, the beauty of their binding, the grandeur of the embossing on the leather covers. She loved to hold them, to organise them, to set them in their proper place, grouped by author and subject, alphabetically arranged in set order. She loved returning them after use to their rightful positions on the shelves in the double-decked cases of the Picton Room, setting them in perfect alignment and restoring the pleasing symmetry of the rows.

But most of all, Jane loved to read them. The content of the books, those she had read and those she had yet to discover, filled her heart with a real excitement. It was a time in which new novels were appearing with great regularity. She could not hope to keep up with all the new arrivals, though she devoured as many as she could. She would look to make her first choices among them as each batch of new books was delivered to the library. Or, when any were already requested by other readers, she would make a note to seek them out as soon they again became free. She was an avid follower of Dickens and Thomas Hardy; she adored Thackeray's *Vanity Fair* and Wilkie Collins' *Moonstone*.

She was inspired in particular, though, by women writers, from Jane Austen's *Emma* to Mrs Gaskell's *North and South* to Charlotte Brontë's *Jane Eyre* and her sister Emily's *Wuthering Heights* and—oh glory!—Mary Shelley's *Frankenstein*. She was lost in wonderment at the skill and imagination of these women who could conjure up such visions of other worlds.

Her most treasured book of all though was Lewis Carroll's *Alice's Adventures in Wonderland*, which she had read five times, each time delighting in its flights of fancy all the more. She rejoiced in the wit that flowed from Carroll's pen and repeated her favourite line from the book to herself at least once a day: "Why, sometimes I've believed as many as six impossible things before breakfast." She found Alice's proclamation encouraging and empowering.

It was in books that Jane had to find her main stimulation in life because, socially, her life was unrelievedly dull. She was keen to meet a man and start a relationship. She wanted to be married, to be a mother and to bring up a family, but the combination of opportunity and chemistry, which she so longed for, had somehow never arisen. Her parents had taken her on many occasions to functions organised by the Birkenhead Orange Lodge, where Tommy was established as an official of some importance, and Mary, as a committee member's wife, was also held in respectful esteem. But the company there did not interest Jane. The Orange Lodge seemed to her a closed and airless world. They were all Protestant people like herself, of course, so there was certainly a shared religious following among the members. But somehow as she attended its functions, and particularly its dances, she found it increasingly stifling.

On the face of it, there were lots of potentially eligible young men there. They were the sons of the men and women who were the Lodge's members. Their sisters regularly came along, too. But Jane found none of them exciting. None of them appeared to have any experience that went beyond her own. She at least had been brought up in Glasgow so had seen another place. She at least had an interesting job and a love of books that transported her mind to other places. The boys in the Lodge seemingly all lived in Birkenhead and had always lived there. Their conversation was halting and limited. They didn't read, they weren't at ease with girls, or seemingly at all interested in what they thought or had to say, and they didn't have half Jane's wit. She conjured up a nightmare vision of somehow waking up one day married to one of these boys and their then continuing to attend the Lodge functions together for years. They would then bring their own sons and their daughters to the family occasions and the future dances until her daughters married the sons, and her sons married the daughters, of other members of the same closed group and did the same thing all over again. To some girls of her age, that would have been attractive, reassuring, even a dreamy outlook. To Jane, it was a mortifying prospect.

Some of Jane's colleagues in the Central Library found the requirement to work all day on Saturdays trying. They had families at home who were neither working nor at school that day, and they begrudged having to give up time they might be spending with them in recreation. But the library was always at its busiest on a Saturday, so it had to be fully staffed. Most of the public were not required to work that day and could come and spend time finding interesting things to read and to look at. The library was free of charge and a diverting weekend day out in beautiful surroundings for aspirational families who were encouraging their children to read and learn outside school. Saturday was also the day when working men, without the time to read for enjoyment or advancement during the weekdays, would come to enjoy private time, catching up on the week's newspapers, leafing through magazines or devoting themselves to books. Saturday was by far Jane's favourite day of the week.

One regular Saturday morning attendee in the Picton Room whom Jane had come to notice was a tall young man with thick dark hair and a broad moustache. She must have seen him three or four times in their Saturday crowd. He was always well dressed, with a starched collar and fully-buttoned waistcoat that reached within two inches of his bow tie, showing just a flash of a white shirt below. He wore a dark tweed suit and well-polished handmade shoes. He had taken to sitting each week in the same place at the lower end of the room, not far from Jane's counter, where she attended to inquiries from the public and collected up returned books ready for replacement on the shelves. She found herself wondering on this Saturday morning what was this smart young man's story. Others in the library wore their easy casual weekend clothes, this man looked as well dressed as anyone she'd come across. He even had a bowler hat, though she'd not seen him wear it inside the library. It was placed instead on the table beside him as he read.

As her imagination played with notions of who he could be, she found herself intrigued to know what book he was immersed in. One of her jobs was to wheel a trolley through the room and pick up books that were clearly finished with and had been left lying on the tables by people who had departed the library. She noticed that there were now several abandoned volumes scattered on his table, so she decided to make the short journey over to gather them up and, while doing so, to see if she could discover what the man was reading. As she approached, she leaned across the table to pick up the first unwanted work and sneaked a glance at the cover of the book he was absorbed in. It was Dickens' *Great Expectations*. As she tried both to look and reach at the same time, she fell into the man's line of sight, and he looked up at her at just the moment she was intending to pull away undetected. He caught her gaze with a pair of bright brown eyes and a warm smile. Jane's curiosity to find out the man's choice of book had not extended to preparing what she might say if he caught her in the act of stealing a direct look. In a slight fluster, she succeeded only in knocking the book she was reaching out for towards him, to a point beyond her reach.

"Oh, please let me help you," the man said quietly, handing her the elusive volume. Composing herself, Jane thanked him modestly and asked softly if he was enjoying what he was reading.

"I am finding it spellbinding, to be honest," he whispered in reply. "It is only my second Dickens after *Oliver Twist*, but it is so beautifully written I can hardly wait to turn the pages. But at the same time, I can hardly bear to let them go either!"

Jane smiled broadly at him and rejoined, "You've made a good choice there. Do you not have much time to read?" The man replied, his hand shielding his mouth, "Not as much as I would like. My family work in the building trade, and I'm very busy all week. So I really look forward to Saturdays when I can come here and lose myself in a good book."

Jane again smiled approvingly and was about to move away when the man said to her, "I hope I'm not being too forward, but I thought I might go across the road to a teashop I know for a little lunch in a short while. You wouldn't care to join me, would you? I'd love to talk to you some more."

Jane had only a second to think how to reply but she was ready with an instinctive answer. "Well yes, how kind. Thank you, that would be very nice. I have a break for just one hour at midday if that would be suitable?"

"That would be wonderful," said the man. "I will come over to your desk at noon. My name is William by the way. William Garston."

"It's nice to meet you, William," said Jane. "I'm Jane. Jane Gemmill." "I'll look forward to seeing you then."

Four

There are those who still doubt whether there is such a thing as love at first sight. None of those doubters would harbour any question of it had they witnessed William Garston and Jane Gemmill's first lunchtime meeting.

They fell into each other like lovers restored from long separation. Their fevered conversation never flagged for a moment. Over and again, they surfaced mutual enthusiasms, they hung on each other's words, and were delighted by them. They surprised and intrigued each other in turn. They laughed together like children. They drew one another in. No remark that either made sounded a single flat note for the other. It made them hunger all the more for each other. In under one hour, they found themselves sharing intimacies, some of their innermost thoughts, that they had never dared breathe to another soul before.

They instantly trusted one another implicitly and were electrified by that recognition. By the time their brief lunchtime was over, they noticed neither had touched their food or, in truth, even looked at it. They already had to rush to get Jane back to her desk on time. They ran across the square to the library, hand-in-hand, like young teenagers.

"I'm not coming back in there," said William as they reached the door to the library at two minutes to one o'clock.

"I had planned to come back for the afternoon, but there is really no point me coming in now. I know I will spend the afternoon looking over at you and won't take in a sentence of my book, that one that was holding my whole attention before. It will also be an unfair torture not to be able to come and stand with you while you work. Can I wait outside for you instead and take you somewhere for a drink when you finish this afternoon?"

Jane, laughing, said, "I would love that, William, but I have not told my family that I might be late. They will be expecting me home as usual and they will worry."

"Well, tomorrow then?" said William, not to be deterred. "I could come to see you somewhere near you on the other side of the river. Would you meet me for an ice cream on New Brighton pier tomorrow afternoon at two? The sun is bound to shine for us!"

"That would be lovely," said Jane, smilingly offering him her cheek. He touched her pale skin lightly with his lips, breathing her in fleetingly as he did, before she skipped away up into the building, her hand waving gaily over her right shoulder as she disappeared from his view.

They met at the agreed time and place the following day. Jane simply told her mother she was going out to meet a friend, which was true. They enjoyed a blissful afternoon together. The sun, as William had promised it would, shone unbreakingly. William was a good conversationalist. He told her about working with his brothers in the family asphalt business and what it was like to work for your father in a family firm. She could sense as he described it that he was torn between devoting his life to the family business or moving on to do something new and quite different. Instinctively, she found herself wanting to encourage him to strive for something beyond what he had. She wanted to say he was worth much more than road building but she held back at the last.

He had travelled, which Jane was thrilled by. He had been to London with his father and stood under Big Ben as it chimed midday. He had seen the Tower of London. He had been to Dublin and visited Trinity College, where he saw the ancient Irish relic *The Book of Kells*, the thousand-year-old gospel manuscript. Jane had never heard of it but was enthralled to hear him describe its complex patterns and its vibrant colours. He had even been to Paris, where he had visited Notre Dame Cathedral. They immediately both confirmed amid laughter that they had read and loved Victor Hugo's tale of the Hunchback. William told her he had also stood up close to see the work in progress on Gustav Eiffel's incredible new tower. "It was an unbelievable sight and it is a stunning engineering feat, but it was only half built when I was there, Jane," he said. "Maybe we can go together to see it when it is finally finished?"

"I would love that," she replied, excited by the very thought of it.

For William, Jane was different from any girl he had ever met. He had been introduced to many attractive young women in and around the family home in Crosby but none had ever offered him any challenge. They were comfortable, home-loving girls who wanted to marry within their own community, good Catholic girls looking out for a good Catholic husband. Jane, though, knew more than he did about many things. He had seen that already. She was far better read than him and, while she had not seen much of the world, she had studied and learned a great deal about it from her reading. She was quick and intelligent, with an informed opinion on most things, even matters he thought he knew well. She was more than he was, if anything, certainly not less. He saw her immediately as his equal, his partner, not some doting dependant. She would help him to make the best of himself, and he already wanted to do that, both for her and with her. She was a woman that he longed to know completely. He needed her in his life. He had never before felt such a clear and powerful compulsion.

With William's place of work in Crosby, and Jane's long days in William Brown Street, it was hardly practical for them to try to see each other during the week. Instead, they met each Saturday at the Library and took lunch in their now regular haunt where they had become instantly well known to the staff. On their second visit, the cafeteria owner, taking their food order, joked with them to Jane's embarrassment. "Going to eat it this time, are we? It's a terrible expense for you to go to if you're not even going to look at it. Especially after we've taken all the trouble to make it for you!"

On Sundays, they alternated between meeting in Liverpool or William coming across to her side of the river. So engrossed in each other had they been that, somehow, after a month, the question of religion had never arisen between them.

Jane knew no Catholics and she lived in a world dominated by her father with his virulent views of Irish Papists. These two words were one and the same thing in Jane's mind.

Catholics were Irish. Irish were Catholics. Neither was any good as far as her family was concerned. William was a Lancastrian Englishman. She was a Scot. It never crossed Jane's mind that he would be anything other than a Protestant.

So it was without warning when her presumption was shown to be quite wrong. She had been talking to William about the Orange Lodge and her father's role within it. William had not yet met her parents and, after these several weeks when they were both so obviously in thrall to one another, it had occurred to Jane that maybe she could ask William to come with her to the next Lodge dance. It would be a good opportunity for her to introduce him to her mother and father in a pleasant social atmosphere of enjoyment.

William looked at her and said, "I'm not sure they'd let me in, Jane." As she looked at him uncomprehendingly, he added, "You do realise I'm a Catholic, don't you?"

Jane was dumbfounded by the revelation. Her first sensation was to feel humiliated, an utter fool. Why had she not realised or asked? How had she missed the signs that must have been there? It stopped her flat in her tracks. He was English. He must be Protestant. It only dawned on her now how stupid and empty an assumption that had been. She was struggling to assess the turmoil of implications of what she had just heard and could not yet begin to process them all. But she knew one thing for sure amidst all this new crisis of uncertainty. She loved this man as she had never loved anyone, and she wanted to be with him. She did not want to give him up. She did not want to lose him.

"Is that a problem for you, Jane?" asked William.

Jane thought for a moment and said, "I don't know. It would be a huge problem for my father. My mother, too. They are strict Protestants. That is who my Pa is."

"What about you?" she asked. "What would your family feel to have a Protestant in their house, William?"

William said, "I don't know either but in all honesty I think they also might have great difficulty with it. We're a Catholic family going back hundreds of years in Crosby. It is an important part of my parents' English identity and their culture. My father has very little to do with the Liverpool Irish but he is most definitely a Catholic patriarch. It is fundamental."

Jane's eyes welled up with tears as he spoke. She could instantly begin to see this deliriously happy and life-changing relationship crumbling away before it had really even begun. "Is that how you would feel, too?" she asked in complete trepidation.

William wrapped his hands around hers. "If you're asking would I give that all up for you, Jane, yes I would. I love you and I want to be with you always."

Jane gasped. She did not know where that took them, but her body was suffused with grateful emotion that their relationship was at least still intact. Now hugely challenged for sure, but still alive. Thank God.

William then asked her the obvious next question. "Do you think your parents would accept a Catholic into your family?"

Jane again thought a moment and replied, "My father is a proud and uncompromising man. I honestly cannot see him ever doing that."

"So where does that leave us, Jane?" asked William now becoming the anxious one. "Would you take me against his wishes?"

After a pause, Jane looked into his eyes and took his hands in hers. "Yes, William, if you'll have me, yes I would."

Five

The following week was excruciating. William and Jane went back to their separate day lives and their work but neither could think of anything else. They were not able to see one another, or otherwise be in touch, until the next weekend. Jane considered writing him a letter and she made several attempts to put down on paper what she was thinking and wanting to ask him. But all her efforts ended up screwed up in her hand and abandoned. She was normally so good at writing. There were times when the written word could be no substitute for conversation.

The biggest issue that could possibly confront them had emerged so early in their young relationship, and it had placed an indescribable strain on their freshly established bond of trust in one another. Separated by a distance of several miles at this most critical juncture, they were both racked with fears and concern. What if the other was now thinking better of the lovestruck commitments they had made to each other? Could they really ask this extraordinary thing of the other? Were they truly certain of their own conviction that this was the right step to take after so short a time? When they would at last meet again this coming Saturday, would they find a different, colder person to the one they had held in their arms last week? The uncertainty was unbearable torment for them both and that week of separation was the longest of their lives.

When Saturday finally came, William met Jane outside the library at twelve o'clock. They were nervous and tentative with one another, their confidence shaken, neither wanting to be the first to declare their feelings after a whole week of elapse of time, for fear of rejection. William suggested they could walk together for the hour, and Jane, who had been thinking exactly that, readily consented. They agreed they would go down to the river and walk along the front.

"I can't bear it, Jane," William broke, as they left the Library square. "All those things we said last week, do you still feel the same? Before you answer, I want you to know that I do, with all my heart. But if you have decided against me, I promise you I will understand though it would devastate me. But I must know how you feel."

Jane stopped him and threw her arms around him. She stroked his anxious face to sooth away his fears. "Of course I feel the same, you silly thing. I could not bear to be without you, and we must face the consequences of that if you feel the same way."

"My love, I do," he replied.

That exchange ended their first and most acute agony of not knowing if the other's intentions had entirely changed. But it did not answer what their next steps should be.

William took the lead.

"I am sure you will have thought deeply about it, Jane, and you may well have come up with a better plan than I, but let me at least start by telling you what I have thought," he said. Jane nodded and listened intently.

"Neither of us has even met the other's family, so we cannot have much idea of them or what they will say. It seems to me, though, that, as far as we two are concerned, there is no advantage to our simply asking them whether they would approve of this in principle. It seems almost inevitable they would both say they absolutely do not and would try to compel us to stop seeing one another. If that happened, we would just have to run away together. I simply could not bear to be without you."

Jane was about to interject when William asked to be allowed to tell her the rest of his thought.

"I have also come to the conclusion there is no merit to our telling one family and not the other. Whatever the reaction of whichever family we might choose to begin with, would still tell us nothing about the other's reaction. We could be delighted by the first one and then confounded by the second, or the other way around. I think we should tell them we plan to marry, and tell them at the same time."

Jane heard the words but could not immediately visualise how that could happen. "But how can we do that since we would need to be in two places at once. Unless you are thinking of getting them all together for this?" she said, appalled at the very idea of such a thing.

"No, that was not my plan, Jane!" said William, laughing out aloud for the first time since they had met again. "I think we each need to tell our own family what has happened. That way we can give them the time and the space to give vent to whatever reaction they have within their own house, with only their own family present. That way we can give them time not just to react but to think. If it goes even passably well with either or both families, we can then introduce ourselves to the other's family the next day. Do you think that is worth trying?"

Jane had not focused on the logistical implications of the conversations with the two families, although she had imagined countless times her father screaming at her.

"That seems a good plan, William," she said after a few moments. "I think you are right. It would be better we break the news to our own families alone and, yes, I do think that is better done without an introduction being pressed on them at the same time. They might well need a period to consider their responses. Having you or me sitting there, with our knees pressed together, while the other's parents try to come to terms with the shock of this for the first time, could be truly awful."

"The other advantage of doing it that way is that we will know at the same time what the position is and what our next steps must be," said William.

"What if they throw both of us out?" asked Jane. "Have you considered that?"

"I have," he replied. "If that happens, I have money for us to stay separately from one another in two hotels. We could then make plans together to marry as soon as we practically could."

Jane was impressed with the thoroughness of William's planning. She could at least now envisage how this might all be played out in practice, even if she had the gravest forebodings about the whole experience. But she had something important still to say to William.

"William, I think you have thought that through well, and I think that is a plan that could probably make the best of what is going to be very awkward for both of us and for our families. But I have something to ask of you before we go there, which I must say to you and which we have not discussed. I hope very much that you can agree to what I am about to ask you because, if you cannot, then I cannot go ahead with this."

"What is it, my love?" asked William, his brow furrowing with apprehension.

"I would love to be your wife and I would love to raise a family with you, but only on one condition," said Jane. "I have read a great deal in the past week about the Catholic religion, its practices and the requirements that it has. It is very clear that Catholics, even when they marry outside their religion, are expected by the Church to bring up their children in the Catholic faith. I am not a Catholic, William, and I never will be. I have been brought up in the Protestant faith and it runs deep within me. I will not become a Catholic, and I could not, and I will not, bring up my children as Catholics. We would have to be a Protestant family."

She fell silent for a moment to allow her momentous words to sink in. After what seemed an eternity, William spoke.

"I have already considered that Jane. I understand and I agree. My parents' nature is such that I think there is a strong probability that simply suggesting I wish to marry a Protestant could spell the end for me as part of the family. They have been Catholics forever. That is who they are. It is clear that one of the two of us will have to give up our faith if we are to marry and bring up children together. Your belief is stronger than mine, and we have to decide upon one or the other. You have made it clear you would not convert to Catholicism. I respect that position. I am prepared to become a member of the Anglican Church if that is the only way I can have you as my wife."

For Jane, this was the ultimate test and it had been passed. William had clearly spent much time in the past week thinking of how they would answer the "How?" questions they faced, how they would clear the immediate hurdles in front of them. It was helpful that he had done so. She had given barely a moment's thought to those tactical details. They would be resolved one way or another, she knew. Instead, she had devoted almost all her thinking time to the "What?" issues. What would their marriage be? What would be the basis on which their family would live? What did she want from her life? What would she accept and what could she never surrender?

As she worked through her own thinking, her resolution had hardened. She recognised that she was prepared to go against her parents' wishes in marrying William if that proved necessary. She was not beholden to them in choosing her future husband, the man she would spend her life with. She had seen their ideas of her suitable choices—the dim, dull boys at the Orange Lodge—and not only was she completely unmoved by them, she was also rather insulted that her parents, her father in particular, might ever imagine that she might be interested in them. The suggestion that one of those boys should be her lot in life was oddly dissonant with how he had brought her up: to aspire, to reach beyond the obvious, to insist on being the best. When she had hugged her tearful friend Elizabeth goodbye on the bench in Cambuslang, the fact of her departure from Glasgow had not come at all as a surprise to Jane. It had been the logical next step on the path to discovery she was already set upon. Now, in these last years, she felt she and her parents were no longer travelling on an open road. She felt they had arrived at a destination. Her parents had settled in Birkenhead and they had settled for it. They expected her to do the same. She would not accept that.

But nor could she accept the self-betrayal that being asked to adopt the Catholic faith would entail. There was nothing about that doctrine that resonated with her. She loathed all the pomp and circumstance, she found the ritualism absurd and, most of all, she decried what she saw as the Catholic lack of discipline and moral fibre. She believed in responsibility. She believed everyone answered to their Maker for their actions on the Earth. He would sit in judgement upon everyone on their final day. There was no eluding that, there were no easy escape routes. He was all-seeing and He would hold everyone to account. So the Catholic practice of the confessional was anathema to her. It smacked to Jane of weakness and self-deceit. Commit a sin, visit a priest and have it wiped from the slate seemed to her both a religious abomination and a practical outrage. She would never bring up children with such laxity or permit such spinelessness.

So that had completely answered for Jane the "What?" questions about her potential future with William. The question she had put to him was, in effect, an ultimatum. For all the powerful surging of love she felt for him, if he had replied in any way to suggest a milky compromise or some necessary accommodation to the religion of Rome, she would have halted the relationship there and then. She had been fully ready to do that. She was clear-eyed about it. She was quite decided.

So when William confirmed that he accepted her terms, she felt both delighted and vindicated. She had through her own conviction and emotional strength put herself into a position to resume her expansive journey in life. She could see the road ahead again now clearly; she could see William and her having a family together. Theirs would be a family built upon firm ground, not deflected by the opinions of others or disoriented by specious concessions.

"Will you marry me, Jane?" said William, dropping onto one knee in front of her. "I will, William," she said. They kissed to seal their bond.

Six

At the agreed hour of seven o'clock the following evening, divided by the river and ten miles of road, Jane and William began their separate conversations with their parents.

"Now what is it you want to talk to us about, Jane?"

"Very well, William, your mother and I are listening."

"Are you mad, girl?"

"I can't believe what I am hearing, William."

"This cannot happen. You have lost your senses."

"How long has this relationship been going on?"

"How long have you known her?"

"Are you pregnant? Is that what this is all about?"

"Is she with child?"

"Have you even stopped to think what this means?"

"We would no longer be welcome at the Lodge. It would be the end. I would have to stand down."

"Would you throw away 500 years of family history on this one girl?"

"What is wrong with all the young men among our own people?"

"You must never see him again."

"You should go away. Take time to think before you make a terrible mistake."

"Will she convert?"

"Will he convert?"

"If you do this, we can have nothing more to do with you, do you know that?"

"If you do this, you realise it means you will have to leave our family?"

"You will have to leave our house."

"You will have to leave the firm. Are you ready to give that up, too?"

"You will have to leave this town."

"I cannot believe you have repaid us in this way."

"After all that we have been through. This is so disloyal."

"These are not our people."

"These are not our people."

"You must reconsider."

"Will you reconsider?"

"I am so very angry."

"I am so very sad."

"I don't know what to say."

"There is nothing more to say, is there?"

"Pack your bags and be ready to leave this house tomorrow first thing."

"If your mind cannot be changed, we must live with the consequences and so must you."

It had not gone well, in either house.

Seven

When William met her at noon the following day, Jane was white. No sign of tears but deathly pale. She had packed her bag as she had been instructed by her father and had brought it with her to her place of work. She had made no arrangement for where she was to stay. She had some money, and she planned to find lodgings for the night, or perhaps the next few days, after she finished at the library for the day.

They shared their experiences of the night before and found they were remarkably similar. The respective reactions of the two families, while not unexpected, were at the same time quite shocking. Neither of them had been met with any understanding or sympathy. Both had been accused of being out of their minds and of standing on the brink of a dreadful mistake.

But what was most devastating to both Jane and William was how quickly the door had been closed on them. There were no offers of support or expressions of concern. No suggestion had been made of meeting the other family or of being introduced to their prospective marriage partners. Neither family had even asked to know the surname of the other party involved. Both sets of parents had quickly concluded that their prodigal children were wholly and disastrously in the wrong. They also made it very clear that what they planned to do, in crossing the religious divide, meant they would be disowned. There was no other way for it. They would not be welcome to stay within their family confines. If they were going over to the other side, then they would have to make it there on their own. If they chose to make their bed there, then they would just have to go lie in it.

Two Christian religions, which had such apparently important and vehement differences on so many things, were quite as one on this issue, it seemed. Both sides completely agreed this was as bad as it got. William and Jane were proposing to do an unthinkable thing.

William came back to the library with Jane and collected her bag from her. He had made his excuses at work that day, and he undertook to use the afternoon to find Jane some suitable lodgings so that when she emerged from work she could at least go straight away to decent accommodation and not have to walk the streets in search for it. William would then meet her at the library door at six o'clock and would walk her to her new temporary home.

Her bag in his hand, he walked up the hill towards Rodney Street, the well-appointed area above the city centre where well-to-do professionals and artists lived. It was also the site of the Scottish Presbyterian Church of St Andrew, which he thought might be a comforting neighbouring presence for Jane. Along the street there was one building he noticed had been dedicated as a guest house, with a sign saying 'Rooms Available' in its window. After surveying it outside for a few moments, William elected to go in and was met in a smartly decorated panelled hallway by the hotel owner, a small neatly attired gentlemen wearing a pince-nez who was seated at a Georgian walnut reception table.

William told him he was looking for a smart room for his niece who was working in the Central Library for a few weeks. He wished to make arrangements to pay for her room in advance, and also to leave funds on account for her to cover both her lodging expenses and a breakfast and evening meal at the hotel each day. The owner showed him up to a room that, while compact, was both clean and bright. The linen on the bed was crisp white and well laundered, and the room had a fine view from its casement windows over the town below. William accepted it and handed over two guineas to the hotelier to cover Jane's costs for the next two weeks. Should his niece require to extend her stay, or purchase anything from the hotel in addition, she would be able to pay for that directly herself, he confirmed. Taking the room key, and leaving her bag with the hotelkeeper, William departed.

That evening, Jane was hugely grateful that he had made things so easy for her. She found the room pleasing, the hotel was spotless and safe. William's prepayment of her stay, and his creation of a simple and plausible explanation of why she was there, had made what might have been an awkward series of conversations very straightforward.

To avoid any embarrassment at the hotel, William had booked them a table at an eating house in town that evening. As they sat in the small family-run establishment, over a comforting plate of hot beef stew, they were finally able to speak about their next steps, about their future.

"My father has said I can stay in Crosby in the family home until I decide to tell anyone other than my parents about our plan," William said. He explained that his parents had told him they themselves would not mention a word of it to anyone, in the hope that he would have a change of heart and the unfortunate matter would all blow over.

"They don't really believe for one moment that it will blow over," William said. "They just don't want to make it any easier for me to leave. But I think that actually might suit our purpose. If we can use these next weeks to find a church that will marry us, then we might be married within a month. We can then find somewhere where we can be together. Could you bear to stay in that hotel for a few weeks while we do that?"

Jane agreed that she could, and she told him that she had managed to do some researches of her own during quiet moments in the library that day.

"There is a church in Kirkdale called St Mary's that is two miles from here and only five or so miles from Crosby, which I think would be perfect for our wedding," she said.

"The vicar seems to be a wonderful man called Canon Thomas Major Lester, who has been curate there for more than 30 years. He is renowned all over the city for good works with children's charities and for helping the poor. I think he would be a perfect person to marry us. Would you be happy if I made some inquiries there?"

"That sounds perfect!" said William, before asking, "Is the vicar a soldier?"

Jane looked blankly at him for a second before she got it. "No, he is not a major, you big booby, that is his name: Thomas Major Lester." They both fell into fits of uncontrolled laughter before William said, "I've obviously got a lot to learn about the Anglican Church, haven't I!" Their shared hilarity rinsed away for the first time the strain they had living been under for so many days, like waves breaking joyously on a shore.

"Is he a soldier?" Jane repeated aloud, before dissolving again into a fit of giggles.

Jane used her lunch hour the next day, the fourth of February, to visit Canon Major Lester at St Mary's to see if he would be willing to marry them. Kindness personified, he confirmed to her he had not the slightest problem with William's Catholic heritage and would be delighted to preside at their wedding. He instantly recognised Jane's strong Protestant roots, and said he would be more than happy to welcome William into the Anglican Church as her husband. With a mischievous grin that set Jane's anxiety fully at rest, Canon Major Lester told her conspiratorially he was 'always glad to win one over from the other side'!

They agreed a day for the wedding at the first possible date, which was 18 days hence. They were to be married on Sunday, February the 22nd in the year 1885. The third reading of the banns for their marriage would be held at St Mary's morning service that day, and their wedding would take place immediately after the service was over. Canon Major Lester said he looked forward to welcoming Jane to the congregation on the coming Sunday, when they would be able to hear the first reading of the banns taking place. He looked forward to meeting William then, too. Jane thanked him profusely and hurried from the church to catch the horse-drawn bus that would return her to the centre of the city.

She made it back through the library doors within the hour with just moments to spare. Things were now really on the move.

Eight

They were married on that appointed day at St Mary's Church, Kirkdale. Canon Major Lester, who presided over the service with gentleness and good humour, had recognised, without being told, that the happy couple's biggest concern was that they would have no guests to see them married. With gracious insight, he had approached them on the Sunday before, when they came to hearing the second reading of their banns.

"I hope you won't mind me asking you this," he said. "But the St Mary's congregation loves nothing more than a good wedding. Would you consider allowing me to tell them at the end of the service today that your wedding will take place immediately after the morning service next week? If you would be prepared to allow that, I would very much like to say to them that the bride and groom would be pleased to welcome everyone who would like to stay on to witness the happy event itself?"

Jane, who prided herself on the control of her emotions, felt her eyes welling at the vicar's proposal. The only apprehension she had felt about the wedding was the thought that it might take place, as if shamefully, in front of only a handful of church people. Neither family would be sending anyone. They had not invited any friends. The churchman's suggestion in the circumstances was perfect.

"Canon," she said, seeing the immediate agreement in William's eyes. "We would be delighted to share our occasion with the congregation."

Their simple wedding ceremony was consequently witnessed on the next Sunday by a full church. After the service, the two of them returned to Jane's hotel and enjoyed a wedding breakfast of oysters and saddle of beef together, washed down with a bottle of French champagne. The hotel had made them, as a gift, a small special white-iced cake, which they took as their dessert.

William's father, when his son had left their house for the last time the day before, had handed him a cheque for £50 and wished him good fortune. William was grateful for the gesture, and for the money itself, but both men knew there was something of a settling of an account in the parting gift. William had been his father's most likely successor as the head of the asphalt business. His decision to marry Jane had cost him not only his family, but also his livelihood, his income and his future prospects of prosperity. The £50 meant the newly-weds would not want for money for a while, but William knew he needed a proper plan now to replace what he had just lost.

As they savoured their champagne, he told Jane his thoughts.

"I have been thinking about what I should do with regards to work," he said. "I know the asphalt contracting business but, beyond my father's gift, I have no capital whatever to buy the equipment I would need to start me out. In truth, I also feel no attraction to resuming exactly what I have been doing, and what my family does. It seems to make a mockery of our hopes for an entirely new life together. I also would be very uncomfortable competing for business against my father and my brothers. It would pour salt into the wounds that my leaving has opened up. So I think I must find something new. In my work in the firm, I have learned how a business is run and how to manage it carefully. I understand very well, for example, the great importance of cash. You need it to keep your business alive, so you cannot afford to grant your customers extended credit, tempting though that may sometimes be. If they don't pay you, you don't eat."

"So are you thinking about going into a new business?" Jane asked.

"I am," he replied. "I would like it to be a business in which you and I could work together. I am sure the two of us would have a much greater chance of success than me alone. I would like it to be a business where, if we are blessed with children, you could look after their needs while still helping me when you could. I would like us to have a business that we could manage from our own home. I am thinking of opening a shop."

Jane was used to dealing with the public for her work in the library and she enjoyed those interactions. It allowed her to be efficient in resolving questions and providing service. So the prospect of running her own retail businesses with William was not at all unappealing. "What type of shop do you have in mind?" she asked.

"A general store," said William, "and I have a particular place in mind." He told her he had seen a shop advertised in the *Liverpool Daily Post* in the Anfield district of the city. It was not an expensive lease. It was a run down and unloved property but it did have six rooms above it. They were certainly in need of repair and decoration but they provided potentially a substantial living space.

"I thought before we have any little arrivals of our own, we could supplement our income from the shop by renting out one or two of the rooms," he said.

"What is so special about this place, William?" asked Jane. "There must be hundreds of shops that are available to rent. Why is this the one we must have? Is it just because you want to get on and be seen to be doing something, or is there some special reason for it?"

"There are some special reasons," he replied. "One, we can afford it, which is a good place to start. Two, it has the living space which would allow us to bring up a family. Three, it is in a poor state, and we can improve not only the living rooms but also the appearance and the space of the shop itself, which should help to improve its fortunes. And number four, it is in a good location."

"By the fourth, you mean there are lots of houses nearby with customers we could serve?" asked Jane.

"Yes, there certainly are," said William, "but there is something more than that. The shop is in Walton Breck Road at number 140. It stands right outside a football ground which the city's football team, Everton Football Club, has just moved into over the last few months. The pitch is owned by a very wealthy local businessman called John Houlding, and he has plans to develop it with the construction of large stands to accommodate lots of spectators, both seated and standing. Once that is done, the Anfield stadium will be able to hold tens of thousands of football supporters."

"It means we would be there from the very start, Jane. Everton is already a popular and successful team and the plans for the new stadium will mean it should prosper in the future. A shop serving food, drinks, newspapers, tobacco and all manner of other things should do a roaring trade each time the team plays and crowds of thousands flock to the ground. There is virtually nothing to see there now but, in a year's time, I think the whole area will be transformed. I want to rent the sad, grimy, unloved shop that will be sitting right in the middle of all that positive change when it happens."

Jane leaned forward and took both his hands in hers. "That sounds to me like a wonderful project, William. If you decide you want to do it, then you can count me in."

"Now did you mention something about hoping to be being blessed with children?"

Nine

William's departure from his family was treated by the Garstons rather in the manner they might have adopted if he had died in unspeakable circumstances. William's name simply ceased to be mentioned by the family who carried on their lives much as if he had never been there. If pressed by persistent customers or family outsiders for news of him, the stock answer given by Peter Garston and followed by Eleanor and by William's siblings was simply that he had 'moved away'. People quickly realised that the subject of William Garston was now taboo in the Garston family. There was no further discussion of him to be had. The matter of William had been quietly and permanently laid to rest.

Jane's departure, by contrast, served only to inflame further the already fevered mind of Tommy Gemmill. He had poured all his hopes and aspirations into his daughter. As his eldest child, she had been the focus of all his fatherly energies. He saw her as completing his own rise from the poverty of his youth to the middle class status and financial well-being he had managed to attain. She would mark the next step forward for the Gemmill family. She would create his real legacy.

That she was a girl had only redoubled his determination to ensure that she would achieve in life and become truly exceptional. As a female, she would have more hurdles in life to clear than her three younger brothers, so Tommy became fixated on equipping her to overcome all challenge. He sought to imbue in her a sense that there was nothing she could not do. When she reported small successes at school, or in her place of work, his regular response to her was that such recognitions were only to be expected. "Of course, you are top of the class," he would say. When she had begun work and told him on occasion that she had received some praise from her superiors, his comment was, "It is no surprise your managers congratulate you. So they should."

Achievement for Jane, therefore, became not a cause for celebration but rather just the next milestone along the road of her life. Falling short was not an option. No prospective task, no matter how mountainous or unreasonable, was beyond her ability to complete. What was more, she should expect to be able to do it quicker and more effectively than anyone else. That was what her father told her and, therefore, that became what she believed, the standard she had to hit. Fortunately, for the most part, Jane managed to live up to those vaulting expectations that he set for her. She experienced perhaps less joy along the way from what she achieved than others less gifted than her would have done with less frequent successes. She moved quickly from every goal she accomplished to the next one. Life to her was a ladder she just had to keep climbing. As she put her foot on one rung, there was always the next one appearing above. Because she had little or no experience of her step ever failing, however, her ability to recover from life's setbacks had never been truly tested.

Such was his undiluted concentration on Jane that Tommy had little time or belief left for his three younger children, Andrew, George and Richard. He left their upbringing almost entirely to his wife Mary. He rationalised this in his own mind that, as boys, they would just have to make their own way in the world. They did not need any mollycoddling from Tommy. He had managed perfectly well without any from his own father, after all. As much as he was entranced by his daughter, he was unmoved by his sons. Where they had shortcomings or lacked application, he put that down to a fundamental lack of motivation and purposefulness. He had no patience for it. Where they fell short, Tommy often recognised in them deficiencies of his own. He had managed to overcome those failings without any help, and now so should they.

The boys were unexceptional students and none of them was manly enough for Tommy's liking either. He saw them as Mummy's boys who showed too frequently signs of weak will. As they reached their teenaged years, it became clear that what interested the three of them most was music and especially singing. To Tommy's barely disguised disdain, they had formed a singing trio. They called themselves 'The Singing Gems', and began to have modest success as entertainers touring local taverns to perform, and even appearing down the bill at some of the smaller music halls. Their act was amusing and risqué. They finished each set with a harmonised and ribald version of Marie Lloyd's popular song *The Boy I Love is up in the Gallery*, which never failed to bring the house down. At the time of Jane's departure, her three younger brothers had already left home and were pursuing a life on the road as travelling minstrels. Their mother missed them dreadfully. For Tommy, they were out of sight and out of mind.

Jane was banished, too, but in a different way. Tommy was appalled and angered by what had happened. As time went by, his private version of the story changed its shape as it pickled away in his vat of bile. His daughter had been spirited away by Irish, who had got into her mind in their evil way. It confirmed everything he had ever known and said about that awful breed. He had not needed further encouragement to boil up more anti-Catholic poison, but he now had reason of his own to add to his lifelong vigorous defence of the Protestant cause. His enmity to the Church of Rome now knew no bounds. His hatred of Popery could now go unchecked.

The division that existed in Tommy's mind was exactly mirrored on the streets of Liverpool. The city was now part of the largest Roman Catholic diocese in England with over 400,000 members. Irish Catholics made up more than one third of the city's population. The year of William and Jane's wedding saw Liverpool become the only British mainland constituency ever to elect an Irish Nationalist as its member of Parliament, when the Catholic Thomas Power O'Connor. 'T.P.' was returned for the Liverpool Scotland constituency. He went on to hold the seat for 44 years.

At the very same time, the presence of the Protestant Orange Order in the city was enormous. At the annual Twelfth of July parade, there were almost a hundred lodges from the city and surrounding counties represented with a turnout running into the tens of thousands. A few years earlier, the number of Orangemen and supporters on the city's streets for the Glorious Revolution parade had been estimated at 150,000. Liverpool was by far the largest Orange city in mainland Britain. The meetings of the national Grand Lodge of the institution were dominated by the Liverpool lodges. At one national annual meeting, it was reported that of the 34 officials from around the country who had attended 28 had come from the Liverpool lodges.

Liverpool had become the place on the British mainland where Protestantism and Catholicism collided, where the immovable object grindingly met the unstoppable force.

It was a huge friction point, wanting only a spark.

Ten

William and Jane got their shop. Jane carried on working at the library for three months, while William carried out the heavy work to paint and decorate the living rooms, and clean and reconstruct the selling space itself. He painted inside and out in brilliant white. He scrubbed down the long unwashed windows to free them from the mud and grime from the street outside, and the grease of handprints inside, which in combination had rendered them almost totally opaque. He erected shelves around three walls and built a handsome glass fronted counter cupboard with four internal racks that opened from the rear and would allow customers to see the fresh foodstuffs he planned to display. Jane came home from work each evening and lent a helping hand with the painting and cleaning. Finally, their work was almost completed, and Jane served her last day at the library.

Their efforts had transformed the appearance of the shop. To apply the final touch, William, whose handwriting script was beautiful, had made a template of the new name of the shop, cutting it out carefully with scissors from a large piece of strong cardboard. After testing it several times, by painting over it to check the stencil would emerge faithfully onto a paper below, he gave Jane the honour of putting the new name onto the paintwork above the front window of the shop outside.

Handing her a small tin of black paint, he held the ladder steady as she climbed to the right height, on a level with the template he had secured firmly into the correct place. She dipped in the brush deeply and drew it from left to right and back again three times across the stencil. As she climbed back down, William then stepped up quickly in her place to lift away the template to reveal the single word, in black bold italics, now standing proud against the white background.

Garston's. They were open for business.

For several reasons, the shop proved to be a very shrewd choice for William and Jane. Commercially, it quickly became a success. William's predictions about what would happen to the local area, now the football club had moved into the ground just yards from their front door, were shown to be completely right. The popularity of Everton FC grew exponentially. It became one of the founder clubs of the new national Football League and was a highly successful team. It attracted followers from all over the city and the surrounding areas. It provided an important new focal point for all the people in Liverpool and not for one religion rather than another, not for one nationality but for all. The Blue and White colours of Everton FC began to transcend the fierce divisions of the Protestant Orange and Catholic Green. Football was a uniting entity for the city and the people in it.

Twice a month on Saturday afternoons, when the team played a match on its home turf, the area was engulfed by supporters for hours before. As many thousands of people milled around the ground waiting for the match to begin, the Garston's shop across the road had more custom than it could possibly cater for. Jane turned over half the shop on those afternoons to selling hot and cold drinks—cocoa, beef extract, tea, coffee, lemonade, ginger beer, cream soda. They sold no alcohol, but there were local public houses to meet those needs. So substantial was the custom for their drinks, together with the pies, pastries and sandwiches which they stocked up for on those big days, that Jane had to bring in two day girls, local sisters Miriam and Joan Eastbrook, to help them meet the huge demand. It amounted to a completely exhausting few hours once a fortnight, but the shop's takings on each of those match days were enough to meet all the family's expenses for a whole month.

But beyond its financial success, the shop served another equally important purpose for William and Jane. It placed them at the centre of a community. Both of them had grown up in strong family environments. Jane had her three brothers as well as the constant vigorous presence of her father and the reassurance of her mother. Now she had none of those. For William, his break was even more extreme. He had grown up not only in a large group of siblings with his parents, but also in the midst of a hugely extended family in the surrounding roads of Crosby. Suddenly, almost overnight, all that had gone. William and Jane were ready to hunker down as an isolated couple, but nothing in their upbringing had prepared them for that.

The Garston's shop, and the active trade it saw everyday serving local people, made their transition much less abrupt. They were accepted into the neighbourhood community and quickly became embraced by it. Local families were delighted to have such a store on their doorsteps, and William and Jane between them bought their stock wisely. They recognised their customers were not wealthy but that they appreciated good things.

Garston's had lots of low price items, all the staple needs of fresh sliced meats, eggs, fruit, bread, cheese and a wide selection of good quality but inexpensive tinned food. It also offered cigarettes as well as sweets and small treats for children. Jane especially worked hard to ensure that everything they stocked was good quality and represented good value. She did not sell anything she would not buy herself.

William also recognised early on that the strict approach his Crosby family had taken to providing customers with credit in the asphalt business could not be transferred to a business like Garston's. They had to recognise that, with household cash in short and often irregular supply, there were occasions when their regular customers needed time to pay.

They managed the process carefully and worked hard to ensure that no-one built up debts they could not meet, but William and Jane's account book became a well-used and well-thumbed part of the Garston's business. That they recognised this need from the outset played a big part in their becoming accepted by the Anfield customers. Families who were often struggling to make ends meet made sure they settled their bills with Garston's as their first priority as soon as they could. They needed the shop's door to stay open to them, and especially valued continued access to it when the change in their pockets ran out.

Jane was more respected than loved. She knew all the regular customers' names, but she always addressed them by their surnames. Women unused to such courtesy and formality elsewhere became Mrs Beckett, Mrs Strother and Mrs Whiting as soon as they crossed the Garston's door. Jane would greet them with a smile and was happy to exchange brief pleasantries with them, but she was never a gossip and she shared little of her own private life, and almost nothing of her thoughts, with her customers. Everyone held her in high regard, but no-one presumed so much as to call her a friend.

William, on the other hand, was an easy-going character who quickly endeared himself to the locals. With his handlebar moustache, and always sprucely turned out in his immaculate apron, he looked like a shopkeeper who could grace the Fortnum and Mason's grocery in London's Piccadilly, let alone Garston's general store in Walton Breck Road. His smart appearance, and the cleanliness and neatness of his shop, raised the spirits of the area. William visibly enjoyed his work and took an interest in the families of the men and women who shopped with them. He referred to Jane as 'The Boss' and told everyone who asked, and many of those who didn't, that she was the one who made all the important decisions in the shop. His regular joke was that there were good decisions and bad decisions made every day in Garston's, and he was in charge of the second group.

He enjoyed companiable relations with all the frequent customers and struck up close friendships with three men in particular. The four of them took up playing cards and dominoes together, wagering a shilling or two, every Thursday evening. They came from very different walks of life but enjoyed each other's easy company. George Corfield was a railway engine driver, Harold Preston was a local plumber and Seamus Scullion worked as a foreman overseer at the Liverpool port's Huskisson dock.

It was not long before William and Jane started a family of their own. The following year, Jane gave birth to their first child, a boy. She wanted to give their son his father's name so they christened him William Henry and called him both names. William the father, William Henry the son. Two years later, came a daughter, Ethel. In 1895, Jane gave birth to a third son they called Alex, and in the first year of the new century, their family was completed by the arrival of a fourth baby boy, Albert. Each of the children was christened by Canon Major Lester at St Mary's Church. In just under 14 years, William and Jane had replaced their lost families with a complete family of their own. Jane had achieved what she wanted: her own new family fully established, and her children all brought up in the Protestant faith.

The shop continued to thrive, though Everton Football Club left the Anfield stadium not long after they arrived when a new club was formed to take its place in the ground. Named Liverpool Football Club, it was established by the chairman of Everton FC, who owned the Anfield ground. John Houlding gave the Everton club notice to leave his stadium after falling out with the board of directors. The celebrated Blues had to relocate to a new ground across the nearby Stanley Park, called Goodison Park.

The new Liverpool club was run by men who were members of the Orange Lodge and it had a distinctly Protestant feel to it. They recruited their players from Scotland and were consequently referred to as the 'Team of Macs'. William and Jane rented out rooms to the new footballers who were arriving in Liverpool for the first time to play for the new team. They served many of them ginger beers from their shop after they finished their daily training sessions. Jane's Caledonian roots played especially well with the Scottish players, and Garston's quickly established itself as the shop of choice for all the team.

Liverpool played in red and white and, once again, the football-going public quickly crossed the religious divide. Liverpool FC, just as Everton FC had done, found followers from across all sectors of the city's communities.

The divided city had now developed a new rivalry in football, but one that would be played out on elite sporting fields, not through fist fights on the streets. Oranges and Greens were now to be found standing side-by-side on the terraces, cheering on lustily for the Reds or the Blues as their favourites played out their tribal battles on the football pitch against opposition from Manchester, London and the Midlands.

Eleven

One August morning, shortly before their youngest Albert's fifth birthday, a letter addressed to William arrived at the Garston's shop. When he picked it from the floor in front of the door, William immediately thought he recognised the handwriting on the envelope.

Yet such a time had elapsed since he had last seen it that he could not be quite sure. As his eye scanned the envelope looking for further clue of its sender, he saw the stamp bore a Crosby postmark. It was from his brother Jack. William returned to the kitchen table, where he had been sitting sharing a pot of tea with Jane. He opened the envelope, which contained a single page. He unfolded it and read.

Dear William

I hope this letter finds you in good health. It has been a long time. I am writing to you on our mother's behalf with some sad news. Our father passed away two weeks ago. He contracted a dose of pneumonia and I am sorry to tell you it took him quickly. We had the funeral last Saturday at Saint Peter and Saint Paul's church here. The service was very well attended and he was given a good send off. We thought you would want to know.

Before Father died, he asked me to take over the running of the business so I am now doing that. Brother Edward is of course still working hard in the firm. John and Peter Junior have joined the company now, too, so things go on.

I heard you have children. I am sure they will bring you happiness. Stay well. Good wishes

Your brother
Jack

William let the letter drop on the table and gazed at the kitchen wall, a feeling of hollowness descending over him.

"What is it, William?" asked Jane, concerned at his expressionless response. William did not reply but, with a gesture of an open hand, passed her the letter to read for herself.

Jane read it in silence before standing and embracing her husband around his shoulders from behind. She gave him her condolence.

"I am so sorry, William," she said. "Why didn't they tell you sooner so you would have had opportunity to go to see him or at least attend the funeral?"

Since William did not reply, Jane continued to fill the silence of the room. "I have to say that is bad of them and I must say it is also typical. They are all so pious and righteous about what is appropriate and what is not, but when it comes down to it, they just do what they want, no matter who it hurts. Then they trot along to ask for forgiveness on Sunday and the world is supposed just to move on. It really is too much."

William was only half hearing what his wife was saying. His mind was elsewhere. He had learned in their marriage that there was nothing to be gained by engaging her in conversation about the Catholic faith and the people who practiced it. Her views were strident and unwavering, and anything he said to counter or check them only risked adding fuel to her fire. Some might say he was passive or weak-willed to take such a stance, but William had long ago decided that there were some battles in life that were simply not worth fighting. Any small victory in argument with Jane on this topic, he had already discovered, could only be pyrrhic.

William's overriding sensation at the news of his father's death was one of emptiness. He searched in his heart for some flickering emotions of sadness or regret that he could capture and seize hold. But those faintest twinges were quickly extinguished by the reflection that, if he had really meant anything to his father, there would have been a reconciliation of some sort or at least some resumption of polite relations. He could hardly lay claim to sudden genuine feelings of grief today when they had been no interaction at all between them for almost 20 years. The physical distance between them during that time had been less than ten miles; the emotional distance had been impassable and infinite.

This letter was the first correspondence he had received from any member of the family since the day he left the family house. That was the day his relationship with them had truly ended. Christmas and birthdays had since gone unremarked.

His father's death, rather as the tone of his brother's letter had conveyed, was simply an event, an item for the diary, a formality. They were notifying him of his father's passing for the record, for his information. There was no assumption of any special bond or emotional connection, still less any real recognition of a bloodline. His entitlement was much less than that. It was not greatly more than what would be due to a passing acquaintance who might be interested to read Peter Garston's obituary in a newspaper. William had seen more emotional engagement in letters from his bank manager than he saw in that advice from his younger brother.

The narrow threshold he had crossed when he had departed Crosby to marry Jane had proved to be a chasm. He knew it, but his brother Jack's letter, with its few sparse sentences, came as a haunting cry from the other side.

Twelve

"It is altogether an anomaly and a crying evil in a Christian land that two communities whose members dwell side by side within the sound of the same bells... should in many respects be practically as wide apart as if they resided in two separate quarters of the globe."

Report of the House of Lords Select Committee on the Means of Divine Worship in Populous Places, 1850. *Comment on Liverpool.*

Relations between the Protestant and Catholic communities in Liverpool continued to deteriorate and, if anything, become even more tense. Faced with the challenges of the grinding poverty in which so many of their number continued to exist, Catholic priests, almost all of them English-born, busied themselves, creating charitable networks within the Irish Catholic community to help the most needy. The increased insularity that this brought with it only aroused further suspicion and antagonism from the Protestant side, much of it stirred by the Orange Lodge.

Connections between Belfast and Liverpool were strong, and certain firebrand preachers from Ulster, whose antipathy to their Catholic brethren was visceral, found ready audiences for their invective in Liverpool. The first of these evangelical demagogues was The Very Reverend Hugh M'Neile, an Antrim-born, fiercely anti-Catholic preacher who had been first appointed to Liverpool's St Jude's Church as a young cleric in 1834. He was appalled by the ingress of Irish Catholics that followed, and he lost no opportunity to whip up ill feeling towards the immigrant masses.

To M'Neile, the Roman Catholic Church was the enemy of Christianity and he believed the Pope to be the Antichrist. So extreme were his views that he would not bring himself to use the term 'religion' to describe Catholicism. And his call on all Protestants to wage a constant fight to oppose the Church of Rome was uncompromising. He stopped short of inciting violence against individual

Catholics, who his doctrine told him were simple, unwitting victims of a grand deception, and who needed help to find true religion. But he held poisonous views against Catholic religious rituals such as the use of wafer bread and mixing water and wine in the holy chalice during services, the wearing of priestly vestments, the practice of absolution, the making of the sign of the cross and bowing at the name of Jesus. All these practices were abominations in his eyes.

M'Neile was an articulate and powerful orator, and he had a large following in Liverpool who took his words as confirmation that popular street prejudice against Catholics was part of a righteous spiritual crusade. He had so many grounds of difference on which to bring contest with the Catholic faith that it made him a highly combustible speaker.

To men such as Tommy Gemmill, M'Neile's rhetoric gave form and dignity to their basest tribal instincts. He gave their abrasive tendencies the cloak of a great and noble cause. In practice, a great many of the men whose sectarian passions were roused by M'Neile's invective were infrequent attenders in their own Protestant churches. The details of ceremonies which took place in Catholic churches—what the priests wore, the devotional signs of the cross they made, and even confessional procedures—were matters that would never have perturbed or even crossed the minds of most of them, had they not been made such exaggerated causes of contention. But those pious differences allowed an unholy mixture of other resentments to unload and coalesce into a single undiluted loathing.

It was one of many ironies lost on most that the newly arrived Irish Catholic inhabitants of Liverpool were, in general, not very regular churchgoers themselves. Their frequency of church attendance, as distinct from that of the indigenous English Catholic middle class, such as the Garston family in Crosby who maintained a consistent and committed rate of religious practice, was very far from complete. The high church ceremonies that M'Neile railed so furiously against were, therefore, not even being witnessed by most of the ordinary Catholic residents of the city.

Another inconvenient truth that went unaddressed in M'Neile's sulphurous speeches was that the Catholic Church in England was actually a very English creation, presided over by an almost exclusively English episcopate and a predominantly English clergy. While four fifths of the Catholics in the country were now suddenly Irish by birth or descent, the Catholic Church they were deemed to be synonymous with actually had relatively little in common with them, their history or their culture. But because Irish and Catholic were deemed one and the same thing by their Protestant opponents, the very English minority Catholic Church helped to preserve a distinctive sense of Irish self-identity in Liverpool when, in practice, it had little interest in doing any such thing.

But small details such as these did not trouble the likes of M'Neile and his followers as they fomented sectarian strife. Every charge man could lay against another was laid against the Irish Catholics. They were criminals, they were filthy, they lived in squalid conditions that shamed the city and spread disease. They wanted no part of the union and were all plotting for Home Rule, they wanted to overthrow the Church of England. Public money spent on their schools and churches amounted to 'Popery on the rates'. They were feckless and idle, and almost all their working men were unskilled labourers, so there were always ten men for every job in Liverpool, and wages for ordinary good men consequently could never rise. And what was more, they were always favoured over Protestants by the police.

M'Neile, in time, moved on from Liverpool to St Paul's in London, and his departure left behind a space for a new voice of the Protestant hard-line to emerge in the city. M'Neile's brimstone pulpit was then filled by a young pastor called George Wise. Inspired by M'Neile and sharing very similar views, Wise was, if anything, still more inflammatory in his intent. He took his oratory outside his own church and into the streets, especially those that lay along the fault lines between Catholic and Protestant districts. Wise took his anti-Catholic hatred right onto the frontlines.

Thirteen

Tommy Gemmill, together with his regular drinking partner Jocky Johnstone, never missed a George Wise lecture. They became confirmed Wiseites. Since Jane had been stolen away from him by a Papist, giving vent to his anti-Catholic feelings in demonstrations and forums had become the prime purpose in Tommy's life. He was easily whipped into a fever by Wise's militant oratory, and it delighted Tommy that the pastor's outdoor addresses frequently spilled over into street violence and indiscriminate physical attacks on Irish Catholics. Any retaliation to this aggression coming from the Catholic side was met only by a redoubling of aggression and venom towards them.

Tommy still harboured a seething resentment at two Fenians who had attempted to bomb the Liverpool Town Hall, though their device in the event injured no-one and caused only mild damage to some external brickwork. He was also driven to fury when, during a Protestant parade, a small boy dressed up to represent King William was hit by a stone thrown by a Catholic protester, causing him to fall from his horse, howling in pain. A window that displayed Wise's portrait was smashed by some thugs, to Tommy's great anger. On another occasion, a Catholic mob stormed a mission hall where Wise was conducting a harvest service, leaving Tommy bursting for revenge. No incident or slight caused by Catholics was ever forgotten or forgiven. In Tommy's boiling mind, every such instance was a provocation calling for wholly justified, disproportionate, response.

Eventually, this led Tommy to start to hunger for some grander gesture that he could make to express his opposition to all things Irish Catholic. After one Wiseite demonstration, he and Jocky sat in a quiet corner of a public house near the river taking a whisky before they boarded the ferry to return home for the night.

"I've been thinking," said Tommy. "I think someone needs to do something more to take this game to the Papists. Pastor Wise is telling us every time he speaks what a threat they are to our way of life and everything we hold dear. He couldn't make the case any louder or any clearer. We all know that it's true. But what does anyone really do about it?"

"Well, you and I have given one or two of them a good hiding over the years, Tommy!" said Jocky. "You never leave any of them in much doubt what you think of them, do you?"

"That's true, but I am growing tired of all the words and the little skirmishes. I want to make some more impact. I think it is time. I want them to sit up and pay notice. I want some of them to realise, once and for all, they are not welcome here and would be better off packing their Popish bags and leaving. I want to send them a warning that they will all recognise."

"What are you thinking of?" said Jocky, craning forward.

"I'm thinking of an explosion," Jocky. "Timed to coincide just right with one of their infernal parades. So there is no doubt about what it means."

Jocky drew a deep breath and leaned back in his chair. "You're not thinking of killing people, Tommy?"

"No," said Gemmill. "There doesn't have to be any killing if it is done properly. What I want is to send a message. I want to do something to make them feel they have had a lucky escape this time, but that it won't stop there. I want to do something that will have them in fear of their lives and put some of them on the boats back where they came from."

"So are you thinking of a bomb?" asked Jocky incredulous. "Do you even know how to make a bomb? Where did you get this idea from?"

"There's a new man who just started in our yard at work. I don't know if you've come across him yet. He's been in the same gang as me for the last couple of weeks. Good man by the name of Sam McKiver. He's come from working in the Staffordshire lead mines. He was involved a bit in the blasting there. I asked him the other day whether he might be able to get access to a couple of sticks of dynamite for the right money. He told me that he might, provided there was enough in it for him. I'm going to talk to him."

From a mining contact in Staffordshire, Samuel McKiver secured two sticks of dynamite for Tommy Gemmill. He also obtained for him a percussion detonator containing mercury fulminate, and a short length of fuse wire. In return for these materials, Gemmill paid him £10.

As he handed over the bag, McKiver said, "Listen, I don't know you, or anything about this material, or why you want it, and I don't want to. I am selling it to you on the basis that you never mention my name in connection with this material, and that this transaction has never happened. You have learned from somewhere else, and not from me, how the detonator works and how to use the explosive safely. You have also learned from somewhere else what damage this quantity of dynamite could do if it is allowed to explode in the wrong place— and particularly if it explodes near people."

"Thank you Sam. All agreed." said Gemmill. "You have my solemn word I shall never mention it to a soul."

Fourteen

All Saints Day, a Holy day of Obligation in the Catholic Church, is celebrated on the first day of November. That year, 1908, saw it fall on a Sunday.

To mark the occasion, Catholics from the Scotland Road area planned to make a formal procession from their district down into the city. Their goal was to attend a special service of mass at The Chapel of St Nicholas, the church that served as the city's Catholic Procathedral. Their planned route was to descend Scotland Road, turning left as they reached the edge of the centre of the city into Hunter Street, before then turning first right onto Islington and then left into London Road. From there, they would continue straight down onto Seymour Street and finally into Copperas Hill to the Chapel.

Tommy Gemmill had selected this day as the moment to make his mark. Accompanied by his constant companion Jocky, he had selected a small alley called St Vincent Street as the place to lay his home-made device. St Vincent Street was a narrow passage running between London Road and Lord Nelson Street. The Catholic processionists would pass right in front of it just as they turned from London Road into Seymour Street in the final leg of their journey.

All Saints Day had not been favoured with kind weather. It was a cold dark overcast day, and heavy rain had threatened all morning. As Tommy and Jocky made their way early to St Vincent Street on foot from the river, the heavens opened into torrential downpour. The two men darted in and out of doorways as best they could, but there was no escaping a thorough drenching in such weather. The uncomfortable soaking conditions only added difficulty to their task of laying their device.

The weather also caused the Scotland Road processionists to change their plans. What had been intended to be a bright, flag-waving, leisurely-paced parade with an accompanying band, was no longer feasible in such storms. Instead of enjoying a joyous procession through the town, the worshippers would now want to get out of the howling wind and rain as quickly as they could. The organisers in Scotland Road, in response, announced a revision to the procession plans. They would still follow the same route, and all walk down together, but they would start half an hour later to allow people time to return home and get suitable outer clothing for the elements. Given the inclement conditions, the new timings would also give everyone a chance to cover the ground more quickly.

Tommy carried the device in a hessian bag with two handles long enough to drape over his shoulder. As he and Jocky arrived at St Vincent Street, they were encouraged by the protective half-light of the gloomy afternoon. As the rain continued to pelt down, they made their way through the alley to a point halfway down where there was a deep recess set into the brickwork. Tommy set down the bag and had Jocky stand guard over it as he walked to the other end of the street to the junction with London Road to survey the impact point that he had envisaged. There were already a few tens of people making their way down London Road in the direction of Copperas Hill, so Tommy took that as sign that the main body of the parade would be soon on its way. As he looked up the road to his right, there seemed to be thickening of the crowds, with more people joining and making their way down into the centre.

He went back to Jocky and whispered, "Let's give it ten more minutes."

As that time elapsed, Tommy could see the footfall passing the opening of St Vincent Street on London Road was increasing. It was now time. He opened the bag to give himself access to the dynamite inside. The two sticks were bound tightly together with tape, with the detonator secured between them. From the detonator, there protruded some four inches of fuse wire. McKiver had told Tommy that each inch of fuse would take about one minute to burn through, giving anyone lighting it a few minutes to vacate the scene before the flame reached the mercury in the detonator and the explosion triggered.

Stooping down low, Tommy fished into the bag for the box of Lucifer matches he had brought to light the fuse. His hand grasped the box, and he realised instantly it had been reached by the rainwater from the deluge that continued to pour down on them. He took out a match from the top layer of the box, and it crumbled instantly on contact with the striking strip. Three more matches suffered the same fate, breaking and falling to the ground at his feet. Tommy looked up and saw the crowds walking by were now building up further. His short fingers burrowed deeper into the box and he drew out a match from the middle of the pack. It felt harder, more intact, as if the seeping water had not reached it. He struck it, and it lit. He shook it out in his hand. That was all he wanted—to know that at least some of the matches would still ignite. He only needed one to do the job.

As he and Jocky crouched together, each on one knee shielding the bag between them in the dimly-lit recess, they now just had to steady themselves. Once the fuse was lit, setting off the brief few moments before the explosion would hit, they needed to stand up smartly, walk briskly down to the bottom of the alley, out into the main road and into the crowd, and then, without drawing attention to themselves, ensure they were far enough away from the seat of the explosion to be at a safe distance. And all that within two minutes.

"Are you ready then, Jocky?" Tommy whispered to his co-conspirator. "Aye, Tommy, when you are." he replied. Tommy drew breath and reached back into the Lucifer pack. He took out a match that again seemed to have escaped the ingress of water. He prepared to strike it.

At that moment, the two conspirators heard a sudden huge commotion coming from behind them, from the direction of the Lord Nelson Street end of the alley.

"Hoi! You two! Stop there! Police!" went up the deafening shout.

They turned and, to their horror, they saw the cry was coming from a mounted policeman on a huge grey horse that seemed almost to occupy the full width of the alley behind them. The horse was careering towards them at full tilt, the policeman blowing his whistle as he came. Jocky didn't need any invitation. He snatched the bag out of Tommy's hands and ran, getting to the Seymour Street end of the alley and disappearing out into the crowd before the horse reached Tommy. Gemmill's reactions seemed momentarily dulled by the shock of what was happening. The high pitched shrieking of the policeman's whistle, the din of the shouting, and the horrific sight of the great beast approaching him fast, rainwater splashing off its head and its sides, all combined to transfix him to the spot.

Suddenly he recovered his senses, freed himself from the instant of paralysis and turned around and ran full pelt in the direction in which Jocky had disappeared.

"You! Stop there now!" roared the mounted policeman behind him. Tommy paid him no heed and hurtled forward as fast as he could. "Stop! Police!" came the cry for the third time.

Tommy was now at the verge of the junction with the main road and was preparing to dive out into the crowd when his exit was suddenly barred by the massive presence of a second police horse being hard driven up into the alley by its rider, who was clearly responding to his colleague officer's cries and whistling. Running as fast as he could, and seeing his path suddenly blocked without warning by such a huge obstacle, caused Tommy's step to falter, and the sole of his right boot slid on the soaking cobblestone underfoot. He started to fall forward into the path of the horse. The animal reared, frightened by the threat of the headlong rush of the falling man before him, just as it was adjusting into its hard turn into the unknown narrow alleyway. The horse's front legs flailed in panic into the air and, as they did, its rising left hoof found thundering connection with the falling Tommy's head.

The force of the blow was quite enough on its own to have broken his skull. But as he dropped, Tommy fell under the panic-stricken horse, which was desperately trying to recover firm ground. As the animal tried to bring its hooves back down onto the stones, it succeeded only in catching Tommy's head twice more with the full force of its weight. Gemmill's already lifeless body lay crumpled on the ground as the two policemen, arriving together from either end of the alley, dismounted at speed to attend to him. It was immediately clear from the bloodied mass of his face and head, with his blood already flowing heavily into the gullies between the cobbles and mingling into the still driving rain, that there was already nothing to be done for him.

Jocky Johnstone, the feverish sweat pouring from his forehead being flushed away in the storm, walked as steadily and calmly as he could manage among the crowd making their way to the church. He did not know whether the contents of the bag over his shoulder would go off at any moment. He did not know whether Tommy had been successful in sparking the fuse alight, or whether the dynamite might just explode at any second anyway without warning. What he did know was that, if he was caught with it or seen disposing of the bag, he would likely face a very long prison sentence or maybe even the gallows. He had had the presence of mind to take the bag from Tommy and to get quickly away. He had had the presence of mind not to run and make it obvious he was escaping from the law. He had managed to meld into the moving crowd without arousing suspicion. He hoped Tommy would not be far behind him and that he had not been apprehended by the police. If Tommy had been arrested, it wouldn't be long before the police would come looking for him. He realised that he must get rid of the bag, but he had to do it safely without being noticed by anyone before he was stopped.

Jocky parted from the crowds as they headed round to St Nicholas' and walked as robustly as he dared, without breaking into a run though that was what every fibre of his being wanted to do, through the still pouring rain down towards the river. As he did, he caught sight of pile of large stones on the kerbside. Pausing and turning around quickly to make sure he wasn't being observed, he stepped over to them. Dropping to his knee for five seconds before rising again, he picked up two of the heavier stones and slipped them unnoticed by any onlooker into the bag. They transformed the weight of the sack at once, and it now hung heavily on him, biting into his shoulder.

Jocky continued to walk on down the dock road towards the ferry, soaked through to his skin and terrified of being apprehended with the damning evidence still in his possession. At last, his temples pounding, he reached the waterside and, walking beyond the landing stage where the ferry would dock, he moved 100 yards further along the riverside. The rain continued to lash down, agitating the black river water in the descending gloom.

Finally, when he judged it safe, after looking furtively all around him to be sure he was not being watched, he took the bag from his shoulder and tied its two handles tightly together into a single knot that hard fastened over the opening. Gripping the large knot in his fist, Jocky held his arm out over the retaining wall and dropped the bag into the River Mersey. He leaned over to witness it hitting the water, breathing out heavily for the first time in many minutes as he saw it plunge instantly to the depths below.

Fifteen

The tragic incident had occurred too late to be reported in the next day's publications. The following morning, however, it was on all the front pages.

At seven o'clock, William's first task of the day at Garston's was always to pick up the parcel of newspapers that was hurled onto their front step in the early hours by the newstrade distributor from his horse-drawn cart. As William cut open the string binding the package containing their usual selection of daily papers for sale, his eye went straight to a story on the front page of the *Liverpool Daily Post*.

Orangeman dies at Catholic parade

By a Daily Post reporter

A prominent Orange Lodge official was killed in mysterious circumstances during the Catholic All Saints' Day parade in central Liverpool on Sunday.

Thomas 'Tommy' Gemmill, aged 60, the secretary of the Birkenhead Orange Lodge branch, was trampled to death by a police horse in St Vincent Street as Irish worshippers processed towards The Chapel of St Nicholas for a service of mass.

Sergeant Walter Ion of Liverpool Police said Mr Gemmill fell under his horse as he came running out of St Vincent Street towards London Road. A second policeman, Constable Arthur Mellor, who was also mounted on horseback, had called out to Mr Gemmill and another man to hold their ground when he discovered them in St Vincent Street.

Constable Mellor said, "I saw two men crouching in the gloom in the alley and I wanted to know what business they had there. I called out to them to halt where they were."

On hearing the constable's instruction, one of the men immediately ran off and disappeared into the crowd. He was followed by Mr Gemmill who appeared to slip on the wet ground at the end of the alley. This caused him to stumble and he fell under Sergeant Ion's horse, which was at that moment entering St Vincent Street from the direction of London Road.

"Your eggs are ready, William! You're supposed to be folding those newspapers for the rack, not reading them. You're not back in the Picton Reading Room now!" Jane called out from the kitchen.

"Just a second, my love," William replied quietly, as he returned to the final paragraphs of the article.

Police obtained no description of the second man, who was seen fleetingly with Mr Gemmill before the accident and have asked the public for any information to help find him.

Tommy Gemmill was an active member of the Orange Lodge in Birkenhead and a respected official of that institution. He was known to hold strong Protestant beliefs.

He leaves a widow, Mary, aged 58.

William made his way into the kitchen holding a copy of the paper out of the way low down by his side. Jane's back was turned as she finished off frying the eggs on the stove. The family was assembling around the breakfast table. William Henry, now come of age and working as a legal clerk, looking characteristically neat and tidy in his starched shirt and immaculate bow tie, was sitting at the table poring over an arithmetic book trying to help his 12-year-old brother Alex solve an intractable homework problem. Ethel, 14, tidily dressed, already brushed smart and ready for school, was seeing to young Albert, at eight years old his hair still unruly from his bed, his shirt not properly fastened and his socks still askew around his ankles, boots not yet on. It was just the normal beginning of a normal family day.

Jane was spooning out the eggs onto six plates when William went up close to her and said quietly. "There is something you need to see, love." Turning to his eldest children, he said. "Will, Ethel, could you finish off what your mother is doing here, please. Just put ours under a couple of plates."

Jane was about to protest that what could be so important that it couldn't wait for them to have their breakfast first, when she saw the look on William's face as he pointed her towards the sitting room. She patted down her apron and went through. William closed the door behind them and gestured for her to sit down.

"It's your father, Jane. You had better read this."

Jane took the paper and read the short article, her left hand covering her mouth as she read. When she finished, she let the paper fall and sat grim faced, her eyes glazed with tears. She said nothing.

"I am so sorry, Jane," said William.

"Well that's it then," she said finally. "I shan't see him again now. He was a good father to me. He helped me to become who I am. He had his principles and he stuck to them. That never made him easy company but, I tell you what, I'd rather trust somebody with principles than someone without them."

She dabbed her eyes briefly with her handkerchief, looked up at William and, composing herself, said, "Life goes on. Let's go and have those eggs before they spoil."

Sixteen

The police had little or nothing to go on. They found five spent matchsticks trodden underfoot in the puddles in St Vincent Street but nothing else. Neither of the two officers involved had seen the face of Gemmill's companion nor noticed anyone joining into the passing crowd at the busy scene. They telephoned Cammell Lairds as Gemmill's employer, having found his union card in his pocketbook. They asked his foreman whether Gemmill had any particular friends at the yard who might know anything about who he might have been with on the fateful day. The foreman told them that Jocky Johnstone was certainly his closest mate in the yard, and they were welcome to come to talk to him if they wished.

Sergeant Ion and Constable Mellor went across to the Lairds' yard in Birkenhead and met Johnstone in the canteen. He was obviously very upset to have read the news of his friend's death. But he knew nothing of the circumstances and he hadn't seen Tommy since the end of the Saturday morning shift, he told them.

"So you weren't with him in Liverpool on Sunday afternoon, then?" Sergeant Ion asked.

"No, I wasn't, Sergeant," came the reply.

"So where were you on Sunday?"

"I was at home," said Jocky. "The weather was filthy all day. I just rested up at home, finished off a good bottle of whisky and got myself an early night."

"Is there someone who can vouch for that?" asked Constable Mellor.

"Not really," said Jocky, in a matter of fact tone. "I live alone and I didn't go out. It was raining cats and dogs all day. Who would want to go out in that unless they had to? Lucky it was a Sunday, and I could stay inside. I wouldn't have wanted to be out working in that rain."

"Did Tommy tell you he was going to Liverpool on Sunday?" ventured the Sergeant.

"No, but then again he wasn't generally in the habit of sharing his travel plans with me."

"Can you think of anyone he might have been with?" asked the Constable, who was fast running out of questions.

At this, Jocky Johnstone leaned back in his chair and his face cracked into a grin.

"What is this? Some sort of parlour game? Alfie, Billy, Charlie? Danny, Eddy, Fred? Maybe his neighbour or his cousin or someone he just met? No, Constable I cannot. Presumably, it could have been anybody?"

The officers were silenced by his words. They went right to the heart of the hopelessness of their quest. Jocky leaned forward to press home his advantage.

"Let me tell you something now, gentlemen. From what I read in the papers, it sounds as though it was your horse that killed Tommy Gemmill, Sergeant Ion. I lost a good friend and workmate on Sunday. A decent British Protestant man who died at the hands of the British police while they were escorting an Irish Catholic march right into the heart of a British city."

"It is you who should be answering questions about that, Sergeant Ion, not wasting people's time playing guessing games. But, of course, you won't be, will you, because it doesn't work like that does it?"

"Now if you have no more questions for me," said Jocky, "I have a job to hold down here and I am letting my gang down outside while I'm sitting in here talking with you."

The policemen closed their notebooks. "Good day officers," said Johnstone, as he rose from his chair and left the room.

That interview concluded the police investigation into the circumstances surrounding the unfortunate accident leading to the death of Tommy Gemmill. The police had been seen to make due inquiries. They had been unable to find the identity of the missing second man. That trail was completely cold. There was no suggestion of any wrongdoing by either policeman, who corroborated each other's versions of what had taken place. No crime had been committed nor reported. It was recorded as a death by misadventure.

There was nothing further to be added. The case was therefore closed.

A few days later, Jane received a letter from Elizabeth.

My dear Jane

I was so sorry to read the news of your father's death. It must be so upsetting for you to have lost him so suddenly in such tragic circumstances. I know you have not been in contact with one another so I can only imagine that must make it even more difficult. I'm sending you all my love and kindest wishes. I have such fond memories of your father when we were all together in Glasgow. He loved you so much and was so very proud of you. I remember the look on his face when you got the job in the Cambuslang library. He was properly fit to burst. He was such a good friend to my dear father too. I do hope they are together in Heaven now. God rest both their souls.

I don't know if this is good timing given the sadness of what has happened and please just tell me if it is not but I am writing also to tell you that my daughter Janet has got wed. She has married a lovely young man called Archie Rogers who works in something to do with photographs. You will surely understand it all much better than I but he is what they call a process engraver. It sounds all very technical and skilled. Anyway, small world! Archie is a Liverpool man. He lives in his own house in Toxteth and he and Janet are setting up their married home there. I imagine that cannot be so far away from where you are?

I wondered if you would mind if I gave Janet your address? She doesn't know anyone in the city other than Archie of course and I thought it would be nice if she could bring him to meet you and William and your family one afternoon? I know you are terribly busy in the shop on Saturdays with all the football custom so maybe one Sunday afternoon if you weren't doing anything else? Let me know if that would ever be convenient for you. I'm sure you'll want to leave it a while for the moment but it would be lovely if you could get together one day.

Meanwhile, life goes on here. I am delighted for Janet that she is starting out a new life. She is very happy and she so deserves it. For my part that leaves me with just the two boys now. Both of them are dead set on joining the army as soon as they're allowed. They are so committed to it I cannot stand in their way. They would not pay any attention to me even if I tried! Donald has been out of that Industrial School for six months now and it seems he is gradually coming out of himself. He was really very quiet in the early months I had him home. He still says very little about his time there. I hope all will work out for him. I still feel such an awful guilt about it all.

I hope William is well and the children are thriving. How wonderful for you to have a 21 year-old son! I am sure William Henry is a great pride to you.

Write soon to tell me your news and to let me know about Janet. My sincere condolences again Jane for the loss of your dear father.

Your ever friend Elizabeth

Three days later, Elizabeth was delighted to receive a reply from Jane by return.

Dear Elizabeth

Thank you so much for your kind letter. It was a sad day for sure. I had such fond memories of him too but of course these last years since William we'd not be in touch. Such is life I suppose. The world moves on. It is nice to think of him and your father back together again up there.

We'd be delighted to see Janet again and to meet Archie of course. Shall we say next Sunday afternoon at three o'clock? We will have the kettle on ready for them!

Love Jane

Seventeen

As the sitting room clock struck three the following Sunday, the Garstons' front door bell rang. It was Janet and her new husband.

"Hello, Aunt Jane," said the visitor on the step. "It's Janet, Elizabeth's daughter." Archie shyly shook Jane and William's hands and introduced himself, too. "It's Archie, Archie Rogers, Mr and Mrs Garston. I'm honoured to meet you both." He had brought a large bunch of blue delphiniums for Jane and, as he handed them to her, confirmed instantly a place for himself in her good books. Janet had also brought an offering. "Aunt Jane, I've made you a cherry cake," she said. "How delicious," said William eagerly taking it from her. "I think we have a few people through here who will be very pleased to help us with that!"

They showed Janet and Archie into the front room where the whole family was gathered in their Sunday best to greet them. "Come and say hello to William Henry, to Ethel and to Alex and Albert," said Jane.

Over tea and Janet's cherry cake, which met with universal acclaim, the conversation flowed freely. Archie told the story of how he and Janet had met and of his work in photographic production. They spoke of their wedding and their new life together in Archie's Toxteth house.

"How are you finding Liverpool, Janet?" asked Jane. "All very different from Scotland I imagine. Are you missing Dundee?"

Janet paused, and the family noticed her look shyly at Archie before responding.

"Of course, I do miss Mother and Donald and David, but I was very glad to leave Dundee, Aunt Jane. It was not an easy life there for any of us and I am pleased to be somewhere new. I am hoping that Mother and the boys will come down and join us here one day, but that's for the future."

"Have you managed to make yourself comfortable here then, Janet?" asked William.

"I'm so pleased to be here with Archie, of course, and the house is lovely. But I must say I find Liverpool quite an angry place," Janet replied.

"Since we've been here, there have been quite a few disturbances, and I don't feel happy going out at night time. Dundee certainly had its problems, and you're used to a bit of strife, but here it seems a bit worse. The Protestant and Catholic problems really didn't seem to exist in Dundee. There were a lot of Irish women working in the mills, of course, but everyone mixed in together pretty well. Here it seems as if there are different parts of the city where people live, depending on who you are, and there's regular fights and even some rioting go on. I don't much like any of that, I must say."

It was Ethel who spoke next. "Yes it's a real problem here, Janet, I agree. It's because there are so many Irish here that the city has got very overcrowded and un…"

"Look out! Here she goes!" said William Henry, cutting across his younger sister. "You've started something now, Janet! Ethel has some quite firm views you'll find!"

"Yes, well," interrupted Jane, "there is a time and place for everything. We do know what you mean, Janet. Liverpool is not always an easy place to live and it does have its troubles. Might you think of moving somewhere else one day, do you think?"

It was Archie who took the opportunity to reply. "My work is based in the city, Mrs Garston, though I imagine it would be possible to move somewhere new with the skills I have in due course. But we are thinking about going across the river to be honest. Janet loves the beach and the seaside attractions in New Brighton. We might sell up and move over to Wallasey. It would be easy enough to get over to this side on the ferry for my work, and the atmosphere there is very different. We are thinking it might suit the two of us a bit better."

"Ah!" said Jane, "what an interesting idea. I used to live that way when I first came to this part of the world, and I thought it was lovely. I must say I think it is a nicer place to be than here in the middle of the city. Not so many people for a start. A bit more civilised.

Who's for another slice of this lovely cake?"

William, keen to change the subject, asked Archie if he followed football. He replied that, yes, he was an enthusiastic supporter. "So are you a Blue or a Red, Archie?" asked Alex.

"I'm a Red," said Archie. "What about you, Alex?"

"Boo! I'm a Blue!" he replied. "Hooray, Archie, I'm a Red like you!" chimed in young Albert. "Up the Reds!"

William said, "We were all Blues when we first came here because the ground opposite was Everton's. We're almost all Reds now though, aren't we, Jane?"

"Absolutely!" came her reply.

"Who's your favourite player then, Mother?" asked Alex mischievously.

"I don't know… what's the name of that nice Scottish captain of theirs? Alex somebody?"

"It's Alex Raisbeck, Mother!" said Albert. "He comes in the shop sometimes."

"Oh yes!" said Alex. "Whenever Raisbeck comes in for a ginger beer, Mother is always the first to jump up to serve him." "Oh yes Mr Raisbeck, do sit down Mr Raisbeck, here you are Mr Raisbeck, thank you Mr Raisbeck!"

"That's quite enough of your cheek, young man!" said Jane blushing and cuffing her son over the head with a smile.

Janet and Archie stayed for almost two hours, comfortable in the welcoming company of the Garston household, before they made their farewells.

"Thank you both so much for coming, it was lovely to see you Janet and to meet you Archie. And thank you for the flowers and the delicious cake," said Jane.

"Come on then, Gladys, time for me to get you home," said Archie as they moved to the door.

"Gladys?" said Jane, "who's Gladys?"

"It's what he calls me, Aunt Jane," said Janet embarrassedly. "He says I look like Gladys Cooper!"

"She does," said Archie, "but this one's even better looking!" They all laughed as they waved goodbye.

"Who's Gladys Cooper?" asked Albert when the door had closed.

Eighteen

Over the course of the following year, 1909, sectarian tension and aggression in Liverpool was reaching crisis point. The divided city found itself ensnared in a vicious descending circle, in which provocation was met with violence, which triggered retaliation, which in turn gave rise to further provocation.

The rabble-rousing George Wise continued to send out his haranguing messages of hate from his public meetings, and his voice was doubled by a second splenetic lecturer named John Kensit, who took a vehement anti-ritualism platform to preach his own brand of anti-Catholic hatred. Outbreaks of violence became so frequent and recurrent that all connection to specific cause was eventually lost. Wise was imprisoned for four months for causing public disorder. Some 100,000 of his followers walked with him to the prison to proclaim his martyrdom. Furious at his incarceration, they then plunged headlong into further violence and troublemaking in response.

During the course of the summer, the Provincial Grand Lodge of the Orange Order organised a counter demonstration to a Catholic procession that broke up into a wholesale riot. Hundreds from both sides of the divide were arrested for assaults and waves of vandalism in the weeks that followed.

For the Garston family, life in Liverpool was becoming increasingly disquieting. Ethel, in particular, was starting to be much disturbed by what was taking place. She read voraciously, scouring each day's papers for reports of the latest incidents of violence and affray, the arrests, the court cases, the imprisonments. She had inherited her mother's uncompromising views of the rights and wrongs of the issue, and she read into every article some further confirming reason to condemn the Catholic population of the city. But her absorption in the whole subject was also making her increasingly nervous about the family's safety.

"It feels like we are living in a war here, Mother," she said one day. "I fear for you and Father and the rest of the family. I fear for myself. I don't want to go over the door any more, and certainly not alone." A talented musician and pianist, Ethel had gained admission to the London School of Music. She had begun earning good money to put away to fund her forthcoming studies by giving pianoforte lessons to local children and some of their mothers. That meant she did not have to leave the house for her work. It also meant she was in danger of becoming imprisoned by her fears.

The final straw came late one evening in September when someone threw a brick through the Garston's shop window. The whole family was already in bed, but William and William Henry were down the stairs quickly, ready to tackle any intruder. They found no-one. The incident was the first serious problem they had ever had at the shop, but the family saw it as a telling sign.

William Henry tried his best to calm the situation. "It could have been just a mindless piece of vandalism. It might have been children out playing dare, or some drunk out of his mind on the whisky. We've been very lucky so far never to have had any problem. Let's not get too upset by it."

"That's just it, Will!" cried Ethel, clinging tearfully to her mother. "We've been lucky so far, but we aren't going to be lucky any more. It could have been vandalism, but do you read the papers? Do you know what is going on? It could also be a warning, and who is to say it won't happen again and be much worse next time? You don't have to ask me to know who I think did it, and I know they will be back."

William sent the family back to bed and swept up the piles of broken glass from the floor. He hammered in six planks of wood as best he could across the window frame to cover the gaping aperture. He then put on his coat and sat in guard of their vulnerable shop for the night.

"I think it is time, William," said Jane the following morning. "It's enough. We need to go."

That Thursday evening, William sat down to his usual card game. That week, it was the turn of Seamus Scullion, the dock foreman, to host him and their two friends, the engine driver George and plumber Harold.

"I've some news and something to ask you about, Seamus," said William. "We're thinking of not renewing the shop lease and moving over to Wallasey. Jane is not happy being over here any longer with all the trouble that's going on. William Henry could get to his work in the city from there on the ferry, and so can young Alex, who just started out last month at a fruit brokers in town. But that leaves me. I need to think about what I am going to do next. I was wondering about dock work. What do you think?"

"I hope we aren't going to lose you from the Thursday card school!" cried Seamus, shocked at the sudden news. He was quickly reassured by William that no such thing would happen.

"Well, what can I tell you? The employment, as you know, is all casual. Men turn up and wait on stands every morning in the hope of getting picked for work that day. Each dock has got its own stand. My dock is the Huskisson, and it's my job as foreman there to select the men we need for the day. It's done in half-day shifts, but I usually only hire men in the afternoon if we are busier than we thought, or if some of the men we took on in the morning need replacing. I have my regular men who I pick out every day and then I select some extras where we need them. The work is quite heavy, and you have to keep your wits about you loading and unloading cargo from the ships. There are lots of things moving around, and daydreamers can easily get hurt. But it's certainly not bad money, if you work regularly."

"How much do you pay?" asked William.

Seamus smiled. "I have been there for 20 years and the pay has never once changed. And it never changed for the 20 years before I arrived either. That's because, even though the docks are all usually very busy, there are always far more men turning up seeking work than there is work for us to give out. So the employers in the port have never had to raise the wages. They know they'll be turning away dozens of available men literally every shift. So there's no need for them to pay any more. It's four and six a day. Not much if you only get one shift in a week, but if you are working five and a half days full out, it's well over a pound a week—one pound, four and nine. It all depends if you're a regular or not."

"How do you get to be one of those?" asked William.

"If you were serious about this, William, you would come on my stand because I know you and I would pick you out on a regular basis. If we didn't have work for whatever reason, I could also get you work on one of the other docks with friends of mine who run their stands. So you could bank on a pound a week and more. You would need a union card, though. I always pick union men first. I could help arrange that for you, though, too."

"You don't think I'm too old for the work do you? I'm 46 now, you know." William asked.

"No, we take men of all ages. The older ones are usually the ones who get the pace and the rhythm right. It's not about running around like a mad thing doing everything double quick to show how tough you are. The ones who try to do twice as much as they should don't last. The bright ones soon learn. You're going to get four and six for the shift whatever you do, so you work the normal pace. Just like Goldilocks, not too fast and not too slow!" said Seamus laughing.

"Are there ways people can get on and earn a bit more then, Seamus?" interjected George.

"That's one of the bad things about it," Seamus replied. "There are no prospects for anyone on the docks. You either get the work that day or you don't, and it is what it is. Then you come back the next day and hope you're lucky again. That way they keep all the workers in their place. That's why you've got to know someone on the stands who can help you."

"I imagine there must be a few shillings greasing palms on the QT to make that happen?" said Harold.

"There is, unfortunately," said Seamus. "Believe it or not, I have never accepted a penny from anyone. It's dirty money and I couldn't take bread from another man's table that way. You do see some of the foremen leaving on Saturday afternoon with their pockets bulging with bribe money, though. I have nothing to do with the bent ones. You soon see who's straight and who's not."

"How does it all work with regard to religion?" asked William.

"Again, it differs from dock to dock. Some of the foremen who are hard Protestants operate an informal NINA policy: No Irish Need Apply. But other docks have appointed Irish foremen, and they tend to go the other way and give all the work to Irish. Some of the docks, mine is one of those, are open to all comers, mixed. They just try to get good men and don't worry which pub they drink at."

"So, William, that's the story." said Seamus. "If that money appeals, and you can put up with going through the morning stand hire shenanigans every day, then you should consider it. It's a simple life, you're responsible for yourself and the others on your team, and that's it. You do your shift, you go home. Come back the next day and do it again. If that is what you want to do next, I'll be happy to help you."

"Thank you kindly, Seamus, I think that is very interesting. I might well take you up on that offer," said William.

"Now what's it to be? Hearts or Whist, gentlemen?"

Nineteen

The Garstons moved to a house in Kingsley Road, in the Poulton district of Wallasey, in the spring of the year 1910. While it had not been pre-arranged, their new home was not far from Janet and Archie Rogers' new home in Morley Road.

William took up Seamus's offer of help and began to present himself for hire at the Huskisson dock. True to his word, Seamus picked him out from the stand each morning, and William quickly accustomed himself to the work. He was tall, strong and fit, and muscles he realised he had not used since his contracting days on the asphalt were surprisingly soon reactivated. It was unskilled labour in that supposedly anyone could do it, but it still required precision, strength, constant attentiveness and an ability to work cohesively in a small team. William found he rather enjoyed it. The money for five and half days work was almost as much as he and Jane had taken out of the shop between them but, with none of the worries of the ordering, the stock-keeping, the book-keeping and watching the bank balances, on top of actually running the shop and serving the customers. When he walked off shift now, his day's work was done. As Seamus had promised, it was a nice simple life.

William travelled over to Liverpool every morning on the busy Seacombe ferry with William Henry and the new young apprentice fruit broker Alex.

William Henry, who was now 24 years old, was progressing well with his work. He was employed in a clerical capacity in the General Post Office in its very grand newly opened city centre building on Victoria Street. His profile in the organisation had been raised greatly in the last few months after he entered a national handwriting competition and, to his great pleasure and surprise, was awarded second prize. The results of the competition were reported in the *London Times*.

His managers were highly delighted to have a national prize-winner suddenly in their midst, and the work he was then given to complete had become both more various and more interesting, as he became revered as the office penman. Whenever a special notice, a certificate or an official contract needed to be crafted, it was to William Henry they now turned first. His departmental manager, Mr Arthur Potts, had also recognised William Henry's achievement by raising his weekly wage by one shilling to thirteen shillings and sixpence.

Outside of work, William Henry's life was a little quiet. He was an easy-going young man, his father's son, and he enjoyed his family life. Now they had moved from the shop and out of Liverpool, though, he was beginning to get a stronger sense of having outgrown the family nest. Wallasey and New Brighton were pleasant enough residential places, with some attractive family entertainment spots, but he missed the restless hubbub of Liverpool. For all its problems while he was there, he had felt he was living in the middle of things. He now felt, all of a sudden, distinctly suburban.

It was also striking him that the abrupt break from the Walton Breck Road house and shop that he had grown up in had had another dislocating effect for him. At 24 years of age, William Henry now felt like an overgrown schoolboy in the Kingsley Road house.

While they were all running Garston's together he would regularly work in the shop on Saturdays and, in the evenings, he would happily help his parents count the takings of the day and bag cash for the bank, as well as do various other writing and accounting jobs wherever they were needed. He realised now that part of his identity had been about being the eldest son in a family business. That was suddenly no longer there. Instead of him growing quickly accustomed to his new surroundings, they now seemed to him empty and faintly repellent. He did not really have a role any more, whereas he had never had cause to question that before.

He also found the religious discussions in the house increasingly trying. His mother at times, and now his sister, were both strident and presumptive in their views and their statements. Their moral certitude and their various disapprovals troubled him and, if anything, drew him to taking the opposite view to them, almost whatever that entailed. Things were not generally black and white to William Henry. There were always alternative views, different shades to consider. The concept that some people were Good and some people were Evil actually seemed to him ridiculous. People were just people, they had their good sides and their less good sides, their good days and their bad days. You had to get to know them. Some people you'd like more than others. You had to learn to take the rough with the smooth. Life was not a strip cartoon. People were not caricatures.

William Henry had taken to treating himself to a lunch once a week on a Friday. He liked to buy himself a newspaper and find a quiet place for a small hot meal away from the office, with the luxury of a bit of time and space to enjoy it. When he arrived at work this particular Friday morning, he was immediately summoned to Mr Potts' room.

"Come in, William Henry, and do sit down," said the usually doleful clerical manager looking, for him, most uncharacteristically cheerful. After 36 years with the same department in the General Post Office, first as a clerk and then as a clerical manager, it now took a great deal to excite Cecil Potts. His long GPO race was nearly run, but today he seemed very animated.

"William Henry, I have some splendid news to impart! You have come to the attention of the general manager Mr W. T. Armitage himself. He was made aware of your success in the national handwriting competition, and he asked personally to see samples of your work for the department. I am delighted to tell you that he was most impressed. He is proposing to promote you! He wants to create a new position of GPO calligrapher especially for you. You will be doing all the important writing tasks for the whole of the Liverpool General Office. You are to be granted a short audience with Mr Armitage on the top floor on Monday morning at nine fifteen prompt to welcome you to your new position. He has asked me to tell you that it will carry a raised salary of £42 pounds a year. That is 16 shillings a week, William Henry! Congratulations to you, Mr Garston, your success reflects very well on you, on this department and, if I may say so, in my own small way on myself as your manager. I think you are the very first person ever to be promoted out of this department during my entire time here, so this really is a most special day. You should feel very proud."

William Henry thanked Mr Potts profusely and went to his desk to take stock of his new situation. What a delightful surprise! This was certainly progress. He decided straight away he would treat himself to a special lunch today. He would go to the Adelphi Hotel, quite the grandest venue in the whole city, and order himself a celebratory meal. If you couldn't celebrate on a day like this, then when could you?

Full of the positive bonhomie that tends to be engendered in recipients of recognition and gratitude, William Henry handed in his hat and coat at the Adelphi cloakroom and made his way through to the restaurant. It was a truly spectacular room, lavishly decorated with chandeliers and adorned with ionic columns, marble panelling and grand arches. William Henry felt his shoes sinking softly into the thick pile of its luxuriant Turkish carpet as he walked across the room. He was shown to his table by the maître d'hôtel, guided most solicitously into his chair, and presented with the day's menu. The hotelier inquired whether he might bring sir a glass of champagne while he was making his selections. William Henry, on the verge of automatically declining, caught himself at the right moment somehow forgetting that this was supposed to be his day of great celebration. He accepted as though a glass of champagne with his lunch was quite the most normal thing in the world. As he surveyed the room over the top of the menu, sipping at the perfectly chilled bubbles, William Henry felt as though he was walking on air.

Suddenly a young waitress in black uniform with a white apron over came up to the table with her notebook and pencil at the ready. "Good afternoon, Mr Garston, may I help you with your choices, sir?"

William was momentarily startled, wondering how on earth the young woman knew his name. Had he met her before somewhere? He looked at her smiling face and said, "Do we know each other, Miss?"

As the words left his mouth, he realised he had been asked to give his name at the front desk when he'd requested a table. The waitress would, of course, have been given the names of all the guests seated at her tables. This was by far the grandest place he had ever been.

"I'm sure not, sir," said the waitress blushing. "I do hope I have pronounced your name correctly."

William Henry suddenly became aware of the young woman's pretty features. Her hair, which fell in dark luxuriant curls under her white lace cap, her small and, he thought, very kissable retroussé nose, the bright grey eyes and her shy, soft-lipped smile. He wasn't sure whether it was the happy occasion, the grandeur of his surroundings, the champagne or her physical presence—or perhaps some intoxication of all four—but he found himself thinking, she was possibly the loveliest thing he had ever seen.

Recovering his composure, but without losing eye contact with her for a second, he said "You pronounced it quite perfectly. I wondered for a moment whether we had met before but, if we have not, then I am so very pleased to meet you now."

"Honoured I'm sure, sir," the young woman replied. "May I ask if you have made your selections?"

William Henry looked down at the menu and saw the "Adelphi's celebrated turtle soup, made from turtles kept live on the premises." This was clearly to be a day of firsts, so he ordered a bowl of that to begin with, followed by a roast beef and gravy with vegetables. He also ordered himself a glass of claret to accompany his feast.

"Will that be all, sir?" asked the waitress, noting it down.

"One more thing, if I may," said William Henry. "May I know your name?"

"Of course, sir," she replied, smiling at him. "My name is Fanny. Fanny Inglis. I will be back directly with your luncheon."

They flirted lightly with each other throughout the meal. The waitress playful and witty but always politely deferential to the hotel guest, as her role required. William Henry increasingly drawn to her, wanting more. When he came to ask her for his account to settle, he barely noticed that his lunch had cost him more than six shillings.

"Would you come out with me?" he asked her, as he put down a ten-shilling note on the small salver she had laid in front of him. "There are two films showing at the Palais de Luxe in Lime Street this week. They are showing *Ben Hur*, and there is a new comedy to precede it called *The Blue Bird*, which is supposed to be very funny. Have you seen them?"

"I have not," said Fanny. "But I should love to. I have never been to a picture house."

Twenty

William Henry and Fanny's relationship galloped away over the next weeks. Two young people with not so much experience of the opposite sex, they found themselves quickly besotted with one another. They decided quickly together that they had found true love. They were also both of an age when decisions about the future could be made—and needed to be made. Fanny was living alone in lodgings in Liverpool. William Henry was, increasingly awkwardly, still in his parents' home in Wallasey. Both their situations were ripe for change.

Fanny had long since left her parents behind in Holyhead in Wales to come to Liverpool. She wrote to them once a month to stay in touch, but she was very much her own woman. Her new relationship with William Henry was not a matter for her parents' approval or otherwise. She made her own decisions in matters of the heart, as in other things now. She would let her parents know of her new relationship in her own time, when she was good and ready.

For William Henry, still living at home, the communication of his relationship with Fanny to his parents was a rather more pressing and problematic matter. This was chiefly because of one significant issue.

Inconveniently, Fanny was a Catholic.

William Henry tried to describe to Fanny as best he could the strong religious convictions of his family and, most particularly, his mother. He realised as he tried to convey it that he found it tricky to explain. His own approach to most aspects of life was comparatively so calm and balanced that he was a poor man to articulate an extreme position that was not based on evident sound reason. He did his best to do the attitude some justice but recognised, as he heard his own words fall from his lips, that some of it must sound almost incomprehensible, even laughable. It was, though, no laughing matter.

Fanny listened carefully but she could hardly imagine any of this was going to be much of a problem, given how down to earth and relaxed about most things William Henry was, and especially given the fact that she herself was very far from a doctrinaire or even devout Catholic. It had been some time since she'd even been over a church threshold, she reflected, with a slight twinge of guilt.

William Henry resolved in time that the moment had come to broach the news with his parents. He was not sure quite how it would be received, but he took the opportunity to raise the matter one mid evening when he had them alone after the evening meal in the Kingsley Road dining room.

"Mother and Father may I tell you something."

"Yes, of course, dear. What is it?"

"I am in a relationship with a lovely young woman. Her name is Fanny."

"That is marvellous news, William Henry! We are so pleased. Can we meet her?"

"Yes, of course. I am sure you will like her."

"I'm sure we shall! How did you meet her?"

"She served me lunch in The Adelphi Hotel. She works there as a waitress."

"How romantic! Will you bring her to meet us?"

"There is something you should know about her first."

"What is it?"

"She is a Catholic."

"No! She cannot be! That cannot happen."

"She is not a strict observer and it is happening."

"She is pregnant, isn't she? That is what it is?"

"Of course, she is not pregnant."

"In that case, you simply must not see her again. We are a Protestant family. Catholics are not our people."

"I want to marry her."

"Don't be so ridiculous. That just cannot happen."

"I am 24 years old, and it can."

"You would not defy us! You know that a Catholic girl is bound to bring up her children as Catholics? It is the law of that church! Your children would all be Catholics. It would mean the break-up of this family."

"I am sure if you meet her."

"I will not have her over the door of this house, William Henry. William, tell him!"

"Your mother has very strong feelings about this son."

"I know that she does, but they are not my feelings. I love Fanny and I want to marry her."

"If you do it, I will disown you. You will leave this family and I will have nothing to do with you ever again. Do you understand?"

"I hear you but, no, I do not understand you. But I will, of course, obey your wishes. I am at an age where I should have my own lodgings anyway. I can afford to support myself now I have had the promotion."

"Don't do this to me and to us, William Henry it is not worth it!"

"I do not understand what those words mean, Ma. I love this woman and I want to marry her. I hope you will come to know her and to love her as I do."

"I will never ever allow her in this house."

"Very well. With a heavy heart, I will make arrangements to leave, so I can be with her. I am sorry it has caused you such a hurt. I hope in time that you will come to understand. Thank you for listening to me. I love you both."

It had not gone well.

William Henry Garston left the Kingsley Road house in Wallasey two days later, having taken new lodgings in Snowdrop Lane, Liverpool where he was joined by his fiancée, Fanny Inglis. They immediately set to making plans for their wedding.

Twenty-One

In Dundee, in the year 1912, David Simpson finally achieved his lifelong ambition of joining the British Army when he enlisted in The Royal Highlanders' Black Watch regiment. He was following in the footsteps of his elder brother Donald, who had signed the self-same forms one year earlier.

David's application had not proved problematic. He presented himself in the weeks before his 18th birthday. The Dundee recruiting sergeant was only too glad to sign up an applicant who was evidently fit, strong, energetic and focused.

Dundee was not an easy place for the army to recruit. This was not for any shortage or reluctance of the menfolk of the city. On the contrary, Dundonian men were applying to enlist in their droves. But many of them were simply not fit to serve. The scarcity of jobs for men in the city, and the consequent very high unemployment among them, left many impoverished. Many were in poor physical condition when they presented themselves at the recruiting office. Often they were not only small in height but also thin, weak and plainly chronically under-nourished. A large number showed signs of a dependency on alcohol. The army was hungry for recruits, but it had to send almost half of the Dundee applicants away on grounds of lack of fitness to serve. It was a sickly city.

David, a notable exception to that rule, was sent off to York to begin his training as a professional soldier. Donald, who was by now entering his second year of service, was already in training in barracks in the south of England, at Farnborough.

Now that both of her brothers had left their home city, leaving their mother alone in Dundee, Janet increased the pressure on Elizabeth to come to join her and Archie in their new Morley Street home in Wallasey. She wrote:

You really have no reason to stay there now, Mother. There is nothing for you in Dundee and, now that they've enlisted in the army, Donald and David will not be there for at least six or seven years, apart from perhaps short leaves. They might even find they want to spend those somewhere else too you know!

We have a lovely house here with four bedrooms. You would have your own room and we could be together again. Who knows, if any children were to come along for Archie and me how nice it would be to have their grandmother with them, not living alone hundreds of miles away. Will you come? Please say that you will?

As Elizabeth read Janet's words, she accepted that the case for her to move was becoming increasingly compelling. Dundee was not her city. She had lived and worked there purely by happenstance. It had been James' place. It had been his parents' place. She had received no contact at all from her two eldest children since the family was divided into two. Perhaps Dundee was still their place, too, now for all she knew. But they may just as likely be long gone. She had stayed to provide for her remaining children when James had left. Then, when Donald was sent away to that school, she had to stay to wait for him and to bring him home. There had been no question of her doing anything else. But now what real reason did she have for remaining? Her children were all now grown adults. None of them needed her any longer as they had. They certainly did not need her to be in Dundee.

Like many mothers when their young leave the nest, Elizabeth now had to adjust to very changed circumstance. Her purpose in life while the children were all growing up had been very clear. The long struggle she had eventually won against the odds to keep them healthy and together had been all engrossing. It had defined who she was. It more than justified her.

But now that purpose was fulfilled. Gone. With its passing, she felt a chill not only of loneliness but also of uncertainty. She reflected that all her decisions for as long as she could remember had been very clear, and almost all made on behalf of others, not herself. Now her decisions had to be about her, about what she wanted to do, where she wanted to go, who she wanted to be. She was no longer in the background of her own life. She was floating into the centre stage, into the limelight. She now had to find herself, to decide who she was. She had to make decisions for herself alone. There was no-one else to worry about any more, no-one else to stand behind. She picked up a pen and wrote.

My dear Jane

I hope you are well. It is an age since I heard from you. I have news. David has now joined Donald in The Black Watch and has left home to do his army training. Janet has been badgering me forever to come to live with them and I have always found some reason to put her off and to stay here in Dundee.

Now they've all gone I have realised I really don't have any reason to be here any longer. I am going to write to her to say I will come to live with her and Archie in Wallasey. I'm daunted at the prospect but I think it is the right thing to do. I want to do it for myself! I can't remember the last time I had the feeling of saying that. It's somehow both frightening and liberating to make a selfish decision just for me alone.

So my dear we might be neighbours again. Janet tells me her house is not far from yours! It will be just like being back in Cambuslang again. I'm out of practice with skipping though and I'm not sure I'll be quite as good at hopscotch as I was when we were children!

I wanted you to know first and I do hope you think I am doing the right thing and are happy with my decision. I so look forward to seeing you again.

Your loving friend
Elizabeth

Jane's reply came swiftly.

Dear Elizabeth

That is such lovely news and I am quite sure you are doing the right thing! It is wonderful that you can think about what you want for yourself after so long looking after everyone else. It would be marvellous if Janet and Archie do have children for you to be with them all and I will so look forward to having my very best friend in life so nearby once again.

I have some difficult family news to share that I have been intending to write but now it can wait until I see you. There is nothing to worry about and nobody is ill. I will tell you when we are together.

Let me know when you can when that will be. I will be so pleased to see you. How exciting!

With my love
Jane

As Elizabeth Simpson prepared to pack her bags to join her daughter and son-in-law in Morley Road in Wallasey, a tall, richly dark haired and notably handsome man in his late middle age stood in the middle of Limekiln Lane, a few yards down from Janet and Archie's home. He was inspecting the newly arranged window display of his large double-fronted grocery shop on the street.

He lived there with his wife Georgina and their six daughters, and had done so for more than ten years since he first opened the shop. It had proved a great commercial success, and he had also proved a great personal success in the town. He had been elected as a Conservative councillor and was a much-respected man in Wallasey. A member of the Masonic Lodge, he was a person who had made much of himself from very modest beginnings.

Orphaned by the death of his mother when he was only eight years old, he had been sent into the care of a Ragged School in Liverpool. His upbringing had been paid for from the public purse. He had, however one looked at it now, more than made good upon the public's investment in him.

His name was Joseph Steggle.

Book Four
David France and Flanders 1914–1918

One

Before it all kicked off, I'll be honest, I had never heard of the Archduke Franz Ferdinand. I might have been able to tell you Sarajevo was in Serbia. But if you'd asked me to point it out in an atlas, I couldn't have done it. I can now. For a time, you couldn't pick up a newspaper without seeing a map reminding you where it was.

The papers were full of articles all that summer about the rising tensions. Arguments seemed to be flaring up every week across Europe. It felt like there were several countries jostling for position, some of them spoiling for a fight. I tried to read it all up. It was complicated, not easy to pick your way through. Eventually, you realised there were so many agreements between nations, to support one another in the event of any trouble, that even a small spark could start a fire across the whole continent. It was precarious and unstable. A tinderbox.

The Germans were belligerent. Empire envy some called it. There was plenty of newspaper speculation saying Germany was jealous of the British Empire, ambitious to acquire more overseas territories of its own. I remember thinking we would never go to war with the Germans. Not with the same royal family.

Then the Archduke was on all the front pages. Serbia mortally offends the Austrians and now they're straight away in an argument with the Germans, too. The Russians are protectors of Serbia and they also have a treaty with the French. Britain seemed to be on the edge of it all. We just wanted little Belgium to stay independent, so it could continue to be a buffer for us between Germany and France. So no-one could use it to come at us from the Belgian ports.

After Ferdinand and his wife were assassinated, and it all started to blow up I had an unworthy thought. I thought two people have died there, and that is obviously very sad. But we can't bring them back, and a lot of men are now going to die trying. I did my best to quash that feeling. It felt weak and unpatriotic. I was ashamed of myself for having it. I am not ashamed now.

In the beginning, it was like a holiday.

Just as if it were yesterday, I remember waking up that first morning in Aldershot. It was the middle of August. My brother Donald was in the bunkbed below me. There were 80 of us in our caserna at the Oudenarde barracks. The reveille was sounded at four thirty. The piper struck up the battalion's good morning refrain "Hey, Johnnie Cope, are Ye Waking Yet?" and right on the opening note, all the lamps went on. There was no first light reluctance. No groaning or clinging to sleep. It felt like the whole room had been lying on full alert in the half-light, just waiting for the call. Everyone slept in their full kit. The men on the top bunks were all in an instant sat bolt upright, with their stockinged feet hanging down over the edge of their beds, ready to drop down to their waiting boots. The lads underneath were scrambling to get out, picking their way through the forest of trailing legs. Packs, caps and rifles. Everyone had them all in place, ready by the side of their beds.

Within five minutes everyone was stood, shod, loaded up. Good to go.

I cannot speak for them all, but certainly Donald and me and our two Dundonian pals, Jimmy Weir and Tam Miller, we all felt the same. It is hard to imagine it now, but we were excited, like kids we were. Donald had done nearly three years of training, and I had completed my two. We were both fully-trained professional soldiers. Now at last, all the tedious getting ready work was done. All the square bashing, the brass and the leather polishing, the fieldcraft, the rapid fire shooting with blank ammunition, the digging in at speed, the bayonet exercises, all that practising was now going to be behind us. Now we were going. Finally it was real.

We marched the three miles to Farnborough. Twenty eight officers and more than a thousand men of the Royal Highlanders' Black Watch First Battalion, under the command of Lieutenant Colonel Adrian Grant Duff. By all accounts, he was one of the most gifted soldiers in the whole British Army. At Farnborough, we piled onto two special trains to Southampton. At the port, we boarded the 'Italian Prince' for the short voyage over to Havre. We got there a little after midday. We marched to a rest camp in a village called Harfleur, about five miles away.

Next day, it was back to Havre and onto a train to a town to the north-east, Le Nouvion. From there, we made a short march to our billets in a village called Boué, which was so beautiful. I think of it sometimes still, bathed in the August sun. The local people were all delighted to see us. They lined up to cheer us over the next four days, as we did our practices and route marches around their streets.

One mademoiselle came out of a doorway the second morning, clapping and laughing and trying to keep up with us. She ran alongside me for a moment and planted a kiss on my left cheek as we marched. I didn't dare look at her or pause for a second, so much as I wanted to. All I remember is the pink flowers on her dress and the sweet scent of her, and then the corporal, a few paces behind me, barking out, "Keep your eyes to the front!" I ought to have forgotten her by now. Except, I never have. In the dark times, in the trenches, on my own, trying to sleep, I would touch my own cheek lightly with my fingertips to try to recapture the softness of her lips, to summon up her kiss again. She helped me to get through, there is no doubt of that. She helped me to stay alive.

There was a reservoir in Boué in which we men swam on those few midsummer evenings. I can picture it now. Rays of sunshine breaking on the dark water in the dying embers of those hot days, creating embracing warm currents below. Water-boatmen hovering and then, standing, legs splayed, defying gravity, on the water's surface as you swam. The villagers sang "God Save the King" and the "Marseillaise" when we left. They showered us with flowers, wine and all kinds of food. We left them some cap badges for the children as souvenirs. They made us feel like heroes. Someone told me later that boue is the French word for mud.

We joined in the great forward movement north. We stopped another overnight somewhere called Cartignies, and the following day, we marched all day long, 22 hours in all, a lot of it on cobblestoned roads. That was hard. Blazing hot, fully loaded up carrying 60 pounds of kit, and most of us had new issue boots that were not broken in. After a while, the foot blisters were killing. Some of the boys just took their boots off and carried them, preferring to walk those hard-pitted roads with their feet wrapped only in their puttees. We finally arrived, exhausted, in a place called Grand Reng, outside the Belgian town of Mons. As we were marching in there, we could hear the sound of gunfire in the distance. Our heartbeats lifted, our pulses quickened. We would soon be getting at Fritz now. Holiday over.

To everyone's irritation, after all that marching, we were told we were being held in reserve. We saw no action that day. The nearest we got was talking with some of the troops who were on their way back through us from the frontline. I spoke to a lad from the Middlesex. He was a Cockney called Charlie and he called me 'Mac'. He was in good spirits. What he said to me were the first words of the war I heard.

"We've taken a lot of them down today, Mac. They came at us from a salient all closed up in tight formation, like they were on a parade ground. Captain gave us the order for rapid fire at a thousand yards, and we just let them have it. At first, I was trying to take proper aim, but they were giving us such a wide, dense target to shoot at, we all soon just concentrated on speed of fire. We were mowing them down, and the strange thing was, as they dropped, they just refilled their lines from behind and we shot them down again. I tell you, Mac, if that's the way this war is going to play out, you'll be done, out of here and back home with your sweetheart by Christmas."

You'll be back with your sweetheart by Christmas.

The next day, we were told we were retiring. "Blimey!" Jimmy spluttered. "Retiring? We haven't even started work yet!" We were given no explanations, but seeing how far we'd come to get there, it can only have been the scale of the opposition we were encountering ahead. What it turned out to mean was us walking back all the way and further than we'd come.

The first village we passed through was Villers-Sire-Nicole. We were on high alert at that stage to being attacked from the rear by German pursuit. As we marched through the village, we were going the wrong way now for the liking of some of the locals. A few old men called out to us several times, "Perfides!" Over my shoulder, as we marched, I asked Tam what it meant. He had a bit of French. "Are they calling us cowards, Tam?"

"Not so much cowards as traitors, Davy," he said.

As we continued to march south on the third day, we came under rifle and artillery fire between Étreux and Iron. It was not sustained, but we did suffer losses, our first of the war. After two more days of marching, we were then allowed to rest up at Saint Gobain.

The summer heat was unrelenting and it was taking its toll on many of us. We had been on constant move by then for eight days. The word was passed round that the Commanding Officer had said if anyone wanted to hand in their greatcoats they could. About half the lads did, glad to be rid of the suffocating weight, not thinking ahead. Donald, who was really struggling, was about to hand his in. I stopped him and said I would carry it for him rather than that. He decided to keep hold of it. Thank God. As we resumed the southward march, we *left behind us a blazing bonfire of the hundreds of greatcoats that had been handed in and had no-one then to carry them.*

Over the next few months, some of those men who left their coats to the flames on that sweltering day had cause to regret their decision many times over. First, we were soaked in incessant and torrential autumn rain and then we were exposed to freezing cold as the blistering winter set in. For many of them who had given up their coats, it was only when an opportunity eventually presented to take an unwanted coat from the back of a man who no longer had need of it, that they had proper protection against the harsh conditions we faced.

We crossed the Marne River and reached Le Plessis. We'd marched almost 300 kilometres south. We saw a sign in the hedgerow along the way that said Paris 30 kilometres away. We were a long way from the Belgian frontier we had come to defend, we were now pushed back deep into France. That was, though, as far south as we went. Our next order was to move east. We were turning back.

"Who's in charge here?" Jimmy whispered to Donald and me with his big toothy grin. Jimmy always had a quip in him. "Is it the Grand Old Duke of York, do you think? He was the one who marched them up the hill and then back down again, wasn't he?"

But all our spirits lifted with the turnaround. We had come here to fight the Hun, not run away from him. The next few days saw us come through several skirmishes as we swung back north. But we really got our wish at last on September the 14th. At a town called Vendresse on the River Aisne, we encountered the enemy properly established and determined not to yield any more ground. It was a day of close, fierce and hard street fighting in heavy mists. Our vision was badly hampered, but we were active throughout. We did what we could to keep them pinned down with rifle fire. But there was damage. We lost the commander, Lieutenant Colonel Grant Duff that day, and several other officers went, too. There were many casualties among the ranks. We had our longed-for welcome to the war. We were blooded.

Over the next four days, we dug in our positions on the Aisne valley. Our weapons were now spades, as we began to entrench. Ours were some of the very first spadefuls of that long, long line of holes in the ground that, in the end, stretched from Switzerland right across France to the sea. I remember an officer describing the trenches to us as 'stabilised warfare'. He should have given it its real name: stalemate warfare.

That was when it started. Very early. We had been there for barely a month.

Two

The British Secretary of State for War, Field Marshal Lord Horatio Herbert Kitchener, took few prisoners in life, either in war or in peace. Strident, robust and uncompromising, vastly experienced in military campaigns, he was no politician. It wasn't that he didn't suffer fools gladly; he didn't suffer them at all. What is more, he found himself constantly surrounded by them.

Kitchener's appointment to the cabinet of Herbert Asquith's Liberal government, three days after Britain entered the war, was, therefore, a bold and, some thought, reckless step by a prime minister with a reputation for governing by consensus. There were those who thought Asquith a procrastinator. That was not a charge anyone had ever levelled at his new minister of war. Kitchener was by no means everyone's favourite. One of his predecessors in his new role, the now Lord Chancellor Viscount Haldane, described him damningly as 'a man of great authority and considerable ignorance'.

Once he found himself appointed to the War Ministry, Kitchener lost no time in declaring that, contrary to the belief of many others in politics, the press and indeed the majority of the Great British public, there was no possibility whatever that the British Army would be 'Home by Christmas'. Unlike most of his starch-collared colleagues in parliament, he understood and did not under-estimate the scale and strength of the German military machine. As a veteran of many war zones, including Sudan and the Boer War, he had no romantic view of armed conflict. He was aware of the devastating power of the new technology of warfare. To the dismay of his new Cabinet colleagues, who were presuming the war would be a short-lived affair, Kitchener immediately predicted it would last at least three years, and that Britain would be required to contribute millions of fighting men in order to win it.

Given that, at the start of the war, the full complement of the British Army stood at fewer than 250,000, Kitchener recognised the strengthening of the country's ground forces was a matter of extreme urgency. In matters of defence,

Britain traditionally looked first to the Royal Navy, the senior service, for its security. The army was a far smaller force, used chiefly for the policing of its Empire territories. Before the declaration of war, one third of the British Army's modest manpower was stationed in colonial India. This stood in stark contrast to the might of the German regular Army, which was deploying more than one million professional soldiers in its initial invasion of Belgium and France, a complement roughly equal to that available to the French commanding officer General Joseph Joffre. While there was a case to be made that the British Army was the best trained and best equipped land force in the world, there was no questioning the fact it was very far from the biggest. In the initial confrontation on the western front, Britain was, in manpower terms at least, a very small presence.

Taking matters largely into his own hands, Kitchener announced a national call for civilian volunteers to join his 'New Army'. He set the immediate target for new recruits at 500,000 and launched a ubiquitous poster propaganda campaign, featuring his own imposing moustachioed visage calling on patriots to enlist. His clarion call, "Your Country Needs You," rang out up and down the land.

It was met with enthusiastic support from the British public. Such was the success of Kitchener's call to arms that by the end of 1914, more than one million volunteers had signed up. Many were encouraged by the prospects of fighting alongside their friends, neighbours, workmates and relatives in battalions that promised to keep locally recruited men together. They wanted to ensure Britain won the war and were willing to play their part in achieving it. They also sought adventure and the opportunity to brighten dull lives, and most thought that the British bulldog fighting spirit was all that would be required for victory. For many of the new recruits, the regular wage on offer was attractive too.

By the time the new volunteers had received the basic training they needed to take up combat roles, the regular British army, who made up the Expeditionary Force that had first arrived in France that August, had been almost completely obliterated. That grim reality was obscured from the view of the vast numbers of New Army volunteers by a virtual news blackout on events from the Front, which was ruthlessly imposed by Kitchener. The picture house newsreels and the newspaper reporting trumpeted British successes. They minimised, or did not record at all, their many setbacks or their legion casualties.

Among the countless households energised by Kitchener's call to arms were three families on either side of the River Mersey.

In Snowdrop Lane, Liverpool, William Henry Garston was telling his young wife of the recruitment campaign being sponsored at his workplace, the General Post Office. The Post Office was the largest employer in the world, with more than a quarter of a million people on its payroll.

"They are calling for volunteers to join the Corps of Royal Engineers, to manage the postal service on the Western Front in France and Flanders, Fanny. The Post Office section volunteers who join them will sort and deliver all the letters and parcels to and from the soldiers at the front. I want to enlist and get involved."

Fanny was quite terrified at the thought of William Henry enrolling in the fighting army, but she was at least partly cheered by his description of what he would actually be doing.

"Does that mean you won't be involved in the shooting?" she asked.

William Henry reassured his wife. "No, we will be providing the postal service for fighting soldiers, but we won't be combat troops ourselves. There is a separate Post Office regiment they are recruiting for now, called the Post Office Rifles. They will be regular infantry. But I'm not going to join up there. I will be doing what we do here in our everyday work but just dedicated to the soldiers at the front. So don't worry, my love, I will be quite safe!"

William Henry felt this was absolutely something he should do. Communications with loved ones at home would for sure play a vital role in maintaining the morale of those on the frontline. It might not have the glamour of active deployment on the firing lines, but it would be an important behind-the-scenes service that would allow him to help the country's war effort. He had already been told that by virtue of his newly promoted position to the manager grade at work that he could expect after his training to be appointed as a non-commissioned officer, most likely as a Sergeant. This would give him a supervisory role over the rank and file men working in sorting and running letters and parcels to and fro.

In December 1914, William Henry Garston, then 29 years old, enlisted with the Royal Engineers East Riding division and presented himself for training. His army training, in practice, was brief and peremptory. It was the basics only. The volunteers of the Royal Engineers Postal Section, known by everyone as REPS, would remain under the control of the GPO. They would wear the King's uniform, but the Army was only in nominal command of their work. Just as William Henry had described to Fanny, his job would be managing letter flows, not killing Germans.

In Morley Street in Wallasey, Archie Rogers, was preparing with rather more reluctance to leave his wife Janet and their two children: Harry, who was now four years of age, and their newly born daughter, Bunty, barely one year old.

"It is only right for me to go, Janet," Archie told his wife. "I should do my bit and I want to. It won't be long anyway before there will be no choice about it. They ask for volunteers first, of course, but just wait pretty soon they will introduce a draft and everyone will get called up to go, whether they want to or not. This is a chance at least to enlist in a battalion I actually want to serve in."

"Which one is that?" Janet asked, recognising that her husband's decision was already made.

"The artillery, sweetheart. If I'm going to go, I want to man the guns," he replied.

Archie Rogers, who gave his age as 31, enlisted in the Royal Field Artillery (West Lancashire) division and was assigned to the C Battery 286th Brigade as a Gunner.

He prepared himself for six months' training, learning the operation of the modern long-range shell-firing guns with which both entrenched sides on the western conflict were already hammering each other mercilessly, as if there would be no tomorrow.

Three

The departure of so many volunteers to the war front had an unexpectedly beneficial effect on the financial position of the household of William and Jane Garston.

William was of that fortunate age, too old to be considered as a volunteer for the army, but fit and agile enough still to perform daily dock work. That labour was also increasingly important as the port of Liverpool processed the country's vital wartime import and export cargoes, as well as the Atlantic passenger ships coming through its docks.

Large numbers of the young and fit men of Liverpool had by now volunteered to join up with the forces under Kitchener's programme, and their mass departures from the city meant the dock stands each morning were now only lightly populated with men hoping for a day's work. Instead of the throngs of workers queuing for hire, who had always far exceeded the number the dock employers actually needed each day, there were now barely enough men turning up seeking work for the jobs that were available. Moreover, many of those who did present themselves for shifts were not strong enough for the physical tasks they had to perform. They included many who had already failed the army's minimum fitness criteria.

As a result, and for the first time in two generations, the balance between the supply of labour and the demand for it in the Liverpool port swung from constant surplus into regular shortage. The dock employers, who hadn't changed the rate of daily pay they offered for 45 years, since 1870, now had to start putting up dock wages regularly to attract in the sort of men they needed. William, a proven and valued hand, who was used to being picked from the pen every day without fail, found he could now earn ten shillings and sixpence a day, more than twice what he was being paid for the same work before the country went to war.

These improved circumstances for William and Jane were also aided by contributions from the earnings of their three remaining children they still had living with them. Ethel was continuing her music studies and now making a good income as a pianoforte teacher, coaching students of varying levels on the piano in her parents' front room. From her earnings, she was able to contribute ten shillings a week to the family budget, in return for her board and lodgings. Alex, now well established as a fruit broker, was able to match his sister's weekly contribution. Their younger brother, Albert, who had just started work as an apprentice provision merchant, learning the trade of keeping shops stocked with goods, could find five shillings from his modest wage for the family kitty.

All this good fortune in employment meant the Garstons could afford to live as well as the times allowed, and Jane was able to enjoy, for the first time since she first began working, a period as an at-home mother and housewife. Helped by Ethel, Jane saw her husband and her two young sons off the premises each morning with a cooked breakfast inside them, and ensured they had a good home-prepared meal when they returned from their employment in Liverpool in the evenings. Meat three times a week, a piece of fish on a Friday and a roast dinner on Sunday was their regular regime. Beyond this daily routine and her other household chores, Jane found she had the luxury of a little time to herself, to socialise and to read.

But this more comfortable time was not without its disruption, and it came in the form of an increasingly fractious relationship between Jane and her middle son, Alex. A number of Alex's work colleagues and school friends had already signed up for the army and had left the area, either for training or for the front itself. Alex was impatient to join them. He had taken to bringing up the subject at almost every opportunity.

"I want to go to the recruiting office to see if they will sign me up, Mother," Alex said, as the family sat after their evening meal at the dining table. Jane had already made clear she was horrified at the prospect and she refused point blank to countenance it.

"That is not happening, Alex. I have told you several times. You are far too young. You know perfectly well that you have to be at least 18 years old to attest and here you are, barely 17."

"Well, there is only a few months in it now and I am sure they will overlook it," came Alex's counter.

"That is not the point, Alex. There is a good reason they want men and not boys and, anyway, they also say that, even if eighteen-year-olds enlist, they will not be allowed to leave the country until they are 19. So you'd be sent off somewhere in the south of England to practice marching up and down for 18 months on some parade ground before you'd even be allowed to go. Is that what you really want? The war will probably be over by the time you would get to go anyway."

Jane glared across at William, who was inspecting his pocket watch for evidence of dust and clearly doing his best to stay out of the conversation.

"Don't you agree, William?" she said, staring across hard at him and offering him very little choice in the matter.

"Perhaps you could explain to your son why he cannot join the army?"

When Jane looked at Alex, she saw a boy in the first flush of his youth, filled with a childish sense of excitement and wanting to join in an adventure that he thought others were enjoying without him. She saw a youngster who was a world away from being ready for the dangers of combat or being put at peril.

When William looked at him, he saw a grown young man, maybe not yet quite adult in strict *anno domini* terms, but more than mature enough to make his own decisions. He had watched Alex on football and rugby pitches playing against fully-grown men much older than himself, and had seen him more than holding his own. In William's eyes, Alex was no longer a child and, if he was set on signing up to serve his King and country, then who was he to stand in his way? He strained to find something he could say that would not have either his wife storming out into the kitchen in rage or his son walking out the front door and banging it behind him. Choosing his words as carefully as he could he said:

"Your mother is quite right about the age limit, Alex. When you are 18, you will be legally allowed to enlist and able to do as you choose. In the meantime, why not do some volunteering here instead? The Post Office is looking for lads to deliver telegrams in the evenings, to replace all the fighting-age postmen who have signed up. Why don't you make that your contribution to the war effort until you can sign up?"

"I will do that, but you do know I don't have to, Father, don't you?" said Alex, getting up. "May I please leave the table now?"

Albert, who had been sitting silently, waiting for a chance to escape, took his opportunity to slip away from the fraught scene at that same moment, and Ethel, equally keen to get out of the room, efficiently gathered up the finished plates and left William and Jane together.

"You could be more supportive, William!" Jane hissed exasperatedly as soon as they were alone. "I have to force you to speak before you will open your mouth. You know perfectly well he is not old enough. And whatever did he mean by 'you know, I don't have to'?"

"I don't know, my dear, but hopefully volunteering on the telegram deliveries might take his mind off it for a bit now."

William may have told his wife he didn't know what his son had meant by his remark, but he knew perfectly well. There were plenty of lads of Alex's age going into the recruiting offices, saying they were over 18 and being signed up without hindrance. William was well aware that his son could go and do that any day he wanted. No recruiting sergeant looking at Alex was going to turn down a fit, well-muscled young rugby wing forward who said he was old enough to fight and was ready to sign on. William thought it wise not to share that particular insight with Jane.

Jane and Elizabeth, meanwhile, had resumed their relationship of old. Elizabeth was now living not far from the Garstons with her daughter Janet and her two children in the house that Janet and Archie had bought in Morley Road. The two old friends had morning coffee or afternoon tea in each other's houses two or three times a week.

Elizabeth had much to relate of her times in Dundee to Jane. The truth of her troubled relationship with James, her struggles to keep body and soul together and to bring up her children, her work at the jute mill, and the agonising experience of losing Donald for all those years to the Industrial school. Most excruciating of all, though, she found explaining how it was that she and James had come to give over her two eldest children, Robert and Ada, to her husband's parents.

"How could you have done that, Elizabeth?" Jane asked her when she heard the story. "I'm not sure I could ever have brought myself to do such a thing. Whatever were you thinking?"

"It is the biggest regret of my life, Jane, and not a day goes by that I do not think about them. But sometimes, you have to do what is best, not what you want for yourself with all your heart. I was very afraid that, if we tried to keep them, it would be the ruin of us all, and we would all find ourselves thrown in the workhouse and the children taken away from us. For good or for ill, I decided I could not deprive those children of the chance of a safe upbringing with their grandparents, when I couldn't even guarantee to keep a roof over their heads for more than a few weeks."

"That must have broken your heart. And then after you did that, then you lost Donald for all that time as well. Poor you! It all must have been so awful," said Jane, before adding for good measure, "That James of yours, of course, what a good-for-nothing he turned out to be!"

Jane's brand of sympathy was scant comfort to Elizabeth, who felt the sting of thinly veiled barbs in her remarks. She was only too aware of James's shortcomings as a husband and father, and she did not need Jane's crushing verdict, based only on what Elizabeth had shared with her of the details of their marriage. She would have wished for a little more understanding and caring, but she also had to acknowledge that the choices she had made in her life were far from beyond criticism. All she could say was that she had tried to do the best she could. It was all one could ever do.

While Elizabeth bravely shared her painful stories freely with Jane, the same was not true in reverse. Jane was sparing with the details of the circumstances of how she and William had come to be married, how they had both lost touch with their outer families since, and the subject of William Henry and his whereabouts now was absolutely taboo. William Henry had left home and was progressing his career elsewhere. William and she were no longer in regular contact with him, but they knew he was quite well. That was about as far as Jane would go. Elizabeth just had to accept that there were some subjects that she could not go near in her conversations with Jane.

In other circumstances, those differences might have put paid to the two women's relationship altogether. But they had known each other for a long time. They had grown up together, they had known each other intimately from the earliest ages, and they had shared a lot of experience. They were deeply fond of one another. If Jane had parts of her life she wasn't comfortable to discuss yet, then that was not end of the world for Elizabeth. Perhaps she would share more when she was good and ready. Life wasn't easy, she knew well enough herself.

Nor did Elizabeth think she should be above hearing her trusted friend's honest views on the life decisions that she had made. Their friendship could withstand more than that after all these years. With the exception of those few subjects that were plainly no man's land for Jane, they otherwise enjoyed easy conversation together about their families, their feelings and their everyday lives.

They were glad to have recovered their relationship and both of them were enriched by it.

Four

It had taken Cedric Blumenthaler almost eight weeks in the autumn of 1914 to persuade the powers that be at *The New York Times* to allow him to travel to northern France.

Now a senior and seasoned writer on the newspaper, Blumenthaler's career had taken off following the success of the series of articles he had written from the heart of the British Empire almost 20 years prior. His writing on the women of Dundee, in particular, stood high in the newspaper's all-time pantheon of journalistic achievement. Since then, Cedric had gone on to write extensively on politics, economics, social issues and the arts.

He first took his proposal to be sent to report from France to the newspaper's managing editor, Carr Van Anda, in early August, just as the hostilities were beginning and the scale of the potential conflict was becoming clear. Van Anda was a scientist by training, a physicist and an astronomer. His greatest claim to fame in journalism was the *Times*' world-beating scoop of the sinking of the *Titanic* in the Atlantic two years earlier. Van Anda was obsessed with reporting every major story in great detail, and he was a proud standard-bearer of the *Times*' iconic slogan 'All the News That's Fit to Print'. For all that, he was undecided when Blumenthaler came to him to ask if he could become the newspaper's war correspondent.

"The English are controlling journalists' access to the fighting very tightly," Van Anda told Cedric.

"There are no British newspapers with authorised correspondents at the front. They are all banned. The censors are vetting everything and they are putting out an official line on all matters. It sounds like they are coming down very hard on anyone who tries to break ranks. Kitchener is threatening to arrest journalists who flout his rules. Churchill, who is running their Navy, has said this war needs to be 'fought in a fog'. This is very heavy duty political intervention, Cedric."

"All that is precisely why we need to go, Carr," was Blumenthaler's response. "It is not the job of a great newspaper to lie down in the face of official prohibition. This is the biggest story in the world. We can't just rely on self-serving propaganda and publish it uncritically, with no context and no verification. We can't just have a couple of rookie sub-editors sitting in our office in Manhattan, cutting up and pasting government statements onto our pages!"

Van Anda fully recognised the strength of Blumenthaler's case, but he was concerned for his reporter's safety. Moreover, he could see the *Times* quickly finding itself at the centre of a major diplomatic incident if it carried articles that brought London and Washington into confrontation. Relations between the two countries were delicate enough already, with Britain an active protagonist in the war and America maintaining its neutrality.

Just as he had done 20 years before, when he offered to part-fund his ground-breaking reporting trip to Europe, Blumenthaler then made a suggestion that broke the deadlock.

"Look Carr," he said, "I know you know all the arguments, probably even better than I do. How would it be if I resign my position on the paper today, and I go there under my own steam, paying my own way?"

"I will send you all the stories I produce while I am there on a first refusal basis, and you can either decide to publish or not. If you decline my copy, I will be free to offer it to other papers. If you accept it, you can publish it under an anonymous by-line, if you like. You can say it's 'From a Special Correspondent'. That way, you are employing no-one to do this and you are not commissioning any writing. I will simply give you first view of what I produce. You will know you can trust it. Anything you decide to carry, you pay me by the word. How does that sound? Deal?"

Van Anda, after a prolonged consultation with the newspaper's owner, Adolph Ochs, finally agreed to Blumenthaler's proposal. If the man was determined to do it, and the newspaper had full control and first refusal over whether to publish what he produced, and if it could say in complete honesty that none of its employees was in France, that might just work. If they published nothing that he submitted, it would cost them nothing. Blumenthaler would be going entirely at his own risk. And, if and when the tough reporting restrictions were eventually lifted as things progressed, they would then have a well-informed and well-qualified man of their own immediately on the spot. There did not seem to be anything for them to lose.

American public sympathy in the early months of the conflict had swung heavily behind the people of Belgium, who were facing impending starvation. The invading German army had requisitioned much of the country's food and livestock to feed their own troops.

Britain, meanwhile, had instituted a naval blockade of Belgian ports to prevent war materiel falling into the invaders' hands. Responding to the growing civilian crisis, Herbert Hoover, an American mining engineer and businessman, had established a body to coordinate relief for the suffering Belgian citizens. The Commission for Relief in Belgium, from its New York base, was in the process of setting up an international network of port agents to co-ordinate charitable fundraising and the shipment of food into the embattled country.

Carr Van Anda was well aware of the work of the fledgling organisation and, in wishing Blumenthaler well in his adventure, he pointed him towards the CRB.

"I understand they are actively welcoming non-aligned American volunteers to help distribute food in Belgium, and that might be a way for you to begin once you are there. I believe they have already begun food and clothing shipments from New York to Rotterdam and Antwerp on chartered vessels. Would you like me to make a call to Hoover to see if he can get you a berth on the next one to depart? Remember that would be just a friendly favour and absolutely not a *New York Times* request. As we have agreed, you are completely on your own now, Cedric."

In mid-October, Cedric Blumenthaler disembarked one of Herbert Hoover's ships when it docked in the port of Antwerp. He paid for his free passage from New York with three days' labour, working in the port with the CRB's hub distribution of the food cargo he had just accompanied on voyage. The contacts Cedric made during those three days with the onward road transport providers proved invaluable. They enabled him to obtain a lift by road deeper into the Belgian hinterland. He was heading into west Flanders beyond Ghent towards two towns, the larger of which was called Kortrijk.

The name of the second he had not come across before. It was Ypres.

Five

I learned over the next weeks that much of our life in the trenches was dull beyond belief. Donald and I moved up and down the lines every few days, from the back forward through the reserve trenches, up to the support trench, and then finally into the firing line, where we spent the least time of all. Two days at most. There was always work to do wherever you were, shifting supplies, repairing the trenches, exercising, day-to-day existing. Some of the trenches were little more than glorified ditches and, as the winter rain started to pour in, we found ourselves struggling to keep a foothold on the treacherously slippery duckboards, or else standing shin deep in cold muddy water itself, soaking.

Those first days I spent in the firing line, I can tell you, I found terrifying. The shelling was constant, deafening noise, explosions coming at you from all directions. It was mayhem. One minute in front of you, then behind you. Now to the left, now to your right. It made me feel like a nervous wreck. My pulse was racing, and I felt constantly light headed. Always waiting for the next blast and fearing the worst. I couldn't wait for each short stint at the front to be over, and to get back out of direct harm's way.

My brother's reaction was quite different. It was like Donald had seen it all before. I never saw him flinch or duck or pay any heed to any of the racket. He seemed never to be startled by the violent ripping of the earth all around us, or the fire flashes. It was if he couldn't hear it or see any of it. He looked almost completely unmoved. I began to worry that maybe he was suffering from shell shock. When the day's bombardments finally fell silent one evening, I checked how he was.

"Are you OK, Donald? I'm worried you don't seem much affected by any of what's going on. I don't mind admitting it, I am scared stiff and I just want to know that you are alright."

"Don't be scared, David," he said, "it is not good for you and there really is no need. Think about it. When you take a peek, when all's quiet, at the German lines, what do you see?"

I replied, "Nothing. I don't see anything. There's nothing to see."

"Exactly," he said, "we can't see them and they can't see us. Now take a look at this trench of ours. How wide would you say it is?"

I gauged it was no more than six feet across.

"And how long is the passage we are in, before it turns hard to the left or hard to the right?"

Again I looked up and down the line of the trench to either end, where it changed direction to form its zig-zag twists. That was also a few yards at most.

"Now think about Fritz the artilleryman, sitting more than a mile away shooting at something he can't see. How likely is it that one of his shells actually lands inside this short narrow little slit in the ground? It probably has about the same chance you would have throwing a dart in the air ten yards away and it landing in the eye of a needle. I'm not saying a shell couldn't land right on top of us, but do you know what that would be, if it did?"

I shook my head.

"It would be Bloody Bad Luck, and the thing about Bloody Bad Luck in life is that there is absolutely not a blasted thing you can do about it. If your name is on a shell, Davy, you're done for. If one lands on us, I promise you and I will have absolutely nothing to worry about. The next thing you'll know, we'll be sitting together outside the Pearly Gates waiting for The Big Man to let us in."

"So don't worry about Bad Luck, David, and don't waste your energy fearing it. Fear is not your friend. Fear makes you erratic. Fear makes you run when you should walk. Fear paralyses and weakens you. It stops you thinking straight. When you are afraid, you can easily bring misfortune onto yourself. So my advice is go about your business as best you can and keep your wits about you. Trust in your own good judgement and your own good fortune. That is what has kept you alive for 20 years so far. Believe it will continue to keep you safe here."

As Donald spoke, it dawned on me for the first time that these hellish, stinking, rat-infested, mud soaked holes in the ground were giving us protection from danger, even on the brutally bombarded front line. I had felt only their oppression and their filth before and not their sanctuary. I had hated them. Donald helped me to cross a line. We had been in far more peril fighting out in *the open streets before we entrenched than we ever were now. My brother's words calmed me, and I never thought of the trenches in the same way again.*

I stopped cowering. He gave me a way to think. To survive.

Six

Cedric Blumenthaler boarded the first of three food aid trucks paid for by the Commission for Relief in Belgium in the port of Antwerp bound for Kortrijk. He had been formally registered as a Volunteer with the CRB and given the stamped papers to prove it. These, coupled with his American passport, should suffice for him to pass unhindered in this country at war. Neutral by nationality, and committed to humanitarian work, Cedric and the convoy of three trucks in which he travelled had all the documents they required for free passage through Belgium.

Each truck flew a Red Cross flag on its front right wing. Each had the letters CRB emblazoned across the top of its windshield, and a six-inch by four Stars and Stripes flag fixed in the passenger side front window. It was clear and very necessary precautionary identification. Belgium's largest port was now in the hands of the invading army from Germany. It had taken the German troops, supported by massive artillery firepower, just ten days from late September to dislodge and rout the Belgian army, who lost 30,000 men in their unsuccessful defence of their port fortress.

Now Antwerp was overflowing with German presence, and it was clear to Cedric as the three trucks eased their way out of the port confines and onto the roads beyond that the bulk of the German strength was already on the move out of Antwerp onward into Belgium in the direction of the French border. As the trucks edged out into the city roads, it was plain that a great force was mobilising. When they finally found their way out on to the main Kortrijk road, for their 100-kilometre journey, it became apparent to Cedric and his fellow aid workers that they were going to have substantial military accompaniment along their way. The German Fourth and Sixth Armies were marching west.

Their trucks were squeezed right to the edge of the road by the breadth of this mighty moving formation. The German forces were marching four abreast, and there were men on the flat terrain ahead of the trucks as far as the eye could see. It was certainly tens of thousands of soldiers and they were bringing plenty of heavy armament with them. The rolling artillery presence was everywhere they looked, hundreds of long-range guns pounding along the roads alongside the infantrymen on the march. The equine presence was also huge. There were many hundreds of horses moving with them.

The German soldiers, buoyed by their overwhelming victory in the capture of Antwerp, seemed in high spirits, breaking out into frequent song as they marched. Hearing *Die Wacht am Rhein* and *Heil dir im Siegerkranz* being lustily chorused by so many men would have daunted many an adversary. The rousing singing reverberated deafeningly inside the aid trucks as they edged past the marchers.

The Belgian driver of Cedric's vehicle, who had introduced himself as Jean-Claude Villeneuve, was sweating profusely and looking distinctly uncomfortable as he tried to keep his vehicle from falling off the edge of the road while also steering clear of the track of the marching soldiers. If he ever strayed too close to the marching men, there would be the sound of fists beating the side panels of his truck. The blows were usually accompanied by some deep-throated Germanic roar of disapproval and warning. Each time it happened, Cedric could see Jean-Claude wince, not knowing whether he should be pressing accelerator or brake. It was going to be a long and trying journey.

We had been in the Aisne Valley, dug in for three weeks, when word started to go round the trenches that we would soon be on the move again. We heard tell we were going north and would take up a position at the far left of the entire Allied line. That felt more like what we had been expecting to do. That would mean we would be defending the Channel ports and preventing the Germans from securing them. From a British point of view, that was paramount in importance.

Shortly before dusk, when we got the orders to prepare to move, Donald, Tam, Jimmy and I exchanged our views on what we might expect next.

"My money is on seeing some more of these luxurious trenches!" laughed Jimmy.

"That's a safe bet," said Tam, "but if it's true we've been told to position ourselves on the left of all the French forces, you know what that means don't you? It means it will be up to us not only to defend and hold the ports, which is a big enough job in itself, but we will also have to stop Fritz outflanking the

whole Allied line and getting in behind us. I wouldn't mind betting the Hun will
have exactly that same idea. Because why wouldn't he?"

"This could be the big one," agreed Donald. "This might make what we have
just been through so far look like child's play. Just a warm up act."

As we gathered up our kit, it struck me that this next stage was a fight we
could not afford to lose. If the Germans were allowed to sweep through northern
Belgium into northern France, securing it and enveloping the Allied forces in
the process, then the advantage in this whole war would swing heavily in their
favour. With a gain like that, the odds of an early and outright German victory
would rise considerably. We weren't going to be alone trying to hold it off, but
the sense of responsibility we bore was already palpable.

Cedric's convoy reached Kortrijk after a journey of nearly four hours. Eventually, they had reached the head of the German marching formation and recovered the open road. Jean-Claude breathed easily then for the first time since they had left the port and pressed his right foot down, keen to put as much distance as he could between them and the advancing army.

On their eventual arrival, the three trucks pulled into the market square and were met by CRB organisers on the ground. They had arranged for a major food distribution from the trucks to take place outside the landmark gothic monument St Martin's Church in the centre of the town that late afternoon. As he prepared to help with the handouts, Cedric was beginning also to try to compose his thoughts on what he might write for the *New York Times*. How should he capture what he had already seen in the last hours on his journey from Antwerp? It was clearly building up into a potentially major confrontation on the battlefield.

"How far from here do we think the French and the British are?" he quietly asked one of the local aid organisers as casually as he could. "Not so far," whispered the man in reply. "I live only about 30 kilometres west of here, and they are certainly present there in good numbers, thank God." Cedric had his answer. Thirty kilometres west of Kortrijk was Ypres. He had to get there before the marching force he had driven through that morning.

We Black Watch men were part of a general advance of the British force. As
we had heard, we were moved up to the left of the Allied Line and closer into the
French forces to shorten the communication lines. Other British and French
troops came in on our left and provided us with strengthened coverage to the

313

sea. After a long manoeuvre north, we rested up at Hazebrouck, south west of Ypres and, the following day, we took up a position at Pilkem, a mile or two north of the town. We found ourselves lined up alongside the Cameron Highlanders and the Coldstream Guards as we faced repeated German attacks. At first, they threatened to push us back, but we rallied and recovered the position. Again the Germans came back at us in the night, but we again saw them off, though not without our casualties, as well as inflicting theirs. We were then moved a short distance to another threatened sector barely a mile away, to a position just south of Ypres. We managed to hold it against further German onslaught and we entrenched that night.

All the time, though, we were losing men, and the toll being taken of our officers was heavy. Of the nearly 30 we had in our number when we set out from Aldershot that early August morning, I could now account for only seven still standing. The whole area around Ypres seemed to be infested with rolling battles. This was not one joined up confrontation, but eruptions of heavy fighting in five or six places seemingly at most a few miles apart. We could hear firing in the distance from several directions at once. We sustained severe losses on the 29th of October from several more aggressive frontal attacks. I heard we lost more than 200 men that day, and more officers went down, too. We were holding our own, trading blow for blow with the Hun, but at what cost.

This attritional, rolling fighting continued for several more weeks as we resisted the German efforts to break through us. The battle finally reached conclusion in a heavily wooded area to the immediate east of Ypres, where our artillery again repelled another German advance. That seemed to mark enough for the Hun, and their guns finally, thankfully, fell silent.

After 18 days of almost continuous hard fighting, we were withdrawn from the line. We were replaced by some of the Territorial regiments that were now beginning to arrive in France. What came to be known as The First Battle of Ypres had been won. The Germans, despite applying massive force and energy to the task, had failed to break us.

Over the next years, we were to return several times to fight in this area but the line we held there remained intact through the whole war. The Germans never took Ypres. But in all the fighting in our successful defence of the Ypres salient, with its vast toll in casualties on both sides, we never made much progress either. Our eventual advance from this first line, such as it was, could *be expressed in hundreds of yards and not in miles. We literally fought each other into the ground.*

Cedric Blumenthaler bought a bicycle in Kortrijk and cycled through uncontested roads and country lanes to make his way to the town of Ypres. On his arrival, he volunteered as an ambulance driver. The British Army Medical Corps, struggling to cope with the numbers of casualties being brought back from the various fighting grounds around the town, were only too happy to accept an American with stamped humanitarian relief papers to help them.

Cedric's job was to help move the wounded out of the field stations in the immediate area to permanent hospitals behind the lines. Those who needed to be taken out of the firing line, but were fit to travel, he could help deliver to the hospital boats back to Britain from Dunkirk or other Channel ports.

He had hoped on arriving in Ypres to find his way to the front. But he quickly realised once there that the fighting was so diffuse, so fierce and so fluid that there was no obvious means of getting that close to the action. To try to do so would also likely put him into highly dangerous and volatile situations, where his amateur presence might even imperil the lives of others. He contented himself with the important ambulance relief work and absorbed events around him. He had a strong sense of being right in the centre of things at least. The eyes of the world were on Ypres.

But Cedric was already beginning to appreciate the acute difficulty of reporting this story. He had written a light colour piece on the aid ship en-route for Antwerp and, once he arrived, he had tried to do an eye-witness description of what he saw of the German occupation of the city. But as his normally fluent pen scratched repeatedly to a halt, he realised that, beyond the initial description, the real news was something he could not impart. He could not describe the German forces on the march, the morale of the troops, their direction of their travel, the regiments they represented, the scale of their presence, the details of their weaponry. These were all details that were strictly forbidden to disclose.

Cedric also began to see that, in the context of no other news outlets reporting much information at all, he risked being alone, the only on-the-ground reporter potentially divulging highly sensitive information. The general news blackout meant that anything that was published independently of the official censors was certain to be avidly scoured by both sides. He could see himself stumbling headlong into the unknown world of military intelligence. He could not know the context into which his words would fall.

What if the French and the British didn't know the Germans were advancing towards Kortrijk? Would a news report of their advance cause either side to change their plans at short notice? Might the Germans then change course and attack another place instead? What if their position was already well known to the Allied defenders? Would a potential Franco-British trap, that was already perfectly set awaiting the invaders, then be rendered useless by a last-minute change of the enemy's plan because of something he had written? If they had not known of the German advance before his article appeared, would a diversion of Allied forces in response to his reports then leave undefended another place which the Germans could then pour through uncontested? There were so many impossible questions to answer, and so many possibilities of dire consequences. It made his head spin even to think about it.

Cedric could see that, quite quickly and unknowingly, with even the most innocent, shallow reporting he could become directly responsible for people dying needlessly, soldiers and civilians both. The simple journalistic ideals of honesty, accuracy and transparency, professional by-words that had so far guided and served him so well in his career, might in this arena of war cause catastrophe. He could be signing scores, even hundreds, of death warrants here with a single naive blundering sentence that escaped from his pen. It was a journalist's job to report the course of a war, not to shape it.

But where did that leave him? If he could not be a proper reporter, what the hell was he doing here? Was he some ghoulish voyeur, here to watch the suffering and death? He knew he was not that person, and it caused him reflect hard on what it was that he could report.

As he sat in a cafe on the town square taking a coffee, a division of British soldiers filed past, their kilts swirling. They were Scots Guards. At that moment, it dawned on Cedric what he could do here.

How could he have been so obtuse?

Seven

Cedric Blumenthaler's independent status at the western front became his salvation. Had he remained on the *New York Times'* payroll, he would have been harried daily by a news desk in Manhattan, hungrily demanding his latest despatches. But he was not there on their dollar. He was answerable to no-one other than himself. That allowed him to choose exactly how he would conduct himself in that place: what he would write, what he would not.

So it came as a great relief to Cedric when he hit upon an alternative to daily reporting that would still allow him to remain true to his calling. He would continue to work in a volunteering support capacity, assisting with the wounded and the sick. As he did that, he would gather material to produce an article, or a series of them, which looked at the war through the experiences of a particular group of people. These articles could be published when the fighting was over, perhaps in six months, or maybe a year at most, when surely the world would have come to its senses and would have halted all this carnage and destruction. The way to do that was staring him in the face as clearly as if it was his destiny calling. What better group for him to tell the story through than soldiers from Dundee?

If he could produce a companion work to the award-winning writing he had produced all those years earlier about the women of the Dundee jute mills, by writing the Great War's story through the experiences of the menfolk of that same city, it could be a completing act for him, a perfect symmetry. A lifework. The second grand series of articles could continue and confirm the themes he had explored in the first, illustrating the courage and resourcefulness of the people of that same Scottish city; in war as it was in peace, first through its women and then by its men.

This idea took Cedric out of the immediate, away from the pressure to be on constant alert for new developments he should report. It calmed him. He set himself, over the next months, to his ambulance driving and the other assistances he could render each day to the continuing torrent of casualties returning from the front. He began to make discreet inquiries about Scottish soldiers and divisions, to try to locate a suitable group from Dundee who might become the subject for his work.

He became a much-valued member of the medical support teams. His willingness to help, and his cheerfulness despite the grimness of many of his encounters and the challenge of his daily tasks, made him a popular and well-regarded presence. The respect and affection in which he was held in many eyes was redoubled by the fact that he was a volunteer from a neutral country. He didn't have to do what he was doing; he was doing it genuinely to help. He wasn't even being paid to be there. In the eyes of those around him, 'Yankee', which was how he came universally to be known, was special because he seemed content to be doing good for good's sake.

For Cedric, it was not that at all. Almost the opposite, in fact. He was doing the work because he had to. It was his raison d'être, it had become his reason to be there. He was no longer a lurking outsider at a stranger's funeral; he had proper purpose. He had come as a reporter, but he was now an actor with a real role in alleviating pain and saving lives. It would provide a platform for his writing, but that could wait.

The send-off given to the Fourth Battalion of the Black Watch when it was called to France to join the British forces on the 23rd of February 1915 was second to none. Thousands turned out to see the battalion they knew as 'Dundee's Own' as they marched from their parade ground at Dudhope Castle to Dundee's Caledonian Railway station.

The Fourth battalion was unique in that it was made up entirely of Dundee men, officers and ranks alike. A Territorial force, it numbered 860 men led by 30 officers drawn from the businesses and professions of the city. It was commanded by Lieutenant Colonel Harry Walker, himself a son of the founder of one of Dundee's leading jute family businesses. The Walkers' Caldrum Works was one of the major employers in the city.

The spirit of the Fourth Battalion embodied the spirit of Dundee. It generated a particularly powerful outpouring of emotion as the city's men departed for the front: pride, local fervour, national patriotism, honour, excitement, love. Dundee, the city, now had an indisputably intense involvement in the conflict. Its attitude to the war would be read through the fortunes of the Fourth.

Women from Caldrum and most of the other jute mills—wives, daughters, and sweethearts—thronged with the men as they marched down through the city streets. At the station, the crowds were so heavy that the departing soldiers had to practically fight their way onto the platforms. The three trains that carried them were sent off to the strains of the bagpipes playing *Heilan Laddie* and *Bonnie Dundee*. They were given a send-off for heroes.

At the front, Cedric awaited the arrival of the Fourth Battalion with great anticipation. He had been made aware of their impending arrival when he found himself in conversation with a lightly wounded soldier in one of the field hospitals. Private Jimmy Weir of the Black Watch First Battalion had sustained a painful but mercifully shallow shrapnel wound in his upper right arm. After he was tended to and bandaged up, he chatted away with the American ambulanceman who told him he had once visited Dundee and was always interested to meet Dundonians at the front. Jimmy had been able to tell him that the Fourth were on their way.

"You're in luck, Yankee! I've a few pals from home coming out here soon in a battalion they call 'Dundee's Own'," he told Cedric. "They're territorials, and the whole lot of them are Dundee boys. My mates have written to me saying they're impatient to come out here. I didn't have the heart to reply to say don't be in such a hurry lads. Wouldn't have got past the letter censors if I had. Anyhow, it sounds like they're on their way. So look out for them when they land if you get the chance. If they come to this area, there might be more Dundee men around then than just about anywhere else outside the city itself!"

It was several months after the Fourth Battalion arrived in France until Cedric finally came into direct contact with them. They were pressed quickly into battle action at Neuve Chapelle, where they sustained their first half dozen losses, and at Aubers Ridge, where 38 more men fell and over a hundred of their ranks were wounded. The Fourth were then taken out of the firing line and Cedric had no cause to encounter them in his active relief role until September, when they were called upon to play a significant role in one of the war's major confrontations: The Battle of Loos.

Eight

As we sat together one evening in the reserve trench, I decided to ask Donald about his experiences in the Industrial School. He had barely spoken a word of it since his release, and I wondered if he needed opportunity to offload whatever it was he had bottled up inside him about those years away. I was also aware of the passage of time, and that we neither of us knew how many days we still had left to share.

"What happened to you there, Donald?" I said. "However hard it was, I guess it must pale now in comparison to this?"

My brother looked down and then quickly up at me again and replied, "Davy, if you offered me the choice of a week here in these trenches or another day in that place, I would take the first one in a heartbeat. At least here, I have a name. I have respect. I have a job that needs doing. I have money in my pocket. I am the master of my own destiny. In that place, I had none of those."

Donald drew himself up. He seemed to have decided that in the midst of the filthy conditions we were enduring, with the stench of death around us, he could now afford to tell his brother what he had been through.

"I don't really know why I didn't go into school that day. I had some stupid argument in the playground, which I don't even remember now, and there was some arithmetic I couldn't do. I just decided to have a day to myself, to be free to go roam the streets. I wasn't running away. I'd have gone back into school the next day. When that man with the hook for a hand took me to the police station, my feet left the ground and they did not land again until the door of that place was closed on me."

"I did what Mother had always told you and me to do if either of us ever got into trouble. Stand up straight, be polite, always call your elders and betters 'sir' or 'madam', say thank you, answer questions truthfully, never tell lies. I did all that with the policeman, and I told him my address and my birthday and my name and all the things he wanted to know. When he asked me about Father, I told him

he had gone away when I was one year old and I did not know where he was. I was then taken to stand in front of the sheriff with big side whiskers and a wig, who asked me the same questions all over again, and ten minutes later, I was in the police carriage being carted off to the Industrial School."

"I did not understand what was happening to me when they gave me a number to replace my name, and took my clothes and gave me the school clothes to wear. They would not tell me when I could go home. I asked them many times over the first months, and they never said. So at the end of each day, I hoped that the next day would be the day they would let me go. But that tomorrow never came. I think now that maybe that was for the best. If they had told me when I was nine that I would be kept in there until I was sixteen, I think I would have done myself a harm."

"They told me I was there to be improved. I had to be reformed and taught to be better. I asked them what I had done wrong, and they said I must have done something wrong or I would not be there. When I tried to press it, they told me that the fact I didn't know what I had done to deserve to be there showed how much I needed to be there. If I didn't even know the difference between right and wrong, I had a lot of correcting to do in the school until I could tell the difference between the two. They said I was fortunate that I would have the opportunity to be made into a better person than I was, and that would only happen with hard work over time. I would find out how much time that would take in the future, when it was decided that the improvement I needed was completed."

"I tried to follow mother's advice to be as good and polite as I could be, thinking that maybe that would make them think I was improved and they would let me go. But it didn't make any difference. Whenever anything went wrong, you were punished. I remember, in the first month, I dropped a glass bottle when it slipped out of my hand and it smashed on the floor. They took me away to a room and had me take off my clothes, and showed me the tawse they were going to beat me with. I was scared and humiliated standing there naked, and I wet the stone floor. So they beat me six times for the bottle and then six more times for making a mess. Afterwards, I had to clean it up with soap and water before they would give me my clothes back. The next time, I wasn't as terrified because I knew the pain then, but I was still frightened. The third time, and all the other times, I just stood there and took it because then you know what they have got. It is not the beating, it is the fear that kills you. Once you have conquered the fear, then you can survive."

"It was the same with the dark room. They had a room they would put you in if you were late into class, or you got lost somewhere, or you spoke when you weren't supposed to, or you didn't pay attention. It was pitch black, and there was nothing to sit on so you just had to sit on the floor. The first time they put me in there, I didn't know what else might be in the room, too, and I was terrified. I couldn't see my hand in front of my face. There was actually nothing else in the room with me, but I was still trembling when they eventually let me out. The second time, I dreaded to go back in there, but then you begin to realise that it is only time. In the end, they will let you out. The third time, and after that, I just took the punishment and did not allow it to upset me. You can learn to live with it when you know it."

"One of the men in the school liked to interfere with the boys. He would come and get you from your bed at night and take you off to his room. He would make you undress and then touch you and intrude into you. He made you do things. I just let it happen, but I must have done something right because he only ever came for me twice. Some boys he would come for over and over again. I never went to sleep until I heard him come to get a boy and then bring him back afterwards."

"After a time, I just learned that, to get through, you didn't want to stand out. There was no escape possible by trying to show you deserved reward. There was no reward; there was only punishment. So I learned to sew, I learned to tease horsehair for cushions, and I made many paper bags. I kept my head down, I never volunteered for anything, I never looked an adult in the eye in case they took it for insolence."

"I never heard a single word from outside the school. It was my only world. In fact, Mother wrote me a letter every week, but they never gave them to me. They opened them all and read them, but they only gave them to me on the day they let me out. They handed me a parcel of them all tied up with string and told me it was mine. They didn't say what was in it, so I just took it and carried it. When I went out through the door, I felt like someone leaving a hospital after an operation to have all their insides taken out. I felt like a hollow person. My legs were empty. It was all I could do to walk out of the gate."

"I didn't expect anyone to be waiting. I had spent almost half my life in there, and I didn't know what had become of you, if you had gone away, or forgotten about me, or if Mother was even still alive. I did not hope for anything. When I saw her outside, I didn't recognise her. She was very different from the picture

of her I had kept in my head. Maybe she had changed, maybe it was the picture that changed in my memory. I only knew it was her because she came over to me and hugged and kissed me, and told me who she was. I wasn't used to hugging and kissing. I didn't know what you were supposed to do. I was pleased she was there because maybe it meant I would have somewhere to go that day.

The people in the school had only told me to turn left when I passed through the gate and make my way down the hill."

"I remember walking down it with Mother. I was in quite a daze, and she took me to a cafe and asked me what I would like to eat and drink to celebrate being out. I couldn't think. In the end, Mother chose something for me to eat. It was a pastry with raspberry jam, and I devoured it. It was the best thing I had ever tasted."

"No-one had asked me to make a choice like that, or be part of any decision, in all the time I was in there. I had lost any ability I had to decide anything. That was how they broke you down: to correct you, to make you right and not wrong anymore. They weren't interested in any of your wrong opinions. So they didn't ask for any. I just did what I was told or I was punished if I didn't do it to their liking. They warned us every day that if we violated the school's rules we would be put before a judge who would condemn us to prison and when we'd served our sentence we would be committed to the reformatory in Montrose. That threat, that constant shadow over us, it made us all comply."

My brother fell silent at that. His story left me stunned, dry mouthed, without any words. I felt sick with an overwhelming feeling of guilt. I was only eight years old when he was taken but I could have stopped it. I should have made sure we were together that morning when we set off for school. If only I had let Janet go on ahead and had just waited for him. If I had just gone into the other room to get him, he would probably have come with me.

All that torment, all those wasted years, would have been saved. Why didn't I do that? My tiny, unthinking, stupid, careless decision caused all of it. I was struck dumb by the awful sense of responsibility that I felt seeping, like ice water, all over me.

Suddenly, I was jolted out of my agonised thoughts when the air around us was rent by shouting. An unholy noise in a foreign language I didn't know seemed to be surrounding us. As Donald and I looked at one another quizzically, we looked up and saw a man ranting and raving and now standing right above us on the trench parapet. He seemed delirious, out of his mind. We recognised *from his uniform that he was a German private, and he was holding a stick grenade in his right hand. He leapt down between us to the floor of our trench. He turned to confront me and carried on roaring a stream of angry, incomprehensible words, spluttering them into my face. He must have come a long way, lost in the dark, to find us so deep behind our frontline position. I was startled by all his noise and the shock of his sudden arrival. I had not yet moved a muscle in response when I saw my brother moving behind him. He had picked up his bayoneted rifle and with a perfectly executed and immaculately balanced forward lunge, he drove his bayonet up into the left-side middle of the German's back, puncturing his heart. The madman dropped down silently, uncomplainingly, to his knees. He remained semi-upright, frozen now in time, his trench delirium finally extinguished by the clean thrust of Donald's blade as the last breath left his body.*

I saw Donald calmly lay down his rifle with great care and, dropping onto one knee, he gently prised open the fingers of the German's right hand and slowly drew out the stick grenade from the dead man's failing grasp. Taking the weapon from him, and into his own hand, Donald then hurled it high over the parapet and into the vast empty ground in front of the reserve trench. It exploded immediately as it landed.

I went over to my brother and I hugged him. "You saved my life," I said. "That's what brothers are for, Davy." Donald replied.

Nine

On the night of September the 24th, 1915, Cedric Blumenthaler, ambulance man and now sometime stretcher carrier, found himself surrounded by Dundee men huddled together drinking hot sweet tea in the trenches at Loos. It was the night before what was to be a great Allied assault on the German stronghold positions in front of them, and the men of the Black Watch Fourth Battalion, 'Dundee's Own', were in good spirits, ready for their call to action the next morning.

For the journalist Blumenthaler, the arrival of so many Dundee fighters in the same place was a Godsend. He explained to them the circumstances of his earlier visit to their home city, and his plan to write a companion article about Dundee's men at war. He found the potential subjects of his writing only too willing to help.

"Did you all volunteer for the army when Kitchener made the call?" Cedric began.

"No, most of us were already signed-up territorials in Dundee long before the outbreak of the war. We were only 350 men short of the complete establishment," said one ruddy faced private named Jack. "But once war was declared, we were fully recruited inside two weeks. You'll know from your time there that work was very scarce for menfolk in Dundee, it was too good an opportunity for lads to miss!"

"I did actually have a job in the marmalade factory," said one red-haired fellow who gave his name as Willie. "But most of the lads who enlisted were out of work, and I tell you I got some heavy grief for not making way for one of them that had no work so they could sign up instead of me."

Cedric noticed the range of ages of the men. Many looked fresh faced, little more than late teenagers, but among the group there were several who might have been their fathers, even their grandfathers. "How old are you if I may ask?" he enquired of one man with a heavily lined face who wore the three stripes of a sergeant on his sleeve.

"I'm an ancient warrior called George and I'm 54 years of age," he said, peering down at the piping hot tea in the tin mug he held between his mittened hands, his fingers blackened with dirt. "I reckon I'm one of the oldest territorials in Scotland. I've been in The Black Watch more than 30 years, longer than many of these lads have been drawing breath, and I'm still here to tell the tale," he said with a grin.

"Shouldn't you be at home with your feet up by now?" Cedric asked the veteran with a smile.

"There's plenty more who are not so far behind me here and I dare say even a few older," he replied. "And anyway, if I wasn't here who would get these young shavers out of their fourposter beds every day and bring them their tea and the morning paper?"

Blumenthaler scribbled away as fast as his shorthand would permit him, marvelling all the while at the easy camaraderie of these men: friends, workmates, relatives, neighbours. All born in the same streets, many of them grown up together in the same town, taught together in the same schools, worked together, drunk together, played together, lived together, loved together. Now they were prepared to die together.

"Did they give you a good send-off when you left to come here?" Cedric asked the men.

"They did us proud," replied a dark headed lad in his early twenties named Angus. "The girls all walked through the town with us, all the way to the station, cheering and singing, hanging on to us they were. When the band struck up *Scotland The Brave* as we neared the trains, it almost made me burst with pride. I'll not forget that day as long as I live."

The next morning at five fifty, a British bombardment of the German lines began and, eight minutes later, two mines that had been planted under the forward German position by tunnellers were detonated. On that signal, the infantry rose and advanced in their masses from the British trenches.

Dundee's Own men, with Cedric watching them from their trench, poured out across no man's land towards the German positions but almost immediately faced intense fire. Many were stopped in their stride, dropped and pitched forward motionless. Others were wounded and either lay where they fell or struggled forward until their strength gave out. But their comrades carried on.

At this moment, the British released 150 tons of chlorine gas from more than 5,000 cylinders onto the German lines. The Germans had used gas to damaging effect on several occasions over the previous six months, but this was the first time the British had tried to deploy what was referred to euphemistically as 'the accessory'. Tragically, those responsible for its release had misjudged the wind. Much of the gas intended for the enemy lines blew back and engulfed their own men. Cedric watched with horror as he saw the advancing infantry disappearing into a yellow fog, blinded, unable to see a foot in front of them, wheezing, choking and coughing, suffocating.

In the confusion and chaos, some of the Dundee infantrymen made it through to the German front-line positions. Battle cries of "On the ball, Dundee!" and "Marmalade!" were heard as some of the Dundee men in numbers got through to attack the enemy positions hand-to-hand. They successfully captured some of the German frontline and support-trench positions, and took many prisoners. But their advance was not supported from behind, and those Dundonians who got that far forward found themselves without following reinforcement. Increasingly, heavy German artillery fire and counterattacks were trained upon them as the morning went on.

Many of their rifles proved unworkable, clogged with mud. Many of their ball grenades, which needed lighting with a match before throwing, were faulty and would not light in the damp conditions. They were also so heavy that they were hard to throw any distance. The stick grenades the Germans were armed with were far better suited for hurling accurately over distance, and many found their deadly mark. Isolated and bombarded, the men of the Fourth were eventually forced to give up their hard-won advanced positions and withdraw. They made repeated stands, halting and firing as they retired, incurring further heavy casualties as they drew back under withering machine-gun fire.

From the safety of the British trench, Cedric Blumenthaler watched on in speechless horror, an unprepared eyewitness to the brutal carnage of the day. The Fourth Battalion began that morning with 423 Dundonian fighting men including 21 officers. By the end of the day, all but one of those officers and 230 men were either killed or wounded. Among the fallen was the battalion's commanding officer, the jute baron, Colonel Harry Walker.

Cedric had his Dundee article now, just not the one he wanted. He had hoped to write inspiringly about heroism in the face of adversity, of the indomitable nature of the human spirit, of the victory of comradeship and the untold bravery of friends. His story could contain some of those elements but their setting would be in Dundee's darkest day.

Sickened and dry throated, Blumenthaler reached down and felt the reassuring outline of his notebook, buttoned up safely in his breast pocket. Those spirited men he had been inspired by in the trenches the night before, those men whose words he had faithfully recorded, would never see their city again. It would fall to him to write their epitaphs.

Loos was to prove the Black Watch Fourth Battalion's last act as a separate unit. Its deeply depleted ranks were amalgamated into the regiment's Fifth Battalion shortly afterward.

Ten

I shall never forget that day. July the 19th, 1916. The Somme. My brother's Last Day.

We had spent the previous evening talking to an American. Cedric Blumenthaler he was called. He was a neutral, the Americans still hadn't come in by then, but he was a brave man who had been volunteering, he said, for a couple of years on the ambulances, and now as a front line stretcher bearer. Jimmy had met him before when he was sent back to get a dressing for his shrapnel wound. It was Jimmy who brought him over to meet us.

He told Donald, Tam and me he had been in Dundee a few years before. He knew the city quite well, and he had written a big article for his newspaper in New York about the place, the jute mills and all that. He was very interested to talk to us about our lives there and he asked us if he minded if he took notes. He was hoping, when it was all finished, to write another big article.

We were glad of the chance to talk about home to be honest. It all seemed far away and, for all its mixed memories for us, it didn't seem such a bad place now looking out over these barren mud fields, littered with the fallen, that lay between us and the Germans. Donald told him a bit about his time in the Industrial School, and I told him about life working on the jute. He took plenty of notes. My word, his pencil was whipping through the pages of his thick leather-backed notebook. He looked like he had enough for a full book in there, not just one article.

He told us he had been with the Fourth Black Watch at Loos and he'd seen the carnage there. He told us about the disaster of our own gas blowing back on our troops. He'd witnessed it all at close quarters, and it had obviously really shaken him. Those poor Territorial lads were almost totally wiped out. I think he was glad to talk, to be able to speak to a few regular army Dundonians who were still at the front. Tam and Jimmy chipped in with a few reminiscences and wisecracks, too, and together we had quite a time of it. We must have been chatting away for a couple of hours. I remember seeing Blumenthaler finally put his pencil down, and I watched him button his precious notebook into his left breast pocket.

"Thank you gentlemen, that has been quite invaluable. I will try to do you all credit when I write this all up," he said. "When this bloody war is over?" Jimmy trilled, right on cue as usual.

The following morning, Donald and I were split up into different units. His was being prepared to go over the top for an advance into no-man's land. The officers felt we were gaining the upper hand in the previous days, and they wanted to try to press home the advantage while it was there. I was put in a unit a couple of lines back. It was our job to provide cover for the advance to keep the enemy busy while our men got forward.

The Germans had been using gas frequently since the Somme fighting had started, so Donald and his pals were given instructions to put on their gas masks. Those tube helmets we were issued with were hoods that fitted close over your head down to your shoulders. They were horrible to wear, the chemicals they were treated with to counter the gas stank, and the hoods restricted your breathing. You had to peer out of two mica eyepieces, but they sometimes steamed up so you could hardly see. But they were the only protection that worked against the phosgene the Germans were now using against us. Phosgene was evil stuff. At least with the chlorine they had used before, you could smell the stench of it coming a mile off. This phosgene was much harder to detect and, actually when you could get to smell it, it even seemed quite pleasant, like newly mown hay. Nice newly mown hay that would kill you.

I watched Donald as he put his mask on at the sergeant's command, and I saw the captain leading their attack first raise his arm, pistol in hand aloft, then mounting the ladder out of the trench, and up and out they all went. We watched them as they scurried out, covering the early yards still several hundred yards from the German positions. I glanced over to my right in the trench, and I saw the American Blumenthaler there, crouching, his eyes totally focused on the moving figures of Donald and the rest of his attacking platoon, their heads and shoulders dropped, moving in zigzag pattern forward.

Then we saw it. A great white cloud rolling forward from the direction of the German trenches towards us, and quickly engulfing our advancing men. As it covered them, it seemed to halt their progress almost immediately. We opened rapid fire, high over their heads, hoping to give them some protection from the

German rifles and machine guns which were picking them off now they were no longer moving at speed. I saw several of our lads tearing at their gas masks, and some were even taking them off altogether. They must have been struggling to breathe or see, or both. The masks didn't work against tear gas, we had found that out already, so it may have been that this gas attack was phosgene with tear gas combined. You couldn't know why it was all happening, but you knew that it did not look good. I had lost sight of Donald, but it seemed that Cedric Blumenthaler had not.

I heard him shout out, "Donald!" and I saw him leap up in one bound onto the firestep, and up and out, over the top. I watched him run towards the advance line, maybe 100 yards, towards a single fallen figure. I watched as he got to him, as he raised the man up, as he threw the casualty's arm around his neck, grabbed him round the belt and began to drag him back towards us. The Germans were now following their gas assault with hails of bullets, but Cedric and his man were zigzagging, at least giving the enemy guns a moving target, not a fixed one. On they clambered until finally they reached our trench, and Cedric, exhausted, passed over his stricken casualty into the hands of two of our lads, who eased him down into the trench. I could see immediately it was Donald, and he was in a very bad way. He did not appear to have been hit but he was ashen. He had no mask on and he was shallow breathing and retching fearfully. He was alive but you could see he was right on the verge.

My attention was solely on watching my brother being lifted down to two medics who were waiting, their arms raised, to take him. So with my gaze concentrated there, I did not see the moment itself.

The American, having handed him down, freed of his weight, must have stood back up momentarily watching before preparing to jump down himself. At that exact instant, he had caught a German bullet in the back. I looked up and saw him at the moment of his death, still holding at his full height for a few seconds, his tunic already flooding vivid red at the left breast. The expression on his face I cannot properly describe, but I can see it still and I can tell you that he looked so calm to me. I even thought I saw the outline of a smile as Cedric Blumenthaler sank to his knees and fell.

They saved my brother. Because Blumenthaler had got to him so soon, and carried him back so fast, they could treat him successfully with oxygen therapy in the medical tent in the reserve trench. The medic I spoke to three days later told me that there was no doubt at all that Cedric's prompt actions had saved

Donald's life. He was still desperately sick, but he would live. A few days later, Donald was invalided out of the war, discharged with honour. He was transported back by hospital ship to England, where he went to join our mother and sister in their house in Wallasey, to convalesce where they would nurse him back to health.

Cedric, a civilian of a neutral country, died a hero's death amid so much wasteful death at the Somme. I lifted his body down from where it had fallen over the lip of the trench. He had died instantly. There was nothing that could be done for him. As I looked at his face, I remembered our conversation of the night before, and I recalled his bulging notebook that contained so much of his scribbled writing, and that he had so carefully buttoned away. I reached into his bloodstained left breast pocket, and I found it there. The bullet that took him had passed straight though the middle of the notebook. It was wrapped in a light muslin bag, to protect it from the elements. It had protected it on this day from the gushing of Cedric's blood. I took the notebook out and opened it up at its first page, and I saw his name inscribed there, written in ink in an elegant copperplate script.

Cedric Blumenthaler, Journalist
The New York Times
New York
United States of America

A few days later, I wrote a short letter that I addressed to the editor of The New York Times and posted it, together with Cedric's notebook, to New York.

Dear Sir

I write to you from the British war trenches in France to return to you the notebook of your reporter Cedric Blumenthaler.

I am very sorry to tell you that he was killed by a German bullet in an act of true heroism while trying to help a fallen soldier. He ran out unarmed into heavy fire and successfully recovered my brother Donald, a Black Watch infantryman, who had fallen in no man's land after a gas attack, and brought him back to safety in our trenches. There is no doubt that his prompt action saved my brother's life, and Mr Blumenthaler is assured of my family's eternal gratitude for his act of selfless bravery.

You will see that the notebook, which he kept buttoned in his breast pocket, sadly bears the mark of the bullet that killed him.

My brother Donald and I were honoured to know Mr Blumenthaler, and to have spoken to him at length the night before he died about our lives growing up in Dundee, Scotland. He told us that he had once written an important article about Dundee in your newspaper and that he planned to write another one when this war was over. We were only too pleased to help him in his researches.

I hope you will find a fitting place to keep Cedric's notebook, which I thought only right should be returned to you.

Yours respectfully
Pte David Simpson
First Regiment
The Black Watch, France

I received a reply by telegram a week later from the managing editor of The New York Times, a Mr Carr Van Anda. He thanked me graciously for sending it, and spoke of the newspaper's great sorrow at the loss of their colleague.

He said he would see to it that Cedric's notebook would be put on display in a glass case on the newsroom floor.

Eleven

David's correspondence with New York from the front passed through the Royal Engineers' Postal Section's clearing station in Boulogne where William Henry Garston had been serving for almost 18 months.

He wrote regularly to his young wife Fanny in Liverpool, each time reassuring her that he was quite safe in REPS and was really a long way from the action of the war. And so it was. William Henry was in military uniform under the nominal command of the British Army and he was certainly located on French soil. But to all intents and purposes, he remained an employee of the British Post Office, carrying out their exact same peacetime functions they had in England, just relocated to the edge of a conflict.

The chores of collecting, sorting and distributing letters and parcels were largely unchanged, though no-one doubted the importance of keeping the frontline soldiers in contact with loved ones at home; nor the significance that had for maintaining the morale of the fighting men—and the spirits of those waiting anxiously for their safe return. The volumes of mail were huge. Almost 20,000 mailbags a day were crossing the channel to the depots in Boulogne, Le Havre and Calais.

They were frantically busy every day, but William Henry was becoming bored. He had seen Fanny only three times during his posting, when he was given leave, and he was missing her badly. What was more, he had never so far been even close to a shot fired in anger, let alone been part of the action itself. That was exactly what he had promised his young bride would be the case when he signed up to 'do his bit'. But after a year and a half of inactive proximity to the western front, he was beginning to feel something of a fraud.

Some 12,000 of his Post Office colleagues had opted to join the GPO's own territorial battalion, the Post Office Rifles, and they were now at the front seeing action daily. Those like William Henry, who had opted instead to join REPS, were really just clerks in fatigues, kept safely a long way behind the lines. He was beginning to wonder whether he had made the wrong choice.

William Henry's rising frustration was as nothing though compared to what Archie Rogers, Janet Simpson's husband, was feeling. He was still stuck in England, his training on the big field guns he had signed up for being seriously delayed by a critical lack of arms and equipment.

He had enlisted in the 57th West Lancashire division of the Royal Field Artillery in late 1914 as one of the first wave of Kitchener's volunteers. But by July the following year, he had still not laid a finger on the guns he would be required to learn to operate. None was available for training purposes. Everything the army could lay hands on was being shipped to the front. That month, for the first time, they had finally received two guns they could train with, but they were smaller than the modern issue arms they would encounter at the front and, to Archie's exasperation, they came without sights. It was humiliating.

The division had finally received the modern 18-pound BLC guns they would be deployed with—and some four and half inch howitzers—in January, so proper training had at last begun. But there was still no sign of their deployment. Archie was really regretting his enthusiasm for signing up early. He should have waited for the call. He had been so insistent to Janet that he wanted to go promptly, so he could sign up with the regiment he wanted to join, rather than wait to be conscripted. He had so much wanted to be a gunner, but he had committed far too soon. That decision had cost him 18 months away from home, away from Janet and their two children. Most of that time he had spent kicking his heels. His troop was now in the Emergency Reserves and training in Aldershot. But they were still waiting for the real thing.

At this same time, William Henry's younger brother Alex, after his long and attritional daily arguments with his mother in Wallasey, had finally worn his mother down and got his way.

"I give up, Alex!" Jane finally had said, furious and at the end of her tether.

"I will stand in your way no longer. I do not want you to go. You are not old enough, and you have some stupid, childish, romantic notion of what you will find if you are sent abroad to action. But your father clearly does not agree with me strongly enough to forbid you to go, and I have tried everything in my power to stop you. I have pleaded with you, but you continue to defy me so go. You must do what you will do."

Alex was bursting with excitement and enthusiasm at the prospect of enlisting. His mother was, of course, right about his age. He was not strictly old enough, but he did not care.

He was still only 17 years old, and the minimum qualifying age was 18. It was also true that young recruits had to be over the age of 19 before they could be posted abroad. But that was not enough to deter Alex. He sensed that his father could see he was determined to go to the front. William had made it clear with his passive attitude that he wouldn't stand in his son's way. Alex took it as his silent blessing. His mother, though, had been much more difficult, a much tougher nut to crack.

Having extracted at last his mother's grudging and despairing concession, Alex was not about to invite any more conversation or wait for a moment longer to see if she changed her mind. He made his way the very next day to the army recruiting office in Liverpool and gave in his doctored details to the recruiting official on duty, Sergeant Percy Didlock, who looked him up and down, took in at a glance that he was a fit, healthy and strong lad, and led him briskly through the formalities.

"British subject?"

"Yes, sir."

"Trade?"

"Clerk, sir."

"Married?"

"No, sir."

"Ever served before?"

"No, sir."

"Willing to be vaccinated?"

"Yes, sir."

"Willing to do general service?"

"Yes, sir."

"Height?"

"Five foot six, sir."

"Weight?"

"One hundred and twenty pounds, sir."

"Age?"

"Nineteen, sir."

"Nineteen exactly?"

"Yes, sir."

"Oh well, Happy Birthday then, lad! You're in. Next!"

On the basis of this less than forensic interrogation of his eligibility, Alex Garston was enlisted into the 21st (Reserve) Battery of The King's Liverpool Regiment. Six months later, his training complete, he was transferred into the Sixth South Lancashire Regiment.

They had sustained heavy losses in the ill-judged and ill-fated Gallipoli campaign in Turkey earlier in the year, and they were now in need of urgent reinforcement.

Alex had fully expected, once his training was over, to be following in his brother William Henry's footsteps and to be heading to the western front. So he was greatly surprised when his transfer to the Sixth South Lancashires was completed and he heard the news that he was not heading to France at all, but to Mesopotamia, to the city of Basra, to fight the Turks. Alex was beside himself with excitement. He had never left England before, and his first voyage was going to be a real life Boy's Own adventure. Such thrills!

Seventeen days later, he was on his way. That same week, he allowed his 18th birthday, for reasons of discretion, to pass quite unremarked.

Twelve

Elizabeth and Janet welcomed back Donald, the returning hero, to Wallasey with open arms. He was still weakened by the effects of the phosgene gas he had ingested but, by the time of his return, he was through the worst of it, and the doctors assured him that he should have no lasting weakness.

The medics had explained to him that, because the toxic phosgene was heavier than air, it sinks in the atmosphere when it is released. Lying flat on the ground was therefore the worst possible place he could have been. Cedric Blumenthaler, by pulling Donald up, throwing his arm over his shoulder and leading him quickly away from the gas cloud, had ensured that Donald's symptoms, harsh though they had been for a time on his breathing, his sight and his skin, had not cost him his life. His injuries, though, were more than enough to earn him his honourable discharge. He had been signed off, without demur, with his papers stamped with the endorsement that he should not be called upon to return to the army.

Elizabeth could barely conceal her joy at this outcome, but she knew her son well enough not to fuss too much over him, nor to express any joy or relief that he was now home from the war and finished with it, his life spared.

Donald did not want to discuss his experience at the front at all, and it was plain that he was actually greatly pained at being withdrawn against his will from the combat.

"The job is not done yet, Mother, and I did not complete it. I am ashamed to be here when I know that Davy and my friends are still out there fighting every day for this country, and I am not there. It makes me feel weak and useless."

"You should know that you are neither of those things, Donald," said Elizabeth. "You have served your country valiantly. There are thousands of others going out now every day to take their turn. They are ready to take your place in the lines, and to complete what you have fought for so bravely over the last two years. It will surely not be long now before this war is ended. Who could have thought it would go on so long? Two years! When it all began, people were saying it would all be finished by Christmas."

Elizabeth knew that she could not afford to leave her son too long to ponder his new situation, and that a return to an alternative but purposeful life as quickly as possible was going to be essential if he was not to sink into potentially damaging depression. Her friend the local grocer, Joseph Steggle, was quick to step in to offer her help.

"I have an opening in the shop for a storeman when Donald feels fit to return to work, Elizabeth. It's a strenuous job and a busy one. I had two young lads doing it before, but both have now been called to join up. If Donald would like the job, it is his, and we could pay him one pound a week."

Janet, encouraged by her mother, was also active in making sure her brother did not become a solitary inward-looking soul.

"Donald, I want to introduce you to my friend, Annie Dodds. She works in the munitions factory in Aintree. She lives three roads away and she is a keen dancer in search of someone who could become a regular partner for her. I think you'd like her."

Donald was the very definition of a reluctant dancer, but Annie, an effervescent and always cheerful young woman with blonde bubble-curled hair, an infectious smile and a kind word for everyone, was exactly the sort of partner that Donald needed. He had never had a serious relationship before. He had gone from the school to the army and with the army to the front, and he had had little or no experience of women of his age. The chemistry between them was instant. Annie was drawn to the challenge of this quiet, self-contained and reserved man, whose life experiences had clearly scarred him in many ways. She felt that her love could help to heal him.

Donald, meanwhile, though he was not yet brave enough to express it, fell utterly in love with her and, when they were apart, found himself seared, longing for her company and her touch.

While Elizabeth had recovered her invalided son from the war, and had been able to play an important role in getting him back onto his feet, her friend Jane was feeling quite bereft. She still had her husband William, who was bringing home good money now from his dock work, and they had Ethel and young Albert still with them. But the hollow pain she felt at the absence first of William Henry, whom she had banished and still could not bring herself to contact, and now

Alex, who should never have been allowed to sign up to this bloody war at all, was becoming acute.

The circumstances of Alex's heading out to Mesopotamia had been highly corrosive to her relationship with William. She felt disastrously let down by him, that he had been weak when he should have stood up and been a man and told his son what to do. If the army had only known Alex's real age, he would have been training in Britain for another year at least. Instead, days after his 18th birthday, he was on a ship on his way to some filthy place on the other side of the world to fight against Turks. He wasn't even fighting the blasted Germans. What on earth was it all for?

Had she still had Alex by her side, Jane would not have felt the absence of William Henry so painfully. She felt she had to make the stand she did when he was so determined to leave for that Catholic girl. She had always been very clear with William where she stood on that issue of religion in the family, and once again her husband had been less than fully supportive. He had let her carry the strain of telling William Henry that it was up to him to make the choice between that girl and his family. She never expected her son actually to make the decision he did. She mourned his loss, but she, of course, had to stand by her principles. Who would she be, what would she be, if she did not?

Her husband, though, in neither of these huge moments in their lives, had stood firm beside her. She and William had had stern words over both instances at the time, but now they did not speak of them. Jane lay the blame for both departures at William's door. He could have stopped both of them going. He didn't, and now they were both gone. She grieved their absence from her life in bitter privacy.

William Garston missed his two sons terribly, too, but he did not see things the same way as Jane. Their views were so opposed on the matter that he now avoided discussing the topic of the boys with her altogether. Rather as his own family had handled his own departure when he went off to marry Jane, he felt it was simpler and probably better to draw a complete veil over things and let events see through their course.

While he never addressed the subject with Jane, William did share his innermost feelings with his card school friends Seamus, George and Harold during their still regular Thursday evening games.

"What's the news of your two boys at the front, William?" asked Seamus one evening. "Have you had recent word of either of them?"

"We're not in regular contact with William Henry, who is at the western front, as you know. Jane has totally closed her heart to him since he decided to go marry his Catholic girl Fanny. Jane has not seen him since."

"I've had a couple of quiet drinks with him after work in Liverpool, once just before he signed up to join the Royal Engineers Postal Section and was posted out to France, and once when he came back to be with Fanny on leave. He's in Boulogne, and he's working on the sorting and distribution of letters to the front line and the collection of all the troops' return mail. It's a massive endeavour. So he is busy and he is safe enough, because he's a long way from the front line where he is. But I also thought the last time I saw him that he was sounding a bit unfulfilled, wanting to be closer to it all. I don't know how that will play out."

"And what about your other boy, William, he's just been posted to Basra, hasn't he?" asked Harold.

"Yes. There was a hell of a row over him. He's only just 18 but he was desperate to join up and do his bit so he told them he was 19, and they shipped him off literally as soon as he'd completed his six months training. Jane is beside herself about it, and she blames me for not backing her and for not forbidding him to go before he was of age."

"Why didn't, you William?" asked George. "You could have put your foot down if you'd wanted?"

"I suppose I could have, but what would that have achieved? He'd have been miserable for a few more months and then he'd have gone anyway. I admired his guts and his determination, and I didn't feel I had the right to get in his way, given how resolute he was about going."

"Must have made things very awkward for you with Jane though I guess?" said Seamus.

"It has, and here's the thing with it," said William. "When I think about the two lads going, I feel I stood back and allowed Jane to give William Henry an ultimatum. It was the same ultimatum my parents gave me when I told them I wanted to marry Jane: if you do that, you leave this family."

"Having gone through that awful rift myself, I could never have done that to a child of mine. Never. Jane felt exactly the opposite. She'd given up her Protestant family for me, and it seemed to her only right that she should make her son do the exact same thing if he now wanted to go the other way and marry a Catholic. She'd told me before we were married that it was only on the condition that we raised the family as Protestants, and I'd agreed to that, but I honestly never saw this happening. It never occurred to me we would play out with a child of ours the very same act of destruction that both our families had put us through. To be frank with you, lads, it shocked me and it broke my heart."

William paused to take a stiff draught of his glass of whisky, and Seamus moved to deal the cards before William said, "Wait just one moment, because there something else I want to get off my chest and it's not easy to say. But now is the moment to say it and then it is done."

"When you asked me, George, why didn't I put my foot down with Alex, and prevent him going to the Army when Jane didn't want to allow him to go, part of the truthful explanation is this."

"I didn't stand in Alex's way when Jane wanted me to because she had not shown any sympathy at all for William Henry when he desperately needed some. Some dark part of the reason I was happy let Alex go off to the war was because Jane so desperately wanted him to stay. Jane's refusal to compromise had already cost me one son, and I think I wanted her to know how that felt. I am ashamed of that, it was ugly and horrible, an irrational base sentiment I know. But it was there, it was undeniably part of the reason. There, I've said it now. I can only apologise for myself. I'm not proud of it, but if I can't tell you, my oldest friends, then who can I tell? And I don't want that poison bottled up inside me any longer."

"Right, Seamus, enough of all that, we've not come to talk about me and hear all my woes. Let's see what the cards have in store for us tonight. Deal your worst!"

Thirteen

As cholera is more or less endemic on the Tigris, it is remarkable that it did not occur in epidemic form when we consider the possibilities of infection and the ignorance of the soldier in matters sanitary. Frequently, men filled their water bottles at the nearest creek rather than wait a little longer for a purified supply. Even in hospital, I intercepted a patient going to the creek to fill a feeding cup for one of his fellows. It is also very difficult to prevent men patronising the native vendors of cold drinks, sweetmeats and other commodities that are all potential germ carriers.

It is difficult for anyone at home to realise the amount of pollution to which the creeks of this country are subjected. They are at once the sole water supply and the main sewer. Every sort of abomination is thrown into them, and it is the commonest of sights to see offal floating on the surface. I may mention that within 25 yards of the place from where our water supply was pumped, there was a wooden bridge, and during the course of its repair, a human corpse was found in a high state of decomposition.

Major G Grey Turner

Medical and Surgical Notes from Mesopotamia British Medical Journal July 14, 1917

MEDICAL CASE REPORT
British General Hospital 33 Basra
Mesopotamia December 31, 1916
Disease: Enteric.

Illness began seven days before admission with a shivering fit. On admission, patient complained of feeling weak but with no pain or headache. His temperature was one hundred degrees which rose by five thirty pm on the day of his admission to one hundred and four, point eight. Spleen enlarged, not tender.

Film examination confirmed no malaria. Complained of sore throat. Tonsils were swollen and also glands in neck. Swab examination—negative.

Although throat cleared up, patient did not improve but became weaker. Several examinations of the blood were made, all with negative results. A culture was eventually made which in many particulars behaved like a *B-Typhosus* and a diagnosis of Typhoid was then established. The case had been regarded as probable Typhoid from about the fourth day.

The condition was serious from the beginning. Although patient was cheerful and always assuring one that he was better, he was obviously going downhill. The case was transferred to C ward on December 24, 1916.

Lieutenant AE Finney

On admission to C ward patient was in a very low condition, typical typhoid state. Pulse very quick and very weak. Put on strychnine hypodermically but pulse did not react to treatment. Given saline injections. Temperature on the 25th was normal but patient did not show any signs of rallying, gradually going downhill until his death on December 31.

In my opinion, the disease was due to and contracted on active service in the field.

Lieutenant A Lyons

Name of deceased: Alexander Garston
Rank: Private
Unit: Sixth South Lancashire
Service: One year one month.
Date: December 31, 1916.

Fourteen

The families of fallen officers of the British services received notification of the death of their relatives in personal telegrams sent as promptly as possible from the war fronts on the confirmation of demise.

The registered next of kin of rank-and-file soldiers who died received an army notice partly-typed in a standard form with the name, rank and number, and circumstance of death, handwritten in ink into the spaces between the typewritten words. It was often several days before those notices were posted out and received. There were a great many of them to dispatch.

Their envelope dropped, unannounced, onto the doormat of Jane and William's Kingsley Road home in Wallasey on the morning of Monday, January the 8th, 1917.

William saw several letters being pushed through his letterbox, and fluttering to the floor in front of him, as he made his way downstairs for breakfast. It always amused and pleased him if ever that happened. He took the coincidence of timing as a sign of good luck, as if the postman had deliberately timed his personal delivery so he wouldn't have to break his stride as he reached the foot of the stairs. It put a smile on his face if he could scoop up the just delivered mail with barely a pause on his way into the morning room, where Jane would be preparing his eggs.

On this day, Ethel and Albert were already seated at the breakfast table and, while he was between the front door and the breakfast room, William could hear Ethel scolding her young brother for putting the milk bottle straight onto the table instead of pouring the milk out nicely into a jug. This was not a done thing in the Garston household. It was one of a number of small but unacceptable domestic faux pas that Jane and her daughter would refer to as 'the height of ignorance'.

"Manners maketh gentleman, remember, Albert!" Ethel cajoled her brother.

"The proper expression is 'Manners maketh man', Ethel," Jane corrected her from the cooker as the eggs sizzled before her in the hot fat in her pan.

William had now made his way into the room and, sifting through the postman's delivery, he had instantly seen an official looking envelope among a couple of bills and what looked like another catalogue promotion. With two sons at the front, William was very wary of official letters. He tried not to allow himself to think about the prospect of ever receiving one of these notices, not to torture himself unnecessarily. Instead, he concentrated on reassuring Jane at every opportunity that nothing was going to happen to either Alex or William Henry. They were smart boys and they would be coming home safe. Both their sons would have good fortune on their side.

As he saw the letter, though, William already knew what it contained. He knew one of them was lost. He just did not know which one. As he slid his finger under the lip of the envelope, he felt ice cold and light-headed. The bickering between Ethel and Albert was continuing, filling the air with nonsense, but he could no longer hear what they were saying. He opened the letter and drew out the single page notice with the typewritten words interspersed with the ink of the handwritten script.

The first four words of the notice were enough to confirm it: "It is my painful duty…" William's eye dropped three lines below to see his younger son's name, Alex Garston, written in ink, leaping out from the page. The rest was a blur. He saw other words: 'Rank', 'Regiment', 'which occurred on', 'Sympathy and regret of the Army Council', 'If any articles of private property left by the de…', 'when received they cannot be disposed of…'

He suddenly felt the bile rising overwhelmingly in his throat and, doubled up, he stumbled past Jane out of the back door into the yard where his body immediately and violently disgorged the contents of his stomach onto the cobbled ground. Jane ran out to him, horrified. She had been preoccupied with serving up the breakfast eggs and bacon to the plates and had not seen that William was already reading the morning post.

"William! What is it? Are you ill?" she cried in alarm. She had hardly ever seen her strong, upright husband even looking off colour, let alone being dramatically sick. He had never missed a day's work since she'd known him. "Do we need to get a doctor?"

"No, love, it's not me," said William, as he drew the back of his hand across his mouth and stood up slowly to look her in the eyes, the notice still clutched in his left hand. At that moment, time for Jane began to shudder to a complete halt.

"It's Alex," Jane.

"They're telling us he has died. Of disease.

In Mesopotamia.

Typhoid."

Jane Garston—Jane Gemmill, so stiff backed, so proud, so self-contained and the last person in the world to cause a public fuss, never a woman to draw attention to herself, privacy personified, always the one who kept her business and her family's business to herself—let out a scream that pierced their back yard and would have been heard by everyone in the entire neighbourhood. When her visceral cry finally took the peak of her breath and began to falter, it was followed immediately by another, just as loud and as long lasting as the first.

Jane dropped to her knees, her body folded in two, her face buried in her hands, now sobbing uncontrollably into her skirt. It was as if her insides were being torn out of her. She could not speak. There were no words. She didn't question it. She didn't ask William for a detail or any explanation. She didn't ask him if he was sure. If it was true.

She was engulfed by it. She was drowning in despair.

Fifteen

Jane did not tell William she blamed him. She didn't need to. William bore the responsibility for their son's death as heavily as if someone had placed a beam over his shoulders and nailed it into place there. Throughout all those long attritional exchanges she had had with Alex, prior to her finally relenting to allow him to enlist, Jane had made it abundantly clear that she was looking to William to intervene to prevent their son joining up before his time. He had not done what she wanted and, eventually, she had given up and let Alex go. Now as a result of that, he was gone forever.

For weeks in the aftermath of the news, she and William barely spoke beyond the basic necessities. Jane's face bore a pallor somewhere between ash and stone; her skin grey, her eyes lifeless. She continued to carry out her daily tasks just as before, but now mechanically and with no semblance of pleasure or pride in anything she did. William looked drawn, under-slept, perhaps even unslept, he lost weight, his appetite gone, deeply lined bags appeared beneath his eyes. He was existing rather than living, dragging through the motions of life.

Elizabeth Simpson did her very best to be the companion and friend that Jane needed over the following weeks. She visited her each day with some little gift that she thought might help to cheer her. Jane accepted them all politely, but when Elizabeth returned the following day, she saw the little bunch of flowers she had brought the day before had not found its way to a vase and lay just as she had left them on the sideboard. Or the few raisin biscuits Elizabeth had made especially for her on another occasion were still wrapped on the counter. Or the small jar of home-made raspberry jam stood neglected and unopened. For a time, their conversation was so sparse that a lesser woman than Elizabeth would have taken it as clear sign that her company was not welcome. But she knew Jane, and she persevered for her.

For a long time, Jane would not discuss it at all, but Elizabeth knew that she had to continue to try to encourage her to share something of her feelings, to open up and to let the agony and the poison seep out. If she would not speak to her privately, her oldest friend, then who else could help her? It was clear that her relationship with William had been shocked into a standstill. Elizabeth knew of no-one else to whom Jane could turn.

As they sat together over tea one afternoon, the complete silence punctuated only by the unrelenting tick-tocking of the wooden framed clock that stood on the sitting room mantlepiece, Jane finally spoke.

"I feel dead inside, Elizabeth," she said. "I feel numb and I feel appalled." Unprepared for the last word, Elizabeth replied, "In what way appalled, Jane?"

"I'm appalled at the waste of a young life taken before it had been lived. I'm appalled at William, who could have stopped it, but was too weak to do so, and I am appalled at myself for letting it happen."

"It's neither of your faults, Jane, it's just a dreadful tragedy. You mustn't blame yourselves for it."

"I blame myself most of all, Elizabeth. It's a terrible reminder that when you know something is right, then you have to stand by your principles, absolutely. If you cave in, then disaster happens. I gave up and I didn't stand firm, like my father always taught me to do. And sure enough, this is what happens when I do. Alex should never have been there in that godforsaken place. He died before he was even of the age to go. If only William… if only I…"

Jane's speech broke on that word, tears flowing down her face, her throat choking.

"We can never really know the consequence of our decisions, Jane," said Elizabeth. "We can only do what seems right at the time. It's a fine line we tread, and often we end up making decisions between two alternatives when there is actually no one answer that is better than another. Sometimes there is no 'right' answer."

"If you had stopped Alex going, you'd have no way of knowing what would have become of him. You do know, though, that you'd have made him very unhappy and very angry.

You and William did what you thought was best for him. Alex was determined to do what he could for his country, and he gave his life gallantly trying. What you should be feeling, alongside your grief of loss, is immense pride in your fallen hero of a son, not recrimination."

Jane looked up at Elizabeth and said, "That's very easy for you to say, Elizabeth, when you have your Donald safely returned from the war in your sitting room at home."

Elizabeth stood up and reached for her coat, her eyes smarting at the barb, but recognising the acute personal grief that spited her friend's reply.

"Yes, I count my blessings for that, and for the good fortune that saw him rescued before he had succumbed completely to the German gas. Another brave man made a decision there that saved my son's life, but which cost him his own. What if he hadn't seen Donald fall, or if he had hesitated for a few moments, or had just decided he had to leave him to his fate? I have wondered about that many times. Perhaps these things are meant to happen for some higher reason. We can only thank our blessings when these fine calls help us unimaginably, and do our best to think only our best thoughts when they do not. I could not possibly have blamed that American man if he had not run out to save my Donald, but if he had not done so, he would possibly have been alive today and my son almost certainly would not have been."

"Listen," said Elizabeth, feeling her emotions rising and tears starting to well in her own eyes. "I'll come by to see you again tomorrow afternoon, Jane. Take care."

With that, Elizabeth kissed her unmoving seated friend and made her own way out from her house.

With a heavy heart, William recognised he should write to William Henry to inform his estranged son of his brother's death. He wrote briefly to tell him of the circumstances of Alex's untimely demise and expressing his sorrow for William Henry's loss. He addressed it to his son's Liverpool home in Snowdrop Lane, imagining Fanny would forward it to him in France.

He was surprised to receive a reply the following afternoon when a mail boy brought a telegram to their door. The boy waited as he read it in case of any reply.

Father. Devastating news. Returning France tomorrow. Grapes at 7? WH.

"Any reply sir?" asked the boy. "No, none needed," said William.

William and his eldest son met at their appointed hour in the Grapes public house that had become their favoured, though now infrequent, meeting place since the great falling out. As William Henry entered the bar, dressed in his Royal Engineers uniform, his three sergeant's stripes on his arm, he saw his father, looking thin and drawn, hunched over an untouched glass of ale. William rose as his eldest son approached, and the two men embraced silently, holding each other close, united in their loss. At length, William withdrew from his son's clasp and went up to the bar to bring William Henry a drink.

Taking the glass of beer from his father between the fingers of his two hands with a nod of thanks, William Henry spoke first.

"I am so terribly sorry about Alex, Father. It is such awful news. He wrote to me in France not two months ago. He was upbeat and positive, just as he always was. Not a word of complaint. Mentioned the heat, but he made nothing of it. He was doing what he always longed to do, serving his country. He wouldn't have had it any other way."

"I feel dreadfully responsible for his death," said William. "Alex lied about his age to sign up, and I could have stopped it if I had acted and taken his papers in to show them."

"Listen, Father, what good would that have done? He went a few months early, but once he was 18, there would have been nothing you could have done about it. He was quite determined to go, and he would have been called upon to serve anyway. At least, you allowed him to do what his head and his heart was telling him."

"Your mother doesn't see it like that, I'm afraid," William replied, his eyes cast down.

"No, I am sure, but then Mother has strong views on many things, as we know only too well. How is she coping?"

"Not well. She is distraught, and I think she holds it against me, which doesn't help matters. We are barely talking to one another. But I'm hopeful time will heal eventually, and she will come to accept it. I really hope, if there is any scrap of good to come out of it, that it might be the way we can get her to reconcile with you and to accept Fanny into the family. Let me know when you will be next back on leave and I will see if we can get the four of us together to meet so we can try to end this senseless division."

"If you can do that, Father, I would be delighted, and I know Fanny, who still cannot make out our family at all, will be mighty relieved if she can establish something like a normal relationship with you, if such a thing is even possible with Mother!"

"Leave it with me," said William, not wanting to be drawn towards making a commitment that he did not even know if he could fulfil. "How are you and Fanny doing anyway?"

"It is a terrible thing to say in the context of my losing my closest family over her, but Fanny is the best thing that has ever happened to me, Father. We love each other so deeply and we miss each other terribly while I am away, but we look forward with great optimism to when we can be truly together. We have just spent a blissful ten days together, and I know I'll be counting the days until I am with her again when I get on the train to go back tomorrow morning. When this bloody war is over, and it can't be long now, we can't wait to have a family of our own together."

"That's wonderful, son. I wish you well with that. And how is it at the front for you now?"

"I'm not really at the front, Father, and I never have been. I'm still in Boulogne organising the same post office work that my workmates used to do here in Liverpool. I know it is really important, and it does a lot of good to help real soldiers and their loved ones to keep in touch, but most of the time I don't feel I am in the war at all. Alex's death has brought that home to me even more. My brother was killed in action in Basra, fighting for his country. Meanwhile, I am sorting mailbags in a distribution office on the French coast, a long, safe distance from any conflict. I feel like a fraud in this uniform, sometimes, Father, I really do, like an imposter.

I feel I should be doing more, like Alex was willing to do."

Sixteen

We of The Black Watch ended up staying in the Somme area for almost a whole year after my brother Donald was discharged. The Somme valley had been so devastated by shellfire that it was nigh on impossible to move in large numbers. So we went back and forth in and out of line, wiring, working and training in the muddy back areas. It was monotonous in the extreme, but at least it showed we had achieved our objective with those hugely costly attacks in the summer of 1916. The Germans now realised they could no longer maintain their position on so wide a front, and in the middle of March, they finally fell back, leaving us to advance into the areas they had evacuated. By late April, we were freely moving from place to place, carrying out salvage work, reconstructing roads and railheads that had been destroyed in the German retreat. With the Somme now quietened down, we were ordered to move north to the coast, pausing briefly to participate in what was a quick and seemingly complete British success at Messines, before we moved up to some seaside locations near Dunkirk in June. After so long staring only at the mud fields of the Somme, I tell you it was a blessed relief to see the sea and sandhills. As we marched past the promenade cafes at Oost Dunkirk, Tam, Jimmy and I were whistling "Oh I do like to be beside the seaside."

They made Tam and me up to Sergeant while we were there. It was a very proud day for me. Jimmy, our always joking Jimmy, too many jokes Jimmy; they kept him as a private.

"Look at you two!" he said, when he saw us. "Got your stripes have you now, hey! You know why you've got them, don't you? It's only because you've been here since the bloody beginning and somehow you're still alive!" "FLASH stripes, I'd call those: First Landed And Still Here!"

"If that was the only qualification, then you'd have been made a Sergeant, too, wouldn't you Jimmy? I seem to remember you came out on the same boat as us!" Tam shot back.

Jimmy leaned forward conspiratorially to us and whispered, "Look, I'm sworn to secrecy on this, but they called me in and said they were actively considering me for a promotion to a General, but they'd realised just in time that I was far too on the ball for that, and I would never fit in with the others. So they asked if I'd mind staying on as a private where I could make myself more useful to King and country by actually killing some Germans!"

"I don't know what we'd do without you, Jimmy, so try not to get your daft head shot off so we don't have to find out!" said Tam, knocking his knuckles twice on Jimmy's tin helmet.

"Aye, aye, Sergeant!" said Jimmy, grinning back, quick as a flash.

It was an easy few months we enjoyed up there, with little hostile action to speak of. Make no mistake, though. Our posting there was a total mercy. Had we not been charged with holding on to those quiet coastal positions the French had held since the very start, we would have surely been sent south to Passchendaele to fight in the most attritional and hellish battle of the war.

"I wish to apply for a transfer, sir."

"A transfer, Sergeant Garston? From the cushiest job in France? What on earth for? Men across the country would give their eye teeth for your job here, and you want to give it up? You're well regarded here, Sergeant, and the men respect you. You'd be mad to throw this away, wouldn't you?"

William Henry was not to be moved by his officer's objections. His mind was made up. He had given it another few months in Boulogne since he had returned from home leave, to see if his feelings would change, but they had not. If anything, they had only firmed up further. He felt like a charlatan, a toy soldier, serving years near the front but never seeing an enemy combatant. Pretending to be at war. His younger brother had died killed in action. He owed it now to Alex to pick up his fallen brother's weapon.

"I want to request a transfer to the Post Office Rifles, sir. I am ready to play a more active role in what remains of this war. I don't want to go home in a few months' time as a civilian dressed in a soldier's uniform."

Major Arthur Hedges could not help but respect his sergeant's stand, and it was certainly not his place to try to dissuade a respected and fit non-commissioned officer, engaged in support work, from volunteering for more active service on the front line with the Post Office's fighting regiment.

"Very well, Sergeant, if you are decided on that course, then I can only salute your integrity and your resolve. I will see if arrangements can be made. Report back to me here at this time tomorrow."

It was August 1917, and there were then two battalions of Post Office Rifles active on the western front. The First Battalion had just played a heroic role in the outstanding success the British army had achieved at the Battle of Messines, in which three lines of enemy trenches had been captured across a front of nine miles, with over 7,000 German soldiers taken prisoner. The First Battalion was for now being withdrawn from the front line.

The Second Post Office Battalion, which had not long arrived in Belgium, was heading for a village named Passchendaele to enter a battle that was already one month old. It was to the Second Battalion that William Henry's wished-for transfer from the quiet monotony of the daily routine of the Boulogne postal section was granted.

When he finally reached the firing line of the western front, more than two years after he had first landed in France, William Henry Garston was met by a sight for which nothing in his experience could ever have prepared him. The battlefield of Passchendaele was a desolate and devastated killing ground for as far as the eye could see.

Drenched for more than two months by torrential rain the locals had never seen the like of, five times heavier than it had been in either of the previous two years, the delicate drainage system of the area had been overcome. This land had, at the same time, been subjected to the most brutal artillery bombardment of the war, as the British commander-in-chief General Douglas Haig pursued his long-held dream of achieving 'the Northern Offensive', which would connect up the Allied forces in the fields of Flanders with the Allied held channel ports, thereby driving the German invaders back to the sea. The German positions around Passchendaele, though, were tenaciously held, and artillery fire from one side was met with equal ferocity from the other, each falling shell pitting the soft ground between them with wide, deep holes, creating great unnatural craters, which filled quickly with thick green muddied water.

As William Henry gazed out across this blighted scene, his eye was drawn first to the scattered remnants of the long blasted away agricultural terrain. Those few trees that still stood in what had once been verdant fields and orchards, were now just blackened charcoaled skeletons, stripped of every inch of their foliage, their twisted bald branches looking for all the world like hands grasping upward, fingers clutching desperately at the sky.

While he stared out over this bleak morass, struggling to take in, let alone make sense of, what he was seeing, the merciless artillery bombardment continued uninterrupted.

William Henry noticed, as he tried to follow the enemy shells in the vicinity of the trench that he occupied, that, as each one landed, it caused a great eruption of debris and mud, which was hurled into the air all around its impact point. It was only gradually, as his eye adjusted, that he realised that this jetsam was not only huge quantities of mud from the waterlogged ground, but also the severed limbs and sometimes the whole bodies of fallen soldiers, repeatedly jolted from their sleep by the unhalting battery of the enemy guns.

In the last days of October, with the insistent rain still falling, the Post Office Rifles were ordered forward into the front line, in preparation for the battle for Passchendaele village itself. The infantry was to advance in platoons behind a 'creeping barrage', moving smartly behind the fall of their own artillery shells, which would be fired over their heads to land protectively in front of them as they progressed towards the German line.

As dawn broke on the day of their assault, William Henry was given a section of six men to lead forward, carrying two Lewis light machine guns between them. As they stepped out of the trench from which they began their advance, William Henry led his section, which was positioned furthest to the right of the whole advance, skillfully forward, picking his ground quickly but carefully to try to avoid the most obvious and treacherous mud hazards. As the seven men moved forward together, they saw and heard many of the comrades in front, alongside and behind them not being so fortunate in their progress.

Many were finding themselves caught in sinking mud, sometimes sucking them in up to their waists, trapping them and holding them fast as helpless sitting duck targets for the waiting German snipers. The cries of the wounded and dying filled the air all around them.

William Henry continued to take his men on without mishap, halting only when it became clear that the shells of the creeping barrage were beginning to fall perilously close to their advanced position. Finding himself and his section furthest forward of all the attacking party, William Henry beckoned his men forward and jumped feet first into a waterlogged shell hole. He then signalled to them to pass down the two Lewis guns, which he held aloft out of the water while his six comrades shinned down into the mud and the slime to join him. Once all were in, they set the two guns at either forward extremity on the lip of the hole, pointed towards the German defensive positions.

As he looked around him, however, it became quickly clear to William Henry that he and his small group had come by far the furthest of all those who had set out from the trenches. They were now unsupported, and even the overhead artillery fire from the rear was now falling behind them and reducing to a halt. The strength of the German position was also abundantly clear. At the slightest hint of any movement, a torrent of gunfire from in front of them would be instantly unleashed. The section returned fire from their two Lewis guns, seeking out a barely visible but lethal enemy above the line of their shell hole.

Suddenly, after almost half an hour of heated exchange, there was a huge explosion in their watery hole as a German mortar bomb found its target. It took out not only one of their two guns, but all three men William Henry had detailed to man it. The three were killed instantly by the direct hit, their bodies blown backwards into the water of the pit, blood from their wounds billowing into a fast-expanding red cloud invading the grey green sludge in which they lay.

William Henry's three remaining men—all privates, a London postman called Alfie Strong, a Scot named Kenny McLean and Nick Thompson, a huge bear of a Geordie man—were now looking urgently to their Sergeant for instruction. Waist deep in water, under constant and continuing heavy fire, their three section colleagues now dead in the dank water they stood in, and with none of their supporting troops seemingly anywhere in sight, the desperateness of their position was not lost upon any of them. It was clear to all four men that, now the enemy had found their target range upon them once, it was only a matter of time before they would find it for a second time.

William Henry gave the men his order. "Lads. I want you to retire now. Make your way, the three of you, back towards our line. We've come too far, too quickly, here and these German positions are too strong for us to break through. The best bet is to recover our ground. So ready yourselves now, and make your way to the rear of this hole, ready to move back."

Grim-faced, the three men picked up their rifles and, holding them high over their heads, began to wade to the back of the pool.

"Alfie," said William Henry, as they turned away from him, "wait, would you do something for me? Would you carry this back and send it for me?"

The private turned around and saw William Henry reaching into his breast pocket, drawing out a simple, leather folded purse and extracting a postmarked stamped letter inside. He took a stub pencil from the same pocket and wrote on the back of the envelope.

My darling Fanny

I love you with all my heart. I long for us to be once more in each other arms and I will wait for you for all of time until we can be together again.

Please know that I did my very best. I will love you always.

Evermore Your
William Henry

Handing the letter to Alfie, William Henry said, "Her name is Fanny Garston, and you'll find the address on her letter inside. I know you're a good Postie, Alfie, and you won't let me down!"

Alfie took the letter in silence and fastened it carefully into his tunic pocket. "Aren't you coming with us, Sarge?" he said.

"I'm going to stay here a while and give these Germans something to keep them occupied. That should keep them out of your way as you three make your way back. I'll come back when the coast is clear. Off you go, Alfie, and thank you for sorting that special delivery for me."

Strong, Thompson and McLean clambered out of the back of the shell hole and instantly heard William Henry firing up the surviving Lewis gun, as they moved back up onto flat ground and started their hazardous return to British lines.

Two hours later, all three men were recovered safely into the British trenches.

Seventeen

For the next two days, Alfie Strong searched up and down the trench system for William Henry, hoping against hope that he might be able to return his letter, unmailed, to its intended sender. He asked the subalterns if they might have seen or heard anything of his Sergeant, but without result. Reconciled eventually to the awful truth, he wrote a short note that he enclosed with William Henry's letter, which he addressed as he had been instructed, and committed it to the service post.

The divisional commander came to address the men and informed them that the day had been a great success. The village of Passchendaele itself had been captured by Canadian units, which had succeeded at last in breaking through the German positions. The Post Office Rifles were also to be congratulated for how they had diverted much German firepower away from the main seat of the day's assault. They had not been expected to achieve much headway in any of their objectives, given the overbearing strength of the enemy positions they were going to encounter. And, indeed, no headway at all had been achieved, but nonetheless their bravery in occupying such heavy German forces had certainly played a part in securing the success of the real advance, the general proclaimed, attempting an encouraging and upbeat tone.

"I always thought you were a lot of stamp lickers," he said jovially "but the way you fought you went over like bloody savages."

The men listened in stony silence. The Second Post Office Rifles Battalion had lost 120 men that day in their doomed diversionary attack. Their casualties, which were recovered by the troops advancing to take over abandoned German positions following the capture of Passchendaele, included four men found in an advanced shell hole close to the German lines. Three of them were recovered from the dark water showing clear signs of being blast victims of an enemy mortar bomb. The fourth man was found slumped forward at the lip of the crater, his body spread protectively over an embedded Lewis gun, its magazines emptied of all ammunition. It was Sergeant William Henry Garston. He had been shot through the head by a single bullet from a sniper's rifle.

Two days later, at Snowdrop Lane, Liverpool Fanny Garston received her husband's final letter to her and, with it, Alfie Strong's note of explanation.

Dear Mrs Garston

My name is Alfie Strong and I am a Private with the Post Office Rifles. Your husband was my Sergeant and the last time I saw him, some days ago now, he asked if I would be sure to send this letter for him to you. I am so sorry to tell you that I fear that may have been his last request on this earth. Please find what he wrote to you in this envelope.

He was the best and bravest of men and I am sure you loved him just as dearly as his letter shows that he loved you. His selfless actions on that day saved my life and two other of his men too and I want you to know that we none of us will ever forget him. You can be very proud of him. He was a true soldier. With heartfelt sympathy at your loss.

Pte Alfie Strong
Post Office Rifles

In the same post, Fanny received the Army's standard letter of notification of death to the nominated next of kin, beginning with those dreaded ever-present words, "It is my painful duty…"

Having read her way agonisingly word-by-word through William Henry's intimate farewell to her, and then absorbed Alfie's considerate summation of her husband, Fanny's eyes were swamped in tears that ran in silent rivulets down her cheeks as she sat numbly at her kitchen table. She could barely read the official letter, squinting at it as she held it up awkwardly in her two hands, as if she might somehow be able to support herself on it.

Only his name and three words, handwritten in ink, registered through the fog: Killed in Action.

It took Fanny, in her stunned and grieving state, two more days to realise that since she had received the formal Army notification, it meant that William Henry had named her as his next of kin, and that his family therefore would not yet know that their son and brother had been killed. There was no other way for it. It would unavoidably fall upon her to inform them.

Fanny found it a desperately difficult letter to write, not only for its grim message but also because it was the first communication she had ever had with William Henry's family since they had shunned her so completely without ever meeting her. After several failed attempts, which she screwed up and hurled onto the morning room fire, she settled on a short, polite form that she made as warm as she could for parents-in-law to whom she had never been introduced.

Dear Mr and Mrs Garston

I am afraid I write with some terrible and very sad news. The Army has notified me that William Henry has been killed in action in Flanders. I have also received word from one of the men in his platoon professing his great appreciation of William Henry and giving him credit for saving his and two other men's lives. He described him as 'the best and bravest of men' and 'a true soldier'.

I am so sorry to be the bearer of these tragic tidings. I am beyond distraught to lose my ever-loving husband, and I can only extend my heartfelt sympathies to you in this our shared and irretrievable loss.

Sincerely
Fanny Garston

Jane opened the handwritten letter and read it in silence as William ate his breakfast across the table. When she had finished, she folded the page and replaced it in its envelope. Standing, she passed the letter across the table to her husband and, without further explanation, said only, "There. Now it is over." She left the room, walked without hurry up the stairs to her room and closed the door quietly behind her.

William had no cause to expect such news from what looked to be a personal letter written seemingly in a woman's hand. He was not then at all braced for what he read as he opened it. Ethel and Albert watched their father in silence, aware from the expression on his face, and the sepulchral silence of the room, that this letter contained something of great magnitude.

"It's your brother. I cannot bear to tell you, but William Henry has been killed at the front."

Ethel shrieked and, in floods of tears, ran from the room and straight up the stairs. Albert stood and did his best to comfort his father, who sat, shoulders slumped, his once handsome features creased and twisted with strain and grief. He looked a full decade older than his age as he sat, his head bowed, forehead cupped in his hands. A dejected and defeated man.

Though he was only a casual worker on the docks, William never failed to attend the pens each morning, ready to offer himself up for a day's labour. No well-paid permanent employee could have had a better record of attendance at his place of work than William. He prided himself on his regularity and his reliability. He also wouldn't ever let down his friend—the dock overseer Seamus, who had given him the chance of this work in the first place—by not turning out. Come hell or high water, William Garston would always be there. Never be an absentee, he always told his children.

Today, however, he made an exception. William put his pipe and tobacco into his jacket pocket and went out of the front door for a day-long walk, in search of air.

Over the next weeks, Elizabeth visited Jane every day, trying again to bring some comfort to her friend. Much of their time together was spent in silence. Elizabeth recognised the symptoms of shock and deep depression in her friend's demeanour, and knew that she did not have the capacity to shake herself from it through conversation. Instead, she gave Jane her company, sitting next to her in her sitting room's second armchair, sewing and making the occasional mild comment that invited Jane to say a small something in response. Most often, Jane just let Elizabeth's words fall like passing dust on the room without responding, seemingly without hearing.

When she learned that Jane had found out about William Henry's death from a letter from Fanny, Elizabeth asked Jane if she could read it. Jane passed her the envelope without comment and allowed her to absorb its words. Elizabeth, as she read it, took care to make a mental note of the Snowdrop Lane address from which Fanny had written.

"That is a kind letter, Jane," she said afterward, "she must be utterly distraught at his loss herself."

Eliciting no response, she pressed on gently. "Did you write in reply to her?"

"No," said Jane. "What have I got to say to that Catholic woman, who took my son?"

Elizabeth paused for a moment, wondering whether to let the topic go, before making the decision to try to drain her friend's still-poisoned wound.

"She was your son's wife, and she clearly loved him very dearly. You have not met, but the two of you have an eternal bond, now if not before, in your shared loss. Perhaps you sharing your grief, and showing some kindness to someone who is suffering much as you are, might be a good thing for both of you, both to give and to receive."

"It is a bit late for that now, Elizabeth," said Jane turning away.

"I am not sure that is true, Jane. Maybe that is something you can think about."

A few minutes later, Elizabeth judged it the moment to take her leave of Jane for the day.

"My, is that the time? I must make it over to Steggles to pick up my piece of ham before he closes. I will come and see you again tomorrow, Jane, my love."

William's card-playing circle had not seen their friend for three weeks. William had written to Seamus at the dock to explain his absence from the pen. He had not worked since the day he heard of William Henry's death. He had continued to leave the house at the same time every day and to return each evening as before, but he spent his time walking, along the river promenade, into the sandhills of Leasowe, through the central municipal parks in Wallasey and Birkenhead, often in a trance-like state, sick, pale, alone with his thoughts.

William tormented himself repeatedly with the questions of responsibility and blame for what had happened. Perhaps Jane was right in laying it at his door? Perhaps it all was down to him. Why, when he could have forbidden Alex from going to the recruiting office, did he not do so? But also William Henry, when he met him in the Grapes, and his eldest son had made it clear that his brother's death made him feel he had to do more in the war, why had he not sensed the danger and tried harder to dissuade him? Was that the weakness, that Jane accused him of, surfacing again?

Had he let it all go ahead with both boys for petty or high-minded reasons? Had he fallen into idiotic point-scoring with Jane, or was he being principled and pragmatic? Were his actions or, rather, the lack of them, evidence of admirable patriotic duty or was he simply being reckless and foolhardy? Would other fathers in his place have done the same, or would they have acted completely differently? Was it bravery or mindlessness that allowed him to send both his sons off to their deaths? Was this all the result of fault or fate? He replayed those questions again and again in his mind, without ever coming to clear answers on any of them. Grief made William feel a fool. He seemed to have lost his powers of reason.

Seamus had written to him offering his sympathy at his loss, and assuring him that regular work would be waiting for him whenever he was ready to do it again, but also telling him that his card-circle friends were thinking of him. William had not found the energy or the ability to respond. Hearing no reply, Seamus wrote to him a second time.

Dear William

The boys and I are missing you and much wanting to see you again. We would like to give you our condolences in person and to have the opportunity to pay our respects to your two sons. We want to offer you our friendship and some company. There is also a snippet of news about the dock which you might be interested to hear and which I could tell you about. Won't you join us this week? It is my turn to host.

Your friend, hoping to see you
Seamus

William's three friends, Seamus, Harold and George, sat together around an unopened pack of cards on the table in Seamus' parlour that Thursday evening, anxiously watching the clock as it ticked on past their usual meeting time. As it went to ten minutes past the hour, Seamus was about to pick up the deck and start to deal three hands, when there was a knock on the door, which opened to reveal the tall, but bowed, figure of William on the step.

"Good evening, chaps. I am sorry I have been away. Is there a game to be had in here?"

William looked a changed man. Hollow-cheeked and yellowed in complexion, he looked like he had lost twenty pounds in weight since they had last seen him, but none of them referred to it. They welcomed him in, took his cap and coat, and sat him down at the table. All three proffered him them sincere sympathies for his losses, trying to find words that would not ring hollow, but might somehow give him some relief from the pain of piercing grief that was quite plainly eating him away.

"Let us raise a glass here to the two fallen heroes, William Henry and Alex Garston, who gave their lives fighting for our King and our country," said Seamus, as he poured out four large whiskies.

"To William Henry and to Alex," William's three friends said in unison. "May they rest in peace."

The four men took up their card game and, quieter than normal, enjoyed their reunion and one another's company. William said little all evening but appeared politely engaged and mostly attentive when his friends spoke. As the evening neared its closing, Seamus turned to William and said, "I must just tell the piece of work news I mentioned to you."

"We have a very famous ship coming into our dock tomorrow. No-one knows about it yet, but they will sure enough tomorrow morning. It is the *SS Carpathia*!"

"The *Carpathia*—wasn't she the ship that picked all the survivors from the *Titanic* out of the ocean?" asked Harold, startled at the mention of the famous name.

"That is her, the very same," said Seamus with a proud smile. "We are unloading and loading her tomorrow. What celebrity, hey! I was just wondering, William, if you were thinking of coming back in for work soon, whether tomorrow might be a good day for you to return? If you had a day working on that ship, one of the best known in the whole world, well that would be something you could tell your grandchildren about one day, wouldn't it?"

"What do you say then, William, will you come in?"

Eighteen

That night, for the first time in many weeks, William Garston slept soundly through. The cumulative effect of so much prolonged insomnia, coupled with the previous evening's physical and emotional exhaustion of first dragging himself across the river to Seamus's house, and then managing somehow to get through the evening with his well-meaning friends, had sent him into deep unconsciousness as soon as his head had met his pillow.

He stirred himself partly awake just before six at the first light, his half-wakened mind confirming first the day of the week, and then recalling some images of the previous evening's social gathering and a card game, before that familiar pall of grief once again descended over his chest, like a shroud. He recalled, though, that he had made the decision last night on his way home that today he would try to go into work. Seamus had made it very clear he wanted to see him back on the dock stand.

The great fuss Seamus Scullion had made over the *Carpathia* was almost entirely an artifice to try to help his hollow-eyed friend shake himself out of his stupor and recover some routine and purpose in his life. To get him to return to work, to earn money, to give him something new to think about. If it did not happen soon, all three of William's friends were agreed, it could become a real worry. Did Seamus care whether the ship in his dock today was called the *Carpathia* or the *Carnation*? Not one jot. He was not at all romantic about such things. He processed hundreds of ships every year, and his only interest was in seeing them unloaded and loaded as efficiently as possible and sent out on their way, on schedule, so the next arriving ship could take the vacated berth. He didn't really care which ship they were handling the next day. They were all the same to him. But did Seamus care about restoring his friend's reason to get himself up in the morning, his reason to be? Yes, he did. Hugely.

William got up lightly and noiselessly, so as not to disturb Jane, who was still soundly asleep, her back turned to his side of the bed as was now her wont.

He made his way downstairs and knelt before the hearth to set the fire in the morning room. This was his longstanding daily ritual, which was another thing he had fallen from doing in the last weeks. And it felt good to him to restore it today. He opened out four sheets of yesterday's newspaper flat on the floor and, taking each one in turn, rolled it from its bottom right corner to its top left until it made a newsprint rope that he then tied up into a loose fat knot, which he laid on the floor of the grate to serve as kindling for the fire. When all four tied sheets were in place, he carefully positioned six small pieces of coal on top of them and struck a match to set his neat arrangement to flame. Once he saw the fire had properly caught, its warmth and rich burning smell beginning to fill the room, he rose to his feet and stood the iron fireguard before it on the hearthstone.

William took Jane up a cup of tea at her bedside and kissed her lightly on the forehead, before descending the stairs to put on his cap and raincoat. Closing the front door gently behind him, he walked down the road to the ferry. He would be early for the stand today, but it was a bright warm morning, and he wanted to use it to get some air into his lungs and to try to clear his head. William was glad the celebrated *Carpathia* at least gave him some particular reason to go in today, and maybe it was something a bit special he could tell others about. It felt like a long time since he had started any conversation. He had almost forgotten how you did that.

He stood alone on the top deck of the ferry as it ploughed across the Mersey, allowing the crosswind to blow into his face. He watched as the ferry drew close at the end of its short crossing and the magnificent *Three Graces* on Liverpool's waterfront—the Port Building, the Cunard Building and the iconic Liver Building—all three built in the last decade or so, hoved clearly and imposingly into view. They made a fine triumvirate, a rich architectural testimony to the importance of this city as one of the great ports of the world, a source of local pride. William stepped off the ferry onto the huge landing stage, the largest floating structure anywhere, it was said, and to the sound of the ever present seagulls cawing raucously as they wheeled overhead, he made his way up the ramp and began the walk round to the dock pens.

As soon as Seamus Scullion climbed up the few wooden steps onto his small, elevated platform above the Huskisson dock stand, from where he could survey all the men in the pen who were putting themselves up themselves for work that day, he immediately made out the unmistakable figure of William standing at the front. Six feet tall, head and shoulders above virtually all the others, straight backed, his hair oiled, and with that resplendent moustache. If you knew him as Seamus did, you would have noted that his clothes were today hanging loosely on his frame, that his belt was pulled into its tightest notch and, if you inspected the colour in his face, or looked closely into his eyes, you would probably see that this man did not look well. But Seamus was delighted and greatly relieved to see him back and, after picking out one or two other men randomly before him, so there could be no possible suggestion of favouritism, he beckoned to William to go through to work.

The unloading work on the *Carpathia* was completed during the morning, and the loading began after lunch. William worked diligently through the first session, though his speed, normally well on the average, was today at best only at basic pace.

He felt like some of his strength had deserted him as he went about his work. His arms felt weaker than he remembered, and he noticed his heart was pumping fast whenever he had to bear a load. He knew he was not at his best, but he was not going to let anyone down. He would finish the shift today and see how he felt tomorrow. He had been wondering for some time if he should go to see a doctor, but he had not gone. What could a doctor do anyway? It was quite clear why he felt like he did; he had just lost his two sons William Henry and Alexander. There was no pill or potion that any doctor could give him that was ever going to bring them back. Jane kept telling him he was weak, but he did not think he was a weak man. He was strong, and it was up to him to restore himself.

He would do it. He would manage to get through as he always did. As Jesus said in Luke, book four, chapter 23, "Physician, heal thyself…"

"LOOK OUT!!"

At that moment, a great wooden beam being loaded onto the ship for the purpose of shoring up cargo, was being winched by a crane onto the *Carpathia* when it slipped out of one of its chains and fell from 20 feet in the air to the ground with a thundering crash. It fell exactly where William was labouring on the deck, lost in his thoughts, his attention far away.

Could William have avoided that falling beam? Probably not. Had he been fully fit and attentive, might he have been able to see the accident as it was unfolding and been able to move from its path? Possibly. Should he have been working this day at all, was he really ready to return? Who could ever know now? The difference between life and death can be a very fine line.

Four of his fellow workers moved quickly to lift the beam from William's fallen body, and the foreman sent for a doctor immediately. He arrived within 15 minutes to attend to William, as he lay there prostrate. But everyone knew he was gone. They did not need any doctor to tell them that.

All the loading work had stopped. The ship had fallen silent.

Every worker on the *SS Carpathia* had already removed his cap and was standing grim-faced, head bowed.

Nineteen

If the losses of Alex and William Henry had the effect of turning the elemental Jane from fire into stone, then the loss of her husband William turned that stone to water.

When the police sergeant and constable knocked unannounced at her door to give her the news of the fatal accident at the dock that afternoon, Jane collapsed. Her daughter Ethel was at home and did her best to assure the policemen that she would be more than able to care for her stricken and hysterical mother. But noting that Ethel, too, had also suffered the shocking loss of her father, the senior officer asked if there was perhaps a friend from outside the family nearby whom he could inform of the tragic circumstances and who might be able to come to be with them? Ethel gave him Elizabeth's details, and the sergeant said they would call directly at the Simpsons' home to make her aware.

Elizabeth appeared within 20 minutes at their doorstep, sick with shock herself but ready to do whatever she could to console her friend and her daughter. She had brought a small bag with some overnight things so she could stay with them in their dark hour and attend, as best she could, to any needs. Albert, too, would soon be home from work and he was still unaware of his father's death.

Elizabeth found a very different Jane than the one she had been trying to comfort regularly since the loss of her two boys. Gone was the fiery uncompromised holder of firm principles. Gone was the stoic stance and the hard-edged, all-excluding, countenance.

In its place was now a woman simply plunging in grief, weeping uncontrollably, dissolving and melting in the face of a third devastating loss, simply desperate for Elizabeth's comfort and words.

"What have I done, Elizabeth?" she cried, as she sobbed into her friend's embrace. "I have lost everything! I have been such a fool and I deserve it all. How can I have been so blind, so stubborn? I have thrown it all away."

Elizabeth kept her arms tight around her and said, "You must not blame yourself, Jane, you didn't cause these things to happen. You don't deserve any of it. Good people don't deserve cruel misfortunes, but sometimes they come along anyway, and that is what has happened here."

"I've been blaming everyone else but myself, Elizabeth," said Jane through her tears.

"I can see it all now. First it was William Henry, and I thought he was being ungrateful and selfish in putting our family at risk by falling in love with a girl from the wrong religion, and I told him so. Then it was Alex, and I thought he was being naive and impetuous, and I forbade him to follow his heart, too. And then it was William, and I blamed him for us losing both of our boys by being weak and not standing up to them. I told him over and again it was his fault because he didn't stand up like a man. He didn't deserve that. He really didn't. None of them did. They were all three of them totally in the wrong as far I was concerned, but I couldn't see their side of the story, or I just wouldn't see it. I didn't even try. I was so sure I was right I wouldn't accept any other view. And now they are all gone, and I have no-one left to blame but myself. I can't believe I did and I said the things I did to all three of them. And now there is no time for me to put any of it right. I feel like this is my punishment and this is the end for me, Elizabeth. I really do. I don't think I can go on another day."

"Jane, we all deserve forgiveness. You must start by forgiving yourself. You did and said what you thought was right each time, and we none of us can do any better than that.

Perhaps in setting your principles and your standards so high, you sometimes made it hard for everyone to meet them. And perhaps you could have been kinder at times to them and to yourself, if you'd just accepted that we all have to make our own way in life and make our own decisions."

"Perhaps what a family is for, really, is not to make the decisions once the children are safely grown up, but to provide support for whatever decisions they make, whatever the repercussions they have, good or ill. What is the line in that Robert Frost poem?" "Home is the place where, when you go there, they have to take you in."

"You have suffered a terrible loss today, and two others in such a short space of time, Jane. At least be kind to yourself now. It will take time to come to terms with it all but, believe me, things will get better."

"I hope so, Elizabeth, but I'm not sure I can survive this. And anyway, I know you're trying to be kind, but how can you possibly know how I'm a feeling with the loss of my two boys and now my husband? How can anyone know? It is so completely devastating."

"I probably cannot know exactly," said Elizabeth. "But, if you think, I have had similar losses myself. I lost my two eldest children when I felt I had to let them go, and I lost my husband, too, also by awful coincidence in an accident on a ship. I am not saying these are the equivalent circumstances to yours, but I do know the searing feeling of guilt and loss and regret, and how utterly hollowing and sick-making that is. You do think you cannot go on, but you can, Jane, and you will. You still have people around you who love you, you have me around the corner who loves you and cares for you and has known you since we were children, and you have Ethel and Albert, who more than ever now will need their mother to be strong. They need you to keep going. It is not only about you, it is about all the others who are still here who need you, too."

Elizabeth paused for a moment and then she spoke again. "And you have one other person to consider too now, Jane, if I may say so."

"Who is that?" asked Jane, drying her eyes with her handkerchief and beginning to compose herself.

"The widow of your eldest son, Jane. The woman who had to write to you to tell you of William Henry's death, who had lost the love of her life and who you have never seen fit even to break bread with. The woman whose letter you felt gave you no cause to reply. If there is any good to come out of this awful tragedy, perhaps you managing to achieve some reconciliation with Fanny might be it."

"If you really feel in any way responsible for what has happened, and feel sorry for decisions you made that you now regret, and want to atone for, then perhaps extending a hand of kindness to another grieving widow, your own daughter-in-law, might be a good place to start?"

Twenty

Elizabeth proved unable to persuade Jane to write a personal letter directly to Fanny. Jane told her she had tried to write something several times, but she just could not find the words to ask for her forgiveness.

Instead, Jane had decided she would place two notices in the local newspaper, commemorating what would have been William Henry's 32nd birthday, in the hope that Fanny might see them. Perhaps that might lead Fanny, if she felt so inclined, to write again to Jane, and then she would be able to reply to her. Jane had decided she would write one notice as if it came from Fanny herself in memory of her husband. This would appear first in the column, and below it there would be a second notice which clearly came from Jane and the family.

On May the 20th, 1918, therefore, two paragraphs, each with a verse of poetry within them, appeared in the In Memoriam column of the *Liverpool Echo*. Both of them had been placed and paid for by Mrs Jane Garston.

The first read as follows.

GARSTON—In loving birthday remembrance of WILLIAM HENRY GARSTON who was killed in action November 2, 1917.

I cannot forget you, I loved you too deeply
For your memory to fade from my life like a dream
Lips need not speak when the heart mourns sincerely
And thoughts often dwell where they seldom are seen.

Sadly missed by his sorrowing wife.

Immediately below it, appeared a second notice:

GARSTON—In loving birthday remembrance of my two dear boys Sgt WILLIAM HENRY killed in action November 2, 1917 the dear husband of Frances Garston (Sadly missed). Also Pte ALEXANDER, South Lancs, who died from enteric at Basra, Mesopotamia December 31, 1916, in his 18th year. Also WILLIAM GARSTON father of the above, accidentally killed on the steamer Carpathia April 8, 1918.

I little thought their time so short
In this world to remain
When from their home they went away
And thought to come again
I do not know what pain they bore
I did not see them die;
We only know they passed away
And never said "Good-bye."

Deeply mourned by their mother, sister and brother at Kingsley Road, Wallasey.

Elizabeth Simpson was not a person who liked leaving things to chance. She did not trust in the serendipity, on which Jane was relying, that Fanny would buy a copy of the *Liverpool Echo* that day and specially seek out the In Memoriam column, in case there was some mention of her late husband in it. Elizabeth instead took the pragmatic view that Jane's carefully crafted and extremely subtle message—that Fanny herself was being 'sadly missed'—would probably go unread by its intended recipient if Elizabeth didn't do something to ensure that she saw it.

In consequence, armed with the details of Fanny's address, which she had taken careful note of when Jane first showed her Fanny's letter telling the family that William Henry had been killed, Elizabeth took it upon herself to write directly to Fanny.

Dear Fanny

We have not met but I am a dear friend of your late husband's mother, Jane Garston. I write to offer you my greatest condolences on the loss of your husband and also to enclose a clipping from yesterday's Liverpool Echo, which carried two notices placed and paid for by Jane.

I believe you knew that, as well as the loss of William Henry, the Garston family also suffered the earlier loss of his younger brother Alexander. But you may not be aware that Jane's husband, William Henry's father, William, was also sadly killed in an accident in the docks last month.

As you will imagine, after suffering three such painful losses, Jane has had a lot to come to terms with, I think it has changed her attitudes and her priorities greatly. Having been so very disinclined to meet with you, for reasons I am sure you have had explained many times, her heart is now changed and I know she would love to meet you and to know you.

I am all too aware that this is not an easy request, and I do not presume at all to anticipate how you will respond to it, but would you be prepared to meet with Jane perhaps over some tea somewhere that you like? I think it would potentially bring some peace to her. I also hope, if it can be achieved, that establishing some relationship between you and her, who share both your great love and your sad loss of your William Henry, might bring some comfort to you, too, in his loving memory.

Please reply to let me know if this would be acceptable to you and, if by chance it was, if you could propose a date, a place and a time, I will do my utmost to make sure that Jane is there to meet with you.

With kindest wishes
Elizabeth Simpson

Two days later, Elizabeth received her reply.

Dear Elizabeth

Thank you for your kind letter and for your words of sympathy. Thank you also for the newspaper cutting, which I thought very charming and was very touched to read.

You can know that I bear Jane no animus at all and, while I never understood her unwillingness to meet me, I can only imagine she must have had strong beliefs which she felt she could not betray. I have always welcomed the prospect of meeting anyone in William Henry's family, and I am so very sorry to hear of the recent death of his father. This has certainly been a terrible time of loss for the family.

So I am happy to agree to your suggestion that Jane and I might meet, and I would like to suggest the Adelphi Hotel next Thursday afternoon for tea at three o'clock, if that is convenient for Jane. It is a special place for me because it was there that I first met my beloved late husband, so it seems a fitting place for Jane and me to meet now.

Unless that is inconvenient, there is no need to reply to this letter. I shall assume that I shall see Jane there then.
With kind wishes and thank you for writing to me.

Fanny
Frances Garston

"I have arranged for you to meet Fanny next week, Jane."

"Oh, did she read the notices and the verses in the paper?"

"Yes she did, and she thought they were charming and was very touched to see them. She proposes to meet you at the Adelphi next Thursday afternoon at three for tea. Are you pleased?"

"Yes, I am very pleased, if a little daunted. How was that arranged?"

"Don't ask me that! Just know that it has been and go! It was done by magic, Jane. By a little white magic."

Twenty-One

The tide of the war changed several times during that last year of 1918. I remember the bleakest day in early March when it emerged that Lenin and his new Bolshevik revolution had signed a treaty to take Russia out of the war and had surrendered vast tracts of their controlled land to the Germans and their collaborators in the process. You didn't have to be a clever politician or any sort of military genius to work out what that meant. Not only had we lost a great empire which had been fighting resolutely on our side from the start, but the Germans were now freed from fighting on their Eastern front and could move their forces from there to double up their presence in Flanders and France. Tam, Jimmy and I, we were all agreed that would mean the beginning of the end. We had succeeded in fighting the Germans to a standstill, and we felt we might even have the beginnings of the upper hand after the successes at Messines and Passchendaele, but we were really still at stalemate. We would never be able to resist a new doubled-up German assault. It seemed to us like we were now staring down the barrel of defeat after all we had come through.

But it is never so dark as one minute before the dawn. One month later almost to the day after that Russian-German treaty, came the miraculous news that we had waited on for so long, but by then had given up all hope of ever hearing. The Americans finally entered the war on our side. They started moving thousands of men each day to the front and, instead of our being massively outnumbered by the Germans, as we had feared, the tables were entirely turned. We were being strengthened at a far faster rate than them. The Americans were sending millions of men over to end the Hell once and for all.

The Americans who landed, those that I saw anyway, were not regular army. Most of them were green, conscripted men and boys with barely a few months training under their belts. They had seen no real combat and knew nothing of how the Western front war had been. Some of the American units who came first and fought independently, were led by commanders who thought a full-frontal assault on German positions might be the quickest way to victory. They received terrible awakenings. Only when the American forces were then used as replacements, and placed under experienced British or French command, did the sheer weight of our increased numbers start to make itself felt. It was not long before the Central Powers knew they could not win the war now and, one by one, they signed peace treaties until, in the end, there was only the Germans left standing. Their end was soon coming.

The news from home also all seemed equally good. Donald wrote to tell me he had asked his girl Annie to marry him and she had accepted. I was so happy for him. He wanted to me to be his best man, and told me they would wait the ceremony until I was home when the war was over. My sister Janet wrote me with news of her children and of her husband Archie, the artilleryman, who had been held up in England for nearly two years stuck in preparation training for lack of the right equipment. She said he was now finally out at the front, and he had written to tell her he had taken part in one major battle supporting a big assault. From the date she wrote, I guessed it must have been at Passchendaele where he had cut his teeth. He would have been manning one of the guns supporting the creeping barrage from the rear. Good for him.

Janet also told me about Mother's friends the Garstons and their three, sad losses. I remember thinking that, with Donald at home, me still here and Archie safe, our family had been so lucky in comparison to them. We were close to the finishing line now.

Jane took the train over to Lime Street in Liverpool and made her way through the station over the concourse and began the very short walk to the Adelphi Hotel, which stood immediately in front of the station. She had deliberately not overdressed. She wanted to look smart for this difficult introduction, but she didn't want to look fierce or daunting to her young daughter-in-law. She wanted to look together, respectable, ordinary. Somebody that she herself would like. Not less than that, but not more. She wanted to be a different person than she had been, a better person. She wanted to be a mother.

As she walked, her heart beating faster than it should in her trepidation, she realised with a start that she had absolutely no idea of what Fanny looked like. She had never even asked to see a picture of her. A new chill of shame at that realisation washed over her.

Here she was going to tea with her daughter-in-law of more than three years and, not only did she know little or nothing about her, she had no clue how she would recognise her.

She opened the door of the hotel's cafe and was relieved to see that it was not busy. There were only three tables taken when she looked around, all occupied by women. One was taken by two shop girls, gossiping and giggling together over tea and cakes. A second was a mother, preoccupied with an infant in its perambulator. And the third was a rather grand looking lady of Jane's own age, sitting alone with a pot of tea. Jane noticed the splendid millinery creation the lady was wearing, and the fact she had not removed her gloves while she sipped her tea.

Having surveyed the scene, it was clear that Fanny had not yet arrived. That was just as Jane had hoped. It was still only ten to three. She had aimed to get there ten minutes early to give herself the chance to get properly settled in before Fanny appeared. She asked the waitress for a table facing the door, so she could observe anyone arriving in good time, and be ready to beckon her daughter-in-law over with a smiling wave when she arrived. She had played out that first sighting in her mind's eye, and practised several times in the bathroom mirror the expression she should try to have on her face until she was happy with it before she set out.

Jane asked for the afternoon tea menu and was sitting looking at it nervously without taking in a word of it when she felt a tap on her shoulder from behind. She turned around to see the smiling face of the young mother with the infant who had been sitting at the rear of the cafe.

"Mrs Garston? It's Jane, isn't it?"

Before Jane could respond, the young woman added, "It's me, Fanny. It's lovely to meet you. Let me come and join you. I'll just bring the pram over. I have somebody to introduce to you."

Jane, uncomprehending, turned and watched over her shoulder as Fanny, elegant in a cloche hat, long black coat and matching patent leather shoes, walked over to the carriage, took the handle into her hands and pushed it over to her table.

Fanny sat down and lifted the young child out of the pram onto her knee. Jane all the while just watched her in stunned silence.

"Let me introduce you first of all to my son, Jane."

Jane let out an audible gasp and put both her hands to her mouth. She still could not speak. Nothing had prepared her for this. The rehearsal that she had gone through so many times of how the conversation with Fanny would unfold, how she would try to explain herself, apologise enough, ask for her forgiveness, hope that they might… All of it, all of it, was being totally superseded now.

"Is he… is he?" she stammered, not daring to ask the question which was pressing on her lips.

"Yes, he is, Jane," said Fanny. "He is William Henry's son. He has his father's name. This is Henry, Jane. Henry Garston. He is your grandson. Would you like to hold him?"

Jane took the baby from Fanny's hands and into her arms. The baby's eye was instantly caught by a gleam of light reflecting in one of Jane's gilt earrings, and he put his hand up to touch it, a broad grin breaking out across his face as he did.

"Oh, he is adorable, Fanny!" said Jane, her eyes misting liquid. "I don't know what to say. My heart is breaking. I just want to say thank you, thank you, thank you. I cannot thank you enough."

"You don't have to thank me, Jane," said Fanny. "I am so pleased that you like him. I hoped that you might, and I rather thought that you would. He is adorable I agree, but then, of course, so he should be. He does come from very good stock after all.

On both sides of his family."

Afterword
Wallasey 1945

Joseph

When the grocer Joseph Steggle made his way back to the trestle table, to rejoin his old friends Elizabeth and Jane, the Limekiln Lane party was well underway. The air was filled with laughter and chattering, as the folk of the neighbourhood, still living under the constraints of post-war rationing, enjoyed food in quantity and quality that most had not seen for years. With the unique opportunity to pool all the ration allocations of the local area to create this single event, the local grocer, baker and butcher together had been able to produce a lavish spread, fitting for this long-awaited celebration of the end of the second war and the welcome of a hopeful new beginning.

As he made his way through children playing hopscotch and jacks on the pavement in front of his shop, and edged past groups of adults chatting animatedly outside its wide display window, Joseph was preparing his thoughts for the conversation of reminiscence he had promised the two women. He reflected as he did on the long distance he had travelled since that day, shortly after his eighth birthday, when on the death of his mother Sarah, he had been passed into public care by the artist Leonard Cartwright. He remembered that he had come to believe that Cartwright was his natural father during the time he had lived in the man's house in Rodney Street with his mother and his troubled grandmother Ann. But when he was abruptly handed over by him that day into the Liverpool Ragged School, he was told by those who took him in that he was now an orphan who had been left quite alone in the world. It had been a rude awakening.

Joseph was fortunate that his bright eyes, his polite and enthusiastic manner, and his tousled mop of black wavy hair endeared him immediately to the junior mistress of the Ragged School, a soft-hearted Irish widow by the name of Aoife O'Kane. Mrs O'Kane had immediately taken the young Joseph under her wing and resolved to do the best she could by him. The boy's shock at the sudden loss of his mother, coming not long after his grandmother's death, had been redoubled by finding himself cast suddenly into this strange new place. He clung to Aoife O'Kane's embrace and drew comfort from it. She helped the young Joseph to manage his fears of the unknown world into which he had been thrown headlong.

"Come and sit down with us, Joseph! We have saved a place here for you," said Elizabeth, beckoning him over as Joseph navigated himself through the throng, carefully holding the spout of the porcelain teapot he was carrying upright and away from the backs of the people he slipped in behind. Once seated, he poured them out three cups of steaming hot tea. He then honoured his promise.

"So, you said you want to know my story, ladies? It's not so very special, but I do know a little about yours already, so it's probably only fair that I fill in some of the gaps in mine for you, as far as I know them myself, that is. We are all of an age that, if we don't tell each other things now, then maybe we never will I suppose!"

"My earliest memory is of living with my grandmother and my mother in some rooms we had in a very busy house in the centre of Liverpool. They took it in turns to look after me. I remember there were always men coming and going and knocking on our door, so I got quite used to that. Sometimes, my grandmother would be the one looking after me in the kitchen, other times it would be my mother."

"I so loved my grandmother! I remember she used to tell me wonderful stories, and they always made me laugh. She began every story with the same words, "There was once a lovely grandmother called…" and then she would stop and look at me with the widest eyes I had ever seen until I called out her name: Ann! Only when she heard it, would she go on with the story. I discovered eventually that, if I pretended not to know her name, then, after ten seconds, she would tickle me until I ended up in sobbing fits of laughter and couldn't take a moment more of it, and I would give up and cry out her name to make her stop.

Her favourite lovely grandmother story was a fairy tale about a girl called Ann growing up when she was young and beautiful in a big house in some woods where she worked in the kitchen making delicious food and was as happy as could be. She had a lovely daughter called… and then she would stop again until I called out my mother's name, either without or with some more of her tickling. They lived together in the beautiful house until a wicked man who worked there, and who was jealous of them, chased them away. They were sad for a little while, she used to say, but then they were very lucky because Sarah had a little baby boy and he was called… same routine again for me to shout out my own name. And they all lived happily ever after. Years later, I came to realise that story probably carried a semblance of the truth in it, but I shall come back to that."

Joseph then gave Elizabeth and Jane his recollections of his time in Rodney Street at Leonard Cartwright's house, including his childish awareness that his grandmother, who has been so happy in the few rooms in the busy house, was now much less content in the splendid surroundings in which they were then living. He related the sad episode of the deaths of his two mothers, and of finding himself without warning given over by Cartwright to the Ragged School and being cared for by Mrs O'Kane.

"At that time," Joseph continued, "there had not long opened in Liverpool a new orphanage that was exclusively reserved for the children of deceased seafarers. It had been richly endowed by a group of Liverpool shipowners, and it stood in high reputation as a caring institution of education, qualities which were not then always the case among the facilities set up to care for the needy, you might say! Mrs O'Kane, God rest her, set her heart for some reason on my going to that orphanage. But there was just the small problem to overcome that I was not actually the child of a seafarer."

"Whenever I was asked about my parents at the time, I was in the habit of saying my father was a painter because that was what Cartwright was. Mrs O'Leary told me over and over to stop saying it like that, and to practice instead putting the word 'ship' in front of the word 'painter'."

"He was a ship painter, Joseph," she would say to me. "What was he? A ship painter, a ship painter to be sure, that's right, he was a ship painter!"

"Eventually, I learned her new script. Shortly afterward, she said, 'I'm going to take you to meet a nice gentleman and lady tomorrow, and when they ask you what work your father did before he died, I want you to remember to say he was a ship painter. Can you do that, Joseph?' I told her I thought I could."

"She took me for an interview the following day with a gentleman and a lady in a panelled room at the orphanage, and I was completely prepared with what I was supposed to say when I was asked that question. When it duly arrived, I gave Mrs O'Kane's made-up answer quite perfectly. Unfortunately, she had not prepared me for the next question."

"A ship painter? What is that, Joseph?" the gentleman interviewer asked me. "Is that a man who paints pictures of ships or is it someone who paints the woodwork on a ship?"

"I hadn't the slightest clue what the answer to that was supposed to be, and nor did I realise the potential significance of how I answered. The orphanage was not intended for the children of artists. If I answered the wrong way, I was on the brink of being denied admission. I stood there tongue-tied and at a complete loss, when Mrs O'Kane, who was standing behind me, thank heavens, replied for me."

"The reason young Joseph doesn't know how to answer is because his father was very much both of those things, sir and madam," she told the two officials, straight-faced. "He did beautiful paintings of ships, and he also went on ships and he painted them as they sailed along as well."

"He must have been a very talented person, then," said the lady interviewer, with her hand covering her mouth before she asked me if I knew what six times eight was and what was the hardest word I knew how to spell."

"I apparently replied, 'It's 48, ma'am, and the hardest word I know how to spell is brick. B-R-I-C-K.'"

"That's correct, Joseph, very good, the lady said, but that's not really so hard a word is it?"

"Oh it is," I said. "A brick is the hardest thing I know, ma'am."

Elizabeth and Jane both broke up into laughter at this account, and Joseph, chuckling at his own story, said, "Yes the lady laughed as well, I remember, although I didn't know why it was all so funny at the time. She asked me if I could spell a longer word than brick so I spelled out 'extraordinary', I think correctly. Anyway, they must have been quite impressed because they let me join the Liverpool Orphanage where I then had nine happy years."

"I was well looked after and fed, I progressed in my education, was taught manners and good behaviour and was equipped with work skills I could use to gain employment. I worked a lot in the gardens and that prepared me for agricultural labour. I got employment as a farmhand when I left the orphanage at the age of 16, and I stepped out into the big wide world."

"Was it really so happy a memory and so kind a place for you, Joseph?" asked Elizabeth. "My Donald had such a tough time at the Industrial School in Dundee, though, of course, that was a whole generation after you?"

"Mine was a happy memory to be honest, Elizabeth. I have spoken to Donald about his time in the Industrial School, and it was obviously very different for him. All I can say is the orphanage was set up to care for children who had lost their parents. The authorities saw us as unfortunate innocents who needed care and education, and private charitable money was made available to do it. I was very lucky to be in that group. The Industrial School was not at all the same. Donald got sent there by a magistrate, and they were less tolerant times by then. The public authorities saw children of the poor as potential criminals, so the whole nature of those places was about correction and compulsion. I am so sorry for the experience he had, Elizabeth. You would have to say, though, that Donald has turned out to be a fine man, despite that suffering. I don't know how I could have run the Steggle's shop without his commitment to the cause. Incredible to think he'll have worked for me for 30 years next year, Elizabeth, do you realise? How time flies!"

"So go on, Joseph," Jane then interrupted, "I am keen to know what happened to you next. You became a farm worker and then what?"

"This is where the connection to the lovely grandmother story comes in," said Joseph.

"I was always a keen reader, and I continued to progress my learning as much as I could once I started working and was no longer doing everyday book learning. I used to be a regular visitor to the Liverpool Central library on my days off, and I would devour the newspapers. I was so hungry for knowledge."

"It was on one of those occasions, when I was 21 years old, that I saw a public notice in the pages of the *Liverpool Daily Post*. It was headlined 'Notice of Payments and Awards', and it gave the details of ten payments that had been made over the previous six months from a fund established to 'Encourage Enterprise among the Disadvantaged'." As I read it, I saw that grants of between £25 and £75 had been given to a range of humbly-born individuals, to help them start out in a life in business on their own. One award I remember had been made to a young blacksmith, to help him buy his own anvil, tools and furnace. Another one paid for a set of ladders, brushes and a bicycle for a would-be chimney sweep. And a third went to a seamstress to help her buy a sewing machine and material and to rent a premises to start her own dressmaking business.

"The notice in the newspaper finished with these words and I have good cause to remember them well: 'Those seeking to make application for consideration for funds in the next round of awards should write to Mr Arthur Meggs, accountant and solicitor at the address shown below. By the instruction of Mrs Emily Ranelagh, Trustee of the Hugo Ranelagh Capital Fund for the Encouragement of Enterprise among the Disadvantaged.'"

"Those names meant nothing to me. But I was excited to read of the fund's existence and its purpose. I had long dreamed of opening a grocery shop of my own. Without money, that was just a pipedream; an award like this could make it possible. So I wrote an application to Mr Meggs. He wrote back thanking me for my proposal and telling me it would be considered in the next round of grants. He also included with his reply a document which set out the purpose and the history of the fund."

"It had been established by Emily Ranelagh after the death of her husband Hugo a few years previously. Herself now the beneficiary of a substantial income bequeathed her by own late father, Mrs Ranelagh had sold the family seat at Ranelagh Hall when her husband passed. Before she handed over the property to the family accountant, Arthur Meggs, to sell for her, however, she had carved out the 20 servants' houses, and the land around them that stood in the grounds of Ranelagh Hall, and gifted them to the current employees, who were living in them on a lifetime basis for a peppercorn rent. Since some of the houses were then lying empty, she also invited back some of the old loyal retainers who had been required to leave the estate during hard times. And they had the good fortune, thanks to her, to see out their last years in what remained of the Ranelagh estate on which they had worked for much of their lives."

"Mrs Ranelagh was quite plainly a very astute business person and a philanthropist, and she wanted her husband's name and legacy to have lasting positive effect. She decided the fund would not be used for the relief of hunger and destitution because, while that was a huge need, there was not sufficient money in the estate for it to last beyond a short time if it tried to address such an endless requirement. She concluded that if her husband's legacy was to bring longer-lasting benefit, it could do so better by allocating a small number of more modest payments every year to help ambitious people without financial means to get a start in their working lives."

"So when the time come to consider my application, I was called into Mr Meggs' office in Liverpool to meet him and Mrs Ranelagh there. I had to lay out my case, and set out all my hopes and aims to rent a shop and to fill it with healthy and wholesome goods, beginning with good-quality farm produce such as vegetables, fruit and eggs, and gradually extend into a full range of grocery provisions. Mr Meggs and Mrs Ranelagh said they were impressed with my explanation and recognised my ambition to succeed, and they made me an award of £50 pounds. It was the opportunity of my dreams and I thanked Mrs Ranelagh profusely for her kindness. I assured her I would do everything I could to show that her decision to give me the grant was a good use of her precious family funds."

"I was on the point of leaving the office in a state of near euphoria when Mr Meggs asked me about my surname. He said he seemed to remember the Steggle name from his dealings with the staff details of Ranelagh Hall in the past. He asked me whether I was aware of any previous connections my family might have had with the Ranelagh estate."

"I was completely taken by surprise by the suggestion and, having achieved my life's dream by winning the grant, I really did not want to open up any new conversation at all around it, especially if it could complicate things and cause some question around my eligibility for the grant—or give rise to further inquiries that would hold up or even prevent the gifting of the money. So I just shut down the suggestion as quickly and politely as I could. 'I am not aware of any, Mr Meggs, no,' I said. 'But thank you both very much for your kindness today.' I made my farewells and withdrew."

"As I was departing, I heard Mrs Ranelagh turn to Meggs and say something that at the time I didn't quite understand. It was along the lines of 'We are not looking backwards anymore, Arthur. Hugo and I did quite enough of that for a lifetime when he was alive.'"

"This fund now is all about the future, and it is the likes of Joseph Steggle's future that I would now like to help. I do not inquire into nor try to make amends for his, nor anyone else's, past."

"A cheque for £50 pounds, made out to me, arrived at my lodgings the following day, and it was that money that started me out on the journey that brought me here today."

"How fascinating, Joseph!" said Jane. "But wait, what do you think that comment of Mrs Ranelagh's meant? I don't really understand."

"That whole exchange pricked my interest, too, Jane," said Joseph. "So I decided to do a little more research into the Ranelagh family and into Mr Meggs's suggestion of a connection with my family. When I thought about it, it was obvious that Meggs was not the sort of man to throw in idle speculation or half recall. He was a careful accountant, used to confirming close details. Perhaps my mother and grandmother had worked on their estate, and perhaps Ranelagh Hall was the place from which they had been chased by the wicked man in the lovely grandmother stories."

"I did some more research at the Central Library, where it turned out there was a lot written about the Ranelaghs. Hugo's grandfather, Oswald, had been a hugely successful trader and shipowner, and had made his fortune in the slave-trading heyday of Liverpool. His son, Peregrine, Hugo's father, who was the master of one of Oswald's ships, had died in an accident at sea while he was transporting slaves. Hugo, obviously a very different character altogether from his forbears, had devoted his life to good causes and to giving away much of the family fortune built up in his grandfather's day. Piecing it together, I think Hugo was probably very uncomfortable with the source of all his family wealth. I think that must have been what Mrs Ranelagh was referring to when she talked about no longer making amends for the past but trying to help the future instead."

"Interestingly, I also found out from newspapers of the time that there had been a terrible scandal at the estate, after the manager in charge of running it was killed in unexplained circumstances. It emerged shortly after his death that he had been embezzling money for years. They are long gone now, so I cannot ask them the question, but if my grandmother and mother did work on the Ranelagh estate, and if they were made to leave it by some malign individual as my grandmother's nursery stories suggested, then perhaps it was the embezzler in charge of the place who drove them away. Who knows? It is one of those pieces of history that we cannot ever be sure of perhaps. But interesting to speculate nonetheless!"

"Anyway, the Ranelagh money was the beginning that I needed in life. From that first capital grant, over the next 25 years, we established a great grocery business, which we always tried to base on quality, honest hard work and the best possible care for our customers. I married the love of my life, Georgina, Georgina Cowper, who built up the business with me as my equal partner in every respect and who, as you know, bore me six daughters in the process, who are my total pride and joy today. Of course, they include your daughter-in-law, Elizabeth, my second-born girl, David's wife, Florence. Sadly, as you both know only too well, my Georgina was taken from me too early and died at just 52 of cancer of the liver, leaving me a widower."

"So, now you know the story! I think I must deserve another glass of that punch now, don't you?"

Georgina's death had hit Joseph hard and, in truth, it had been his six daughters who carried him through. But a light inside him went out on the day of his wife's passing, which could never be reignited. He placed his favourite photograph—a radiantly smiling picture of her in a wide-brimmed summer hat and a flower patterned dress—into a large gilt frame and set it on the wall of the Limekiln Lane shop, directly behind the till, so all their customers could continue to see her as they had done so often and for so long before.

As Elizabeth looked across at the shop now, she could see Georgina's portrait through the window. She smiled as she looked back to see her son, David, his sleeves rolled to the elbows and a broad grin spread across his face, approaching their table.

David

"Is there any tea left in that pot?" asked David, as he pulled up a seat between Elizabeth and Jane and sat himself down opposite Joseph. "I've seen you all deep in conversation but someone has to do some work around here, so I decided to volunteer for it to be me! Did I hear someone taking my lady wife's name in vain just a moment ago?"

"Not in vain, David, very much the opposite in fact! And quite rightly, too! You're one lucky man to have Florence, and you know it well enough!" said Jane pouring David out a tea, which, for the extra standing in Joseph's pot, came up rust orange once the little cloud of milk had settled in it.

"You're right, Jane," said David, "there's no doubt about my good luck with Florence, that's one thing for sure. I still remember the day not long after I'd started work as a van driver, delivering groceries to a few local shops, when I walked into Steggle's with Joseph's order and saw her sitting in the window, on a break from serving customers, a lit cigarette between those long fingers of hers. She looked up and gave me a half smile and that was enough. I couldn't get back to Steggle's quickly enough each day on my round after that! If that wasn't luck, then I don't know what is!"

"You've just missed your father-in-law's life story, so you'll have to rely on your mother to tell you any of it now that you don't already know," said Jane. "It's a rich tale and not without its mysteries either."

"Before we leave it though, Joseph," she continued, "that Ranelagh connection, how do you think about that? If that was really where Ann worked, and where Sarah was born, if it really was that cheating manager who saw them off, then what were the chances of that estate, years later, with all those connections long severed, suddenly giving you the money that set you up in life? What do you call that? Was that pure chance? Just coincidence? Or did you do something to make that happen? Or do you believe it was destined to happen? Was it the hand of fate intervening, do you think, or something more?"

"Blimey!" said David laughing, "One minute ago, I was down the road putting out three dozen hot sausage rolls onto plates, and now I suddenly find myself in deep philosophical territory. This is my kind of party! What's the answer, Joe?"

Joseph paused for second and replied, "It won't surprise you, Jane, that I have wondered about that over the years. I've often thought, if I hadn't gone into the library that day the newspaper carried the notice of the Ranelagh fund awards in it, then I might never have known about that fund. I certainly wasn't looking for it or for anything like it. I hadn't even imagined such a fund could exist, although, as soon as I read about it, I realised it was exactly what I needed. So, in answer to your question, I don't think I did anything actively to make it happen, beyond going to the library that day and reading the paper."

"No, but you were in the regular habit of doing that, and I don't suppose many other farmhands working with you were regulars in the library like you, were they?" Elizabeth interjected, leaning across to him.

"That's true enough," said Joseph. "But my part in it all feels like complete chance to me: chance that I went that day, chance I took that paper, chance I read that page, chance I spotted the notice, chance I chose to look closely at it without turning the page. Was anything really pre-planned about that?"

"Yet, I also have to admit that the outcome, if there was nothing somehow already determined in it, then it does feel like a huge coincidence. The estate that my subsequent researches suggested may well have featured hugely in my grandmother and mother's lives, in a variety of ways both good and bad, all at once comes into my life with that all changing impact years later. As you say, when it did, it was long after all connection between us had been completely severed, with my grandmother and mother both long gone. Was there divine or human hand involved there? I cannot say. But if you believe that things in life are linked, that events do lead on to other events, you could say that whether that was chance, fate or pre-determination, whatever it was, it is certainly the reason the four of us are sitting here today, with your son, Elizabeth, married to my daughter."

"If you push me further," Joseph went on after pausing for a moment, "I think that suggests that some things are meant to happen, that there is some determination in our lives. And even if we veer off in different directions for a time, we don't in the end escape the magnet that draws us towards the important outcomes that have been already been set for us."

"Anyway, let me out of hot seat, won't you, Jane?" Joseph cried. "Pick on someone your own size!"

Jane smiled and said, "It's such a big subject this, and I'm not sure there are any right answers. I used to feel so certain about so many things, but as I have got older, I have recognised it's not a world of black and white and clear rights and wrongs most of the time, as I thought so clearly when I was younger. Some things have no definite answer. Why certain things happen, and why other things don't, is one of life's great mysteries."

At that, she turned to David and put the question to him. "When you look back on your time, David, how would you explain it all? Is there a God up there or something else directing the world, or are we all just left entirely to make our own free decisions every day? You survived the Great War from the very start to the finish, you must have thought about it a lot?"

"I don't have any certainty about God," David answered. "Though Florence and I do teach children about Him every week at the Sunday School. If I think about what I have seen in my life, I think the most certainty I can get to is that Godliness is the same as Goodness. I believe you should try to make your way through life being as decent and as kind as you can be. That is Good and that is God for me. As far as possible, try to leave no damage to others in what you do, and take what opportunity you are able to, to help those who are less fortunate than you along the way."

Joseph, listening carefully, interjected at that point. "How do you square that though, David, with what you had to do in France and Flanders to stay alive—and I don't know the half of that I am sure. And how does that sit with what the world has just been through a second time in this second war? There's not been much kindness around these last six years, and I'm sure there was not much room for any in Flanders when you were there either?"

David thought for a minute before replying. "I think the First War is an example of something that was completely pre-determined. So many things were on the verge of erupting in 1914, that it could have been almost anything that set it off. I remember feeling ashamed when I asked myself when it began, why do millions of people have to die now because some Archduke we'd never heard of had been assassinated? I decided that was not a worthy thought at the time, and I tried to strike it out, but I'm not ashamed of that feeling now in retrospect. It was utter folly, human madness on a grand scale, but it was humans that created the conditions that made all the devastation almost inevitable. It happened to be an assassination that set it off. But if that had not happened, I'm quite convinced it would have been something else. It was a huge ticking time bomb, just waiting to explode."

"The war we have just been through, in my book, was a continuation of the first. We never really finished the First War, we just stopped it because the sheer appalling madness of it finally overwhelmed everyone, and halting it finally seemed more sensible than carrying on with all the senseless carnage. But, in truth, the conflict was never resolved in 1918, it ended in a bloody stalemate. Just as we made no ground in France, we made no ground solving the issues that caused the war in the first place. The attrition of the first war may well have made some of them even worse. So, I would have to say it was probably also determined that we had to go through the hell we have just been through a second time, to try to change things once and for all for the better. It wasn't an individual decision, or a single action, that caused it all. It was the ultimate effect of multiple longstanding causes determining what happened. Let us hope that we have finally done enough now to stop it."

David drew a long breath before continuing. "How do I square my own part in all that with my conscience and my thoughts about trying to do good? With difficulty, if I'm honest. I conclude, though, that we had to fight, because we decided, twice, that if we did not fight to see off the threat we judged we were facing, then the cost to our people and our way of life would be even greater and longer-lasting than if we fought to defend it. Those were decisions made by King and country, and I, and millions like me, answered those calls to take up arms. It was a particular decision though, and we can never know how things would have turned out if the powers that be had decided differently. If we had done more jaw-jaw than war-war, perhaps fewer brave and innocent people would have died. But would we have seen off the evil we hope that we have now expunged for good? Perhaps not. Probably only history will be the judge of this, and even history can never convey the whole story."

"The fact we won both wars in the end, we take as a confirmation that we made the right decisions in doing what we did. With humility, I do believe we fought on the side of what was right both times, but were we blameless in everything we did? Of course not. War is an ugly, dreadful, unforgiving thing, and it takes everyone down into the pit. To get out of it you have to win. If you ask me, I think I can just about say it was worth it. But then winners always take more satisfaction from an outcome than losers, don't they?

Would a German man of my age reach the same conclusions? Would my fallen comrades, if their voices could be heard, all say the same? I am not so sure."

"Were there personal decisions that you made, David, that you think were critical in changing the course of things in everything you went through?" asked Jane.

"Hundreds and none, Jane, would be my answer. My brother explained the nature of fear to me, and how to combat it when we first went to the trenches, and that had a massive effect on me. Donald showed me that conquering your fears was essential, a necessary ingredient of the decisions you have to make all the time if you are going to survive. If you are frightened, your decision-making becomes unreliable and you are more likely to suffer and cause others to suffer through your indecision, or hesitation or just dangerous recklessness. So, yes, I made hundreds of little decisions, dozens every day, but none of them was truly important for anything grand, I don't believe, except that maybe they kept me, and perhaps some others around me in the moment, alive for a little longer."

"Life is all about choices, isn't it," said Elizabeth, anxious to lift her son out of some painful remembrances. "I often think about that American man Blumenthaler who saved Donald's life at the Somme and lost his own life in the process." We can never even begin to repay that act of selflessness and kindness, can we?"

"We cannot, and I think of it often, too," said David. "I think Cedric had seen enough of futile war, and he wasn't prepared to see another good man he had just met and spent time with the day before going needlessly to his death. He was an ordinary person who didn't even have to be there, but he showed himself to be an extraordinarily brave man, who couldn't stand back and do nothing while another perished in front of him. Whenever I talk about godliness being the same as goodness, I think of him."

"It chills me, sometimes, also to think that I was in the firing line that day, shooting over the heads of Donald and our other advancing men to keep the Germans occupied as they went forward, and I could have done exactly what Cedric did. I could have left my position and gone over the top to try to rescue Donald. Somehow, I did not. Was that because I was so conditioned to following orders that it did not occur to me to abandon my position? It tortures me, sometimes, that thought. Was that yellow cowardice really, or paralysis, or a semi-loss of consciousness and conscience in the midst of all the noise, fire and mayhem? I promised myself that day that, if something similar ever happened again, I would not stand still and hold my ground, I would get up and run out to save a fallen man, whatever my orders had been. Mercifully, it never did repeat for me, and Donald was saved. If he had not been, I would never have forgiven myself."

Joseph intervened, anxious to move his son-in-law beyond that melancholy thought.

"If you had acted differently, you may not have been here now, David, and Donald may not have survived either, because that would have been a wholly different response to what actually happened. You and Cedric and Donald might all have been killed. Thanks to Cedric's courage and prompt action, Donald lived, that we do know. Cedric, sadly, did not live to tell the tale, but perhaps it was already determined that his life's course was run.

For those of us who do believe in Him, perhaps God's will was done that day. We cannot question that, any of us. When our time is up, it is up. When the last call comes, it brooks no argument. Never doubt your courage for a second, though, son, you are an example to us all and you have all our untold gratitude for what you did. You and your comrades, and those that followed in your footsteps in this second terrible conflict over these last few years, are the reason we are here today."

"I did no more than countless others who were called on, Joe," said David. "But thank you for your kind sentiment. I'll take it out of respect for so many who fell and were not fortunate enough to be spared like me."

Elizabeth

David felt very close to his mother. Their shared intense experience when he was growing up in Dundee, had forged a close bond between them. The years they had lived near one another in Wallasey since the end of the First War, after Elizabeth left Scotland to come and join Janet and her husband Archie in England, had ensured physical proximity helped to maintain their emotional connection. When David had left the army, like his brother Donald before him, there was nothing to draw him back to Dundee. It seemed only natural for him, too, to join his family in his sister's new home.

But as David reflected, and not without pain, on his experience and choices as a young soldier, he felt that deep excavation of memory exposing a void in his understanding of his mother's life. The two of them had never had such a conversation together as Jane and Joseph were encouraging them all to have now. He had never asked nor heard from his mother's lips how she felt about their life in Dundee, and whether she had regrets over events that she might have handled in another way a second time over.

The Simpsons were not a family that looked back much, they were people who looked forward and got on with things. If they faced obstacles, they tried to work through them. They were not great ones for hand wringing or wistfulness. They were no-nonsense people. That, though, made more for easy everyday conversation between them than it did for intimate inquiry of one another.

But taken by the nature of this discussion to a level of soul searching and articulation that he was not accustomed to, David recognised this was a time that might never come again. Elizabeth was now entering her 80s. There might not be many more such opportunities. If he was ever to hear his mother's innermost reflections on the moments of truth in her life, if she was willing to share them, this might be that occasion now. He decided to see if she would engage.

"What does this all make you think, Mother, about all that happened to you and to us in Dundee and since? If you had your time over again, are there things that you did that you would want to change?"

Elizabeth smiled at the question and looked across at her son, and at Joseph and Jane, who were sitting back in their chairs keenly awaiting her reply.

"I'm not one for regretting things really as you know, Davy," she said. "I tend to believe that things that are done are done, and that you have to get on with them and whatever follows. You have to be ready to cope with consequences. I think in life all you can do is make the best decisions you can in the moment they arise. I think it is too easy, and usually not right, to look back on them with the great wisdom of hindsight, and question or condemn them. Some choices turn out well, and maybe that is your good fortune or good luck. Others don't, and maybe that is the reverse. What you cannot ever recreate though is the exact set of circumstances of the moment those original choices were made: who you were then, what you needed most, what was going on around you, what was permitted and expected and what was not, what alternatives you really had at that time. If you are going to revisit history to look to make judgements on it, then you have to be very sure that things that may seem very clear to you now were just as clear then. Only then can you decide whether you could, or would, have made another choice. It's very hard to do that honestly because all our past decisions were made in a precise moment that is now gone forever and will never recur."

"I believe we all have things which lie outside our control and which set the context for our choices. But personally, I think, within those confines, we have complete freedom to act and to decide on what we want to do. Whether that is to turn left or right, or to pick green rather than blue. I am very troubled by the idea that our outcomes are pre-determined, that things happen because they have been decided already. Part of why that disturbs me is that I believe you have to be ready to take moral responsibility for the things you do in life. It feels all too easy for someone to say something happened because it was determined by some greater force, rather than it happened because I chose to do it. We all get to make a lot of choices in our lives, and where we eventually end up seems to me to be a destination determined by the sum of all of our decisions. I believe in God, and I pray to Him for help and guidance, but I still feel responsible for everything I do, and I always have."

Elizabeth then drew breath and paused for a moment, before looking across to Joseph Steggle.

"Can I just say, Joseph, I found your story of Hugo Ranelagh and his wife very poignant, and it resonated strongly with me. He was a man who could not by any stretch of imagination be seen as responsible for all the suffering caused by the cruel actions that his father and his grandfather felt justified to commit during their lifetimes. Those deeds mostly took place before he was even born, and they were brought to an end when he was just a child. Yet he carried the burden of them all throughout his life. That must have been an enormous weight of guilt for him to bear and, ultimately, an impossible debt for him ever to pay off, no matter how hard he tried. Did he and his wife have any children do you know, Joseph?"

"No, I believe Hugo died childless." Joseph replied.

"I am not surprised to hear that," said Elizabeth. "We can't know whether he was unable to have children or he chose not to. But my own instinct would be that he felt the only way for the family's debt finally to be repaid was for him to become the last of the Ranelagh line. I can imagine him deciding that the Ranelagh name should go the grave with his death. His wife managed to give him some legacy with the Fund you benefitted from, Joseph, so there was some good continuing to come from Hugo's life, but I believe he consciously decided his role in life was to consign his family to history in the best way he could."

"What did you mean when you said that all resonated with you, though, Mother?" asked David. "Surely the world the Ranelaghs lived in on their big estate in Liverpool was a million miles from ours, wasn't it?"

"In some ways, yes, David," Elizabeth replied. "But it resonated so strongly because it has make me think about the distinction between things you are responsible for in life and what you are answerable for," Elizabeth replied. "They aren't always the same thing. I just told you I feel responsibility for everything I have done in life, and that is true. I was responsible for my own behaviour, for my decisions, my actions, for my marriage, for the raising of my children, for my friendships and many other things."

"What has always seemed quite clear to me is that we are responsible for things we cause to happen, either by the actions we take or the actions we fail to take. But what this story of the Ranelaghs has made me reflect is that there are things in life, which we haven't caused directly ourselves, but which we still feel we have to answer for; events which we are associated with, and which have our mark upon them, even if we did not cause them ourselves. The feeling of guilt we can all feel at times in our hearts seeks those out for us. Of course, we feel guilty for bad things we have caused to happen, but we can also feel terrible guilt through our association with such things. Our sense of guilt is the judge, both of our responsibility and of accountability, it now seems to me."

"Something I have always struggled to accept responsibility for, for example, was Donald being sent away to that Industrial School. And it is perhaps only now, thinking about the Ranelaghs, that I can find the right words to reconcile it. If Donald had been caught by the police committing some criminal act, and he had been sentenced by the law to years of imprisonment, that would have been a clear sign that I had failed as a mother to bring him up in the right way, failed to teach him the correct way to behave in life. But I don't believe I did fail in that, and I don't believe Donald was guilty of anything more than a childish misdemeanour, skipping school one day. That is the reason I have never been able to come properly to terms with my being truly responsible for what happened to him."

"Until now, though, that has always felt very uncomfortable to me—like a convenient excuse, a self-serving rationalisation of the role that I had in costing my son seven years of his precious childhood freedom. My rejection of that responsibility, that ownership for what happened, has always felt like me salving my own conscience unjustifiably and that made me feel guilty twice over. I think now, what I can say to help me explain that conflicting emotion is, just as Hugo Ranelagh did, I should accept full accountability for what happened to Donald. I may not have been responsible for it happening but I was answerable for it."

"Donald's experience in that harsh school could quite easily have ruined his whole life, and I would have had that cross to bear forever if it had. I believe I was very lucky that Donald emerged from it as the man he did, given that I was unable to save him from what he went through, and I lost him completely at such an important time in his young life."

"What Hugo Ranelagh has caused me to realise is that sometimes your accountability for things can last forever, even beyond your own lifetime. That's what I meant by it resonating deeply for me. You are supposed to learn something new every day. I have learned something today, and I am grateful for it. I am so glad I heard that story. Joseph, thank you for telling it."

"How do you think about James now in that light, Elizabeth?" asked Jane of her friend, inviting her to reflect on her damaged husband and their broken marriage.

"The best thing James did for me was give me five children, and I was very blessed by that," Elizabeth replied. "He was a troubled man, and his vulnerabilities prevented him from being the husband, the father and the head of our family that I had hoped and believed he would be. But would I erase him from my life if I had the opportunity to do so now? Never in a thousand years! He gave me Janet and Donald and David, and also Robert and Ada before them. They were his precious gift to me. He was blown by a gust of wind into my dressmaker's shop that day I first met him, and I often had cause to wonder whether it was providence that blew him in there. There were times I thought it may have been an ill wind, a cruel wind, but now I think only kindly of it and how it enriched my life."

"Do you wish then you had somehow kept the marriage alive longer then, Elizabeth?" asked Joseph.

"Not for one minute," Elizabeth responded without hesitation. "James became unstable and violent because of the drink, and he physically attacked me on several occasions. He inflicted fear and pain on me, certainly, but I probably could have borne that if we had no children to worry about. The fact he did that when we had small children to care for made completely clear to me the case that he had to leave the house. I had made my marriage vows, and I would have honoured them even in the face of his aggression towards me, but I would not put our children at risk. He once knocked me across a room and I came within inches of falling heavily on top of Janet, who was then a new-born baby lying on the floor. And he later on attacked me when I was in early pregnancy with David. In both instances, he could have caused the death of one of our children. The first time, I somehow managed to rationalise it, to excuse him, and I eventually took him back. The second instance was the end. It showed me how much danger I was placing my children in."

"I never actually ended my marriage, Joseph, but I never let him back over the door and I never would have again. I could not have borne being responsible for what might have happened if I had."

"Did you love James, Elizabeth?" asked Jane.

"Yes I did, and I never stopped loving him. I thought when I met him that he was a strong man, but I was mistaken and he turned out to be very weak one. Of itself, though, that made no difference. He was my husband, and we had promised to stay together for better or for worse. I would have done that, but he showed that he could not be safely under the same roof with our children again. Their safety was a much higher calling."

As Elizabeth paused to take a sip of tea, David felt the need to return to the subject of his elder brother and his own responsibility for the fateful day Donald found himself committed into the Industrial School. "I still feel terrible about it, Mother, and I know I could so easily have stopped it happening if I had only made sure Donald came to school with me."

As Elizabeth responded, an unmistakable wince of pain at the recollection crossed her face. "I think that day was a combination of small mistakes, which we all made, and that had awful consequences, which were far greater than those mistakes ever deserved. You should not feel responsible for it at all, Davy, you were eight years old! I left the house to go to work, and I didn't make sure that you all three were all properly set for school when the time came for you to leave. That fault was mine. Janet, who was only a slip of a child herself, with too much responsibility for her young shoulders, was not able to make sure Donald left with her and you that day, and Donald was naughty enough at nine years old to decide he was going to play truant."

"But what happened after that was just wrong, and not in proportion at all to the offence. It was set in motion by forces that were far beyond our control. The powers that be in that day were pre-disposed to quickly condemning a poor child on the street as a vagrant, who would soon become a criminal if he wasn't one already. They did not see an innocent young boy missing a day of school without permission. They saw him as a threat, a future cost to society, who needed to be put away and put right."

"What that showed frighteningly," Elizabeth continued, "was the terrible vulnerability of people who are poor. If it had been the son of the magistrate, or a doctor, who had played truant that day, you could be sure as eggs is eggs that he would not have been bundled off and locked up for years in the way Donald was. If you have no money, you have no influence or connection, you cannot ask or expect any favour. There will be no kind exceptions made for you. Because of who you are, the answer you will almost certainly get to any pleas you make for help has already been decided and it is 'No!' As a pauper, you are someone to whom things happen rather than someone who can make things happen. The poor have no control. That is their lot. It is the way of the world."

"We managed well enough as a family without much money, and, in many ways, not having much money makes life straightforward. You wake up thinking only about the important jobs of putting food on the table that day, making sure you are clean, warm and healthy, and keeping a roof over your head. There is nothing much to distract you from those basic needs so you get on with that. Your life is just about managing."

"Having money makes life more complicated and introduces a host of new decisions for you to make: should we do this or that, shall we buy this today or that? I am not saying poverty makes life easy, it most certainly does not, but it does make it simple. I also think the pleasure from the few things you get to enjoy when you have very little is much greater than that felt by those who can have nice things all the time. Nice things alone won't make you happy."

"But money can buy much more than just nice things. Money can bring you some standing, some power, some element of control over your own life. Without it, you can find yourself easily at the mercy of others, without a voice, and that is not a good place to be."

"So, if we are talking about choice, when Donald was locked up, I had no choice at all in that matter. No choice about it happening, no way of preventing it or changing it, and no other choice in the world but to wait until they let him out. All I could do was to write a letter to him every week, in the hope they would let him see it, and that it would give him some little comfort, so he didn't forget us or ever fear that we had forgotten him. As it turned out, even that small concession was not granted to him. He was handed all the letters on his way out. It was the first time he had seen them."

Jane had one further question for her friend. "I must just ask, what about Robert and Ada, Elizabeth? How did you reconcile yourself to losing them when you agreed to pass them over to James's parents? That must have been the hardest choice of all your choices mustn't it? I have always found that so hard to imagine, and I feel so sorry that you had to make it."

"I think you know, Jane, that that was a dark day in my life, and I remember feeling then I did not know if I could carry on having made that decision. I take complete responsibility for it, and it is a source of unending sorrow in my life that I have never seen my two eldest children again. But I do not regret that decision. James and I were virtually penniless at the time, and the very same public system that a dozen years later decided Donald needed to be locked up in a special school for seven years because he missed a few classes one morning, would have taken both Robert and Ada away from James and me without hesitation if it once decided we were not able to make ends meet or weren't suitable parents to keep them."

"There is not a day that passes that I do not think of Robert and Ada and wonder what became of them. But that was one of those terrible decisions that is both almost impossibly difficult, yet also very clear at the same time. The more I struggled with it, the more it became clear it was really not a choice at all. Perhaps that is what is meant by some of our actions being pre-determined? Sometimes, what you have to decide between is two bad outcomes, and the only decision you really have open to you is, which of the two is the less dreadful. The alternative for me, to have refused to give them up, and to insist on taking them with James and me, would have been selfish and reckless. I put the children's interests first and I still believe I made the right choice in the round, though it nearly killed me to do it."

"I have paid a heavy price for that every day of my life, and I have asked for forgiveness and understanding of it each and every night since. But I have at least had the salvation of my second family of Janet, Donald and David, and who knows whether any of them would even have been born if I had acted differently? So one thing leads to another. One door closes, another opens."

"All I can say is, we have been very happy as a family, and I can only hope and believe that Robert and Ada have been, too, with the different, but I'm sure good, start in their lives that they were given."

"Hear, hear to that!" said David, now keen to move the conversation onto new ground.

"Let me go and bring out a new pot of tea. Could I tempt anyone to a little drop of cherry brandy to go with it?"

Jane

Jane Garston had never found it easy to share her deepest thoughts with others. She considered her private reflections her own business, and she had been brought up to overcome weaknesses, not revel in them. As she progressed into adulthood, this had made her the person she had been: self-contained, resolute, clear-headed. But the tragic events of the final years of the First War had convulsed her. Her three family losses coming in quick succession had caused her to question herself, to question everything.

Bad experiences are often greater teachers than good ones. Good outcomes convince us that all is well with the world; they suggest we are in the right place. They reinforce our convictions, our complacency. They do not drive change because who knowingly disrupts a happy and rewarding position? Bad experiences tend to do the opposite of all those things.

So it was with Jane. The Jane Garston of her second adulthood was an altogether different woman than she had been.

As David returned with the fresh tea, his specially kept back bottle of cherry brandy and four small glasses, the street party music was beginning to strike up. David's eldest, the young Army captain Douglas, had built up an impressive collection of the latest dance records and was playing them gently at first, but progressively a little louder, as the party progressed. Strains of Glenn Miller's *In the Mood*, Cab Calloway's *Between the Devil and the Deep Blue Sea* and Frank Sinatra's *Fools Rush In* provided an undertone of musical accompaniment to all the conversation and the laughter.

"I suppose that leaves only me to say something?" said Jane, when they were all seated together again. None of the others spoke, but their looks of encouragement to her made any reply unnecessary.

"I read quite widely for some time about this question of how far we really have free will in the actions we take. I was desperate to establish whether we are just actors on a stage, playing out a script that has already been written for us, or whether we are truly the authors of our own lives."

"After I lost William and my two boys, I was so bereft and at such a loss to explain anything to myself or anyone else, I submerged myself in that reading. I took refuge in it. I hoped some of the great philosophers, ancient and modern, might be able to help me. But the more I read, the more I saw that philosophy does not provide simple answers. It is not a science, like chemistry or mathematics. It doesn't have hard rules you can learn from.

"Philosophy won't tell you that two plus two will always make four or explain why water disappears if you boil it long enough. Philosophy only offers you ways to think about things that are not certain. It doesn't give you answers; it presents questions. When I first saw that, as I scoured book after book, I became frustrated and angry. I desperately wanted someone to give me some simple certainty, to explain why what had happened to my boys and to me had taken place."

"I came to realise this is a subject that philosophers have puzzled over for thousands of years and will likely for thousands more. Sophocles, who was alive 450 years before Christ, captured it best to my mind when he said, 'All our mortal lives are set in danger and perplexity: one day to prosper and the next—who knows? When all is well, then, look for rocks ahead.'

"I understand that better now, but then, in my hour of greatest need, I was furious with that. I did not want Sophocles' perplexity or his who knows; I wanted answers. Why had so many things gone wrong in my life? I had been so careful, so clear about what I wanted, so sure of what was right and what was not. I had tried to live in the correct way, and bring up my family to do the same and yet, suddenly, all that was gone, just obliterated in a few short months. In the terms of the classical literature I was poring over, had I been too proud, was I guilty of hubris? Had I angered the gods? It certainly seemed like it. My despair, and my own responsibility for it, was confirmed."

"You have all said what you think brought you to this place today on your long journeys. For me, the answer to that is very clear, and it is one thing, actually, in my case, one person. Without Elizabeth, I would not be sitting here today. I was eviscerated by my losses; I could not explain why they had happened. In consequence, I could not come to terms with any of it. It felt like I had been cast overboard from a great ship at sea, with sickening waves of grief and anger and indignation drowning me. I could not get forward, no matter how much I struggled. So after a time, I gave up. I abandoned everything. I had lost the will to carry on. I wanted to be gone, erased from this place. What welcome I had ever had on earth, events had shown me that I had outstayed it. I deserved to be gone."

"But I did have one person who stayed with me through it all. She never wavered, even when I spoke to her rudely or unkindly. I shudder now to think of some of the things I said to her. She says she has long forgiven me. I am not sure I have forgiven myself. But despite all my ingratitude and cussedness, Elizabeth was always quiet, patient and she held me up. She sustained me. The hours we sat in my front room together in each other's company, with barely a word spoken. Only the ticking of my mantlepiece clock marking the passage of the time. I don't know how she did it."

"But during all that period, without ever telling me how to think or what to do, Elizabeth taught me the most important lesson of my life. She was able to do that because, although we had been close friends since our childhoods, I had never noticed that she had run her life in a totally different way than I had run mine. She let me see that as we sat together in my room, and it finally shone a light into the darkness for me."

"What was that difference? Let me tell you. Elizabeth always made people the most important thing of all. To me, it was my principles that were paramount. Where I had doctrines, she had love. She devoted herself to those around her, and set loyalty to others as her byword. Through the good times and the bad, she was a constant for herself and for others. I decided what was important and unassailable to me, and I made everyone around me follow it. Elizabeth understood the constant need for understanding, for compromise and for pragmatism. I dismissed those qualities as weaknesses. I was certain I was right. But I was wrong."

Joseph, David and Elizabeth listened transfixed in silence, their drinks poured but still standing untouched, as Jane continued.

"What that led me to was another dark realisation. I had permitted hatred to enter my soul. I saw those who did not live by my rules, my standards as my enemies. They were people to loathe and despise.

Some of that, I learned from my father, who could not find a good word for any Catholic, and I adopted that same unthinking tack. I decided whole bodies of people were beyond the pale because of who they were, what they believed, where they came from. I was not interested in meeting any of them, because I thought I already knew them and I knew I did not like them. I didn't need to know them individually. There was nothing for me to learn. I could simply compartmentalise them as groups that I would have nothing to do with. I can hardly credit it now when I think back. Can that really have been me, condemning a whole race, a creed, a nation of millions of people at a single stroke? For me, Catholics were feckless, idle and dirty. Catholics were Irish. I thought they should return to their own country. I could not tolerate them. I would have no truck with them. I hated them."

"Once you permit hatred to enter your heart and your words, it is like sulphur in the veins. Your temperature rises, your blood boils, your heart beats too fast, you see only what you want to see, there is no good in what you despise. Once you decide that an entire group of people can be summed up not as individuals but as a mass that can be dismissed in a sentence or two, that is the path to insanity. It is not a long step before that insanity corrupts into evil. We have all seen the horror that can bring in the sickening cruelty and inhumanity of these last few years of war, that has only now been brought out into the open."

"If I am honest, I saw that process of corruption happening in my own father, Tommy Gemmill, who turned from a person of strong conviction into a man of bigotry and violence. I saw that with my own eyes and I heard it when he spoke to his Protestant friends Jocky and the others. He would not use his most venomous language of violence when talking to me. But when he thought I was out of earshot, or he simply forgot my presence altogether, the man he had truly become was laid bare and it was an ugly sight to behold."

"Did that awareness of your father's increasingly extreme views play a part in your decision to marry William, even though he was a Catholic, Jane?" asked Joseph.

"I did not see it in quite those terms at the time, Joseph, but looking back, I believe it did. I was not yet ready to leave behind everything my father had given me in his words about hard work, discipline and principles. They were still mainstays for me. But amid those words, which I thought were wise counsel, there was dangerous excess, even something of the devil in him. I married William because I loved him and I wanted to be with him, but I do believe that, in marrying him, part of my motivation was to distance myself from my father and to get out from under his roof. As it happened, my father's antipathy to anything Catholic was so acute he and my mother disowned me as soon as they heard of my engagement to William. I had made a despicable bed in their eyes, and I would have to go lie in it."

"What became of your mother, Jane?" asked David. "I don't think I've ever heard you speak of her before."

"No, you haven't, and that is partly out of shame, David," Jane replied, looking down. "She died, two years after my father was killed, as an inmate of the Liverpool Workhouse. After he went, she fell on hard times, and I am ashamed to say that I did nothing at all to help her. I thought it was for her to come to me to ask for my help if she wished to, since it was she and he who had cut me out of their lives, not me them. I was too proud to run after her, and I did not want to give her the opportunity to reject me for a second time. So I left her to die in penury. I am not proud of that episode, but then I am not proud of much that I did in the name of my principles during those years. So that is another shameful chapter for me to recall."

"But let me spell out the worst. The episode I have the greatest regret over was the position that I took when William Henry told us he wanted to marry Fanny. I can scarcely explain now how little consideration I gave to my eldest son's wishes, and his happiness, and his complete right to follow his heart whatever direction it took him in. That Fanny was and is a wonderful woman only makes what I said to him about her even more of a calumny."

"Deep down, I was probably terrified that she was spiriting him off into the Catholic faith, and I would never see him or any children he might have ever again. But by giving him such a brutal ultimatum, to choose either her or his family, I brought exactly what I had most feared upon us. I was so certain of my ground, so dead set against any such liaison entirely in principle, that I expelled my eldest boy from my sight and I never saw him again."

"I delivered for him and his father, as well as me, the same awful rupture that William and I had gone through with our two families when we were married. We had been shown the door without compunction by our respective Protestant and Catholic families because we wanted to be together. And two decades later, I repeated exactly that awful act for William Henry.

How blind can I have been to do that? I cannot answer that question. I find it just inexplicable now, and I have been given more than 30 years to ponder it. Was my action predetermined? I would love to think it was, because the moral responsibility for my action, which I have accepted completely, is my life's burden."

"That also cost William his life, I am quite convinced. We had lost Alex to enteric the previous year in Mesopotamia, at barely 18 years of age, and that devastated us both. I know many families lost children in these wars, and my heart goes out to all of them. No-one who has not suffered that experience can know how utterly devastating it is. No parent should experience the loss of a child, and we lost two in the space of nine months. Alex had his whole life in front of him when it was taken away. I can see his sweet face now as I am speaking."

"William should never have gone back to work when he did. He was sick with grief, and he was not fit to go. Doctors nowadays would have had him on strong medication and kept under close observation. I was in no state to stop him or even to recognise what was happening. I was already half way to madness at our losses. I was in a total daze when they came to tell me William had been killed. It was like a final mortal blow for me."

"But you did come through it all, Jane," said Elizabeth, wanting to give her friend the opportunity to end her painful discourse.

"I did, but only with your help, Elizabeth, and, finally, with your prompting and cajoling me to make contact with Fanny. If you had not done that, and thank God I listened to you, I should not have survived the winter that dreadful year. I felt like a ghost, a fraction of a human being. But meeting Fanny connected with all the half realisations I had begun to form about your life, Elizabeth, and mine—and why mine had gone so terribly awry. The dreadful, unacceptable awful Catholic woman I had despised so totally, without knowing a thing about her, was, of course, the dearest of women. I could totally see why William Henry had fallen head over heels in love with her as soon as I met her. I realised, as I spoke with Fanny, that she was not some one-off exception to one of my absurd rules, she was not one individual who could be spared from my prejudice, she was someone who showed me the complete idiocy of my doctrines, the fallacy of my so-called principles, my folly. As Elizabeth had always known, people were good and deserving of kindness. They were not objects to be loathed because of the God they worshipped, the place they were born, or the colour of their skin, any more than by the clothes they chose to wear."

"My convictions, and my sense of incontrovertible right in what I believed, were so strong that I had to be broken completely for me to realise the scale of my mistakes. Those months did break me completely, and perhaps if one believes in the Almighty, they gave me my epiphany."

"I saw that there was a means I could carry on, but I would have to start out anew in a wholly different direction than I had travelled. I still had two children, Ethel and Albert, and I had a god-sent grandchild, Henry, the son of the dearest eldest boy I had shamefully pushed away and lost forever. I had also found a new daughter in Fanny. In their individual ways, they all needed me a little and I completely needed all of them. I came from feeling I was being expunged from the face of the world, to realising that there was still a chance and a reason for me to continue, and so continue I would. I still had a place and some role, and the opportunity to do better. Here I am today, still here, and I am so pleased to be in your company and to share in your love. I owe all you all my heartfelt thanks. You are so much more than I deserve."

"I'd like to stop there now. I think I've said quite enough and I want to finish by proposing a toast," said Jane, raising her untouched glass of cherry brand aloft and waiting for the three others to follow suit.

"The toast is to Elizabeth, my very dearest of friends. My lifelong companion, my love, who showed me, when my road had reached its end, the way to carry on."

After a round of communal singing to Ethel Garston's spirited piano playing, and as the afternoon turned to evening, the younger children began to be ushered away to their baths and beds. As they did, the Limekiln Lane event transformed from an afternoon tea party to a dance night to the tunes being played on Douglas Simpson's hard-working record player.

First up onto the informal dance floor outside the Steggle's shop, to no-one's surprise at all, was Elizabeth's daughter Janet with her husband Bill Bamford, who were accomplished amateur ballroom dancers. Bill, people said, could have made dancing his profession had he so wished, but reluctant to give up his business as a road haulier, which was doing well, he kept dance as a pastime. He and Janet though competed regularly in local competitions and with frequent success.

Janet and he had met in the year after the end of the First War when Janet was still grieving the loss of her first husband Archie, who was tragically killed in the very last days of the fighting in northern France, just two weeks before the armistice to end that conflict was signed. Bill and Janet had three children together, and their family was completed by Janet and Archie's daughter, Bunty. Janet was now still bravely adjusting to a further loss: her eldest child, her son with Archie, Harry, had been killed on active service with the Royal Navy in the third year of the second war. For Janet, going out dancing with Bill, and their all-encompassing enjoyment of music, played an important part in her recovery.

As Bill and Janet danced to Ethel Merman's *I Get a Kick Out of You*, they were joined by Jane's son Albert, who with a charmingly exaggerated bow and an extended hand had persuaded his sister-in-law Fanny Garston up to dance with him. Fanny had never remarried after William Henry's death, and had devoted herself to bringing up her son Henry and to opening and running a successful seaside boarding house in Blackpool. Now fully embraced by the Garston family, Fanny was the greatest of friends with Albert's wife, Lilian. They visited each other regularly and enjoyed an active social life in theatre, amateur dramatics and a shared love for musicals. Fanny, who had never been a religious person, had always joked that she couldn't really lay claim to the status of lapsed Catholic, as she'd hardly ever been an unlapsed one in the first place. She had welcomed Jane's olive branch into the wider Garston family, when it finally came, with grace and good spirit. She had been baffled by her earlier rejection by her husband's family but, by nature a person of happy disposition, she was not one to linger on old ground. Life was too short to worry about old problems that have gone away, she once told Lilian.

Fanny's son Henry Garston, an RAF Spitfire pilot who had served with distinction in the Battle of Britain, the aerial confrontation that had been so critical in forestalling an invasion of Britain by Hitler's Germany, had now become engaged to his sweetheart Daisy Owens. She was a slender, dark haired beauty with a look of the English actress Margaret Lockwood, down to the beauty spot above her right upper lip. Henry and Daisy had missed the afternoon party. But arriving now, he in his immaculate, air-force blue uniform, and she in a bright A-line floral pink dress, to find his mother already dancing with Albert, Henry and his fiancée needed no second invitation to join them.

Encouraged by the sight of the growing number of couples now up and enjoying themselves, Donald Simpson and his wife Annie were next to step in. Annie was a lifelong keen dancer and, over the years, she had taught Donald the steps of all the popular dances. Donald was no Bill Bamford when it came to gliding around a dance floor, and he was never confident enough to be the first up to dance at any function, but he never let the show down when Annie finally got him to his feet.

Donald and Annie and their two daughters, Millie and Lizzie, lived a few miles away in Birkenhead, near the municipal Central Park. Brave as a lion in the First War, Donald had struggled somewhat in the years following his return. He was plagued by a recurring nightmare of suffocation, which his doctors identified early was linked to his experiences under gas attack at the Somme. Many a night in their early years together, Annie would have to wake him from his half sleep to calm his cries of 'Accessory! Accessory!' the term used in the trenches to refer to the toxic weapon that terrified soldiers of both sides of the conflict equally. That trauma had subsided over time, and was now only an occasional disrupter of Donald's sleep. It had become an infrequent but unwelcome reminder of that long period of stress and suffering he had been fortunate enough to survive.

Donald had worked for Joseph Steggle for three decades, as a storeman and driver, but he was now, in practice, working for Joseph's two eldest daughters, Bertha and Nell, who ran the shop these days. The two young managers allowed their elderly father to come in and look proprietorial while tidying shelves that didn't need tidying and charming lady customers with witticisms and small compliments. If neither of his daughters was looking, and Joseph found his path to the till clear, he would regularly call forward his favourite customers and slip in the odd additional item into their baskets, without charge. "You'll be the ruin of this shop, Dad, Bertha would scold him." "It took you 40 years to build this business up, and if you don't stop giving things away, we won't last another 40 days!"

David and Florence, seeing Donald and Annie were up, were the next to join the dancing to their son's music collection. The Ink Spots' *Into Each Life Some Rain Must Fall* was a favourite of theirs, and Douglas, noting that his mother and father had yet to be tempted up from their chairs, had put it onto the turntable for precisely that purpose. The first few notes had been enough to bring them to their feet.

David had served in the Home Guard during the whole of the war just ended and had been colour sergeant of the local platoon that had played an important role especially during the air raids of the German blitz of the Liverpool port. He had retired from the regular army in 1920, after the eight years of service with the Black Watch for which he had originally signed up were completed.

His two comrades and friends, Tam and Jimmy, had, like David, seen through the First War from first to last. Both had retired the service in the same year as David and had returned to their home town of Dundee. Tam had become a manager at Keiller's, the leading marmalade producer in a town famous for its jams. He, in turn, had brought in Jimmy to work in the same firm, and there Jimmy had found his true metier as a salesman. His quick one-liners, his ready smile and infectious personality made him a success with the firm's customers, large and small.

David, Tam and Jimmy had been recalled briefly to the colours in 1926 to help maintain order during the National General Strike. So they had served one further short period in uniform together in Glasgow during that time. They now saw each other only infrequently, but they corresponded occasionally, and unfailingly sent each other a long letter of family news of themselves, their wives and their children each Christmas. Jimmy's letter was always the most eagerly awaited, although David and Tam were in no doubt that fact and fiction were, as often before, quite closely intertwined in the witty lines that Jimmy wrote.

Last of the group to rise, and a little timidly at that, were young Stuart Garston and Josephine Simpson, who had been sitting together on the edge of their chairs waiting for a tune to be played that they knew they had practised the steps for. Finally, it came in the form of a Hal Kemp cover of a song from the Rodgers and Hart musical *Babes in the Wood*.

Trying not to look too shy under the watchful gaze of their two grandmothers, Jane and Elizabeth, who were looking on from the side, Stuart and Josephine moved to the centre of the dancing group. They had met less than a year ago, but all their friends could see that they only had eyes for each other. For Elizabeth and Jane, that two of their grandchildren had met and begun a relationship was a thing of joy.

As the music played, Lorenz Hart's haunting lyrics of *Where or When,* the song of past experience being lived again, sounded mellifluously through the night air as the evening light dimmed.

It seems we stood and talked like this before
We looked at each other in the same way then
But I can't remember where or when
The clothes you're wearing are the clothes you wore
The smile you are smiling you were smiling then
But I can't remember where or when
Some things that happen for the first time

Seem to be happening again
And so it seems that we have met before
And laughed before and loved before
But who knows where or when

As the two elderly ladies watched the youngsters dance their slow foxtrot effortlessly across the ground, Elizabeth reached across to Jane and whispered in her ear, "It seems like only yesterday that we were their age, and with that same look of joy in our faces, doesn't it? A Garston and a Simpson now finally getting together? Wouldn't that be something, Jane?"

"It would, Elizabeth." Jane replied. "I can honestly think of nothing better."